# Into the Dark

# Sharon Smith

*Yellow Rose Books*

Nederland, Texas

ISBN 1-932300-38-4


First Printing 2005

9 8 7 6 5 4 3 2 1


Cover design by Donna Pawlowski


Published by:

Yellow Rose Books
PMB 210, 8691 9th Avenue
Port Arthur, Texas 77642-8025


Find us on the World Wide Web at
http://www.regalcrest.biz


Printed in the United States of America

## Acknowledgments

There are so many people I'd like to thank, I don't even know where to start. To the wonderful staff at Regal Crest, thank you for believing in this novel enough to make it available for the world to read. To Sylverre, for all of your hard work editing. This book would not be what it is without your help. A big thanks goes to Karen "Kas" King and the members of the MerwolfPack list, who helped with the beta reading of the original version of this story. Your support and encouragement is priceless to me. Special thanks to Lori Lake for encouraging me to publish this story, and helping to make it happen. Thank you to FCP for giving me the time to write, and for the daily stress that forced my artistic side to create a character like Jordanna Fox, just to keep my sanity.

## Dedication

To my parents, who selflessly gave all of the tools needed to make it successfully in life. I love and miss you both. To Lorraine, Ruth, and Carol. Since I didn't send my 'shout outs' in the Senior Will of our High School yearbook all those years ago, I'm doing it now. Thank you for being the best friends anyone could ever want. I'm so glad our friendship has continued into adulthood. Last but not least to my partner, Rhonda, for loving me the way you do. This is where it all started.

# Chapter
# One

JORDANNA FOX SAT astride a horse as easily if she had been born in the saddle. The horse trainer looked at the drummer in awe. "I thought you said you didn't know how to ride?"

Seductive blue eyes looked back at her. "I've never ridden *a horse* before in my life."

"Well, you're a natural then."

Jordanna shrugged her shoulders and winked. "I guess I am."

Jordanna and her band, Plenty of Nothing, were on the set filming the video for their upcoming single, "Fight or Take Refuge." They were all dressed as Amazon warriors and sitting high on horses that, with the exception of the drummer, they couldn't seem to control.

"Shit! All this horse wants to do is eat," Kelly Savage, the band's lead guitarist, muttered as she tried to wrench her mount's head away from a nearby tree.

Rachel Simpson, the band's bassist and spokeswoman, wasn't having much luck with her horse either. "You think that's bad, I think Muffin is in heat or something." She laughed. "It keeps sniffing Linda's horse where the sun don't shine."

"Yeah, I think my horse is enjoying it, though. She keeps trying to throw me off." Linda snorted. "This is going to be one hell of a long day."

Irritated, the director of the video called, "Let's break for lunch. We're wasting a lot of tape on this. Give the horses, and the band, time to settle down."

"About fuckin' time," the drummer murmured, easing her sleek, muscled six-foot frame off of her horse. "Good girl," she said, giving the large animal a quick pat and a scratch on its pale mane. She then walked directly over to the horse trainer, put her arm around the smaller woman, and said a few words. Within seconds, the two were headed for the band's trailer.

"Geez, Jordanna's at it again." Rachel shook her head and

laughed. "Is there anyone on the set that our Romeo hasn't been with yet?"

"If the trailer's a-rockin', don't come a-knockin'," Kelly sang cheerfully as she grabbed a sandwich and a bottle of water. "Is there anyone Jordanna hasn't been with yet? Hmm, good question. Well, let's see. First, it was the woman from the audience. After that, the make-up artist. Then I think it was her assistant, which pissed the make-up artist off and she stormed off the set." She put her finger near her mouth. "No, I don't think she's missed anyone. Can you think of anyone, Lin?"

Linda Matthews, rhythm guitarist and one half of the band's vocals, didn't find it funny. "No. As usual, she's done them all. Except for the men, of course."

Kelly walked over to Linda and put her hand on her shoulder. "Still not over her, huh?"

"Fuck you, Kelly."

Kelly laughed. "Real nice, Lin. Guess you just answered my question."

JORDANNA EMERGED FROM the trailer just as the crew was getting ready to start taping again. Rachel grabbed a plate and handed it to the sweaty woman. "You better eat something, Jordanna. We don't want to have to rush you to the hospital like the last time you passed out from low blood sugar."

Jordanna looked at the bassist and smirked. "Thanks, but I already ate," she said, brushing her sweaty jet-black bangs out of her eyes. All eyes went to the blushing horse trainer, who, at that very moment, realized she was needed somewhere else.

Anywhere else.

Kelly got up to throw out her garbage and chuckled. "You really do have a way with the ladies, Jordanna. You screw 'em and then send them all running for the hills."

The drummer grinned. "All in the plan, Kelly, all in the plan. I wouldn't want anyone to grow too attached, you know?"

Linda snorted. "Heaven forbid you'd let that happen, Jordanna. You just might melt or something."

Jordanna looked up and glared at her. "What's your problem, Linda?"

Linda narrowed her eyes. "You, Jordanna," the guitarist answered sarcastically, "are my problem." The drummer got up from her seat and circled around the guitarist like an animal circling its prey. She stopped directly behind Linda and whispered sensually in her former lover's ear. "You know what your problem is?" She took full advantage of her position to tease the guitarist, pinned into her seat and unable even to turn.

"After all these years, you still want me, don't you?" she asked breathlessly into the guitarist's ear. "Don't you?"

When Linda relaxed into the touch, Jordanna laughed and pulled her body away from the frustrated woman. "You need to get laid, Linda. That's what your problem is."

Linda shuddered, and her face turned completely red. She turned around and looked the drummer straight in the eyes. "You bitch! You think sex is all there is, don't you?"

The drummer just stood there, still smirking at the guitarist, very proud of herself. "You might want to think about trying it; then maybe you wouldn't be so frustrated and miserable all the time."

"Fuck you, Jordanna."

The dark-haired woman winked. "You wish."

REBECCA HURLEY COULDN'T wait to get home. After three days in Houston, on assignment to cover a music festival, she drove toward her apartment as fast as the Manhattan streets would allow. "Shit, can't they let me take a shower and get changed first?" she muttered when her beeper went off. She pulled her phone out of her backpack and dialed the number to her boss's office. His assistant answered the phone. "Hi, Janice, it's Rebecca. I was just paged."

"Hang on a sec — I'll get John for you."

John Drake was *Tempo* magazine's editor-in-chief. One of the few people that had been with the popular music magazine since its inception twenty years ago, John could tell any interested listener, in great detail, about the tremendous changes that had taken place in the magazine, and the music business, over the last two decades. Six years ago, John took the chance to hire Rebecca, who had neither a journalism degree nor a college diploma. Now, when anyone spoke of music journalism at its best, Rebecca's name was the first to pop up in conversation.

"I know you just got in, but I need to talk to you about your next assignment. It's big. We're the only ones getting the opportunity for this story and I want you to cover it," her boss barked through the phone. The man was not known for his tact.

Rebecca rubbed her head. "Can't this wait? I haven't even dropped my luggage off, and I haven't slept in over twenty-four hours." She paused for a brief second. "And my flight was great, John, thanks for asking."

"Yeah, yeah. Whatever. I know you haven't slept, kid, but you're young. Hang on for another hour or so. You can get some sleep once we talk." John hung up the phone.

"Asshole," Rebecca cursed. She drove to the next corner and

turned, heading back uptown to the magazine's Manhattan office.

She walked into the building, got on the elevator, and took it up to *Tempo's* offices up on the fifteenth floor. Saying hello to Janice on her way in, she strode into his office, but he wasn't there. Twenty minutes and what little patience she had left later, John still hadn't returned to the office. *He may have all day, but I don't. That's it, I'm outta here.* She got up and made it as far as his door.

"Where's the fire, Hurley? I called you in here for a reason," he said to her as they practically knocked each other over in his office doorway. He walked to his desk and set his cup of coffee and doughnut down.

"Nice time for a coffee break. What's my next assignment, John?"

He pointed to the chair in front of his desk. "Sit down, Rebecca. Damn, you young kids can't sit still for minute. I need you to go home and pack your bags. You're going on a little trip." He grinned at her, knowing damn well her bags hadn't been unpacked yet.

"I can't freaking believe this! I haven't even been home yet and I'm already off again? My daughter will forget what I look like if I keep this up, John. I never get to see her anymore," she cried. "Where the hell will I be heading this time?"

"Chicago." He smiled, so proud of this accomplishment. "I just got off the phone with Jerry Baker, Plenty of Nothing's manager. I called him to see if we could set up an interview with the band, but the only way to make it happen is if you join them on the road for a while."

Rebecca almost fell off of her chair. "What? You've got to be kidding! Can't you find someone else to cover this one, John? I just got home! Next thing you're going to tell me is that you want me to work with Jordanna Fox!"

The popular drummer's attitude toward the press was nothing short of pure bitch, and most reporters left her alone; that was the way she liked it.

John's smile disappeared. "As a matter of fact, yes, it's Jordanna that we're after. She's the most happening thing right now, Rebecca. Everyone wants a piece of her, and we got the job, kid."

"Can't you send old Don Juan over there to cover this one?" Rebecca looked over at her co-worker, Jake Rogers, who constantly boasted of his ability to get any woman he wanted to share his bed. "He's got the hots for her big-time, John. Maybe, this time, he actually will get lucky. Not just in his head," she added with a smirk.

"Rebecca, Rebecca, Rebecca." John leaned back in his chair and sighed. "I'm really disappointed in you, Hurley. Apparently you haven't been keeping up with your homework. Jordanna bats for the other team. She doesn't do the male thing."

*Wonderful. Just my freaking luck.*

"That's just great! So I'll be following some dyke bitch from hell around the country for the next few weeks. What did I do to deserve this honor?" Her hazel eyes shot daggers at her boss.

He took a few moments to mull over her question. "You're good, kid. You ask good questions. You'll see; this won't be that bad. Maybe you and Jordanna will bond. Stranger things have happened."

The young blonde shook her head. "Oh, I'm sure we will. When does my flight leave?" She knew she had been defeated.

A FEW MEMBERS of the crew stood in the lobby of the hotel in Chicago. Jordanna looked at Gary, her drum tech and the band's stage manager. "Did you find anyplace yet?"

He ran his hands through his shoulder-length, dark brown hair. "The doorman told me there's a club downtown," he said in his native New Orleans accent. "It's a bit of a hike, but it will definitely be worth the drive, if you know what I mean."

The drummer pursed her lips and smiled. "Good. I'm definitely in the mood for a little action tonight."

"So am I. Shall we, darlin'?" He opened the front door for the drummer and followed her out into the night.

# Chapter
# Two

THE MUSIC WAS loud and pumping. Flashing strobe lights lit up the drummer's face every few seconds, gleamed blue on her ink-black hair. Jordanna sat in a chair in front of one of the many small stages in the club, watching the buxom blonde in front of her slowly remove her top.

The drummer pulled out a couple of hundred-dollar bills and flashed them to the woman, beckoning her close. She tucked the bills into the dancer's g-string, and the woman winked in understanding.

Gary leaned in and spoke. "She's a real babe. You always find the hot ones."

"I know." Jordanna sat back in her chair, smiled, and sipped her beer, her eyes never leaving the stage. "She's mine, Gary."

"Care to share?"

"Are you suggesting another threesome?" Jordanna laughed, then clasped the dancer's hand when she reached out.

"Well, now that you mention it...yeah." He laughed lowly.

"Forget it, Gary," the drummer said. "Find your own tonight."

The song ended and new dancers took the stage. A few minutes passed before the fully clothed dancer came out and tapped Jordanna on the shoulder. "Hi," she said when the drummer turned around in her chair. "Follow me?"

Jordanna nodded her head at the woman, stood up, and looked at Gary. "Meet you later."

Gary rolled his eyes and laughed. "Have fun, J." He watched the two women walk to the dressing room area, knowing all too well what was going to happen there. "Lucky dog."

"What's your name?" Jordanna asked the blonde as she followed her through a long hallway.

The dancer giggled and batted her eyes. "Bambi."

*So who in the hell does that make me? Thumper?* The drummer suppressed a grin. *Well, thank God I'm not here for her brains, 'cause she seems to be lacking in that department. Lucky for me, she makes up for it in other areas.* "Do you know who I am, Bambi?" she asked, her voice a raspy whisper.

"Yes, Jordanna." The blonde giggled again.

The drummer looked around the room at all the other dancers getting ready. *Mmm, very nice,* she thought as she inspected a dark-skinned woman changing into her costume a few feet away from them. *I wonder if what they say is true? Guess I'll just have to find out.*

She turned her attention back to the dancer, who tugged on her hand. "Bambi, is there someplace, um, more private we can go to here?" She looked at the dark-skinned woman again. *And can your friend come out and play too?*

The blonde looked at her blankly and then giggled yet again. "Uh, there's a room in the back with a large couch." Her tone made it almost a question.

"That'll work," the drummer said, licking her lips.

JORDANNA WALKED THROUGH the backstage curtain, back into the club. Her eyes did a quick sweep of the room for her drum tech, but she didn't see him. Frowning, she thought, then walked through the door of the men's room. Two men exiting the room gave her strange looks. "Gary, you in here?"

"Jesus, Jordanna! Can't a guy take a piss in peace?" her drum tech answered over the sounds of toilets flushing. "Finished with your date?"

"Nope, Gary, ya can't." She chuckled and then leaned against the wall near the bathroom. "C'mon, are you ready to go?"

"Yep, we are," the tech answered her.

*We?*

Gary walked out of the bathroom, and the dark-skinned woman that Jordanna had admired backstage came out of nowhere and latched onto him. Jordanna lifted an eyebrow at him and smiled at the woman.

"Crystal," the woman said, offering her hand to the drummer.

"Jordanna Fox."

"I know who you are," the dancer purred, pinning the drummer with big brown eyes. "We *all* do." She broke the eye contact and ran her finger along Gary's jaw line. "So, tell me, Jordanna, did you like what you saw in the dressing room before?"

"Yes." Jordanna smiled and cleared her throat. "Yes, I did."

"I heard that you were once in the business."

Jordanna lifted an eyebrow again. "You heard correct."

"Then *why* do you frequent these places?"

The drummer snorted. "Can't a woman appreciate a good-looking woman as much as a man can?"

"Is that what you call what you do?" Crystal laughed and continued. "You of all people should know better, how we feel being up there."

"I *do* know how you feel, and that's why I appreciate what you do." She focused her wandering eyes on Crystal again. "You don't *have* to do this, Crystal. There's always another way if it bothers you so much. I got out, after all."

"No, it doesn't bother me. I was just wondering why you do what you do."

"I could always make it up to you. If it did bother you, I mean." Jordanna's eyes turned a deeper shade of blue. "I could *show* you how much I really appreciate what you do up there on the stage."

Crystal smiled seductively. "And how do you suppose you could do that?"

"Well," Jordanna leaned over and rubbed her body against the woman, whispering in her ear, "the limo is outside and I have a nice, comfy penthouse room at the Hilton with a bed big enough to hold," she turned and smiled at Gary, "three."

"I see." Crystal nodded her agreement. "Now, how could I refuse an offer like that?" She took both Jordanna and Gary's hands, and they walked toward the door. "Lead on."

"Did she just snag my date out from under me?" Gary muttered under his breath and shook his head in amazement as visions of that threesome flashed in his mind. "Damn, she's good," he said and smiled. "Oh, yes. She's very good indeed."

REBECCA SAT LOOKING out of the window of the plane. She had spent the last forty-five minutes of her flight reading over some of the more recent articles on Jordanna Fox and/or Plenty of Nothing to familiarize herself with her newest nightmare of an assignment. She glanced up from her reading when the pilot announced that they were currently flying over Buffalo, New York. *Ooh, how exciting.*

In just one more hour, she would be in Chicago. She closed her eyes and leaned her head back against the seat. She wasn't looking forward to this assignment at all, and cursed John up and down for giving it to her.

She'd dealt with many difficult musicians over the years.

She'd fought off drunk guitarists and been invited to join many orgies, which she always graciously declined. Well, all except one, but she didn't want to think about that. Rebecca loved dealing with challenging artists, but Jordanna Fox... *Why her?* She finished reading about the obnoxious drummer's bar brawls, how she'd been arrested for trashing a hotel room in Kansas at the beginning of the tour, hospitalized for malnutrition a few weeks afterward, and, last but not least, about Jordanna's reputation as a womanizer. Just about every article had an accompanying picture of the flamboyant drummer. In each one, she was either holding hands with, had her arm around, or was even kissing a different woman. Rebecca chuckled as she asked herself what rock she must have been under for the past five years; though one of the country's top music journalists, she was not very familiar with the rock world's most popular drummer.

Another question came to her mind: *Why is the country so obsessed with this obviously destructive woman?* She was now determined to find out.

Well, sort of.

The flight attendant brought Rebecca out of her thoughts. "Would you like something to drink?"

She answered without looking up at him. "No, thank you."

He looked down at a photo Rebecca had on her lap. "God, she's gorgeous. It's a shame she's..." He stopped.

"Gay?" she finished for him, chuckling slightly. She thought about what he had said for a moment and then looked up at him. "You really think she's that good-looking?" *And just when did the airlines start hiring pubescent teenagers as flight attendants?*

His face turned slightly red. "Oh, man, yeah, I do."

"Why?"

He made a face at her. "Huh?"

"What is it that you like about her?"

"What are you, a reporter or something?" he asked.

"Good deduction." She smiled at him. "Yes, I am a journalist. She's my latest assignment."

"Wow, how cool." He laughed. "I guess it's the dark hair, the amazing blue eyes, the tight jeans, the leather, the attitude. She's the ultimate bad girl."

Rebecca smiled quickly. "I guess you like the bad-girl type then, huh?"

"Yeah, that and the thought..."

She noticed his ears were turning red as he cut off what he started to say. "That and the what?"

"No, I can't say it." He scratched his chin. "I'll be in big trouble with the airline if I say what I was thinking to a passenger."

"No, you won't. I won't say anything," she looked at his badge for his name, "Gerald." She brushed her fingers gently over his hand and smiled. He was so young.

He stood quietly for a few seconds, then decided that she looked honest enough. He bent down and whispered in her ear.

She laughed a bit and looked back up at him. "Really?"

He nodded.

"Well, guess what, Gerald? You're no different than any other hot-blooded American male; they all think seeing two women in bed together is a real turn-on." She gave him a wink and watched as the red-faced young flight attendant backed away from her seat, clearly embarrassed.

"Hey, wait," she said, motioning for him to come back. When he did, she handed him the few photos of Jordanna she had with her. "Thanks for answering my questions, Gerald. You've been a big help."

His eyes lit up like child at Christmas. "Are these for me?"

"Sure. I think you'll enjoy them a lot more than I will." She spoke with a hint of sarcasm, totally lost on him.

"Thanks. If you need anything, just ask," he said, clearing his throat.

"Thanks, I will."

KELLY OPENED WITH the first few chords of the song, then abruptly stopped playing. "I'm getting some serious feedback in my monitor."

Linda paced around the stage. The band's sound check was almost over and there was still no sign of their drummer. "Where the hell is Jordanna? She knows we're doing the new songs tonight! Has she even practiced them at all? God, she drives me crazy sometimes."

Rachel growled, "Quit your bitching, Lin. She'll be here." She picked up her bass and slung it over her shoulder. "And besides, get over her already, damn it! It's been years now."

"Kiss my ass, Rachel," Linda said sarcastically before she walked away.

Kelly walked over to Rachel. "Do you know where Jordanna is, Rache?"

Rachel nodded. "Jerry asked her to go to the airport with him. He said he had something he needed to talk to her about, and he'd fill us in when they got back."

"Hmm." Kelly looked puzzled. "Wonder what that could be about?"

Rachel began playing some chords on her bass. "I dunno. Whatever it is, Jordanna will no doubt hassle him about it."

Kelly laughed. "Without a doubt." She looked over at Linda, who stood on the corner of the stage. "I think you may have hurt her feelings, Rache. You know how she feels about Jordanna."

Rachel shook her head. "I know. She just pisses me off sometimes, Kel. She has a comment about everything that Jor says or does. I'll be the first to admit Jordanna can be a selfish bitch most of the time, but Linda just takes it too far."

"I know, a woman scorned," Kelly agreed. "Just go easy on her, though. Please."

JERRY LOOKED AROUND the airport at the crowd gathering around them. The moody drummer hadn't responded well to the news that a reporter would be joining them on the tour.

"You have got to be absolutely, positively, fucking kidding me, Jerry!" she screamed, her voice louder with each word. "You *really* expect me to spend the rest of the tour with some reporter following me around like a lost puppy? That's just not gonna happen!" She turned around to walk away, ending the conversation and slamming right into her bodyguard, who stood just inches behind her. "Back off, Lenny! Gimme some fucking space."

"But I have—" The bodyguard started.

She glared at him. "Your orders," she finished for him and softened her voice just a bit. "I know you do. Please, Lenny, just a little space."

He moved out of her way but remained close to her in case anyone thought of trying anything. When he saw Jerry heading towards her, a determined look in his eyes, he stepped forward.

She turned around as Jerry grabbed her arm. "Get your fucking hands off me," she snarled. He let go of her arm and faced her. "It's all right, Lenny; I can handle myself," she said, as the big bodyguard nearly fell over himself to stop the band's manager from touching the drummer.

Jerry waited for everyone to calm down. "Let me explain my reasoning on this, Jordanna," he said in his British accent, while leading her to a private corner. "You know better than anyone that the press you've been getting lately has not been good. In fact, it downright bloody sucks. First, you go and get yourself arrested again, and then you end up in the hospital. Luckily, we could cover them both up before the press could really sink their teeth into them." He looked her directly in the eyes. "It's not good for the band; you know that. I don't want to have to talk to you about looking for a new drummer if your behavior doesn't change. I really don't." He put his hand on her arm gently. "Don't make me have to do that again, Jordanna. I hated doing it the first time," he whispered.

She looked at him, opened her mouth to say something, and then closed it.

"So, please, just go along with this," he continued. "You know I wouldn't do this to you unless I thought it was absolutely necessary."

She shook her head and sighed. "Jerry..."

"And Rebecca *is* the best in the field."

"I know who she is. I've read some of her articles."

He let out a relieved sigh. "It's important that you go along with this. Please, just try to get used to the idea of having someone around you for a while." As he finished his little speech, he caught sight of a small woman with strawberry-blonde hair walking toward them, laminated press pass glinting in the light. "And sooner than later. I think that's her now. Please, be nice to her, Jordanna."

Jordanna snorted. "Yeah, I can be..." Rebecca joined them. The drummer's eyes took the small woman in slowly, starting with her face, down to her feet and then back up into the hazelest eyes she'd ever seen. "....nice," she concluded, suddenly breathless.

*I know her, don't I?*

Rebecca's heart jumped at the sight of the drummer. *Those eyes. I've looked into them a million times before, haven't I?*

Rebecca had seen numerous photos of the drummer but wasn't prepared to find out just how incredibly beautiful Jordanna Fox actually was in person. Yes, the woman *had* been chosen as one of *People* magazine's "50 Most Beautiful People" for the last four years straight, and, yes, that definitely should have been a clue for her. Sometimes, though, as Rebecca read through the list, she wondered what possessed *People* to pick some of the people they chose. But now, standing right in front of her, she knew *exactly* why the magazine had selected this woman to grace the list.

*I just never expected the dyke bitch from hell to be the most beautiful woman — forget that, most beautiful human — I've ever laid my eyes on.* She shook her head, confused by the immediate connection she felt to this virtual stranger.

The two of them just stood there looking at each other, feeling something between them but not really knowing where it came from or what to say about it.

The sound of Jerry's voice broke the spell. "You must be Rebecca. We are very glad to have you join us on the tour." Jordanna flipped him a pained look. "Rebecca, this is Jordanna Fox."

Rebecca blinked and held her hand out to Jordanna. "Hi, nice to meet you."

Jordanna paused for a moment. *Hmm, give me two days...nope, scratch that; make it one day, and she's in my bed.* She slowly took Rebecca's hand. "Yeah, nice to meet you, too."

Jerry picked up Rebecca's duffel bag and threw it over his shoulder. "Come on, let's get your luggage. The limo is waiting out back."

As the two women followed Jordanna's bodyguard to go pick up Rebecca's luggage, Jerry walked as close to Jordanna as he could. "Please try to keep her out of your bed, Jordanna," he said softly. "You've had enough of that kind of coverage, and that is definitely not the kind you need." He knew the raven-haired woman's fetishes all too well, and Rebecca was smart, blonde, and beautiful.

Exactly the drummer's type.

"Is that really what you think of me, Jerry?" She winked and flashed him a crooked smile.

THE RIDE IN the limo was spent mostly in silence. Jerry tried to make small talk, discussing the band's itinerary for the next few weeks. Neither of the women said much. Rebecca looked down at her hands, trying to come up with a way to get the raven-haired woman to say something. Finally, she turned to Jordanna and took the direct approach. "You don't talk much, do you?"

Jordanna was busy reading a magazine and didn't bother to look up. "Don't take it personally. I'm not really a people person. I don't do the chat thing real well."

Annoyed at the drummer's rudeness, Rebecca grabbed the magazine Jordanna was reading and flipped it shut. "Just for the record, Jordanna, I want to be here about as much as you want me to be here."

Jordanna couldn't keep a smirk from her lips. *Hmm, besides being very cute, she's feisty, too.* She looked directly into Rebecca's hazel eyes, put the magazine down, and gave the blonde her full attention. "Okay, you're the reporter, start asking the questions."

Rebecca sat speechless. Not knowing what to say was something she'd never had a problem with before. Silence fell.

Jordanna grabbed her gently by the chin, mocking her.

"C'mon, kid, whaddya wanna know about the big bad drummer? Yes, all the things you hear about me are true." She kept up her mocking tone. "I thought that you wanted to do an interview." She shrugged her shoulders. "Ask away."

Rebecca shook her head out of Jordanna's grip and tried not to flinch away from the intense blue eyes studying her. She felt uncomfortable being scrutinized like that, and shifted in her seat. "Well, first off, why do you have to be such a..."

Jerry cleared his throat and interrupted her. "There's plenty of time for the interview later. We'll be at the arena in a few minutes. We're very late and Jordanna's already missed the sound check. She has to get warmed up for the show." Then he gave Jordanna a warning look.

She lifted an eyebrow and spoke seductively. "Oh, I'm just getting warmed up, Jerry."

JORDANNA SAT BACKSTAGE with her practice pad in her lap, tapping out different sticking patterns to warm up quickly. Once she finished that, she put the sticks and the pad down on the floor, stood up and walked to a corner, and stretched to loosen up.

After Jerry called the other members of the band over to him, he quickly introduced Rebecca to them. "Rebecca, this is Kelly Savage, our lead guitarist." Rebecca looked at the woman with long, curly, dirty-blonde hair and gray eyes and stuck her hand out.

"This is Linda Matthews, rhythm guitarist and vocalist." Linda pushed back a strand of her long, dark hair and said a quiet hello.

Rachel introduced herself. "Rachel Simpson. Bassist, keyboards and resident big mouth." She shook Rebecca's hand, her brown eyes twinkling. "Very nice to meet you, Rebecca. I've read some of your work. It's very good."

The reporter blushed. "Thank you."

A local Chicago disc jockey walked onto the stage and introduced the band as they lined up backstage. Rebecca watched as Lenny, a tall, muscular Italian man that she had met at the airport, practically wrapped himself around the tall drummer, ready to usher her onto the stage. The other band members' bodyguards stood close by their sides, but didn't have them in a bear hold like he had Jordanna in. The reporter shook her head. "That's strange," she mumbled quietly. "I wonder what's up with that?"

"And would you please give a big Chicago welcome to Plenty of Nothing!" the disc jockey announced and then walked off the stage. The band members quickly took their places.

Rachel threw the strap of her bass over her head and walked up to her microphone. "Hello, Chicago! How are you all doing tonight?"

The fans screamed back at her.

"One, two, three, four..." The crowd gave a deafening roar as Jordanna counted them into the opening song, "What Do You Think About That," a Jordanna Fox original from their first album. The song was the band's first hit and the one that had rocketed them straight to stardom.

Rebecca had heard about Plenty of Nothing's stage shows, but she'd never witnessed one. She sat on a speaker on the left side of the stage, just a few feet from Jordanna's enormous drum set. Throughout most of the show, she couldn't take her eyes off of Jordanna. Personality aside, the woman was an amazing talent on the drums with a tremendous stage presence.

Toward the end of the show, Jordanna stepped out from behind the drums. She walked confidently across the stage, shook hands with a few fans in front, and sat down on a stool right on the edge of the stage. Next to her was Kelly, her acoustic guitar in her hands. The lights dimmed. The only lights to be seen in the arena were the two spotlights shining on Jordanna and Kelly and the red glow of the exit signs.

Jordanna looked down and closed her eyes as Kelly began to softly strum her guitar. As a beautiful voice sang out the first few lyrics of the song, the audience went still. Jordanna kept her eyes closed as she sang. When the song ended, she opened her eyes. Some impulse led her to look to the left side of the stage. What she saw was the reporter watching her with a dreamy, far-away look on her face.

At that moment, Rebecca snapped out of her trance, aware of the glare of those intense blue eyes. She looked away when she thought she saw the drummer, who was making her way back to her drum set, wink at her.

*Oh, God, what the hell is going on with you, Rebecca?*

Jordanna climbed back behind her drums and smirked. She felt a jolt of desire shoot through her body. *Oh, yeah, the little reporter is mine. Looks like I bagged yet another one.*

Linda and Rachel rejoined the two on the stage for the last song of the set. When it ended, the band quickly exited the stage. The lights dimmed again, and the crowd spent the next few minutes stomping their feet, waiting for the band's return.

A FEW MINUTES later, four silhouettes walked back out and took their places on the stage. Kelly teased the crowd with a short little guitar solo before she ripped into the opening chords of one of Jordanna's more popular tunes, "Listen to Your Cries." Rebecca found herself smiling as the crowd went wild, recognizing the controversial tune. She watched Jordanna slip a wireless headset microphone on her head and slink to the front of the stage. A good-looking man sat down behind her drum set, and Jordanna introduced him to the crowd as her drum tech. The band played the musical intro of the song.

Jordanna teased and played the crowd as she sang the provocative lyrics, giving them little glimpses of bare skin, damp with sweat, as she lifted her trademark tank top slightly, caressing her own stomach and thighs as the audience looked on.

At one point in the song, she danced provocatively around Kelly with moves that reminded Rebecca of a professional stripper, landing on her knees directly in front of the guitarist. She placed her roaming hands on the guitarist's waist and inched her way down Kelly's body until her hands caressed the woman's thighs.

"I get down on my knees, and run my hands between your thighs..."

She pulled the guitarist closer to her, so close that it looked as if Kelly could feel the heat radiating from Jordanna's hot body.

"I pull your body closer, and listen to your cries..."

She spun around, moving away from Kelly, and slowly eased her body down onto the stage, as if she were easing herself on top of a lover. The band brought the volume of the song down low, so that Jordanna could speak, rather than sing, some ad-libbed lines not on the original recording.

"Your body feels so good under mine, baby," the drummer whispered breathlessly as she rocked her hips back and forth, oozing raw sexuality.

"How does this make you feel?" she whispered, pinning a fan in the front with her blue eyes as she continued to make love to an imaginary lover on the stage.

"Let Jordanna show you a good time tonight. Let me kiss you where you've never been kissed before," the drummer whispered again, as the band kicked back into the song. She crawled to the edge of the stage until she was face to face with the woman she had pinned with her eyes before, and, out of nowhere, she kissed the stunned fan on the lips, a kiss that lasted far longer than it should have. Rebecca noticed that she said a few words and slipped something into the fan's hand when she broke the kiss. The woman looked down and smiled.

Whatever it was made her a very happy woman.

The crowd in front went wild, and she crawled to the other side of the stage and did the same thing, this time finding a male fan to kiss, although this kiss didn't last nearly as long, and she definitely didn't slip anything into his hand.

After that, she stood up and played with the excited crowd some more, ducking as a few bras and panties came flying her way. She caught a pair of black lace panties, resisting the animalistic urge to sniff them before she draped them over her shoulder as she sang, and finally hung them on her cymbal stand when the song came to a close.

As she started to walk back to her drums, an over-excited fan jumped on the stage and ran up to her, wrapping her arms around the startled drummer. Jordanna's bodyguard and several members of the arena's security team ran onto the stage and quickly pulled the kicking and screaming woman off of Jordanna. They forcefully removed the overzealous fan from the auditorium.

Rebecca had seen many musicians tease the crowd like Jordanna just did, but none of them could compare to Jordanna's hypnotic technique. The reporter looked up and found Jordanna's gaze directly on her as she walked by to climb back behind the drums. This time she was positive that Jordanna winked at her.

The band played one more original song, and then the lights in the auditorium went on. The four women accepted flowers, stuffed animals and other gifts from some of the fans in the front row before they left the stage. The reporter noticed Jordanna's bodyguard quickly rush to her side and escort her, almost forcefully, off the stage.

# Chapter
# Three

THE ROOM BACKSTAGE was dark and filled with people. Tables were lined up against the back wall, loaded with food and drink of all kinds. Rebecca grabbed a plate and helped herself to some food as her stomach announced her hunger to the room. She found a chair in the corner and sat down. As she ate, she watched the people in the room with interest. They were all anxiously waiting for the band members to finish showering and come out to join the crowd.

She noticed some people going in and out of another room off to the side. She stood up, threw out her empty plate, and headed that way. As she walked through the door, she saw the room full of scantily clad women and a few men waiting for the band.

*Sheesh, groupies!*

Her thoughts went to the drummer, wondering if she would end up with one of the women that were waiting for her there. Like, what did she really care? She laughed at the absurdity of the thought.

Rebecca sensed a buzz go through the room and realized that someone from the band must have made her presence known. She caught a quick glimpse of the drummer, standing in the corner, her hair still slightly damp from her shower, with at least two dozen women around her, fawning at her feet.

*Oh, please, how pathetic.*

Rebecca shook her head as she watched a woman pull her blouse up so Jordanna could autograph the skin just above a bare breast. The drummer moved in front of the woman to block the view from the others in the room, opened a black magic marker, and went to sign the autograph. The woman moved a bit, probably on purpose, and the drummer's hand grazed a nipple. Jordanna smiled afterward and said a few things to the woman, shaking her head up and down as she did so.

The proud groupie smiled brightly as a friend took a few posed photos of her with the drummer standing behind her, arms wrapped around the groupie's waist and her hands cupping the girl's bare breasts.

Rebecca shook her head in disgust. *The woman's a pig.*

Rebecca then realized that the smiling groupie was none other than the woman from the audience that Jordanna had kissed. She wore a silk backstage pass on her very sheer blouse, and Jordanna planted her hand firmly on the woman's denim-covered ass. *That's what she slipped in her hand after she kissed her, a backstage pass. She's Jordanna's flavor of the night.*

The reporter quickly looked away as Jordanna met her eyes and grinned. Jordanna had caught her staring at her and her adoring harem.

Pushing thoughts of Jordanna out of her mind, Rebecca spent the rest of the time backstage talking with some of the fans, trying to understand the band's appeal. She always did that when interviewing a band for a story. Writing from the fans' perspective always paid off with the sale of more magazines. Who would know what the fans want to read about better than the fans themselves?

Most of the people she spoke to said that Jordanna appealed to them most. She wasn't surprised. She thought that maybe she should write about Jordanna's seduction techniques instead of her musical ability. She *knew* that would be a big seller. Sex certainly worked well enough for the drummer, who had slipped away with the woman from the audience and another woman who Rebecca assumed was a friend of the fan.

As the night wore on, the janitorial crew came in to clean the rooms, and everyone started getting ready to fly to the next city on the tour, Philadelphia. Rebecca figured that she'd better use the restroom before she got on the plane; she had sworn to herself that she would never again use an airplane bathroom. Unless, of course, she was presented with the appetizing opportunity to join the mile-high club, which had so far eluded her.

She walked through the door of the mid-sized backstage bathroom, stopping briefly to look at her reflection in the mirror. *I look tired. Gee, I wonder why. I haven't really been home for a few weeks. Could that be it?*

Her eyes swept through the bathroom; all of the stalls were in use except the last one. As she pushed the door open to go in, her eyes caught sight of Jordanna, standing on the toilet seat with her back slouched, leaning against the wall behind her. Her hands were propped up against both walls, holding her weak body up. Her eyes were closed, and her jeans and panties were hanging from a hook on the back of the door. Her denim shirt was on but partially unbuttoned. The woman from the audience sat, legs straddled on the front of the toilet seat, her face buried between the drummer's swaying legs. Jordanna quickly tangled her hands in the woman's long strawberry-blonde hair, pushing the fan's head deeper between her legs.

Jordanna leaned back against the wall slightly and let out a soft moan. "Oh, yeah, baby, just like that. Work that wonderful tongue for me."

Rebecca got the surprise of her life as the sight caused heat to begin to build between her own legs. She backed out of the stall as quickly as possible, hoping that both women were too caught up in what they were doing to notice that she'd accidentally walked in on them. As she was walking away, she heard the drummer let out a low guttural moan from deep within her throat, announcing her release to all of the other unfazed occupants of the bathroom. Apparently, they'd heard this before.

The reporter stopped at the sink to wash her hands, then ran some cold water, splashed it on her face, and left the bathroom, deciding that she would just have to use the bathroom on the plane, if necessary.

Jordanna's legs were extremely weak, and she could feel herself sliding down the back wall. "That's enough, baby."

The woman sitting between her legs had either not heard her or just didn't want to stop with her ministrations. Jordanna was not one to admit a weakness and couldn't hold herself up any longer. She angrily pulled the girl by the hair and made her look up into ice-blue eyes. "I said, that's fucking enough!"

The shocked young woman moved away quickly, allowing the drummer to jump off of the seat and land unsteadily on the floor. She leaned one hand against the wall, using it as support, and grabbed her jeans and panties with the other.

The woman from the audience adjusted her own wrinkled clothing as Jordanna pulled on her jeans and buttoned up her shirt. She stood there waiting as Jordanna finished getting dressed, not realizing that the drummer was through with her for the night. The dark-haired woman stopped tying her sneaker and looked up at the woman. "You were great, baby, thanks."

The woman remained standing there, just looking at her.

Jordanna glared at her. "What in the hell are you waiting for, my fucking phone number? I said thanks already." She handed the girl her panties. "Here, a souvenir to always remember me by."

The woman took the panties out of the drummer's hand and stomped out of the stall, letting the door slam behind her. Her friend walked up to her and joined her on their way out of the bathroom.

Jordanna whistled as she finished putting on her sneakers and stood up slowly to make sure her legs were working again before she walked contentedly out of the stall, stopping to wash her hands and then fix her hair in front of the mirror.

MOST OF THE band and crew were already settled in their seats on the plane when Rebecca arrived. Still very embarrassed by the incident in the bathroom, she looked around and saw an empty seat next to Linda, who, she knew, was the quiet member of the band. "Mind if I sit here?" she asked.

Linda looked up from the magazine she was reading, surprised to see the young, attractive reporter. "Uh, no, not at all. Um, aren't you supposed to be working with Jordanna?"

Rebecca sat down and took a minute to look at the guitarist's body, realizing that the woman must lift weights in her spare time. "Yeah, I am."

"Why aren't you, then?"

Rebecca blushed. "She's, um, busy."

Linda laughed. "Ah. Say no more."

Rebecca leaned her head back against the seat and closed her eyes, hoping that the image of the drummer and the woman in the bathroom that kept flashing through her mind would go away. When it didn't, she opened her eyes again and looked at the guitarist, who turned her gaze back to the magazine she had been reading. Rebecca cleared her throat. "How long have you been body building, Linda?"

Linda smiled. "Five years."

"It's a lot of hard work, no?"

The rhythm guitarist nodded. "It can be grueling sometimes, but I find it very relaxing."

"I hate working out." Rebecca frowned. "Well, that's not really true. I enjoy working out. I just don't have the time anymore between the job and trying to see my daughter."

"How old is your daughter?"

"She just turned five."

"How old are you, if you don't mind me asking?"

"I'm twenty-seven."

"Ah. I thought you looked kind of young."

"Tell my body that," the reporter said, suppressing a yawn. "So, are there rooms on this thing, or does everyone just sleep in the seats?"

Linda laughed and shook her head. "The plane does have a few rooms in the back where we sleep or go for some privacy." Her face turned red.

"Oh." Rebecca understood the reason for that blush all too well. Hazel eyes immediately scanned the cabin looking for the tall, dark drummer. She was nowhere to be found. *Why am I not surprised?* What did surprise her was a surge of disappointment. The drummer, she decided, was probably in her room—and most certainly not alone. *At least she's behind closed doors this time, thank God.*

"I can take you for a tour if you'd like," Linda offered. "Once we take off and hit cruising speed, of course."

Rebecca turned her head and looked at the guitarist. "Yeah, I'd like that, thanks."

After Linda had showed her around the plane and they were back in their seats, Rebecca decided to see what kind of information she could pry out of the guitarist. "Thanks for the tour. Um, would you mind if I ask you a few questions about the band?"

"No, not at all." Linda rubbed her temple.

"Did you all live near each other when you were growing up?"

"Not really. Rachel, Kelly, and Jordanna all grew up in the same town on Long Island, and they went to school together. I'm from the Bronx."

"How did you end up meeting up with them?"

Linda shifted in her seat. "They placed an ad looking for a lead vocalist, and I answered it. At that time they were practicing in Rachel's basement, so I went to Rachel's house to jam with them to see if it was really her... I mean if they had the sound I was looking for."

*What in the hell? If it was really her?* Rebecca narrowed her eyes. "I guess they did have the sound you were looking for, huh?"

The guitarist smiled. "Oh, yeah. Exactly what I was looking for."

Rebecca wanted to keep her talking. "So you practiced in Rachel's basement. How did you guys end up playing the clubs?"

"Rachel's father is a musician. That's why we practiced at her house. He had all the equipment we needed there, so we didn't have to drag instruments back and forth, especially Jordanna's drums. His band played all the clubs in the area, so he knew most of the owners and got us some gigs. They also knew Rachel because she was always at all of his shows. He really played a big part in it."

"I think about fifteen people came to the first show we did," she continued with a chuckle. "Most of them were our family members. Word spread, and the clubs started getting more and more packed. We played a few shows in the city, but most of them were on the Island. After a while, I got tired of commuting so I decided to move to the Island. Jordanna told me I could stay with her at her house while I was looking for an apartment." She stopped speaking and turned to the reporter. "Hey, I'm gonna get something to drink; you want something?"

"Whatever kind of soda you have would be fine, thanks." Rebecca noticed at that moment that her throat was very dry.

"You got it. Be right back."

Rebecca watched as Linda went to the refrigerator in the back of the plane. The reporter could sense the guitarist starting to feel at ease with her. *This is good. Keep her talking.*

Linda returned and handed Rebecca an ice-cold bottle.

"Thanks." She took a sip of it and continued the questioning. "You were mentioning that you moved in with Jordanna while you were looking for a place. How did you guys get along? She seems so..." Rebecca paused, looking for the right word.

"Unreachable?" Linda interrupted. "Yeah, she's not the easiest person to get along with. She's got a lot going on in that head of hers. It's very hard to read her."

"That doesn't surprise me," the reporter muttered and then closed her eyes to rest.

A loud ruckus startled the young reporter awake. She saw the drummer coming out of one of the back rooms with a woman they didn't recognize. Rebecca cringed. *On to the next flavor, huh, Jordanna?*

The two walked by and took seats in the front of the plane. Linda looked away, her eyes shadowed.

Noticing the change in the guitarist, Rebecca put her hand on Linda's. "Are you all right?"

Linda looked at the hand on top of hers and smiled. "Yeah. It just hurts sometimes when I see her like that."

*Bingo. I knew it.* "You two were involved once?" the reporter asked without thinking.

Linda's eyes opened wide.

Rebecca's face immediately turned red. "I'm so sorry, that's your business. I shouldn't have asked."

Linda sighed. "No, it's okay. It's not like everyone doesn't know about it already." She shifted in her seat. "Not too long after I moved in with her we, um, became intimate. Like so many other people have found out, it's very hard to resist her charm. One day I came home from my day job, walked in our bedroom, and found her in bed with another woman." She stopped and sighed. "She had no remorse. No guilt. Guess I should have expected that but, you know, I really didn't." She tried to smile.

Rebecca was lost in her thoughts. *Let's rewind this conversation a little now, shall we?* "Listen, I'm going to be honest, Linda. I really don't understand your lifestyle, but..." she paused. Seeing the pain on Linda's face she realized how much the woman felt for the drummer. "I can imagine how much she must have hurt you by doing that. But remember, someone like her can only get away with the things they do for so long without having to be accountable."

"Yeah, you're right. She is, and will be, accountable for her actions." An expression flitted over Linda's face and was gone. Rebecca felt a sudden chill. She opened her mouth to say something, she wasn't sure what, but Linda spoke first. "Listen, it's late, and tomorrow is gonna be a long day, so we better get some rest. There should be an extra room available, but if there isn't, you can just crash with me."

They walked to the back of the plane to find all of the rooms in use, except for Linda's and Jordanna's. Agreeing that Rebecca would room with Linda that night, they set out to find her carry-on. When they didn't find it in any of the occupied rooms, they figured it was probably with Jordanna's things, since the reporter had come with her and Jerry.

Rebecca turned to go speak to Jordanna about her carry-on and finally found the drummer sitting in a seat with her starstruck guest standing in front of her, leaning her back against the seat in front of them. When Rebecca got a better look, she realized that Jordanna's hands were slowly working their way up and under the giggling woman's shirt. Embarrassed and uncomfortable that she had to witness another of Jordanna's displays, Rebecca cleared her throat to announce her presence. "Um, Jordanna? I'm uh, sorry to bother you but I, I was looking for my carry-on and was wondering if you saw it in your room?"

Jordanna made no attempt to hide what she was doing to her adoring groupie. In fact, seeing the unquestionably embarrassed reporter there inspired her to put on a better show. She admitted to herself that she had been instantly attracted to Rebecca when she first saw her at the airport. There was something about Rebecca that grabbed her in more ways than one, although she couldn't quite put a finger on it.

What she could put her finger on was the fact that she

wanted to put her fingers and various other body parts on
Rebecca, but the groupie would have to do. For now. Jordanna
noticed that the reporter couldn't take her eyes off her thumbs,
which just happened to be rubbing lazy circles around the
delighted woman's attentive nipples. "You like that, huh?" she
whispered sensually.

"Oh, yeah," the woman answered, but Jordanna's eyes
locked with Rebecca's, making it very clear whom the question
was really directed at.

"I had your things sent to my room, Rebecca. I figured that
you'd be spending the night with me." Jordanna looked at the
woman standing in front of her and winked. "You don't mind
sharing me with the kid, do you?"

Linda, who had followed Rebecca, scowled. "Damn it,
Jordanna, knock it off and grow up already! Can't you fucking
be serious for once in your life?"

A wolfish grin made its way across Jordanna's face. "I am
being serious. I know what it is. You want her all for yourself,
don't you, Lin? That's it, isn't it?" the drummer snorted. "I
know I told you I thought you needed to get laid, Linda; I just
didn't mean that you should do it with one of my women."

*Me? One of her women? I think not!* Exhaustion, confusion,
and resentment combined to ignite her temper. "Don't you ever,
and I mean ever, call me that again, Jordanna! I am not, nor will
I *ever* be, one of your women," Rebecca screamed at the drummer
at the top of her lungs, drawing the attention of the plane's other
occupants. "Just let me get my fucking luggage out of your room,
please?"

Jordanna put her hands over her ears. "Whoa, girl! My
virgin ears!" she teased.

Rebecca didn't see the humor in it.

"Shit, can't a girl have a little fun around here?" Jordanna
got up and headed toward her room. "C'mon, let's go," she
called out to the reporter.

Rebecca walked quickly and caught up with her at the end of
the aisle, following her into the room. She noticed the messy,
unmade bed as soon as she stepped in. Walking past the
drummer when she saw what she was looking for, she grabbed
her luggage.

Jordanna stepped in front of her, blocking her from leaving
the cabin. She leaned down and whispered in the reporter's ear.
"Are you *sure* you don't want to spend the night with me? I
promise, you won't be sorry if you do."

"Not if you were the last person on earth, Jordanna,"
Rebecca said as she walked out of the small room, slamming the

door behind her.

Jordanna sat down on the bed and smiled. *God, she's cute.*

SOME TIME IN the early hours, they arrived at the hotel in Philadelphia. After checking in, most of the band and crew opted to get a few hours of rest.

Unable to sleep, Rebecca decided to relax in the hotel's heated pool. She grabbed a few items from her suitcase and went into the bathroom to change into her navy one-piece before she pulled a long tee shirt over her head. She walked out of the bathroom, grabbed a towel from the linen closet, tied it around her waist, and slipped out of her hotel room, making her way to the pool. She felt very stressed over this assignment and figured that a good swim would calm her nerves. Hoping that there were no screaming children around, she opened the door and made her way through the gym to get to the pool.

Thankful that she heard no screaming when she opened the door, she cut around the corner and looked through the window at the pool, catching a pair of blue eyes looking back at her. The drummer was standing in the pool halfway between the shallow and deep ends, with her back against the wall. She had two female friends with her, so close they looked attached to her like velcro.

*Oh, shit! She saw you. It's too late to back out now.* Rebecca hesitated as she pulled the door open, and noticed the blue eyes were still completely focused on her.

The drummer's heart started pounding as she caught sight of the reporter. She could tell that Rebecca wasn't sure if she wanted to take the swim that she had obviously come there for. "You can come in, Rebecca. This *is* a public pool," Jordanna said.

Rebecca didn't say a word; she just walked over to a chair and put her towel down. Even though her back was turned, she could feel Jordanna's eyes still on her as she stripped out of her shirt. When she turned to walk to the pool, she confirmed her feeling, as her eyes locked with the drummer's once again.

Resisting the urge to dive in to escape the intense gaze, she slowly stepped into the shallow end of the pool and immediately went under the water. When she emerged, Jordanna's lips were locked with those of the blonde attached to the right side of her body. They kissed fiercely and passionately, and Rebecca could see a definite exchange of bodily fluids going on between the two.

And she could feel her own body reacting to the sight.

Rebecca watched the third member of the party as the

drummer and the blonde kissed. "Hey, what about me?" the woman whined, after the kiss had ended.

"C'mere," the dark-haired drummer said seductively, noticing that the reporter's hazel eyes were on her. *She's watching, make this good.* Jordanna smiled seductively as she pulled the woman to her. "Do you really think I would leave you out?" She repeated the same kind of hungry kiss she had just shared with the blonde.

Rebecca didn't want to watch, but she found herself inexplicably drawn to the scene unfolding in the pool. *Why am I finding this so erotic?* the reporter thought as she tore her eyes away from the drummer. *I do not like women.* She shook her head when a vision of the drummer kissing her like that flashed in her mind. *I do not like women! Especially not her.*

She looked up when she heard her name being called. "Come over here," the drummer demanded, rather than asked. "Please," she added, trying her best to be nice.

Rebecca hesitantly swam closer to the drummer and her entourage. "What?"

"I'd like to introduce you to my friends," the dark woman said. "This is..." she paused and a questioning eyebrow went up when she looked at the blonde.

"Cathy," the bubbly woman said.

"This is Cathy," Jordanna repeated. "And this is..." She paused again to look at the other woman.

"Monica," the woman offered.

Rebecca shook her head. She said a quick "hi" before she swam away to do laps in the pool. The dark-haired woman watched her every move, thinking that Rebecca had too beautiful a body to cover up by wearing a one-piece bathing suit.

The door to the room burst open, and Gary walked through it with two other women following him. "Hey, J! Look who I found," he said loudly. "Oops, sorry, didn't know you had other company."

Jordanna laughed and looked directly into Rebecca's eyes. "Don't worry, there's plenty of me to go around," she teased and swam toward the ladder to get out of the pool. "Gary, didn't you meet Rebecca last night?"

"No." Gary looked the small blonde over appreciatively. "I'd remember a woman as beautiful as her, that's for damn sure."

"She's a reporter and she's doing an article on, of all things, me."

"Oh, boy," Gary said. Jordanna's dislike of the media was no secret. "Nice to meet you, Rebecca. I'm the band's stage manager and J's drum tech. If you want the inside scoop on this difficult woman here, I'm the one to ask."

"You wouldn't dare, Gary." Jordanna slowly climbed up the ladder and got out of the pool. "Because if you did, playtime with Jordanna would be over for you."

Rebecca's heart began to pound as she watched the drummer. She wore a black thong bikini that left *very* little to the imagination. *God, what a nice ass*, the reporter thought. She shook her head to clear her thoughts. *Checking out a woman's ass? What in the hell is happening to me?*

Jordanna walked over to a chair, picked up her towel, and began to dry herself off with it. She handed a towel to each of her pool friends and walked over to Gary. "So, who do we have here?" she asked as she rubbed her hand across one woman's back, and areas much lower than that.

The reporter heard bits of conversation as she watched the dark-haired drummer familiarize herself with the woman's form, caressing her in areas that were crying out for attention on her own body. Lost in her thoughts, Rebecca only half-heard Jordanna suggest that they continue their little party in her hotel room. The dark-haired woman turned and looked at the reporter. "You are *more* than welcome to join us, Rebecca," she offered. "Like I said, there's plenty of me to go around."

"Like *I* said last night, Jordanna, not if you were the last person on earth," the reporter responded, before she continued her laps. *You stuck-up, sex-crazed egomaniac!*

"Whoo hoo hoo, J! I do believe a woman has officially refused your advances for the first time ever," Gary said, laughing.

Jordanna looked at him with an amused gleam in her eyes. "It's not the first time, Gary."

"No?"

"She refused my advances last night on the plane, too." She turned and looked at the woman in the pool, who was looking back at her. "But she can only refuse me for so long. I always get what I want. Always."

"Well, there's always a first time for everything. You can't always get what you want," Rebecca mumbled under her breath, but she knew the dark-haired woman heard her when she cheerfully began to sing the Rolling Stones' song by the same name. The drummer then flashed a predatory smile and winked at her before opening the door. "I'm in the penthouse, room 5252, if you're interested, Rebecca. Just in case you change your mind or something." The drummer walked out and slammed the door behind her.

"I won't." The reporter spoke only to her echo in the empty room.

HAPPY TO BE away from the drummer and her friends, Rebecca went into her hotel room and turned the television on before she dialed the office number to give John an update.

"You are going to owe me big time for this one, John." This time it was Rebecca's turn to start off a conversation without any greetings.

"Rebecca? I guess I don't have to ask you how it's going." Rebecca could picture him, head cocked, frowning pensively. "Where are you now?" he asked.

"We're in Philly right now. How much more of this do I have to endure?"

"That bad, huh?" he asked quietly. "You're supposed to travel with them for the rest of the tour. They wind up the tour in New York."

Rebecca's mouth dropped open. "The *rest* of the tour? You've got to be kidding me! Exactly how long is that? I don't know about this, John."

John cleared his throat. "Well, um, how bad can she be, Rebecca? I know she has quite the reputation, but what about the rest of the band?"

She snorted. "Well, the rest of the members of the band are really nice. Linda's been great. But Jordanna..." she sighed, stopping to think about the beautiful drummer. "Everything she says is either an insult or sexual innuendo. Let me tell you, her reputation is definitely not over-exaggerated. I mean, I already saw her..."

"Saw her doing what, Rebecca?" John's voice sharpened.

"I um, saw her..." Rebecca knew that if John found out what she saw happen in the bathroom, he would somehow want that written into her article. After all, sex did sell. "I saw her holding hands with a woman," she lied.

John laughed. "That's it? You saw her holding hands? I didn't know you were such a prude, Rebecca!"

*A prude? Why am I lying for this woman, anyway? Why can't she just behave? She wouldn't have to worry about bad press if she just kept her damn legs shut!* "I am not a prude."

"Think what you want." John snorted. "Keep your chin up, kid. She doesn't sound so bad. You'll be fine."

*Easy for you to say,* she thought as she hung up the phone. She cursed him silently for sending her on this horrible assignment. Then a smile crossed her face. She dialed the number to her ex-husband's Manhattan home. After two rings,

Rebecca heard the very soft-spoken voice of Anna, Rebecca's ex-husband's live-in girlfriend. "Hello?"

"Hi, Anna. It's Rebecca. Can I speak to Cindy?" The reporter surprisingly hadn't experienced any of the problems that most people go through with their former spouses' new significant others. In fact, as much as she hated to admit it, she actually liked Anna. The pair had invited Rebecca over for dinner at their apartment on numerous occasions, giving her the chance to spend extra time with her daughter.

"Hey, Becky. Cindy's not here right now. Dave took her and a neighbor to the park a couple of hours ago. They should be back soon, though." She paused. "So, I hear that job of yours sent you off on another assignment before you could even unpack. What in the heck are you working on now?"

"I'm touring with Plenty of Nothing right now."

Anna screamed with excitement. "Oh, my God! I love them! Have you met Jordanna yet?" she asked, like she knew the drummer personally.

Rebecca sighed. "Yes, I've met her."

"How cool! What's she like?"

The reporter didn't know what to say. "She's, um, she's a great drummer."

"Have you seen her with a woman yet?" Anna whispered, as if someone was listening to the conversation.

Rebecca had to laugh. She'd always wondered why straight people, supposedly so opposed to homosexuality, were so interested in it. "Yes. She's, um, very *open* about her sexuality, Anna. Why?"

"Just curious."

Rebecca closed her eyes and leaned her head back against the hard wall, not really in the mood to discuss the drummer. "I have to go, Anna. Can you let Cindy know that I called and that I love her and will call back later? Oh, and give her a kiss for me," she asked, as an afterthought.

"No problem, Becky, I will. Take care."

Her phone calls taken care of, Rebecca found herself rearranging the things in her suitcase that she had already rearranged three times since arriving in Philadelphia. Bored with that, she lay down on the bed and thought of her failed marriage with David and how much she missed her daughter.

Hours later, Rebecca woke to loud knocking on her hotel room door. She rubbed her sleepy eyes as she answered the door. A road-crew member whose name she couldn't remember stood there. "Ready to go to the show?"

She looked at her watch and cursed, realizing that she had

slept far longer than she should have.  The show was due to start in an hour and a half.  "Shit, give me ten minutes, okay?"

The roadie nodded and started to walk back down the hallway.  "Meet us in the lobby, okay?"

"Yep, I'll be there."

# Chapter
# Four

FIFTEEN PAIRS OF feet ran through the crowded airport, trying to make the now-departing flight. Out of the corner of her eye, Rebecca saw a young girl, no more than seven years old, standing in a corner by a group of phones, crying.

The show had run late, and they were on a very tight schedule. The band members were too caught up in their own lives to have time to worry about someone else's. They all ran right by the young girl, just as Rebecca expected them to do.

What Rebecca didn't expect was to slam into the back of the drummer, who also saw the crying girl and came to a sudden stop. Rebecca stood back and watched as Jordanna walked over to the girl and crouched down next to her.

"Are you lost?"

The little girl looked up at the tall woman, nodded, and started to cry even harder.

"What's your name, sweetheart?"

"Jessie."

"Hi, Jessie." The dark-haired woman smiled and wiped a tear off the girl's cheek. "My name is Jordanna." The girl looked back at her with big, blue, teary eyes. "Are you here with your parents?"

"I can't find my Mama," Jessie said, between lingering sniffles.

Jordanna pointed to a small, emerald-green stuffed teddy bear on the floor next to the girl. "Is this yours?"

The girl nodded again. "Ralph."

Jordanna smiled and picked up the green bear. Tucking it under her arm, she held out her large hand to the young girl, who trustingly slipped her tiny one in it. "You, me, and Ralph are gonna go find your mama now, okay?"

They walked to the closest ticket counter, and the drummer said a few words to the man behind the desk. She stood waiting with the young girl, telling the road-crew member sent to retrieve her to go ahead without her, that she would take another flight out and meet the band at the hotel in Cleveland.

Rebecca heard the page on the airport PA system announcing the lost child and smiled. She then heard Jordanna calling out to her from her place by the desk. "You missed the flight, Rebecca."

"I know."

A dark eyebrow lifted in question. "Why?"

The reporter shrugged. "I don't know." She grinned a little. "I guess I'll have to take the next one out with you."

The drummer turned abruptly as the child's hand was ripped out of her own. "Mama!" the young girl squealed happily. An obviously terrified, yet relieved woman in her mid-thirties had the young girl in her arms within seconds, stroking her hair and kissing her on the forehead.

"Don't you ever walk away like that on me again, Jessie! You had Mama scared like crazy over you, honey."

Jessie pointed to the tall drummer. "She found me and took care of me."

The grateful woman thanked Jordanna, who shied away from the gushing praise the woman was giving her.

"Just glad I could help," the red-faced drummer replied. Jordanna waved to the girl as she and her mother walked away. "Bye, Jessie."

The smiling girl waved back. "Bye!"

The still-embarrassed Jordanna turned around and faced a grinning Rebecca. "Well." She cleared her throat. "Guess we better get ourselves booked on the next flight out to Cleveland."

JORDANNA LOOKED DOWN at her watch and sighed. "We've got quite a bit of time to kill, and the smell of those cinnamon buns is simply making my mouth water. How about we go get one and grab a cup of coffee while we wait?"

Rebecca smiled at the drummer and the thought of two of her favorite things — food and coffee. "Sure, sounds great to me. What about him, though?" The reporter pointed to Jordanna's bodyguard, who had tried, but obviously failed, to mix in with the people in the background.

"You mean Lenny?" Jordanna shrugged. "He's a big boy. He can get his own coffee."

They walked through the airport terminal, following the delightful aroma until they found the small, crowded food court. Jordanna started to walk toward the long line and turned around to face Rebecca. "Why don't you go get a table for us. How do you take yours?"

*Around six feet tall, long dark hair, incredible blue eyes with a body and voice to die for.*

The drummer stood there quietly, waiting for her answer. "Rebecca? You okay?"

"Huh?"

"How do you like your coffee?"

"Light, no sugar, thanks."

The drummer winked at her and then got in line.

Rebecca's body warmed instantly and she held in a sigh. *So, she is a human being after all. And my long-lost libido still works after all, also.*

The reporter was rattled out of her thoughts as a commotion started in the line. "You're Jordanna Fox, aren't you?" she heard a young man exclaim.

The drummer looked up, locked eyes with Rebecca, and shrugged—a gesture that the reporter took as an apology of sorts. "Yes, I am," she answered and sighed heavily as napkins and paper were thrust at her for autographs.

Rebecca watched as Jordanna talked with people, signed autographs, and posed for photos  When she reached the front of the line, she placed her order with the excited teenaged girl behind the counter and signed a piece of paper that the girl handed to her, then went back to signing more autographs and posing for more photos for people in the food court. She paid for the items, grabbed the tray and politely excused herself from the crowd, and walked over to the table where Rebecca sat.

"How do you handle that all of the time?" Rebecca asked as Jordanna set the tray down and slid into the seat across from her.

Jordanna shrugged. "You get used to it. It's part of the job, you know? Actually, it's a very big part of it."

"Well, I don't think I could handle that as well as you just did."

"Sure you could," the drummer quickly replied, and placed the reporter's coffee in front of her. "Light, no sugar," she said, smiling at the reporter briefly.

"Thank you."

"No problem. Dig in." The drummer grabbed one of the two cinnamon buns off of the tray, took a bite out of it, and let out a little moan. "Just heavenly," she said when she finished chewing.

Rebecca did the same. "Better than sex." The words came out before she could stop them. She looked up at Jordanna, who was smiling like the cat that ate the canary.

"Apparently you haven't had sex with the right wom—

person, Rebecca," Jordanna said with a twinkle in her very blue eyes.

Rebecca looked at her with the same twinkle in her eyes, her heart rate increasing ever so slightly. "I walked myself right into that one, didn't I?"

The drummer licked her frosting-covered fingers off slowly, keeping her eyes locked with the reporter's. "Oh, yeah. That you did." She leaned across the table with her napkin and wiped a bit of frosting off of Rebecca's face. "Had a little frosting on your cheek," she said as she sat back down in her seat.

Now, not only did Rebecca's heart rate increase, but she felt a heat starting to build between her legs as her libido got a good kick-start. "Um, thank you."

Jordanna leaned back in her seat and took another bite of her bun, keeping her eyes locked with the young reporter's. "Oh, you're very welcome." *And you're very beautiful when you blush like that, Rebecca.*

"Flight 1435 to Cleveland now boarding at Gate H."

Rebecca snapped out of her erotic haze. "Isn't that us?"

The drummer got up from her seat and put her coffee cup on the tray to throw it out. "Yep, that's us. Let's go."

JORDANNA WOKE FROM her short nap as the flight attendant asked her if she needed anything. She shook her head.

"Do you know if she'd like anything?" the woman asked, pointing to the sleeping reporter, who was using the drummer's shoulder as a pillow. Jordanna smiled at the sight, shrugged, and then shook Rebecca gently on the shoulder. She was rewarded with a muffled, "Just ten more minutes. That's all I need."

"I would say that's a no," the drummer said to the attendant, who nodded and told Jordanna that if they did needed anything, just to ask. She then went to check on the travelers in the seats behind them.

Jordanna turned her head and let her eyes travel up and down the flight attendant's firm body, only to turn and see an older man sitting across from her watching. She winked at the man, and he quickly looked away. She then turned her own gaze to the woman sleeping beside her. Noticing a few stray golden strands in the woman's face, she gently brushed them away from her eyes.

Rebecca stirred at the sensation and her hazel eyes opened with a flutter, only to focus into the beautiful blue ones looking back at her. She stretched her arms slightly and yawned a bit before saying a word. "I guess I fell asleep."

Jordanna laid her head against the back of her seat and turned to face the front of the cabin. "Did you want something to eat or drink? The flight attendant came by when you were sleeping."

"Nope, I'm fine, thanks."

"Rebecca?"

"Yes?"

"How is your article coming along?"

Rebecca closed her eyes again and shook her head. She had been hoping that they might have possibly come to a peaceful treaty while they waited together in the airport. She guessed she was wrong. "Not very good, actually. My subject matter is a real pompous pain in the ass. Why?"

Jordanna burst out laughing. "Just wondering. Pompous pain in the ass, huh? That's a new one, even for me, and I've been called a lot of things."

"I'm sure you have," the reporter answered with a snort.

"I guess we really didn't get off to a good start, did we?"

Rebecca opened her eyes and looked at Jordanna. "I would say that's an understatement."

The drummer laughed. "I was pretty rude to you in the limo, wasn't I?"

Rebecca nodded. "Like I said, a real pompous pain in the ass."

"First time we meet, I'm rude to you," the drummer said and paused. "The next time you see me, there's a woman going down on me in a bathroom stall. That must have been a real shock to walk in on."

Rebecca's mouth dropped open. "You saw me?"

"Nope, I didn't see you. I heard someone walk in." Jordanna smirked. Even with her eyes closed, she could tell the stunned reporter had her mouth wide open. "You can lift your jaw back up; you'll need it to talk."

"How, uh, how did you know it was me?"

"I have many skills, Rebecca. Not much gets past me, as you will find out in the weeks to come." She took a deep breath for effect. "Your perfume. You smell of soft jasmine, Rebecca. Which, by the way, is very, very nice."

"You knew it was me by smelling my perfume? Weren't there, um, other things occupying your senses at the time?"

Jordanna broke out into another smile. "Yep, there sure were."

"Damn, you're good."

Jordanna cleared her throat. "So I've been told." She turned her head and looked into the stunned hazel eyes looking back at her. "Like I said, I have many skills." She wiggled her eyebrows at the reporter. "Like reading people's minds."

Rebecca decided to play along with Jordanna's game. "Oh, yeah? What am I thinking right now, Jordanna?"

The drummer started to impersonate a psychic, pretending she had a crystal ball in front of her. "You, reporter, have lots of thoughts going around in your mind. Yes, lots and lots of thoughts. Far, far too many thoughts...ouch." She rubbed her forehead. "Gives me a headache."

Rebecca laughed at the drummer's goofy antics.

Jordanna continued. "Ah, you laugh at the psycho? I mean psychic? Tch! Are you questioning my psychic abilities, young lady?"

"You sound more like Dracula than a psychic, Jordanna," the reporter said with a huge smile. "And, no, I don't question your abilities. Go on."

"Dracula, eh? Just call me Madam Jorcula, then. Don't bother asking what I come to suck, but it definitely isn't your blood." She let her eyes wander down the front of the reporter's body, coming to a stop at her chest.

Rebecca shook her head. "Even the most innocent of statements, you somehow manage to turn provocative. How do you do that?"

Jordanna lifted a brow. "I'm magic."

"You're magic? No, I think you're insane. Now tell me what else I'm thinking, Madam Jerkcula."

"Jerkcula? Ah, that's very funny, Rebecca. So, she has a sense of humor after all. And stop teasing the psychic or she will have to put a nasty spell on you."

*I think you've already done that, Jordanna.* "I'll stop. I promise," Rebecca said quietly.

Jordanna put her hand on the reporter's forehead. Rebecca raised a questioning brow.

The drummer shrugged. "It helps for me to connect with my subject." Jordanna pulled her hand back suddenly and covered her mouth. "Oh, my, you naughty, naughty girl. You could get arrested for thoughts like that."

Rebecca bit her lip trying to stifle her laughter. She noticed the people in the seats around them were listening in on the conversation.

Jordanna put her hand back on Rebecca's forehead. "Ah, yes, I see it clearly now. You're thinking that in all of the years you have been in the music business, you've met a lot of pigs, but this Jordanna character that everyone talks about, well, she takes the all-time oinker cake."

Rebecca looked at the dark-haired woman and smiled. "One out of one right. Very good so far. Go on Madam Jerk—I mean, Jorcula."

"You are also thinking that as much as you don't want to like the pompous pain in the ass," the drummer stopped speaking briefly and closed her eyes, "you can't help but like her. There's something about her that you are drawn to, right? You just can't put your finger on it."

Rebecca started to speak but Jordanna stopped her. "No, wait, I'm getting more. Like I said, you have lots and lots of thoughts." She leaned over and spoke quietly. "You have also been thinking a lot lately about something that you never really thought of before."

"Oh, yeah, what's that?" Rebecca asked, intrigued by the conversation unfolding.

Jordanna turned her head and looked directly into Rebecca's eyes, holding her gaze. "Being with a woman, and not just as friends."

Rebecca's breath caught for the umpteenth time of the day. As much as she wanted to deny the statement, she couldn't.

"Wait, I'm, I mean, Jorcula's getting more," Jordanna continued, totally into playing around with Rebecca. "You think I'm conceited and completely full of myself, huh?" She looked down and smiled.

Rebecca turned her body to the side. "I will never question Madam Jorcula's psychic abilities again."

"No?"

"No."

Jordanna held out her hand to Rebecca. "Truce?"

Rebecca looked directly into Jordanna's azure eyes. The look in them seemed sincere. She shook the drummer's hand. "Truce."

"Well, then, I think I'd like to start all over again, if it's all right with you. It's very nice to meet you, Rebecca," the drummer said, her smile reaching from ear to ear.

"I'd like that very much. It's nice to meet you, too, Jordanna."

They sat back in their seats, both wondering what had just occurred between them. The easy banter seemed familiar to them both.

"Jordanna?"

"Hmm?"

"What you did for that little girl earlier was a really wonderful thing."

The drummer blinked, but didn't say a word.

"No, I mean it," the reporter said sincerely. "It really was."

Jordanna shrugged her shoulders. "It was no big deal. I just know what it feels like to be alone and scared, that's all."

JORDANNA TRIED HARD to absorb the last few pages of the latest book she was reading. She sat up on the bed in her hotel room, propped up the pillows against the headboard, and then leaned back against them, hoping to keep her eyes open long enough to finish the book.

The phone rang. She jumped, then stretched her long frame across the bed and picked it up. "Hello?"

"Meet us at the bar next door in an hour."

She took off her reading glasses, rubbed her forehead, and looked at the clock. Was it only 8:30? She felt like it should have been 3:00 AM. "Too tired to party, Kel."

"Hel-lo?" Kelly tapped on the phone receiver a few times. "Who is this, and what have you done with Jordanna Fox?"

The drummer laughed. "Really, I'm beat, Kelly."

"She helps one small child in distress and she's exhausted. What's gonna happen when you settle down and have your own children?"

The drummer snorted loudly. "Do you plan on bearing some kids for me, Kel?"

"Not on your life," Kelly said emphatically, and the drummer knew that the guitarist was shaking her curly head. "Well, then, we don't have to worry about what happens when I have children, now do we?" Jordanna heard other voices in the background. "Who is there with you?"

"Just me, Rache, and Linda. Oh, and Joe and Rick flew out to meet us. Rachel told me to tell you there are pool tables here."

"Oh, yeah?" the drummer said with a yawn.

"I can see your enthusiasm," the guitarist snickered. The voices in the background spoke again. "Rache just said she saw a few strawberry-blonde babes walking into the bar earlier."

Rebecca's face popped into the drummer's mind immediately, as it had been doing all night. "Strawberry-blonde? Now you're talking my game, Kelly."

"I thought you'd see the light. Bar next door—an hour."

REBECCA SAT TYPING away on her laptop when she heard a knock at the door. She jumped up from the chair and went to the door, checking through the peephole first. Her breath caught as she saw the drummer standing there. *Oh, God.*

She quickly pulled her hair out of the loose ponytail it was

in and ran her hands through it a few times to straighten it out. *I
have no make-up on.*

"Rebecca? It's Jordanna. Are you in there?"

"Just a minute," she said, and opened the door. She looked
the dark-haired woman over and decided she really liked what
Jordanna was wearing. "You look nice."

Jordanna looked down at her skin-tight black jeans, black-
and-white-striped blouse, and her black biker boots, and
shrugged. She threw her leather jacket over her shoulder and
shifted her feet. "Thanks. Can I, um, come in?"

"Oh, yeah, sure. Sorry," Rebecca answered and backed
away from the door to let the drummer pass. Jordanna walked
in and leaned against a table.

"Everything okay?" the reporter asked.

"Oh, um, yeah. I just came by to see if you wanted to go to
the bar next door for some drinks and maybe something to eat,
that's all. The rest of the band is there."

Rebecca was about to decline when she changed her mind.
"Sure. I just have to take a quick shower and put some make-up
on first. It's right next door?"

The drummer nodded. "Yeah."

"I'll meet you there, okay?" Rebecca said, then grabbed a
small travel bag out of her suitcase and went into the bathroom
to shower.

Jordanna decided she would wait for the young reporter to
get ready. She walked over to the bed where Rebecca had left her
laptop, the document she was working on still on the screen.
With only the slightest feeling of guilt, the drummer read the
piece, smiling as she scanned through it.

It was the article on her and the band. Jordanna was
impressed. The reporter hadn't had a lot to work with, and most
of it bad, but she'd put a spin on it that Jordanna would never
have expected. After she finished the article, she sat down in a
chair to wait.

*I like this little woman.*

The bathroom door swung open, and Rebecca emerged in
only a towel, stopping dead in her tracks when she locked eyes
with Jordanna. "Shit, you scared the crap out of me!" She
watched as Jordanna's eyebrow lifted and the drummer looked
her towel-clad body up and down. When their eyes finally met,
the dark-haired woman smiled shyly, blushed, and looked back
down.

Rebecca felt her breath catch once again when she saw the
drummer's shy smile. It was an incredibly attractive look on the
dark-haired woman. "You didn't have to wait for me."

Jordanna shrugged. "I know." The drummer looked her over again and grinned. "But some things are worth waiting for, you know?"

Rebecca knew her face was red. She could feel the warmth spreading in her cheeks. "Um, I'll be another fifteen or twenty minutes."

"That's okay."

Rebecca went to the closet and pulled out a pair of blue jeans and a sweater, then turned to the drummer and held them up. "Are these okay for this place?"

Jordanna looked the clothing over and nodded. "They're fine. It's not like Studio 54 or anything, I don't think. Kelly said there were pool tables there, so I figured casual would be fine." *Although I think I prefer the towel you're wearing.*

True to her words, Rebecca was ready twenty minutes later. She walked out of the bathroom and toward the door. "You ready?"

The drummer looked her over and nodded lazily before she stood up. "Yep."

They took the elevator down to the lobby and walked out the front door in silence. When the two of them walked into the bar, all eyes turned their way. Jordanna was always an imposing presence. Rebecca noticed the waitress and a few of the bars patrons give the drummer the once-over. Jordanna didn't seem to take notice, though, and they went to join the others.

The rest of the band members were at a table hidden in a dark corner of the bar, drinking beer and munching on appetizers. There were a few people there that Rebecca didn't recognize—a tall, blond man sitting next to Rachel and a shorter man with dark hair sitting next to Kelly. "Who are those men?" she asked the drummer.

Jordanna looked at the table to see whom the reporter was talking about. "Oh, that's Joe, Kelly's husband, and the other guy is Rachel's boyfriend, Rick."

Rebecca blushed. She had assumed, since Jordanna and Linda were both gay, that the whole band was. "I didn't know Kelly was married."

Jordanna saw Rebecca's cheeks suddenly turn pink. *Poor kid. I could embarrass the heck out of you right here.* "She married her high-school sweetheart. They have two kids, both boys. I don't know what the hold-up is with Rache and Rick. They've been together forever. It's like they're married, anyway. You want a drink?"

Rebecca didn't answer the drummer's question. Moments later, Jordanna waved her hand in front of the reporter's face.

"Rebecca? Where did you go? Did you want a drink or not?"

The reporter looked up at her. "Hmm? Oh, sorry, just daydreaming. The last time I drank, I made the biggest mistake of my life. Well, not really a mistake, Cindy is the best thing that ever happened to me, but..."

Jordanna felt a surge of jealousy flow through her. *Cindy? Rebecca has a girlfriend?* "What are you talking about? Who is Cindy? All I asked was if you wanted a drink."

Rebecca looked up at Jordanna; the drummer's blue eyes had an odd gleam. *Jealousy? What in the hell?*

"Damn, I'm babbling. Cindy is my daughter. Shit, forget it. I'll have a cola, thanks."

The drummer nodded. "Why don't you take the table next to them, and I'll be right back, okay?"

Rebecca slid into a booth near the rest of the band and watched them for a few minutes while she waited for Jordanna's return; it wasn't as long as it felt. The raven-haired woman moved across the floor with the grace of a panther, sliding into the seat across from Rebecca and handing her a soda before taking a long pull of the beer she had brought for herself. "Thanks." Rebecca started to pull some money out of her wallet, her eyes never leaving the blue of Jordanna's.

Jordanna put her hand on Rebecca's. "It's on me." The drummer paused for a moment. "You have a daughter? Are you, um, married?"

The reporter blinked twice and shook her head. "I'm divorced."

Jordanna let out the breath she was holding. "Oh, sorry."

Rebecca smiled. "No, I'm cool with it. Dave couldn't handle my dedication to my job. He said that it seemed like the job was more important to me than Cindy or he ever was. I guess, in a way, I can understand why he feels that way." Her eyes were wet, tears forming at the thought.

Jordanna shifted in her seat, not knowing how to react. "What, so you spent more time in the office than at home?"

The reporter swallowed hard and closed her eyes. "You could say that."

Interested blue eyes looked at her. "Where did you meet your ex-husband?"

"I met him in college."

"Where did you go to school?"

"New York University."

"Are you from New York?"

The reporter laughed. "Nope. I was born and raised in Lancaster, Pennsylvania."

"Ah, home of the Amish.  What, um, does your family do, if you don't mind me asking?"

Rebecca took a sip of her soda and then put it down on the table.  "Farmers."

The drummer tried very hard not to laugh.  "Really?"

Rebecca looked down.  "Yeah.  They sorta expected me, as the oldest of three kids, to marry this local boy and take over the farm.  They were very disappointed when I told them I wanted to go away to college and become a journalist."

"You're kidding?"  Jordanna's eyes opened wide.  "Like an arranged marriage?"

"Yeah."

"Shit! Your parents do know it's the 21$^{st}$ century, right?"

Rebecca let out an embarrassed laugh.  "Yeah, they do now."

Jordanna looked her directly in the eyes.  "So, what happened between you and your ex?"

"Hey, I'm the reporter!" Rebecca replied, feeling uncomfortable under the scrutiny.  "How is it that you're asking all of the questions tonight?"

"Since you are finding out a lot about me on this assignment," Jordanna winked, "I think it's only fair that you tell me about yourself. Don't you?"

"Yeah, I guess."  Rebecca shrugged and decided to open up a bit to the drummer.  "After I got my job, I had to travel a lot and wasn't home all that often.  That's when he handed me the divorce papers.  We agreed that it was best if I moved out and Cindy remained living with him.  I haven't even had the chance to see her in between my latest assignments."  She looked down at the floor and wiped at the tear that escaped from her eye.  "I miss her so much."

"Don't be so hard on yourself.  It's obvious even to someone like *me* that you love your daughter.  I certainly understand where you're coming from, even though I don't have kids.  I often wonder how Kelly and Joe handle the situation."  The drummer drew Rebecca's gaze back up to her by lifting her chin with her finger.

Just then, a tall blonde walked up to the table.  She crouched down and whispered something in Jordanna's ear.  The drummer's lip twitched and her eyes glistened.

The woman stood back up to her full height, and Jordanna looked up at her.  "I'm flattered, really, and that's a very tempting offer," the drummer said, and then looked at Rebecca.  "But I can't. Sorry."

Rebecca wanted to scream.  She couldn't believe that this

woman would come and proposition Jordanna right there in front of her. *This bitch really has a lot of nerve. How does she know that Jordanna isn't with me? What if we were lovers?* Rebecca paused mid-thought and shivered at the depth of her jealousy.

The blonde was persistent. "Oh, come on, Jordanna. I'll make it worth your while."

Jordanna shook her head. "I'm sorry, I really can't."

"I'll be by the bar if you change your mind," the woman said before she walked away.

Rebecca put her hand on top of the drummer's. "You can go with her if you want, Jordanna. You certainly don't have to stay and entertain me."

"But..." Jordanna started to say.

"She's a beautiful woman, and I know she propositioned you. I can tell by the twinkle in your eyes."

"But I don't want to..."

Rebecca's heart pounded; she didn't hear the drummer's words. "Don't let me get in the way of a good time that I can't give you, Jordanna," she said sarcastically. "Just go...be with her."

*Good time that she can't give me? I thought she was kinda open to the idea. Fuck!* The drummer rubbed the back of her neck, slid out of the seat, and went back over to the bar.

Rebecca watched the raven-haired woman walk over to the blonde and say a few words to her. The blonde smiled back and ran her hand down the buttons on Jordanna's blouse.

*That was real dumb. She was opening up to you, and because of your jealousy you blew it!*

Linda took the seat the drummer had just vacated. "What happened? Was she harassing you again? Did she just leave you here alone and go off with that whore?"

Rebecca shook her head. "No, she was charming, just like you said she can be. She didn't do anything wrong, Linda. It's just..."

*Just what, Rebecca? It's just that I think I'm starting to fall for her, and I stupidly told her to go be with someone else, that's what.*

She stood up and looked at Jordanna with the woman again. They were still standing by the bar together, and Jordanna had her hand on the blonde's thigh, rubbing it gently. "I think I'll go back to the hotel, Linda."

Linda put her hand on the reporter's arm. "No, forget about her, okay? Don't let her ruin the night. Do you play pool? I need a partner. Kelly and Rache want to gang up on me like they usually do. I suck at pool," she admitted. "Jordanna's the pool shark."

"Why don't you ask her to play then?" she hissed at the guitarist, not meaning to sound so sarcastic. Then, "I'm sorry, Linda. That was uncalled for."

"It's okay, Rebecca." Linda turned to look at the drummer, gesturing for the reporter to do the same. "That's why I won't ask her."

"Oh." Rebecca felt a stabbing pain in her chest when she saw Jordanna sitting at a table with the woman. She leaned up against the guitarist as her weak legs started to give. *You told her to go with the woman.*

"Are you okay, Rebecca?" Linda asked, grabbing the small woman.

"Yeah, I'm fine," Rebecca answered quietly. "I just got a little dizzy all of a sudden. I must be hungry."

"We should get something to eat then, Rebecca. Forget the game."

Rebecca looked over at the drummer again and winced when she saw that she was now kissing the blonde. "No, I want to play."

Rachel and Kelly had already racked the balls and were waiting at the table for them. "You wanna bet on this game, Lin?" Rachel teased. She often said that she could buy the Taj Mahal with the money she'd made off of previous pool bets with Linda. She turned to Rebecca. "You don't look like the type to spend much time in pool halls. You'll probably fool us, though."

"Nope, never really played before." The reporter took the cue Linda handed her and scratched her first shot. "I told you I couldn't play. Maybe you can give me some pointers or something?"

"Jordanna's the one that you would want to teach you," Kelly answered. "She sorta grew up in pool halls."

"I don't think she would appreciate me asking her," Rebecca said solemnly. "She's kinda busy with her friend right now."

Kelly laughed. "Jordanna? Busy with a woman? Nah, never!" She picked up her stick and leaned it against the wall, then walked over to Rebecca. "We can interrupt her. Besides," she said in the reporter's ear, "she can pick another one up faster than you can scratch your next shot."

"I know," the reporter said with a sigh.

The game ended in a slaughter. Linda announced with a sigh that she was glad that she hadn't bet on it. Rebecca was too preoccupied with what Jordanna was doing to care about the game, anyway. Quite a few times while they were playing she caught the drummer watching her. Their eyes would meet and they would quickly look away.

"JORDANNA?"

The drummer ripped the label off of her bottle of beer and looked up blankly. "Huh?"

The blonde got up from her seat on the other side of the table, and slid in next to the drummer. "That woman you were sitting with before isn't your girlfriend, is she?"

Jordanna sighed and looked up at Rebecca, who was leaning far too comfortably against Linda as Kelly racked the balls on the pool table. *Unfortunately, no.* "Do you think I'd be sitting here with you if she was?"

"No, I guess not."

"So, let's get down to business then," the drummer said. She glanced across the room and saw that Rebecca was still leaning on Linda. In response, she leaned down to kiss the blonde. As they kissed, she ran her hand along the inside of the girl's thighs and cupped the heated, slightly moist area between the young blonde's legs. The drummer rubbed her hand against the other woman's jeans, making the blonde whimper for more. Jordanna let her hands roam up to the woman's ample breasts and caressed them through the thin fabric of her shirt, all while sucking on an exposed neck, marking her. She closed her eyes and heard the woman suggest that they go in the bathroom to take their passion a little further, but all she saw in her mind was Rebecca's sweet face. She opened her eyes and moved away from the woman, pushing her out of the seat. "I'm sorry, I just can't. I gotta go."

"WANNA GO ANOTHER round?" Rachel kidded.

"You've got to be kidding! I was pathetic," exclaimed the reporter, blushing.

She didn't see Jordanna leave the table and come up behind her.

"I'll teach you how to play," the drummer offered, her sexy, deep voice sending shivers down the reporter's back. Rebecca turned around to face sparkling blue eyes. "If you want me to, that is," the drummer continued.

The reporter's hazel eyes answered even before her words. "Yes," she said. "I would like that." She turned and looked back at the table where Jordanna had been sitting with the blonde. The fair-haired woman was still there, but another woman was sitting in Jordanna's spot. She looked back at the drummer, who shrugged.

"She wasn't my type."

Rebecca laughed out loud. "Not your type? She's sitting up, and her chest is moving, so she's definitely breathing." She looked at the woman again. "She looks like a female. How can you say that she's not your type?"

"Ha ha," the drummer said slowly, as the rest of the band got a good chuckle at her expense. She bent down and whispered in Rebecca's ear. "She's a transvestite. When I rubbed my hand between her legs I felt something I've never felt on a woman before."

"Oh, my God!" Rebecca's eyes opened wide. "Really?"

"No, but the look on your face is absolutely precious. Do you always believe everything that everybody says to you?" she teased. "C'mon, let me teach you the game of pool." Jordanna walked over to the table. She noticed the sign hanging on it and laughed. Do Not Move Pool Table. "Who the hell is going to move the pool table?" Jordanna said, turning to face the reporter. "Well, I can think of a few ways to make the pool table move, but it has nothing to do with physically pushing it. And believe me when I say that no balls of any kind are involved." She winked.

A blush as red as a stop sign appeared on the reporter's face. Jordanna took that as her opportunity to take the stick out of the reporter's hand and started by showing her how to hold it. She lined two balls up on the table, stood behind Rebecca, and guided her through her first shot. The ball bounced, flew in the air, and landed on the floor. "Easy. Easy. Not so hard," Jordanna whispered in her ear. "Try it again."

This time she wrapped herself around the young woman, putting her leg in between Rebecca's to hold her in place and guiding the small woman's hands with her own larger ones.

Rebecca could feel the drummer's breath on her neck. *Mmm, that feels so nice. She smells so good.* The reporter's knees were getting weak, feeling the drummer's body against her.

This time, Rebecca sank two balls with the shot. "Yes! I did it! I did it! I did it!"

Jordanna eased herself off of the reporter. "Good, you're getting it. Want to try it again?"

"Jordanna?" The young reporter turned around and held the raven-haired woman by the arms.

"Hmm?" the drummer responded, slightly dazed. She felt something that she had never felt for anyone before: She actually cared about this woman, cared how Rebecca felt about her. She had been hurt when Rebecca told her to go with the blonde.

*You're losing your touch, Jordanna. What's going on with you? Let's face it, girlfriend, you like her.* "I like her," the drummer mumbled under her breath. *Yeah. I like her. I don't just lust after*

*her like all the others that I use. Well, I do want her...but it's not just*
*about power or sex with her. I truly like her.*

Rebecca still had her hands on the drummer's arms.
"Jordanna? Did you say something?"

Jordanna shook her head and lied. "No. I didn't say
anything. You were going to say something to me, if I recall."

Realizing that she was still holding on to Jordanna, Rebecca
let go of the drummer. "Oh, yeah. I was just going to apologize
for what I said to you the other day about being a pompous pain
in the ass."

"You were just being truthful, Rebecca. Let's face it, I
wasn't the nicest person I could be when I first met you," the
dark-haired woman admitted. "C'mon, it's your shot."

Rebecca and Linda won this one. "Hey, no fair," Rachel
snorted. "You've got the help of the best pool player I know."

Jordanna laughed. "Fair? Like the first game when you guys
slaughtered them? You knew they couldn't play. Let's talk about
fair." She then turned to the reporter. "You hungry?" It was
after eleven, and they hadn't had a bite to eat yet.

"Famished." Rebecca had a slight hunger headache, her
stomach definitely not used to being ignored.

"Me, too. Do you want to stay here and eat, if the grill is
still open, or get something from somewhere else? That's if you
don't mind eating with me," she asked hesitantly.

Rebecca rewarded her with a huge smile. "I'm kinda craving
an unhealthy old greasy cheeseburger. Probably be better here,
don't you think?" Her stomach growled at that moment.

The drummer felt a surge of giddiness run through her, and
she broke out into a big smile. "A cheeseburger it is, then. Let's
go see if we can get a table."

# Chapter
## Five

JERRY STARED AT the phone in his hand. Phone calls after midnight were never good news, and that call had been worse than some. At least no one had died. Shaking his head, he looked around for his room key. Better tell Jordanna the latest. He walked down the hall that led to the drummer's room, saying hello to the guard on the floor that night. "She alone?" he asked.

The guard shrugged his shoulders. "I'm not a hundred percent sure, but I think so. It's awfully quiet in there if she isn't. Jordanna and her lovers are kind of vocal, if you know what I mean."

Jerry nodded and laughed at the comment.

Praying that she was alone, he hesitantly walked to the door of her hotel room and knocked. After a few minutes a groggy and half-asleep Jordanna opened up the door.

"Jerry, it's three in the morning," she said in a rough voice, rubbing the sleep out of her eyes. "What could be that important?"

"Can I come in?" he asked, looking over at her messy bed, confirming that she was indeed alone.

Jordanna, disliking the vibes she was getting from him, stepped aside. "Sure, c'mon in. Sit down."

Seeing that Jerry chose to lean against the table, rather than sit down, gave her an uneasy feeling. "Okay, Jerry. What's on your mind? Out with it."

"Jordanna, I just got a call from the San Diego Police. It seems..."

She didn't let him finish his sentence. Rubbing her temple, she spoke softly. "Damn it! What has Susan done now?"

"She's been arrested."

Jordanna shook her head. "What for? Lemme guess, something to do with drugs?" she asked, already knowing the answer to her own question.

"Yep, she was having quite the party at your house. She wasn't the only one arrested, I'm afraid." He paused for a moment, then sighed in frustration. "Jordanna, you know that I don't like telling you what you should do, but I think it's time you made a decision. She's been nothing but trouble for the past couple of years. I'm starting to wonder if she is the one behind the death threats you've been receiving."

The drummer looked away in thought. "That has crossed my mind quite a few times. The police seem to think that it's some obsessed fan doing it, Jerry, but as for Susan sending me letters like that, I don't think so. She's not that smart."

Jerry shook his head. "I don't know, Jordanna. She seems out to get you sometimes."

The drummer walked across the room, sat down on the edge of the bed, and ran her hands through her unruly locks. "No, the only thing she wants from me is a place to live and more money to snort up her fucking nose."

"Speaking of threats, you haven't received any more letters, have you?"

"No, I haven't."

Rocking back on his heels, he took in the tired, worn appearance of the drummer. "All right, if I can do anything for you, let me know."

After Jerry left she tried to get back to sleep. She tossed and turned for a good hour before she gave in and got up. She went to her suitcase, pulled out a pair of light blue jeans and a navy denim shirt and quickly got dressed.

Truly out of character, she really felt like talking to someone. She had a specific someone in mind named Rebecca, but she didn't want to wake the young reporter. She had to wonder why, though. What was it about this young woman that intrigued her so?

Her second thought was to go for a run, but she had been warned against going anywhere alone since the death threats had started.

She was surprised at herself because usually her first thought when she was stressed would be to go find a woman willing to take on her rough sexual appetite, so she could release that pent-up energy. But, for some reason, she didn't want to do that this time.

She slipped out of the room, sweet-talked the guards into leaving her alone, and hopped in the elevator. Reaching the lobby, she walked out to the back of the hotel, where there was a built-in pool surrounded by tables, chairs, and lounges. She realized that she probably wasn't doing the smartest of things at the moment, because whoever was threatening her could easily have a gun pointed in her direction there by the pool, too.

She chuckled to herself. *Nobody would miss me if that happened, anyway.*

She sat down on one of the lounges, looked up at the stars and thought about the way she was currently living her life. She went through a list of things that she liked and disliked about her life.

She knew she didn't love Susan, and Susan certainly didn't love her, but the woman did love spending her money.

*Okay, decision number one made. Susan's got to go.*

She knew there were also deeper feelings for Rebecca growing inside her, but she didn't know how the reporter *really* felt about her and figured she would hurt only hurt the young woman in the long run, anyway.

*Wouldn't I?*

If Rebecca did feel the same for her, could she give up the sins of the flesh? Could she love the young woman the way she deserved to be loved? She sighed and looked up at the night sky waiting for resolution to a question that only the two of them could answer.

*Oh, my God. Did I just say* love *her? I only just met her.*

Jordanna's eyes closed after her last thought. She fell into a restless sleep on the lounge, with visions of the reporter and herself trying to live a happy life together dancing around in her brain. The next thing she heard was the voice of the woman she was dreaming of.

"Did you sleep here all night, Jordanna?"

Her eyes fluttered open, and she looked up into the reporter's sparkling hazel eyes. "Huh? Did you say something to me?" she asked, admiring Rebecca's strawberry-blonde hair, shining brightly in the early morning sunlight.

Rebecca moved closer to the drummer. "I just asked you if you slept out here all night, that's all."

Jordanna cleared her throat. "No. Jerry woke me up around three a.m. and I couldn't go back to sleep, so I came out here to think and just fell asleep in the lounge chair. Not the smartest thing to do, huh? My back is seriously stiff now."

The reporter walked up behind Jordanna, put her hands on her shoulders, and started to work the kinks out. "Something happen last night that you couldn't sleep?"

"Mmm, that feels good, Rebecca." The drummer let out a pleased sigh. "Just came out here to think. Jerry took a call for me from the San Diego police. It seems that my lover and a few of her friends got arrested last night for possession. She decided to throw a big party at my house, and it got raided. And she didn't even invite me to the party. Nice, huh?"

"She's an addict?" Rebecca moved her attention to the area in between the drummer's shoulder blades. "You're so tense, Jordanna; just try to relax. She sounds like trouble. She lives with you?"

"Susan does love her cocaine." Jordanna could feel herself relaxing into the reporter's soothing touch. "Yeah, she lives at the house I have here in California."

Rebecca was finding herself slightly turned on by the physical contact with the drummer. "Why don't you lie on your stomach for me? I can get your back better."

Jordanna got up and sprawled out on her stomach, giving the reporter complete access to her back. "Oh, yeah, right there, Rebecca," Jordanna moaned in pleasure. "Feels so good."

"How did you meet her?" Rebecca pulled Jordanna's shirt up slightly as she worked her way down the drummer's muscled back. "How long have the two of you lived together?"

"I met Susan at a club in Los Angeles a little over two years ago. She's an actress. Came here from Iowa looking to hit it big, the same story every struggling actor tells. We started dating pretty much right away. She got me drunk one night and she talked me into letting her move into my house."

"Aren't you from New York? Do you have houses elsewhere?"

Jordanna nodded her head. "Yeah, I'm a native New Yorker. *My* home is on the eastern end of Long Island. I live there during our off-time."

Rebecca laughed at the explanation. "And Susan lives here in California? That's some arrangement. I don't know about you, but if I lived *with* someone I would prefer them to be there with me."

"Most normal people would feel that way, Rebecca, but neither of us are normal. It works out fine for us this way."

The reporter stopped her massage and rubbed her own head. "Doesn't sound like a very loving relationship."

Jordanna burst out laughing. "Love? I'm not in the relationship for love."

"Then why do you stay?"

Jordanna turned around to look the reporter in the eye. "Why do I stay? I don't really know. I know it doesn't make sense, but it helps to know that she's there, even if we don't see each other much. I know all we really do is just use each other."

Rebecca returned the drummer's gaze. "It seems to me that she does most of the using, not you."

Jordanna narrowed her eyes. "Why do you say that?"

Rebecca went back to her massage. "Well, she lives at your home for nothing. You are never there. She's a coke addict. That is not a cheap addiction. If she's a struggling actress, where does she get the money from, Jordanna?"

The drummer's head snapped up. "I do not pay for or condone her use of drugs! I got her into rehab twice last year to try and get her clean. Obviously, it didn't work."

"I didn't mean that the way it sounded," the reporter apologized. "It's just...well, since she sorta lives off of you, you are in a roundabout way contributing to her habit. She probably wouldn't be able to afford it if she had to support herself."

"That's not true. An addict will do just about anything for their fix, Rebecca. Anything. They always seem to find a way." Jordanna lowered her head. "But I guess you're right. Living off of me does make it easier for her. She could support her habit on just the money she saves by not having to pay for rent or utilities."

Rebecca looked directly into the drummer's blue eyes again. "Call me stupid, but I still don't understand how you feel you use her." She shrugged her shoulders. "I'm sorry, I really don't mean to pry into your personal life." She moved back behind the drummer and began massaging her temples.

Jordanna grabbed the reporter's hands and stopped her. "Sex," the dark woman said coldly. "I use her for sex, Rebecca. She's, um..."

"She's what?"

"She's absolutely incredible in bed." Jordanna blinked a few times and continued. "We have an agreement, of sorts. She lives at my house, rent-free, and can see whomever she wants when I'm not home. But when I am home..." she paused. "Well, she does anything and everything that I tell her to do. If I want sex, she drops whatever she's doing and we have sex, no complaints, no questions asked. And she takes everything that I give her sexually and knows enough to thank me for it during and afterwards. You get the picture?"

*Everything that she gives her sexually? What in the hell does she mean by that? I guess I don't get the picture.* "I can't believe that *you* feel you would have to practically pay someone to sleep with you. I mean, look at you! You're rich and talented, and you happen to be the most beautiful woman I have ever laid eyes on." Rebecca flushed with the admission. She couldn't believe what she'd just told Jordanna. She turned to look at the drummer to see her reaction.

Jordanna wore a completely stunned look on her face.

"You...you think I'm beautiful, even after the way I've treated you?"

Rebecca sat down on the empty lounge next to the drummer. "Yes," she whispered softly, unable to look Jordanna in the face.

"I, um, I'm sorry about that, by the way," the drummer managed to blurt out. "I shouldn't have treated you like that. You didn't deserve it."

"Are you apologizing to me?"

Jordanna cocked her head to the side and looked at the reporter. "Yes. Why?"

Rebecca shrugged. "Just didn't expect that from someone like you, that's all." She cleared her throat. "You know, Jordanna, I can see that you actually do have a heart, although you try your hardest to hide it from people. The question is, why?"

"Why, what?" Jordanna asked, not waiting for the answer. "Why I don't show my true self, is that what you're asking me?" She chuckled.

"Yes."

The dark woman smiled and ran her hand across Rebecca's cheek. "You're an amazing woman, Rebecca Hurley. Did you know that? Naïve, but amazing."

The reporter laughed. "Thanks, I think."

They sat in silence for a few minutes. Breaking the silence, Jordanna turned to the reporter. "And by the way, I happen to think that you're very beautiful, too."

Rebecca's mouth dropped open. "You do?"

"Yes, I do," the drummer confirmed. She leaned forward and kissed the reporter on the cheek. A light kiss, innocent. Hearing the reporter's slight gasp, she took Rebecca's smaller hand in hers and pulled her closer. "Can I?" the dark-haired drummer asked nervously.

Rebecca nodded her answer. *Yes, please! Kiss me before I chicken out.*

Jordanna leaned forward again and gently brushed her lips over Rebecca's. Since the reporter made no attempt to break away, the drummer kissed her more intensely, nipping gently on her bottom lip.

Rebecca could hear herself moaning but couldn't stop. "Mmm, yeah." *Kissing David never felt like this. Oh, no, not ever.* "Oh, God," she murmured between sighs.

The drummer intoxicated Rebecca; there was no doubt about that. Her face, her eyes, and her body. Everything about the woman assaulted her senses all at once. The sound of her deep voice, the way she smelled.

Rebecca looked up at her after the kiss ended. "Eternity?" she asked breathlessly. The question came out of nowhere.

"Eternity?" Something in her heart told the drummer to just say yes to the question.

"Your perfume."

"Huh? Oh, yes, Eternity."

"It smells beautiful."

The drummer ran her fingertips across Rebecca's cheek. "You are so beautiful."

The reporter shivered. "So are you."

Jordanna leaned forward again, and their lips met far too briefly for either of their tastes. They broke away at the sound of Linda clearing her throat and stood up quickly.

Linda's face turned red and she stuttered. "Uh, sorry, but we gotta get going soon, Jordanna. We have that acoustic show that we're supposed to do for the local radio station this morning. You do remember that, don't you?"

"Of course I remember," the drummer lied. She hadn't remembered the show. Her mind was preoccupied at the moment, and it was all Rebecca's fault.

The reporter called to the drummer. "Jordanna?"

"Yeah?"

"Before you go to the radio station, I think that you have someone to call and talk to, don't you?"

"Yeah, I guess it's time to evict an unwelcome guest." Jordanna walked over to Rebecca, ran her thumb along the reporter's jaw line and then kissed her quickly. "You know, Rebecca, this is the part where Linda warns you all about the big, bad drummer. For the record, what she's going to tell you is probably true." She turned and started to walk back into the hotel, stopping just shy of the door and looking back at the reporter. "Would you join me later for some lunch?"

Rebecca's heart started pounding, and she nodded. "Um, yes. I'd like that."

"Great. See you then." Jordanna smiled at her, turned around, and made her way back into the hotel.

Rebecca's eyes followed the drummer's retreating form. "So, are you?" she asked.

Linda looked at her and quickly turned away. "Am I what?"

"You saw what we were doing, Linda. Are you going to warn me about her?" She stood with her arms crossed, looking as if she was ready for a battle.

With a sigh, Linda considered and answered the question. "I've already told you about her. You know that she cheated on me, and I'm just one of many, Rebecca. You're both adults and can make your own decisions." She started to walk toward the door, then stopped. "You are a nice person, Rebecca. I just hate to see you get hurt, and, mark my words, she will at some point hurt you. I just hope, for your sake, that you're not just another notch on her proverbial belt, like I was, and all the others are."

Rebecca sighed. "Linda, I'd be lying if I said that I'm not attracted to her, or that I didn't want to get to know her better. I understand what you are trying to say, and I appreciate it, but there is something about her that is so familiar to me, something that makes me feel — no, know that she is worth the risk."

Linda held the door open for the reporter. "Just don't say I didn't try to warn you."

"Consider me warned."

# Chapter
# Six

Jordanna finished dialing the number to her California home and listened to it ring. *Ten rings. Where in the hell is she? Maybe she's still in jail. Ha!*

"Uh. Hello?" Susan's voice sounded like she had just waked up.

"Where were you last night? I tried calling you a few times."

"I was out last night, Jordanna, why?"

"That's not what the San Diego County Police told Jerry when they called." The drummer snorted happily at her lover's misfortune. "So, did you enjoy your night in jail, Susan?"

Silence.

"Are you deaf, Susan? I asked you a question. So tell me, did you enjoy your night in jail? How much was the bail set at *this time?*"

"$50,000," Susan answered quietly.

"You don't have that kind of money, Susan." Jordanna kept her voice low and hid her anger. "Who bailed you out?"

Silence.

"Answer me!" she screamed. "Who the fuck bailed you out?"

"Diane. My friend Diane," Susan admitted.

"And tell me, where exactly does Diane live, Susan?" Jordanna asked, drawing her words out slowly.

Susan wasn't the brightest star that ever shined. "She lives here."

The dark-haired woman did all she could to hold her temper. "In *my* house?"

"Yes, Jordanna, she lives with me in your house. In fact we just finished fucking in *your* bed right before you called."

Jordanna paced around the room. "Get out."

"What?"

"I said get out! I want you and your friend out of my fucking house by the end of the day!" She waited for Susan to object but got silence. "Oh, and Susan?"

"What, Jordanna?"

"Make sure you have my house cleaned and fumigated after you leave, you stupid bitch!"

Furious, she threw the phone across the room where it smashed into little pieces when it hit the wall. *Fuck! Now I know I'm insane!* She paced around the room, trying to tame her anger and release her excess energy.

*I need to get laid. That's it.*

*But what about Rebecca?*

Jordanna's impulses warred, one against the other. Not angels and devils on her shoulder, but two sides of herself, speaking loudly inside her skull. *You need to get laid, Jordanna. That's the only way to deal with this,* her darker half whispered.

*But I care for Rebecca.*

*So then fuck her. You know she wants you as bad as you want her,* came the reply.

*I'm not so sure of that, and she deserves better. She deserves to be loved, not be just another victim of my sexual escapades.*

The darkness urged her on, trying hard to entice her back into its fold. *There are plenty of women downstairs waiting for you, then. You know what to do.*

*No. I don't know why, but I don't want to do that anymore. Don't make me do it.*

*Don't fight with me, you'll lose. You always do. You are not good enough for her, Jordanna, so forget it. Even your own parents didn't want you, so why would she? You're a loser.*

*No. Shut up. That's not true.*

*Yes, it is true. Go get laid, Jordanna. It's what you know best.*

Knowing she had lost the fight, Jordanna picked up her leather jacket and quickly exited the room. Pressing the lobby button in the elevator, she headed down to meet with the fans that camped out in front of the hotel, hoping to get a glimpse of the band. When she made her way into the lobby, she was immediately surrounded by at least twenty fans looking for an autograph, a photo, or something more. She surveyed her prospects carefully, finally choosing a small strawberry-blonde woman as the winner. With nothing more than a look, the drummer headed back into the hotel with the woman following closely behind. "There," she said, pointing to a ladies' room that she hoped was vacant and out of the way of the lobby. They slipped inside. Locking the door behind her, it took no time for Jordanna to slip her jeans off and hop up onto the bathroom sink. The woman just looked at her.

"Well?" Jordanna said, her body throbbing and her temper short. "What are you waiting for?"

ON THE CHANCE that they hadn't left yet, Rebecca went down to the lobby, but didn't see Jordanna. When she heard a fan gush about his quick glimpse of the dark-haired drummer, she turned around and headed in the direction he mentioned — back in the hotel.

She looked all over and did not spot the drummer. Walking down one of the hallways she caught a glimpse of a very sloppy, but very happy-looking woman with strawberry-blonde hair coming out of a bathroom. *Oh, man, she should get a good look at herself before she heads into public. Brush her hair or something, at least.*

She had barely finished the thought when she noticed Jordanna slipping out of the bathroom behind her. Her face was all sweaty and her clothes were a mess. *Huh? What happened to her?* Rebecca put two and two together. *Oh, shit!* It felt as if someone had punched her hard in the gut.

She didn't know how she got there so quickly, but she soon found herself face to face with the drummer. She didn't realize that she had slapped Jordanna across the face until she felt her hand sting. "How could you?" Rebecca looked at the drummer's denim shirt, which was tucked in on only one side. "For Christ's sake, at least make yourself presentable, Jordanna."

The drummer looked down at her shirt and quickly tucked it in. Startled by Rebecca's actions, Jordanna didn't know what to say. "What?" She put her hand on her cheek. She hadn't realized that the small woman could hit so hard.

"What do you mean, what? Didn't you just kiss me this morning? I guess that doesn't mean much to you, because you'd screw anything that breathes, but it meant something to me. Don't fuck with my feelings like that, Jordanna! I will not tolerate it!" The reporter turned and started to walk away, mumbling, "I can't believe I could be so fucking stupid."

"Wait." Jordanna grabbed her arm and tried to stop her. "Rebecca, please..."

"Get your hands off of me, you heartless bitch!" the reporter screamed.

The sloppy-looking woman the drummer was with stood to the side, watching the scene unfold. Feeling the sting of Rebecca's words, Jordanna tried to regain her composure. She looked at the woman standing there. "Do you mind?" she asked sarcastically. "This is private." She turned back to the reporter once the woman stalked away, obviously feeling angry and used. "Rebecca, please calm down. I won't touch you again, okay?" Jordanna sighed, not really sure how to express her feelings. "I, I...um, kissing you this morning did mean something to me; just let me explain it to you."

"Yeah," Rebecca snorted in disgust. "It meant so damn much to you that you ran into someone else's arms the first chance you got. I should have fucking listened to Linda's warnings about you."

"No, it's just..."

At that moment they heard the drummer's name being called. It was Kelly, running toward them. "There you are. We gotta go. We're running very late."

Jordanna didn't want to leave Rebecca without explaining what had happened. Turning to her, she took the reporter's hand and walked away from Kelly. "I need to talk to you. I'll meet you back in your room when I get back. Please say you'll wait for me and hear me out."

Rebecca couldn't wait to hear what the drummer had to say, and what kind of an excuse she'd come up with. "I'll wait for you," she said quietly.

The dark-haired woman flashed a quick crooked smile and ran her hand gently down Rebecca's arm, grabbing her hand quickly and releasing it before she turned and started walking towards the front lobby.

THE BAND FINISHED their acoustic show and rode in relative silence back to the hotel. The drummer stepped out of the limousine and noticed a very welcome sight—a delicatessen across the street. It was well past lunchtime and she could feel her stomach growling. "I think I'm gonna go to the deli and get some sandwiches instead of eating in the lounge. You guys want anything?"

After they politely refused, she ran across the busy street and into the deli. *Now what would Rebecca want from here?* Not knowing what the reporter would like, she ordered a few different types of sandwiches and grabbed a big bottle of soda.

As she walked up to the register to pay for her order, the young boy behind the counter recognized her. "You're—"

She cut him off instantly. "I know, Jordanna Fox, right? Everyone always tells me how much I look like her."

Cheeks pink, he apologized. "Sorry. You do look an awful lot like her, though," he said, handing her the bag of food.

"That's okay. It happens *all* the time," she said with a wink.

Her stomach started to knot as she ran back across the street and walked through the lobby of the hotel. Stepping into the elevator, she contemplated what she was going to say to the young reporter. *I guess I'll just wing it when I get there.*

She stepped off the elevator, said hello to the guard on duty, and walked to Rebecca's room.

*You can do this.*

She knocked quietly and waited. She heard rustling, and then the door opened.

Rebecca looked Jordanna up and down. "Come in," she said quietly, opening the door completely.

"Thanks." The drummer stepped past Rebecca and walked into the room. "I hope you're hungry 'cause I brought lunch," she said, putting the bag down on the table. "I wasn't in the mood for lounge lunch today, and I'm seriously missing New York cuisine, so I picked up a couple of sandwiches. It's the closest thing I could find here. I hope you like them."

"I do."

The drummer's heart was pounding so hard, she thought surely the reporter could hear it. "Rebecca, I'm sorry if I hurt you. I didn't mean to. It's just..."

"Just what, Jordanna?"

"I don't...I don't know what to say to make you understand," she muttered.

"Did you call her?" Rebecca asked coldly.

Jordanna pulled the sandwiches out of the bag, one by one. "Yes."

"And what happened?"

The drummer poured two glasses of soda, handing one to Rebecca. "I told her to get out."

Rebecca looked at the drummer. "And that made you do what you did?"

Jordanna looked down. "No." *You are not making this easy, Rebecca.*

"Then why? Why would you kiss me like you did and then go have sex with some stranger in a hotel bathroom?"

Taking a sip of her soda, the drummer cleared her throat. "Because I was angry."

"What the hell kind of an excuse is that?"

The drummer began to pace around the room like a caged animal. "Because when I get angry, people end up getting hurt. I have to release my energy some way, and sex has always been it."

Rebecca closed her eyes and spoke softly. "You could have come to me."

Jordanna put her glass down on the table, walked over to

Rebecca, and took her hands. "I couldn't."

"But you kissed me, Jordanna."

"That's *exactly* why I couldn't, Rebecca. I don't want to use you." She paused for a moment. *You already mean more than that to me. I just wish I just had the courage to tell you that.* "And that's exactly what I did to the woman in the bathroom," she continued. "That's what I do with all the women that I sleep with. I use them for my own needs."

"So, did she leave?"

Jordanna picked up a sandwich and handed it to Rebecca. "There are other kinds if you don't like that one."

"You didn't answer my question."

Jordanna ran her hands through her dark hair and sighed. "I don't know if she left. I told her to get out by the end of the day. Tomorrow we head to San Diego so I'm going to go and check it out once we're settled in the hotel. The house isn't very far from there."

Rebecca played with her sandwich. "Do you want some company?"

The drummer lifted a surprised brow. "If you want to... I'd like that."

The two women finished their lunch in silence. Jordanna nervously looked at her watch and announced that it was almost time for sound check for the show. "I'll see you in the limo," the drummer said, although her tone of voice made it sound more like a question than a statement.

"Yeah. I'll be there," Rebecca confirmed, as she watched Jordanna walk out the door.

Closing the door behind her, Jordanna leaned her back on it and let her body relax. "I'm so very sorry I hurt you. How can I show you how I really feel?" she said quietly to herself.

AFTER CHECKING INTO the Hyatt Regency in San Diego the next day, Jordanna and Rebecca caught a taxicab and headed out to Jordanna's house in Coronado.

Rebecca rubbed her eyes and yawned slightly. Between traveling and not being home for weeks, it seemed ages since she'd had a decent night's rest, and exhaustion was starting to take its toll. "How come you take a taxi instead of the limo?"

Jordanna took a deep breath to keep herself from yawning, too. "It keeps me grounded."

"What do you mean?" Rebecca asked, and yawned again. This time it was contagious; Jordanna followed suit.

"I don't want to be a spoiled brat rock star."

"But you are..."

"But I'm really not. Spend a little more time with me and you'll see that."

"Uh huh. If you say so."

Jordanna turned and gazed out the window as the taxi sped down the 5 on its way to the small island just off of San Diego. Rebecca did the same, enjoying the view of San Diego, her first time in the area. "What is that?" she asked the drummer, pointing to a small inlet where people were picnicking and just enjoying the beautiful sunny day.

Jordanna turned to look, and smiled. "Mission Bay. See the little white blimp balloon thingy flying in the sky in the distance? That's where Sea World is."

Rebecca found herself getting all excited. "I love Sea World! I like it so much better than Universal Studios. I was a little bored there. Except for the *Back to the Future* ride."

"Maybe we can go there later if we have time. I happen to like it there, too." *I must like her a lot 'cause I can't believe I'm admitting that.*

"That would be cool." Rebecca smiled. "How do you go out in public, though? Isn't it rough for you to do that with people noticing you and all?"

Jordanna thought about the poor boy she'd lied to at the deli the previous morning. "I usually just put my hair up in a ponytail and put on sunglasses, and people don't recognize me. My eyes usually give it away if I have to take the glasses off. I do own brown contacts, and I've used them a few times, but they annoy me, so I haven't used them in a while."

The reporter thought about Jordanna's beautiful eye color. "I can't imagine you with brown eyes. That must look funny."

Jordanna chuckled. "Takes some getting used to, I must say."

"I'm sure you still look absolutely gorgeous, though, no matter what color your eyes are. You're a beautiful woman, Jordanna, but I think that I have already told you that," Rebecca said, slightly blushing.

"You did." Jordanna smiled. "But I don't mind. You can tell me that over and over if you'd like," she said, looking directly into the reporter's darkening hazel eyes. "Whoever said flattery never gets you anywhere was wrong."

The taxi driver looked in his rear-view mirror. "Damn dykes. Is everyone gay in this day and age? I could show them what a real man would do for them. I'd take them both on at the same time, and they'd love every minute of it," he muttered. His eyes followed their curves, and he smiled.

As they crossed the San Diego/Coronado Bay Bridge

Jordanna felt a sick feeling in her gut.

"What is it, Jordanna?" the reporter asked, sensing her uneasiness.

"I just have a bad feeling all of a sudden."

As they got closer to Jordanna's house they noticed all the flashing lights and activity. "What in the hell could have happened now?" the drummer said angrily. The taxi slipped through the open gate, and Jordanna jumped out before it had even pulled to a stop. She ran up to a group of policemen standing in front of the house. "What's going on here, officers? I'm Jordanna Fox. I own this house."

The young officer looked her over appreciatively. "Well, Ms. Fox, it seems that someone has vandalized your house. Your staff found it this way this morning and called us right away. Do you know who would do something like this?"

Jordanna's eyes turned to slits. "Yes, I think I have an idea," she said, not bothering to expand any further. She turned around and walked back to the taxi where Rebecca sat waiting.

"Are you all right? What happened?"

Jordanna shook her head. "Susan happened, that's what." *At least I think it was Susan.* "The house has been vandalized. Come in and take a look with me. Please?"

Side by side, the two of them walked into the house. "Holy fucking shit." Jordanna scowled upon seeing the damage as soon as they walked in.

Rebecca looked around with shock at what apparently must have been a gorgeous home. The carpets were ripped, furniture slashed and turned over, and the glass ceiling lighting fixture in the foyer was smashed to pieces and on the floor. "Wow," was all the reporter could say.

The damage worsened with each room they walked through, and Jordanna's face remained cold and unreadable. She wasn't sure if this was the work of her ex or if this had something to do with the threats she was receiving. "I can't believe this," she whispered to the reporter when they saw the master bedroom. Everything had been dumped out of Jordanna's dresser drawers, cabinets, and closets, which made the dark woman wonder if whoever had done this was looking for something. The sheets and her bed were slashed, and red paint was poured on it, which made her think otherwise. She turned and saw the graffiti on the wall behind her bed in the same red paint that said, "This Ain't Over, My Sweet."

*Oh, yeah, it was Susan.*

The water in the bathtub in Jordanna's bathroom had been left running and had overflowed. The floor was a mess. The wallpaper in the room was ripped, and part of the fan was hanging down. Rebecca took it all in and shook her head. "Nice piece of work. I won't even ask you about the bra hanging on the ceiling fan in your bedroom."

Despite her bad mood, Jordanna couldn't help but laugh. "You don't want to know."

Walking back into the bedroom, Rebecca picked up a smashed picture frame with a ripped photo of Jordanna and a woman she assumed was Susan, taken at a party of some sort. The woman was tall, but not as tall as Jordanna, and her long bleached-blonde hair stood out next to Jordanna's inky black hair. She had a wild, almost psychotic, look about her. Rebecca jumped when the drummer came up behind her.

"That's her, if you were wondering."

Rebecca touched her arm lightly. "So, what do you think? You sure it was her?"

"I'm sure," Jordanna said quietly, looking at the graffiti behind her bed. The drummer had always hated when Susan used the words "my sweet," and she did that quite often.

"She's a sick woman. I can't believe you were with her."

Jordanna snorted, remembering that those were pretty much her last words to Susan when she left for the tour. "I know. I told you why I was with her, though."

"And why is that?" came a voice from behind them. Turning around, they saw a tall, muscular man with long, brown hair and glasses coming towards them.

"That's none of your damn business," the drummer said, annoyed at the intrusion. "Who in the hell are you?"

"Sergeant Robert Johnson, San Diego PD," he said pulling out his badge. "I need to talk to you, Ms. Fox. Would you mind coming with us to the station?"

"Why the hell should I go to the station? I haven't done anything. Can't you question me here?" she asked, her voice loud. "I'm a busy woman." *I have to go to Sea World with Rebecca.*

"I understand that, Ms. Fox. I know who you are. But even you are not above the law." It was apparent to the drummer that he enjoyed throwing his authority around.

"Jordanna?" Rebecca chimed in.

The drummer turned to look at the young woman. Rebecca took her hand. "Cooperate with them, please. Don't make it worse for yourself."

Nodding, Jordanna agreed. "Oh, all right, let's go," she said to Sgt. Johnson. "Rebecca, can you take the taxi back to the hotel and tell them what happened?"

"I'll call them and tell them what happened. I'm coming

with you."

"But..."

Rebecca smiled at the drummer.  "No buts, Jordanna.  I'm going whether you like it or not."

# Chapter
# Seven

JORDANNA GREW IMPATIENT with all of the police's questions. "I told you that three times already! Susan has lived with me for two years now. Yes, she was my lover and, yes, I kicked her out of the house yesterday. Anything else?"

"Did you know that she and quite a few others were arrested the other night, on your property, for possession of narcotics?" the detective asked.

"Yes! I thought we went over this." She rubbed her head. "That's why I asked her to leave. It wasn't the first time she was arrested. Shit, this is absolutely outrageous."

The detective shook his head. "Can you tell me about the death threats you've been receiving? Do you think she may have anything to do with them?"

The dark woman shrugged her shoulders. She didn't want to talk about the threats, especially with the idiot detective. "It's possible that she sent them. I really don't know."

The detective sighed impatiently and muttered something about lippy babes. "Just a few more questions, Ms. Fox, and you'll be free to go."

"What the hell more do you need to know? My fucking underwear size?" she said, jumping up out of her chair to leave.

The detective was at her side, guiding her back to her chair. "You'll leave when we tell you we're finished. Sit down, Ms. Fox."

Two hours later, Jordanna walked over to Rebecca, who had dozed off in a chair in the waiting room. "Rebecca, wake up." She shook the young woman gently. "Time to get the hell out of here."

Hazel eyes fluttered open. "Oh, I fell asleep. You under arrest?" she teased.

Jordanna shook her head and smiled. "You'd think that, wouldn't you? They certainly grilled me enough."

"So, what is the final outcome? Are they going to arrest Susan?"

The drummer scratched her head. "If they prove it was her, yeah. Looks like her friend, Diane, was involved, too. She's got a record a mile long."

"Who is Diane?"

"Oh, that's right. I never did get to tell you about the phone conversation I had with Susan.    Seems that Susan has a girlfriend, and they both were living in my house.  Remember how I told you I was angry yesterday?"

*How could I forget?*    Rebecca shuddered at the thought. "Yeah."

"She told me that they had just finished...uh, well, you know in my bed.  My bed!"  The drummer sighed.  "Don't get me wrong, I don't give a shit that she has a girlfriend.  I just don't like being played for a fool."

"I can see why you were angry.  I would be, too."  The reporter looked Jordanna directly in the eyes.

Jordanna suddenly felt very guilty.  "Listen, Rebecca.  I told you I was sorry about what you saw, and I really do mean that.  I never meant to hurt you.  I just don't think about other people's feelings sometimes."

*That's good, Beck; you're falling for someone so sensitive to other people's feelings.*  Rebecca sighed.  "C'mon, let's go."

REBECCA SAT ON a couch in the hotel lobby, enjoying one of her favorite pastimes:  people watching.

"You ready?"  The sound of Jordanna's voice startled her. She hadn't seen the dark-haired woman approach.

Rebecca looked up at a woman she didn't recognize. Jordanna was dressed in a pair of blue jeans and a plain black tee shirt.  Her hair was up in a ponytail, and mirrored sunglasses covered the drummer's eyes.

"Ready for what?"

The drummer shook her head.  "Don't tell me you forgot about Sea World already."

A smile lit up the reporter's face.  "Sea World?  You were really serious about going there?  With me?"

"I never make promises that I don't intend to keep, Rebecca."

Rebecca tried not to, but looked Jordanna up and down. "You look so different with your hair like that.  Your eyes?" Rebecca wondered if Jordanna had put in the brown contacts.

The drummer took her sunglasses off and showed Rebecca her baby blues.  "Didn't want to wear the contacts."  She grinned. "If you want to see me with brown eyes, I'll put them in for you when we get back."

THE TWO WOMEN walked into the park and stood in front of the large, sand-like sculpture of two children petting a dolphin that greeted all who entered the park. They looked at their map and show schedule to decide what they wanted to do first. "Well, the Seymour show starts in twenty minutes. That's the one with the seals and otters. It's cute," Jordanna said, pointing to the direction that the show was being held.

Rebecca looked at the drummer and laughed. "This is way too funny."

"What's funny? Are you making fun of me? I like to have innocent fun sometimes, you know." Jordanna pouted and started to walk ahead of the reporter.

"No, no. I won't tease you," Rebecca said as she ran to catch up, still laughing at the drummer as they looked at the various water mammals that lived at the park.

Rebecca noticed a large tank of water with a crowd of people standing around it. "Look," she pointed towards the tank. "Let's go pet the dolphins!" She grabbed the drummer by the hand and quickly maneuvered them through the crowd, finding a tight spot for both of them to stand in front of the tank. "There's one over there," Rebecca pointed out. "It's coming this way."

Jordanna looked down at their entwined hands and felt her heart race. "Huh?"

"Aren't they just so cute?" The reporter finally let go of the drummer's hand, climbed up on the small ledge, and leaned her body over the top of the tank, trying to touch the dolphins that swam close to the clear glass walls they leaned on. All she managed to do was get wet.

Jordanna's fingers still tingled from the reporter's innocent touch. Rebecca's small hand had felt more than perfect in her larger one. She already felt a loss of contact, something that was totally unfamiliar to her. *Oh, God, what is happening to me?*

"Jordanna? You okay?"

The drummer snapped out of the haze she was in. "Uh, yeah, I'm fine." She felt the reporter grab her hand again and pull her up onto the ledge, right next to the blonde. At Rebecca's urging, she leaned over and stuck her longer arm out as a small bottlenose dolphin swam by. The animal teased the crowd, coming close to them but not close enough for anyone to touch. Jordanna kept her eye on the small dolphin as it made its way around the tank one more time, and stuck her hand out once again as the porpoise came near. The dolphin popped his snout out of the water and nudged the drummer's hand. Jordanna petted the porpoise quickly, but when the rest of the crowd ran towards them to see, the dolphin swam away.

"Oh, my God, did you see that? That was amazing!" Rebecca said with the excitement of a child. "He came right to you."

Jordanna smiled, enjoying the younger woman's excitement. "Yeah, that was pretty cool."

"What did it feel like?"

Jordanna lifted a brow. "Cold and smooth, kinda like human skin. Not what I expected, though."

"I always wondered what it felt like."

Jordanna stepped off of the ledge and told the reporter to stand where she was just standing.

"Why?"

Jordanna smiled at her. "Trust me."

Rebecca stepped over slightly and stood where the drummer asked her to go. Jordanna then stepped up on the ledge behind her. She took the reporter's hand and linked her fingers with Rebecca's, sticking both of their hands out over the water. A larger dolphin swam by them, splashing water all over them. "Shit! Thanks, Jor!" the soaked reporter screamed.

Rebecca felt tingles go up and down her spine as the drummer's body moved against hers, laughing at the wet woman. "That wasn't my idea. Blame him," the drummer whispered, her breath warm against the reporter's ear.

Jordanna spotted another dolphin heading their way and stuck their hands out again. This time, Rebecca knew enough to get out of the way. As the dolphin started to splash them, she ducked as much as she could and let the drummer take the brunt of the soaking. "Ha ha! Gotcha this time!" She threw her fists in the air.

Jordanna jumped off of the ledge from her position behind the reporter. She climbed back on the ledge, standing next to Rebecca. She grabbed Rebecca by the waist and lifted the reporter up off of her feet. Rebecca looked into mischievous blue eyes, then looked back at the water that she was dangling above. "You wouldn't."

Jordanna wiggled her eyebrows at the smaller woman. "I would."

"Please don't..."

The drummer smiled. "You gotta beg me better than that, Rebecca."

"Pretty please with sugar on top?"

Jordanna lifted her a little higher.

"I'll sleep with you."

Jordanna's breath caught, and she nearly dropped the reporter into the water. "You're going to sleep with the fishies first, though."

"Hey! Get her down from there!"

Rebecca looked down to see a park security guard standing there looking at them and then felt Jordanna gently ease her down until the reporter's feet were planted firmly on the ledge again. They both stepped off the ledge and listened as the guard scolded them like children, threatening to kick them out of the park if they didn't behave. When the guard walked away they both looked at each other and burst out laughing, feeling like a couple of giggling schoolgirls.

The blonde still had a smile on her face as she absentmindedly took the drummer's hand in her own again and started to make their way through the crowd. She turned around to address the drummer. "You wouldn't have really thrown me in there, would you?"

"Would you really sleep with me if I didn't?"

The reporter blushed and turned around, picking her way through the crowd until they found the dolphin show, having missed the first Seymour show. They slipped through the gate, and Jordanna followed Rebecca as she climbed all the way to the top of the metal bleachers and sat down. Jordanna looked around the audience for a few minutes. "I'll be right back, okay?"

"Where you going?"

"To get some popcorn. You want anything?"

"A soda would hit the spot."

The drummer smiled at Rebecca before she turned around and made her way back down the bleachers, jumping the last four rows to the ground below.

Rebecca was deep in thought when Jordanna sat back down next to her, placing the huge bucket of popcorn down between them. She handed Rebecca a giant-sized soda. "I hope you don't mind; I took a little sip of it. I didn't realize I was so thirsty. Sorry."

Rebecca shook her head and took a sip for herself. "No, I don't mind at all. We can share it."

"Have some popcorn."

Rebecca smiled shyly and took a handful of popcorn, feeling like a teenager out on her first date. She watched as Jordanna did the same, smiling back at her.

Halfway through the bucket of popcorn, as the dolphins were jumping and splashing in the water, Rebecca saw, out of the corner of her eye, the drummer throw a piece of popcorn into the audience below. It bounced off of a woman's ridiculous-looking straw hat and landed in a man's lap.

She leaned over and whispered in the drummer's ear. "What

are you doing?"

"I just wanted to see if my aim was still good. We used to do this as kids when we were at the movies." Jordanna grinned and pointed at a bald man's head five or six rows below them. "See Kojak down there? He's my next target."

Rebecca chuckled. "You are bad."

"Yeah, I'm bad," the drummer replied, just as the piece of popcorn bounced off of her unsuspecting target's head.

Rebecca picked out a piece of popcorn from the bucket and pointed below, calling out her first victim. "Man in the ugly Hawaiian print shirt."

*Bounce.*

"Girl with big ears and Metallica tee shirt."

*Bounce.*

"The kid with the bright orange mohawk."

*Whoops, he's got popcorn stuck in his hair. Oh, well.*

"Girl in the Plenty of Nothing tee shirt three rows down, two seats over," Rebecca called out next.

"Ooh, a fan?" Jordanna grabbed a handful of popcorn and smiled wickedly. "Let's really nail her!"

*Bounce bounce bounce bounce bounce bounce.*

They couldn't control their laughter as the people down below started to notice that it was raining popcorn. They both turned their heads as eyes went their way.

"We're going to get ourselves kicked out before the night is over with; you know that, right?" Rebecca pointed out as they stood up with their empty bucket and walked down the bleachers after the show. "You're a real troublemaker, aren't you?"

Jordanna wiggled her eyebrows at the reporter. "Oh, yeah."

Rebecca blushed. "So, where to next?"

Jordanna opened up the map and time schedule of events. "The next Seymour show starts in five minutes. Are you up for a little seal action?"

*I'm up for any kind of action with you, Jordanna.* "Sure, seal action sounds great."

They spent the next forty minutes laughing with the rest of the crowd as the seal, the otter, and the walrus searched for, and finally found, the hidden coin that they were looking for.

As they were walking out of the area, they noticed a food vendor, packed with sweet goodies, parked right next to the show's entrance. The drummer saw Rebecca's eyes light up. "Do you want some cotton candy or something? I think I'm gonna have some."

Rebecca smiled and chuckled softly, pushing a few strands

of windblown gold hair out of her eyes. "I like seeing the lighthearted side of you, Jordanna. It's really, really nice." Her smile never left her face. "And cotton candy sounds great."

Jordanna gave the reporter her best *don't go there* look as she walked over to the counter. "Yeah, well, just don't put any of this in your article, okay? Don't want to ruin my image."

"Your image, uh huh. I won't, don't worry," the reporter said, taking the cotton candy from the vendor and ripping off a piece before handing the rest to Jordanna. "If only the staff photographer were here. A cover shot of you eating cotton candy would be really nice."

The drummer leaned in close and whispered in the reporter's ear. "I could think of something far better I'd like them to photograph me eating, Rebecca."

*Yeah, me, too,* the reporter thought and smirked. *Did I really just think that?* "Like what, Jordanna?"

"Like, um, hey, check that out." Jordanna pointed to a small kiosk, in a sad attempt to change the subject, never expecting Rebecca to call her on the provocative comment. "It says that there's a pearl in every oyster." She walked into the kiosk, looked around, and laid some money out on the counter. "Why don't you pick one out, Rebecca?"

The vendor placed a medium-sized barrel of oysters in front of the two women. Rebecca looked at Jordanna hesitantly and picked one out. The woman opened the shell, and in it was a large black pearl. Looking at it from certain angles, it had a pinkish tint to it.

The woman that ran the kiosk made a big fuss over the pearl, rare because of its shape, color, and size. "You want I could put this on chain for you," the woman said in broken English. "It too pretty not to."

Jordanna nodded and looked at Rebecca. "Yeah, put it on a chain, whichever one this beautiful woman here picks out."

A blushing Rebecca shook her head. "No, Jordanna. I couldn't."

"Please don't argue with me, Rebecca. I want to do this, okay?"

"No, really, I couldn't."

Jordanna lifted a brow at her, and Rebecca gave in and picked out the cheapest gold chain she saw.

"Are you sure that's the chain you really want, Rebecca?" Jordanna noticed the price of the one the smaller woman picked. "I think I can afford it," she teased, and a hint of a smile crossed her lips.

"I like that one. It's simple, yet elegant."

The drummer sighed, but went along with Rebecca. "Okay, if you are sure that's the one you want."

They stood and watched as the woman set the pearl on the chain. "You no wear this for twenty-four hour. Glue need to dry." The woman put the necklace in a small, plastic Ziploc bag and handed it to Rebecca.

The reporter took the small package in her hand as the drummer paid for it. When they walked out of the kiosk, Rebecca bumped her hip into Jordanna's. "Thank you. You really didn't have to do that. It is a beautiful pearl, though,"

*That smile.* Jordanna smiled back at her. *I love her smile.* "I know I didn't have to, but I wanted to. And you're welcome."

They walked together through the park's restaurant area, and the smells of all the different types of foods cooking made the drummer realize she was hungry. "Let's go get a bite to eat. That cotton candy didn't quite stick to my ribs."

As the day turned into night, the two decided they would catch the last Shamu show and then leave. The wind off the bay had picked up some, and the evening had a chill to it. Sitting on the metal bleachers watching the show, Jordanna noticed the reporter shivering. "Cold?"

"Yeah."

"Here." Jordanna moved closer to the reporter and put her arm around her. "How's that?"

Rebecca smiled. "Much better."

Jordanna rubbed her hand up and down Rebecca's arm. "Good."

"Jordanna?"

"Hmm?"

"Thanks for doing this for me. I had a really nice time."

The drummer stopped her movement and looked into hazel eyes. "So did I," she finally said, and looked around to see if anyone was watching them. Seeing that everyone around them was paying total attention to the large, black-and-white fish swimming in the tank in front of them, she slowly leaned down to claim Rebecca's lips with a very gentle kiss.

Rebecca's heart began to pound rapidly as she gave in to the kiss. She didn't know where this was heading, but she couldn't help but feel that it was right. Even the water the killer whale was busy splashing on them couldn't put out the growing fire that was beginning to burn between the two women.

On their way out of the park, they stopped and watched the closing-time firework display. Jordanna looked up at the brilliant colors painting the night sky and then looked at Rebecca, who was looking back at her. *Those fireworks can't*

*possibly compare to how I feel in her company.*
*I'm falling for her.*
*Hard.*
*This isn't good. I don't do things like that.*
*Shit!*

Jordanna looked in the windows of all the little shops that they were passing, and something black and white caught her eye. "Rebecca, I'm going to run in that shop quick and pick up a sweatshirt, okay? I'm kinda cold." She started to head for the door and turned around. "You want anything?"

"No, thank you, I'm fine. I'll go call a taxi and then wait for you right over there by that bench, okay?" Rebecca walked over to a concrete bench and sat down. She watched the dark-haired woman walk into the shop and out of her view. Seeing this rarely seen, playful side of the drummer made her like the woman even more than she had already. She sighed.

Twenty minutes later Jordanna emerged from the shop wearing a white sweatshirt with *Sea World* scrawled across the front in rainbow colors, and *San Diego* written the same way under it in smaller letters. The drummer smiled when she saw Rebecca.

And Rebecca smiled when she saw the drummer. She got up and started walking toward her companion. "What took you so long?"

"Lots to choose from, couldn't decide." Jordanna smirked. "Plus, I had to sign a few autographs. The clerk recognized me."

"I guess your eyes do give you away, huh?" *I could just gaze into them forever.*

"Yeah, I guess they do."

# Chapter
# Eight

THE FINAL SHOWS of the tour were in the band's hometown of New York. They were scheduled to play four sold-out shows at Madison Square Garden and three at the Nassau Coliseum on Long Island.

The flight from San Diego to New York's Kennedy International Airport was a quiet one, with some of the plane's occupants opting to sleep and others watching a movie. Rebecca sat in a window seat, looking out at the clouds. She realized that she had to use the bathroom so badly, she was willing to use an airplane bathroom. "Jordanna?"

"Hmm?"

"Can you let me out? I have to use the ladies' room."

The drummer stood up and moved out into the aisle to let Rebecca through. She sat back down and quickly rummaged through her flight bag, smiling when she found what she was looking for. She put it on Rebecca's seat.

Kelly watched her from her seat across the aisle and grinned. "Well, isn't that cute."

Jordanna glared at her. "Forget you ever saw it, Kelly."

The guitarist rolled her eyes. "You big mushball, you. So that's where you two went? Sea World, huh?"

"Shut up, Kelly," the drummer said as Rebecca was returning to her seat. Jordanna stood again to let the reporter back to her seat but didn't move into the aisle. Rebecca shivered from the contact as she brushed by and then squealed as she saw what was on her seat. "Oh, that is so cute, Jordanna! Is that for me?"

The drummer nodded, her face fire-engine red.

Rebecca picked up the tiny stuffed whale and examined it closely. "Thank you. I love it." She kissed the blushing drummer on the cheek.

Kelly burst out laughing.

Jordanna glared at her again. "I'm warning you, Kelly."

"My lips are sealed," Kelly snorted. "I won't let on that bad girl Jordanna Fox is really a big, romantic mush."

Rebecca clung onto the small stuffed whale and was deep in thought when the drummer asked her if she had any problems with the upcoming arrangements in New York. The drummer touched the reporter's arm. "Rebecca?"

"Hmm? Did you say something? I'm sorry, I guess I was daydreaming again. I'm sure you noticed that I do that a lot," the reporter said, slightly embarrassed.

Jordanna laughed and smiled. "I hope it was about something good, at least."

Rebecca felt herself blushing. "It was," she said, reliving their day at Sea World and thinking about the kisses they had shared.

Jordanna thought she knew what Rebecca was daydreaming about when she saw the reporter's face turn red. "I was just asking if you had any problems with staying at my house when we get to New York."

This was news to the reporter. "Your house?" she repeated, clearly surprised. Since they would be playing in their hometown, only the members of the road crew that were from out of town would stay in hotels, while the band would enjoy their time at home. Rebecca had just assumed that she would stay at the hotel like the crew, or, even better, head to her apartment in the city. She still missed her daughter terribly and was looking forward to seeing her.

The drummer tried to sound innocent. "You didn't know that?" She'd personally made the suggestion to Jerry, who wasn't at all pleased with the idea. She'd used the excuse that the reporter would be able to finish the article for the magazine at her house, and asked him to keep it a secret for fear that the reporter would reject her offer. After all, they hadn't discussed what had happened between them in Los Angeles and San Diego, and she wasn't completely sure how the reporter felt about her, although she knew Rebecca had feelings of some sort.

"Nobody told me that, no..." the reporter stuttered. Her romantic side was doing the happy dance, but her heart ached for the chance to see Cindy after being away for so long. She looked down and tried to hold back tears.

Jordanna felt her insides tearing apart. *I should've known she wouldn't go for it.* "You don't have to, Rebecca."

Rebecca shook her head. "No, it's not that I don't want to go with you; it's just that I miss my daughter so much."

The drummer's stomach immediately calmed down, and she smiled. "I live on Long Island, Rebecca. It's not that far from

New York City. We can go see your daughter whenever you want."

The smaller woman smiled back at the drummer. "Well, then, you have yourself a houseguest, Jordanna."

AFTER THEY LANDED and got off the plane, Jordanna tugged on Rebecca's arm. "C'mon, the limo's waiting for us over there. I don't know about you, but I'm exhausted, and I can't wait to get home."

When they were on the south shore of Long Island and closer to her Amagansett home, Jordanna spent time detailing points of interest to the reporter. To her dismay, most of the attractions were still closed for the winter. It was a beautiful early March day, and a light snow had fallen, coating the ground and the trees. They could see the sun's glistening rays on the long stretch of the Atlantic Ocean.

Rebecca turned and looked at the drummer. "It's beautiful here. I love the ocean. I didn't get to see much of it when I was growing up, but we did vacation in the Bahamas. I can see why you love it so much."

Jordanna closed her eyes and smiled. "There's nowhere else that I would rather live. I grew up on the Island; it's my home. Although my childhood memories are not really good ones." She sighed. "But I didn't live out here then, so..."

The reporter took the drummer's hand in hers and gave it a quick squeeze. She looked directly into the blue eyes that she had somehow begun to love. "I'm here to listen if you ever feel like talking about it."

Jordanna squeezed back and returned her gaze. "Thanks."

The limo made a quick right down a private drive and pulled up in the driveway on the side of Jordanna's house, which was off-white in color and looked more like a country home than an oceanfront house. "This is it," she said, and looked down, realizing that they were still holding hands. She let go right as the limo driver opened the door to help the reporter out of the back of the car. Jordanna jumped out behind her.

Rebecca looked at the house and thought about how out of place it looked in the area. "Wow, it's gorgeous, but it doesn't quite fit in here."

"That's why I bought it." Jordanna walked them to the deck in the back of her house and pointed to the next house, which was about a half mile down the beach from her house. The house was dark gray in color, hidden partially by the dunes, and looked as if its visitors needed to be checked by security to get in. "That looks like a federal building or a library, not a home. I didn't want that."

"I don't blame you. Do you know the owners?"

Jordanna made a face. "Yeah. The husband owns an investment firm in the city. The wife spends her day sitting at home eating bon bons, getting her nails done, entertaining the socialites with her witty personality. Ugh."

"Guess you don't like them much, huh?"

The drummer laughed. "Is it that obvious? Let's put it this way; they don't think very much of me, either. A lesbian rock star living one house over from them? How appalling." Her eyes lit up and she smirked. "I just might lose control and hit on the wifey one day, you know?" she said with a wink. "See how good those bon bons really do taste."

Rebecca laughed and elbowed her lightly. "You're bad."

"Well, that's what they think, Rebecca."

After all of their luggage was safely inside, Jordanna asked, "You want the tour now or are you too tired? I noticed you yawning quite a bit on the ride. Was I *that* boring?"

Rebecca shook her head profusely. "Oh, no-no-no, you are definitely anything but boring. I'm a little tired, but I'd love to see your house, thanks."

"Do you want something to drink first?" Jordanna asked, checking her cabinets and refrigerator to see if her service had been in to stock them recently, which apparently they had. "I have soda, iced tea, milk, juice..." She moved the milk carton out of the way to see if there was anything else to offer. "And beer, lots and lots of beer," she said with a grin.

"I'll have a soda, if you don't mind," Rebecca called out. She stood in the living room, looking around at all of the walls of compact discs the drummer had lined up, in alphabetical order, on her CD racks. "Damn," the reporter muttered as she shuffled through the numerous rap CDs the drummer owned. "I guess you are into rap music, huh?"

Jordanna walked into the room and handed her a glass and a can of cola. She grabbed a bottle of Michelob for herself and took a pull on it before speaking. "I love all kinds of music, but, yeah, rap is definitely one of my favorites. It's so full of expression. Most of it has such a sensual feeling to it, good to, uh, dance to."

Rebecca laughed and bumped into the drummer for effect. "Dance to, huh? I've never really liked rap music much. I just don't understand it." She smiled when she saw Jordanna's collection of classic rock CDs, and pulled out her favorite Led Zeppelin disc. "Now this is more my style," she said, waving it in front of the drummer's face. "Classic rock and roll."

"Don't knock rap until you've really tried it. Who knows, it just might grow on you," the drummer teased and looked Rebecca in the eyes. "Sometimes, if you're around things that you think you don't like long enough, they somehow start to grow on you."

The reporter's breath caught. "Um, yeah, I guess you're right."

Feeling the growing connection between them, Jordanna really felt she wanted to get to know the reporter better. "Can I ask you something personal?"

Rebecca wanted nothing more than to be able to trust the drummer, but after the way Jordanna had treated her in the beginning, she was apprehensive about answering anything personal. "Sure. I can't guarantee I'll answer, though."

Jordanna felt slightly hurt by Rebecca's apprehension. *I guess I deserve it, though.* "Well, it's not that personal, actually, and, um, you don't have to answer anything I ask you if you don't want to. I just wanted to ask you about your daughter. What's she like? Do you have a picture of her?"

A huge smile appeared on the reporter's face. "Yeah, I sure do," she said, getting up to find her backpack and her wallet. She pulled out a photo and handed it to the drummer. It was a family shot, taken just before David handed her the divorce papers. "That photo was taken when Dave and I were still together."

Jordanna looked at the photo of the young family with a bit of sadness, knowing that she would probably never have a picture like that to show to people. *Maybe I should have taken photos of all the women I've screwed so I could show them,* she thought bitterly.

"She's adorable, and she does have your gorgeous hazel eyes," Jordanna said to the reporter with complete sincerity. "Do you still love him, Rebecca?" She pointed to the couch. "Why don't you sit down and get comfortable. We have plenty of time to tour the house."

Rebecca walked to the couch and sat down. Jordanna followed behind her and sat on the chair opposite of her. "This is a beautiful house, seems very relaxing here," the reporter admitted. She was in awe of the view from the living room, which faced the ocean.

Jordanna liked the fact that the reporter was starting to feel at ease with her. Rebecca certainly was easy to get along with, especially when she herself wasn't being difficult. *Easy to start to fall for.* "Hey, you never answered my question."

"Which question was that?" Rebecca found herself truly

taken by this woman. Focusing on that sinfully sexy voice and the drummer's stunning blue eyes, she had forgotten what the question was. She now knew why the rest of the country was so obsessed with Jordanna Fox. Even with her bitchy, bad-girl rock-star attitude, it was very hard not to be. *Just one look into those blue eyes and whammo! God, Rebecca, you're so pathetic.*

"You're far too young for Alzheimer's, kiddo," Jordanna teased. "I asked you if you still had feelings for your ex-husband."

"Oh, yeah, that question," Rebecca said blankly. "No, I don't think that I ever really loved him, to be honest." She wondered why Jordanna would ask that question. "Why?"

"I was just curious, that's all," the drummer responded, flashing an inquisitive smile. "And you don't drink because the last time you did, you got pregnant? Do you think that you'd get yourself into that situation again?"

*Not if you and I were together, Jordanna.*

"I don't like to let myself get in a situation where I'm not in control anymore. I don't like to rely on other people to keep me safe." She winced at the memory. As much as she loved Cindy, she knew that the circumstances leading up to her birth had been a *big* mistake. *Why all the questions?*

Jordanna got up and grabbed the cordless phone. "You know, you can use the phone anytime you want to. Why don't you call your daughter? I can see you really miss her."

Rebecca took the phone from the drummer and smiled. "Thanks, I really appreciate it."

Jordanna started to go into the kitchen so the reporter could make her phone call in private, but Rebecca called out to her. "You don't have to go, Jordanna. This *is* your house."

The drummer shrugged and sat back down in the chair while Rebecca spoke with her family. She didn't want to, but she found it very difficult not to listen to half of the conversation. Rebecca loved her daughter. That was obvious. She felt sad that the reporter felt like a bit of failure when it came to her family.

"Thanks, it was so good to hear her voice again. I really do miss the little pipsqueak," Rebecca said after she finished her phone call.

"How far do they live from Madison Square Garden?"

"A couple of blocks, definitely within walking distance."

"We could always stop and see them when we're in the city for one of the shows, or we could just go there on an off day."

"That sounds like a plan." Rebecca yawned.

"Tired?" the drummer asked, and then yawned herself. "C'mon, I'll show you to your room. I think we both could use a good nap."

Jordanna took Rebecca's hand in hers and walked out of the room, heading towards the stairs. "Let me show you around upstairs a little." Rebecca had to work hard to keep pace with the woman's long strides. After passing by a small bedroom, Rebecca stopped short when she caught a glance of the drummer's computer room. She walked around the room and studied all of the framed Broadway prints and various rock-and-roll memorabilia covering the walls. There was even an autographed 8"x10" photo of Diane Sawyer hanging over her desk. "Diane Sawyer?" Rebecca had to ask.

"I'm a news junkie," the drummer answered shyly, ushering the reporter out of the room before she could ask any more.

Jordanna stopped at the next room. "I have four guest bedrooms, but I think this one is the nicest. You can use whichever one you want, of course. It's up to you." *Or you could stay in my bedroom...that would also be fine with me.*

"This is nice," Rebecca said, looking around the room and noticing the large windows and the view of the ocean. "I think I'll take it."

"Thought you would say that. Lemme go get your things."

Rebecca looked around the room as Jordanna ran downstairs to get her suitcase. She was salivating at the Jacuzzi in the adjoining bathroom when the drummer returned. "Mind if I use this?"

"That's what it's there for, Rebecca. Feel free to help yourself to anything in the house."

Rebecca rummaged through her bag to find her nightshirt. *Anything, Jordanna?*

The drummer turned quickly around as Rebecca began to undress. "Well, I'll leave you alone now. Enjoy your bath."

REBECCA WOKE FROM her nap refreshed and very ready for something to eat. She took a quick shower, got dressed, and quietly made her way downstairs. Walking through the formal living room, she stepped down into the den, then opened the French doors that separated the den from Jordanna's sunroom. "I'd kill for a room like this," she said out loud. "You'd never get me out of here."

"Then why don't you use this room to write your article in?"

The reporter jumped, startled by Jordanna's voice. "I didn't know you were in here." The drummer was sitting on a wicker bench, looking out at the ocean.

The reporter's stomach loudly and angrily made its presence known. Hearing the loud rumbling, Jordanna realized that they hadn't eaten since early in the morning. "Do you want to go out for dinner tonight? I've been craving good pasta for weeks now. I know a great Italian restaurant down on the pier. What do you think?"

A smile made its way onto the reporter's face. "Pasta sounds great to me. I'm starved."

"The only thing is, Rebecca, this restaurant sort of has a couples setting. You know, small table, candlelight, and all. Is that a problem for you? We haven't really discussed some of the things that have happened between us so I want to be sure you feel comfortable being seen with me."

"I have no problem with that at all," Rebecca responded. *Not at all.* "Uh, unless it would bother you."

"No." Jordanna shook her head for emphasis. "I just wanted to warn you. I guess what I'm saying is, expect to get some funny looks because I'm sure at least a few of the people will think that we're a couple," she said in a serious tone. "Sometimes people can be really ignorant and make nasty comments. I must admit, I don't react well to being called a fag."

Rebecca was stunned. "You've been called a fag?"

*Even by my own mother.* "More than once. That's why I just want you to make sure you understand what you'll be dealing with, okay?"

Rebecca sat down next to the drummer and reassured Jordanna that she had no problem being seen with her in that type of setting. "Don't worry. I can handle it, Jordanna. Now, what do I wear to this place? I don't really have anything fancy to wear."

Jordanna put her hand on her shoulder. "What you're wearing is fine." The reporter had on a pair of black jeans and a form-fitting, red V-neck sweater. "You look good in red. It looks nice with your hair. I do, however, have to change out of this," she said, pointing to her ripped blue jeans and a just as beat-up sweatshirt. Running up the stairs to head to her bedroom, she called over her shoulder to the reporter. "I'll be right down, okay?"

After a quick shower, the drummer went to her closet. Rejecting each piece of clothing she pulled out of her closet, she could feel herself starting to get angry. *What am I gonna wear? Black leather miniskirt and lacy black shirt? No. Well, not today at least. I wonder if she'd like me in that?*

Flipping through all the jeans in her closet, she spotted one of her favorite pairs. "Ah ha, yeah, that's it," she said as she pulled out the winning outfit. She slipped on the skin-tight cream-colored jeans and a chocolate-brown sweater. She rounded out the outfit with a brown belt and pair of boots, and she was ready to go.

Rebecca caught sight of the drummer as she came down the stairs. Her heart started to pound, and her palms started to sweat. *Oh, God, she is magnificent.* "You look wonderful, Jordanna."

"Thanks." Jordanna held her hand out to the reporter and led her to the door. "You ready to go?"

They walked to the garage and waited for the door to open. When it did, Rebecca followed Jordanna to the bright red Mitsubishi 3000GT parked in the far corner. Opening the door for Rebecca, the drummer waited for her to get in and buckled before heading to the driver's side.

Jordanna got in and adjusted the seat and mirrors to her liking. She hadn't driven the car since the last break the band had from the tour, around Christmas time. She always made sure that she had someone take her vehicles for a drive at least once a week when she was away so they would be in good shape when she did get home.

Rebecca ran her hand along the stick shift. "This is a really nice car. I'm surprised you don't have a luxury car, though."

Jordanna shrugged. "I know you may find this hard to believe, but I honestly am not much for flaunting status, Rebecca. I used to have a Mercedes SL500 convertible, and Susan decided to take it on a joyride with her girlfriend one afternoon when I was on tour and wrapped it around a tree, so I never bought another car in California for her to drive again. I was hardly ever there, anyway." She sighed. "Now that I'm home, I'm going to look into replacing it. I really loved that car.

"I've always liked this car, though," she continued. "So when I like something I buy it, even if it doesn't quite fit the *image* people have of me. Personally, the Harley is my fave. I love riding it around here in the summer, wind blowing through my hair and the vibration of the engine between my legs. I feel so free. Do you ride?"

Rebecca shook her head. "I've always wanted to, but didn't know anyone who had one. I don't know if I could ride one myself. They seem pretty heavy."

The drummer chuckled at the thought of the small woman trying to ride her Harley alone. "Well, we'll just have to take her out for a spin one day. It's a little cold right now, but we can bundle up."

Rebecca turned and looked at the drummer. "I'd really like that a lot."

AS SOON AS they walked into the restaurant, a small man who looked like he fell straight off the boat from Italy greeted the drummer with a big hug and a kiss. "Jordanna? Is that you?"

The drummer smiled at the older man. "Hello, Mario. Good to see you. You look as handsome as ever," she said, returning the hug.

Mario chuckled and waved her off. "You always were a good BS artist, my dear Jordanna," he said, grinning from ear to ear. He elbowed her arm and motioned to Rebecca. "Are you going to be polite and introduce me to this beautiful young woman, or do I have to do it myself?"

Jordanna took Rebecca by the hand and introduced her. "Mario, this is Rebecca, a, uh, friend of mine."

Mario took Rebecca's hand and kissed it. "I'm Mario, and I'm very pleased to meet such a beautiful young woman."

"Mario owns this place, Rebecca. You have to watch out for him. He's not as innocent as he looks," she said, winking at the man. "He's a real heartbreaker."

"Flattery will get you everywhere, Jordanna. I'll have your old table set up for you," he said, and his smiling face suddenly turned serious. "Did you break up with Susan?"

Jordanna cleared her throat and glanced at Rebecca. "Yes, I did break up with her. Recently, as a matter of fact."

The answer pleased the restaurant owner. "Good, good. That woman was—how do I say this nicely?—creepy. I'm glad you got rid of her, Jordanna. She seemed like trouble."

"She *was* trouble," Rebecca chimed in.

"Ah, now this woman," Mario said, taking Rebecca's hand again. "Make sure you take good care of her, Jordanna." He grabbed two menus and led them into the dining area. "Your table is ready."

It was Jordanna's turn to blush, and she wondered what Rebecca was thinking. She looked at the reporter and saw nothing but a smile on her face. Smiling back at the reporter, she answered him. "I absolutely intend to, Mario, thank you."

He held out the chairs for both of them. "I bring you a bottle of our finest wine. On the house, okay? Roberta will be over to take your order when you are ready."

They sat down at a table way in the back of the room, right next to the window. From their table, they had a perfect view of the Atlantic Ocean. In the distance they could see the Montauk Lighthouse keeping its watch over the people and animals of the sea. "Pretty here, isn't it?" Jordanna said, noticing the reporter taking in the scenery.

Rebecca turned and looked at her companion. "Yes, it is. I

could get lost just watching the ocean. The water is kind of choppy, though. I wonder if there is a storm coming?"

"I did hear something about a nor'easter heading this way, but they never get the forecast right. The weathermen don't seem to want to commit to anything anymore. We'll probably just get rain, like usual," the drummer commented.

Their waitress brought a bottle of wine to the table and poured a glass for each of them. Jordanna looked at Rebecca questioningly. "Would you like something different? I know you don't drink much."

The reporter shook her head. "No, this is fine. One glass won't kill me. Maybe we could get a pitcher of water, too?"

"Sure. I'll take your order when I bring the water," the waitress said, turning to go back into the kitchen.

Jordanna flipped through the menu. "I already know what I'm ordering. Do you know what you want?"

"How is the fish here?" the reporter asked.

Jordanna laughed out loud. "I wouldn't know, Rebecca. I *hate* fish. Yeah, I'm from a big fishing community like Long Island, and I hate fish. I'm weird, what can I say? I feel like I ate far too much of it in a past life or something, if that makes sense." She realized she was babbling and smiled shyly. "I hear it's excellent, though."

Lifting her wineglass up, Rebecca made a toast. "To a new friendship," she said, looking directly into the drummer's blue eyes and then tapping her glass against Jordanna's.

"Yeah, to a new friendship," the drummer repeated, and then smiled.

When their dinner arrived, Rebecca grabbed the wine bottle and poured herself another glass. "Would you like another glass?"

"No, thank you." The drummer shook her head. "I haven't finished my first glass yet. Are you sure you can handle more than one?" she asked, and took a bite of her penne ala vodka. "Why don't you have some water instead?"

Rebecca dug into her seafood platter. "This is really good. I think I can handle two glasses of wine, Jordanna!"

AN HOUR LATER, Jordanna noticed Rebecca shifting her body around so she could unbutton her jeans. "Rebecca, *what* are you doing?"

Rebecca put her hand on her stomach and shook her head. "I am so stuffed. I don't think I should have had that second dessert."

"Or that second glass of wine," Jordanna added. "And don't

forget that you ate most of my dessert, too."

"I ate you as dessert?" the reporter asked tipsily.

Surprised by the reporter's verbal slip, Jordanna shifted in her seat and smiled. "I wish. Now let's get you home before you get us into trouble." Motioning for the waitress to bring the check, she helped Rebecca out of her chair. "Can you walk?" the drummer teased playfully.

"Of course I can walk," Rebecca responded. "Whoa. Floor's slippery."

Jordanna grabbed the young reporter. "You all right?" She picked up the bill and walked behind Rebecca to the front of the restaurant. Taking her credit card back from the hostess, Jordanna added the tip and quickly signed the receipt. The drummer didn't notice that an old couple that had been sitting at a table near them was watching them, but the reporter did.

"What in the damn hell are you looking at?" Rebecca screamed. "Haven't you ever seen two women together before?" She grabbed the drummer by the chin and kissed her soundly on the mouth.

Stunned, the drummer broke away from the kiss. Jordanna looked at the couple and apologized. "I'm sorry; wine goes straight to her head."

"Let's get out of here, Rebecca," she said as she led the reporter out the door and into the parking lot, where a light snow had coated the ground.

When they finally made it to the car, Rebecca managed to pin Jordanna up against the passenger- side door. "You didn't respond to my kiss," the reporter said, disappointed.

"Rebecca, you're very tipsy. Please don't read me wrong, I do want to kiss you," Jordanna said, still pinned under the reporter. "More than anything," she whispered in Rebecca's ear. "Just let me get us home safely, okay?"

"Okay," Rebecca chirped, happily moving away from the drummer. "Whoa. Why are you spinning like that?"

# Chapter
# Nine

REBECCA OPENED HER eyes and felt the room spinning. "Ow!" Rubbing her eyes, she took a few seconds to look around the far-too-bright room. *Where am I? And what truck fell on me?* "Jordanna," she muttered when she remembered where she was. *Jordanna was right. I guess I can't handle more than one glass.*

"Oh, God, I'm gonna be sick!" She ran into the bathroom and threw herself on the floor. She was glad that the guestroom had an adjoining bathroom. Picking herself up off the floor, she went to the sink, ran the water, and splashed it on her face. "This sucks," she said to herself. "I always make fun of my friends when they have hangovers. I'm such an idiot." She noticed that Jordanna had left out a toothbrush, toothpaste, and mouthwash in the bathroom for her. "Is she trying to tell me something?"

She looked in the mirror and saw the long, black tee shirt she was wearing that said *I'll take a little pain with my pleasure.* The shirt had a picture of a leather-clad woman with a whip on the front, and the name of some fetish club in San Diego on the back. She shook her throbbing head. "She's too much," she said to her reflection. "Pain with my pleasure," she snorted. "She knew how I was going to feel this morning, huh?"

Getting as much of the horrid taste as she could out of her mouth, she left the room in search of the drummer. Upon inspection she noticed that Jordanna's room hadn't been touched except that the clothing that she had worn to the restaurant was hanging on the back of chair next to the bed. It was obvious that the drummer had not slept there.

The house was quiet. Holding onto the rail as she went down the stairs, Rebecca cursed herself silently for drinking the wine. She made her way into the den and smiled when she saw Jordanna asleep on a chair. A book was draped over one of her thighs, and a pair of eyeglasses was lying on the floor, near the sleeping woman's feet.

Rebecca stumbled over to the drummer and picked the book and the glasses up, setting them both on the end table. "Holy shit," she said as her eyes caught sight of the scenery out the window behind where Jordanna slept. The light snow that was falling the night before had turned into a blizzard during the night.

Blue eyes shot open and focused on the woman standing in front of her. "How are you feeling this morning?" the drummer asked sleepily.

Rebecca put her hand on her forehead. "Not so good," she muttered and then pointed out the window behind Jordanna. "Check it out."

Jordanna got up to see what Rebecca was looking at. "Holy shit! That's got to be about two feet of snow," she said enthusiastically, and then yawned and stretched her body to get the kinks out. "Guess the weatherman was actually right this time. I'm sure tonight's show will be postponed."

Rebecca sat down on the couch and put her head in her hands. Noticing her discomfort, Jordanna knelt in front of her and began massaging the reporter's temples. "I guess you're paying for last night, huh?" she said sympathetically. "A lot of people can't handle wine. Apparently you're one of them." She cracked a small smile. "How 'bout I make some coffee and get you something to eat."

Rebecca shook her head violently. "Ugh! No food."

"You have to get something in your stomach, Rebecca. Why don't you lay down on the couch while I get you something to eat. Just have some dry toast, okay? It should help with the nausea."

The reporter refused. "Ugh. I can't eat."

Jordanna sighed. "Please, just try for me, Rebecca. I'm the first to admit I don't cook well, but I *can* make toast, and my coffee isn't too bad," the drummer teased.

Rebecca lifted her head and cracked the best smile she could for the drummer. "Okay, but only for you, though."

Jordanna smiled back at her. "Good, thank you. At least I know I'll feel a lot better. I shouldn't have let you drink wine last night." Jordanna stood up and walked into the kitchen.

"Did you just say you *shouldn't have let me*, Jordanna?" Rebecca asked angrily as she got up and followed the drummer into the kitchen, regretting it instantly when her head started pounding like a drum again.

Jordanna watched the reporter grab her head. She tried to talk herself out of the situation. "No, I didn't say that. Well, yes, I did, but I didn't mean it the way you think. I knew that you would probably get a hangover because you don't drink. That's what I meant."

"Oh." Rebecca put her hand on the drummer's cheek. "I'm sorry. I just don't like being told to do things."

Jordanna put her hand over Rebecca's to accept the peace offering and then went to work on the coffee. "Besides, you were just so damn cute last night," she teased.

Rebecca looked into her eyes. "That's what I wanted to ask you. Did I do something stupid? I don't really remember all that much except eating a lot...and you."

Jordanna looked perplexed. "Me?" she said, pointing to herself.

Rebecca laughed quietly. "Yeah, you. I remember that I was thinking how lucky I was to be out with you. I saw the way some of the people in there were looking at you. The waitress couldn't take her eyes off of you. The man at the table behind you was staring, too. He must have thought that maybe he would be the one to straighten you out."

Jordanna felt a deep blush building. "Straighten me out?" She paused and cleared her throat. "If he was sitting behind me, then he was looking at you, Rebecca, not me," she continued, pulling out the toaster. "To be honest, I, um...I was thinking the same thing about you."

"You were thinking that he would straighten me out?" the reporter asked, with a look of mischief in her slightly bloodshot eyes.

"No, silly," Jordanna said, putting her hand on the reporter's cheek. "I was thinking that *I* was out with the most beautiful woman that I've ever laid my eyes on. Rebecca, *I'm* the lucky one."

"Oh."

"Yeah, oh. Now, how do you like your toast?"

THE TWO SPENT the afternoon in the den watching television. Jordanna turned on News 15 to see what the latest was on the storm. "I can't stand Snooze 15," the drummer complained, referring to the local news channel. "They have to be the dullest newscasters I've ever seen in my life."

"Why are we watching it then?" the sleepy reporter asked.

"We're watching it because they have the most accurate forecast for this area since they're local. You just have to fight to stay awake until the weather comes on," Jordanna explained, and jumped up to answer the phone. "But don't worry, if you miss anything you *will* catch it again next hour 'cause most of their stories are taped, and they play them over and over every hour," she said as she walked, her voice trailing off in the distance.

While Jordanna was on the phone, the weather came on. "You missed the weather," Rebecca teased when Jordanna returned to her spot on the couch.

"Figures," the drummer said with a laugh. "That was Jerry. The show, of course, has been postponed. They're going to try to reschedule it for sometime next month. Let's hope we can dig our way out of here by then." *Although I certainly wouldn't complain if we couldn't.*

Rebecca sprawled out on the couch and put her feet up on the coffee table. "Jordanna?"

"Hmm?"

"You never did tell me if I did anything stupid last night."

The drummer laughed. "You really want to know?"

Rebecca sat up straight and opened her eyes wide. "Why? Did I really do something that bad? Tell me, please."

"You really wanna know, huh?" The drummer spoke slowly to prolong Rebecca's agony. "You yelled at an elderly couple that were looking at us when we were leaving."

The young blonde shook her head in disbelief. "I yelled at an elderly couple?" she repeated. "I did not!"

"You most certainly did, Rebecca." Jordanna questioned whether she should tell the reporter the rest. "So, do you want to know what you said to them?"

"Yeah. I think," Rebecca answered reluctantly, not knowing what to expect. People always seem to say exactly what is on their minds when tipsy.

The drummer chuckled. "You demanded to know what they were looking at."

"Oh, that's not that bad." Rebecca sighed with relief. She thought that she had made a complete fool of herself.

"Well, it wasn't too bad until you asked them if they'd ever seen two women together before and then proceeded to scandalize the whole room by kissing me on the mouth!" Jordanna winked at Rebecca.

"I did what?"

"You kissed me on the mouth," the drummer repeated, a wicked grin slowly building on her face.

Silence.

Jordanna narrowed her eyes at the reporter's response, or lack of response. "Are you all right? C'mon, Rebecca, talk to me."

Rebecca apologized. "I'm sorry."

Jordanna narrowed her eyes. "Sorry for what?"

"I can't believe I did that. I don't know what I was thinking." Rebecca got up and walked away from the drummer. She couldn't look at her anymore.

"Rebecca," Jordanna crooned softly, and walked across the room to be closer to the reporter. "We've kissed before."

"Stay away from me!" the embarrassed reporter hissed. Tears were forming in her eyes.

The drummer grabbed the blonde by the arms and shook her. "Rebecca, please! Why are you doing this?"

Rebecca freed herself from the drummer's vise-like grip. "No, I feel like an idiot now. I'm such a fool to think that someone like you could possibly like me!"

"Hold it right there, Rebecca." Jordanna was floored. "What do you mean someone like me couldn't like someone like you? If anything, it's the other way around."

"Why do you say that?" Rebecca asked quietly, her voice hoarse.

Jordanna shook her head and laughed. "Rebecca, I am that woman that everyone's mother warns them about. It's no secret I'm a womanizer; even I admit it. Why on earth would you even *want* to like someone like me?"

The reporter looked into Jordanna's blue eyes. "If you are trying to scare me off, Jordanna, it's not going to work."

The dark-haired woman walked over to the window. "Rebecca, I..."

"How do you really feel about me, Jordanna? Don't try to spare my feelings, I can take it," Rebecca questioned, her eyes following the tall woman as she walked over to the window.

Jordanna closed her eyes. *Just do it.* "I..."

*I can't do this.*

The drummer knew that these new feelings would get her into trouble. She wanted to let down the walls that she had worked so hard to build and let someone in, but with love came pain and rejection.

*There goes that nasty 'L' word again. Just tell her how you feel.*

"Rebecca, I want you. I've wanted you since the moment I laid eyes on you."

Rebecca let out a deep breath. *It's all about sex with her, isn't it?* That wasn't quite what she wanted to hear from the dark woman. "As just another one of your playthings, I take it?" she said, not afraid to let the hurt show in her voice. "I don't want to be just another notch on your bedpost, Jordanna. That's not my style."

"No," the dark woman replied, her eyes following the heavy snow that was still falling. "You see, that's just the thing. I get these feelings when I'm near you that I've never experienced before." She turned around to face Rebecca. "These feelings, well...they confuse the hell out of me."

"What kind of feelings?" the reporter asked.

*Oh, God, this is so hard.* Jordanna swallowed a few times before answering. "It's hard to explain. I have a feeling like I've found something that was lost, except I didn't know I was searching for it. I know that sounds stupid, but..."

Rebecca didn't let her finish. "It doesn't sound stupid, Jordanna. I feel the same way."

"You do?" *Is it possible?* The drummer locked eyes with the smaller woman. "I uh, I also feel like I found feelings again, if that makes any sense. I haven't felt anything for anyone or anything for a damn long time. That's why I've never really had a real relationship and just fucked around; it was easier that way. I can tell you this; I *want* to have a real relationship now...with you."

Rebecca didn't know what to say.

Jordanna felt extremely awkward about revealing any of her inner feelings to someone else and wasn't sure she liked the fact that Rebecca hadn't said anything. She walked over to the couch and sat down next to the reporter. "Are you okay?"

Rebecca looked up at the drummer, and Jordanna noticed that there were tears forming in her eyes. "Yeah, I'm better than okay," Rebecca answered, her face breaking out into a huge smile. "I want that too, Jordanna."

Jordanna sat silent for a minute, relishing Rebecca's words. "You do realize that you'll be entering into a whole new world by getting involved with me, right? Things might not always be that pleasant for us," the drummer warned, laying the cards out on the table for the young reporter.

Rebecca nodded. "I understand that. Not everyone will be that accepting of our relationship," she said, pausing to put emphasis on what she was going to say to the dark woman. "But you know something? I really don't give a flying fuck what people think, as long as I'm with you. I just...well, I don't know if I can compare to the other women you've been with, Jordanna."

"You can't compare to them."

Rebecca closed her eyes and sighed quietly. She'd been afraid that the drummer was going to say that. "I..."

"Shh, listen to me." Jordanna put her fingers over the reporter's lips. "My heart doesn't skip a beat when I see any of those women from across a room. My breath doesn't catch when I feel their slightest touch. Those things only happen when I see or touch you, Rebecca. None of them has ever made me feel like you do. So, no, I can't compare you to any of them. There's no contest. You win, hands down."

Jordanna closed her eyes and a tear escaped. "I've never made love to anyone before, Rebecca," she continued, admitting something that sounded very stupid, even to her.

The reporter laughed. "You've got to be kidding me, I've seen you, Jordanna."

"What you've seen and what I've done has never been done with love, Rebecca."

"What about Linda?"

Jordanna shook her head in shame. "Linda was a big mistake. I didn't love her. I thought she knew that."

"Susan?"

"Rebecca, Susan was..." the drummer sighed. She knew Rebecca deserved to know about her fetishes, and she needed the opportunity to back out before it was too late. "Susan was my slave."

The reporter looked up at her with confusion. "Your slave?"

"Yes, she was my slave. Sexually."

Rebecca looked down at the shirt she was wearing. She thought back to the conversation where Jordanna said that Susan was willing to take anything Jordanna gave her sexually, and knew enough to thank her for it afterward. Now it all made sense. "Your slave. As in whips and chains slave?"

"Yes."

Rebecca swallowed hard. "Why are you telling me this?"

"Because I think you deserve to know the real person that you want to get to know better before jumping into things." Jordanna took the small woman's hands in her own. "Rebecca, you need to think about this carefully. I honestly don't know if I will be able to let go once I give you my heart." The drummer let another tear fall. "I've never felt this way. I've never wanted to give my heart to someone before. I don't know how to handle it."

Rebecca wiped the tear off of the drummer's face. "You want to give me your heart?"

"Yes, I do."

The reporter cleared her throat and smiled. "I want so much to take it, Jordanna."

"That's why you need to know all of this. Just as you don't want to be one of my playthings, I don't want to be just an experiment for you." She got up off of the couch and kissed Rebecca on the cheek. "Take the time to rest and think about this, okay?" Jordanna ran her hand through Rebecca's messy hair, then went to the linen closet, pulled out a blanket, and tucked it around the reporter. She walked across the room and picked up her book and reading glasses. "I'll be in the sunroom reading if you need me, okay?"

Rebecca nodded and then sat back on the couch and closed her eyes. She didn't know if she was still nauseous from the wine, or if it was from fear of jumping into the unknown. She had done that too many times in her life since she graduated from high school, and she didn't want to get hurt, or hurt anyone else for that matter.

She was thankful for the glimpse Jordanna had given her of her heart, and that she cared enough to tell her exactly what she was about. This confirmed what she knew all along, that Jordanna was not the selfish, uncaring person that everyone believed her to be. That person would have just jumped in bed with Rebecca, taken what she wanted, and worried about the consequences afterward, or sent her packing. Instead, Jordanna opted to give her time to think.

She didn't have to think. Her mind was made up. It had been since the moment she looked into the drummer's blue eyes for the first time.

JORDANNA WALKED INTO the sunroom and opened up a few of the vertical blinds. She shielded her eyes from the snow's immense brightness and closed all but one. She sat for a while watching the steadily falling snow, thinking. Her mind threw question after question at her. Some she knew the answers to, and some she knew she would have to search the darkest depths of her soul for.

She picked up her glasses and put them on, opening the book up to the first page. She knew that she hadn't absorbed a word that she had read the previous night, so she started to read it over. Unable to grasp what she was reading again, she sighed, then closed the book and put it down.

After getting up from the couch, she walked into the living room and checked on Rebecca. She could tell by her light snores that he reporter was sleeping soundly. With a content smile on her face, Jordanna walked into the kitchen and started to make herself a cup of tea. An hour and a half later, a shadow made its way across the pages of the book. Jordanna looked up and saw the reporter standing in front of her.

"I've made up my mind, Jordanna."

The drummer's heart began to pound wildly, and she started to speak. Rebecca put her fingers over her lips. "Shh, let me tell you what I've decided."

Jordanna looked up at the reporter, waiting patiently for Rebecca's decision. *I will not be upset if she doesn't want to get involved with me.*

Rebecca ran her hand along the drummer's cheek and then took her glasses off. She set them down on the table next to her and held out her hand to the drummer. "Make love to me, Jordanna."

*Oh, God.*

Jordanna's heart lurched, and a childlike grin formed on her face. She took Rebecca's hand and let the reporter lead her to the couch in the living room. After they sat down, Jordanna turned to the reporter. "Um. Is it," she hesitated, "is it all right if I kiss you now?"

"More than all right."

Jordanna leaned in and captured Rebecca's mouth with her own. It was gentle at first, but as both their desires grew the kiss intensified. The drummer sought entrance into the reporter's mouth with her tongue, and Rebecca willingly let her in. "Mmm," she moaned, enjoying the feel of Jordanna's tongue dancing with hers. She sucked in her breath when she felt the drummer's tongue rub along the roof of her mouth near her teeth. When they broke the kiss, the reporter looked at the drummer through hooded hazel eyes filled with desire. "Take me to your bed," she said quietly.

The dark-haired woman's heart started working double time. She leaned in close and began nibbling on Rebecca's ear. "Are you sure you want to do this?" she whispered in the ear she had just nibbled on.

"Yes, I'm very sure."

Jordanna stood up and offered her hand to Rebecca. The reporter took it, allowing Jordanna to lead her up the stairs to the drummer's bedroom. The dark-haired woman opened the door and followed the reporter into the room, closing the door behind her. Rebecca stood near the bed and waited for the drummer to join her. Jordanna could tell that Rebecca was nervous by the way she was shifting from foot to foot, and realized that there were butterflies forming in her own stomach.

*Why am I so nervous?* the drummer thought, as she was walking across the room. *Let's face it; you've fucked hundreds, maybe thousands, of women over the years, but you've never once made love before, and you* want to *make love with Rebecca.*

She approached the reporter slowly, not wanting to scare her, and also to give herself time to calm down. When she reached her destination, Jordanna wrapped her arms around the smaller woman's waist and pulled her closer. She ran her hands across Rebecca's cheeks and leaned in for a kiss. "Are you really sure that this is — that I am — what you want, Rebecca?"

"Very sure."

The drummer smiled at Rebecca, a smile that went all the way up to her eyes. She pushed Rebecca's hair to the side and began placing light kisses on the smaller woman's neck. Rebecca jumped at the sensual feeling, and Jordanna pulled away, her heart beating faster than she'd ever felt before. "Are you all right?" *Because I don't know if I am.*

Rebecca shook her head. "I'm just a little nervous. I, I've never, you know, with a woman before," she tried to explain.

Jordanna ran her hand along the smaller woman's cheek. "I know you haven't, Rebecca. We'll take it slow, okay?"

The reporter nodded, unsure if her voice would fail her at this point or not. The drummer took Rebecca's hands in hers and eased them both down on the bed, where they lay on their sides facing one another. The dark woman brushed a strand of golden hair away from Rebecca's face and then leaned in to gently kiss the reporter's lips. She saw that the small woman's hands were shaking and took them in her own. "We can wait if you don't feel you are ready for this, Rebecca."

"No, I'll be fine. I just don't really know what to do."

"Were you this nervous when you made love with David for the first time?" the drummer asked, and then a thought occurred to her. "Was David your first time?"

Rebecca squirmed at the question. "Uh..."

Jordanna put her hand on Rebecca's shoulder and gave her an apologetic look. "I was totally out of line with that question, Rebecca. I'm sorry. That's really none of my business."

Rebecca pushed the drummer's hair away from her face. "No, that's okay. It's just that with anyone I've slept with I have never been...um, I was never really satisfied."

Jordanna nodded in full understanding. "I understand, Rebecca." She leaned forward and whispered in Rebecca's ear. "This time an orgasm will be a reality and not a fantasy."

Rebecca's eyes opened wide, and she started to laugh. "My, my. We are the confident one, aren't we?"

Jordanna laughed and pulled her closer. "Well, I've never heard any complaints."

The reporter looked directly into the drummer's blue eyes. "I'm scared, Jordanna."

In all truth, Jordanna was scared, too. Scared of the real feelings she was having, afraid of chancing having her heart broken, frightened of breaking Rebecca's heart, and terrified that she would be unable to make gentle love to the woman. She was afraid of herself. "I know you're scared, Rebecca. I won't hurt you. I promise."

"I know you won't."

*Okay, Jordanna, stay in control of yourself. You want this to work.*

She thought of a way to relax the reporter and took Rebecca's hand in her own. "Rebecca, I want you to familiarize yourself with my body," she said, flashing a small smile.

Rebecca looked at the drummer as if her hair had just turned purple.

"No, I'm serious, Rebecca. This will help you relax. Start with feeling the curve of my hip," the drummer said, laying Rebecca's hand on her hip area. With the drummer's hand still on top of her own, Rebecca began to slowly feel the powerful body under the sweatpants that Jordanna was wearing.

"Now my arms, feel the muscles in them. Think of the way they'll feel wrapped around your body," the drummer continued.

Rebecca ran her hands along the length of the drummer's arms, imagining how it would feel to be tucked securely in them. "Mmm, it will feel wonderful," she murmured.

"Good. Now, my hands, Rebecca."

Rebecca traced the outline of Jordanna's hand with her own, dipping into the webbing between the drummer's fingers as she went along, never losing eye contact with the dark-haired woman. "You have such long, elegant fingers."

"And you have such beautiful lips," the drummer whispered softly, tracing the outline of Rebecca's lips with the long fingers that Rebecca just traced with her own. Feeling slightly more relaxed, Rebecca opened her mouth and bit down gently on the drummer's index finger and took it into her mouth, sucking lightly on the tip of it. Jordanna sighed as the warmth of Rebecca's mouth embraced her senses, making her feel light-headed and dizzy.

Jordanna pulled her finger out of Rebecca's mouth and replaced it with her lips, brushing them gently over the reporter's. After they broke the tender kiss, Rebecca resumed her slow exploration of Jordanna's body, running her hands along the drummer's tight abdomen. She lifted the dark-haired woman's sweatshirt up slowly and traced the same path that she had done just seconds before. She caressed the dark-haired woman's silk-covered breasts, letting out a brief sigh while doing so. She pushed the sweatshirt up and over Jordanna's head and threw it into a heap on the floor.

Jordanna shuddered slightly as warm skin hit cold air, and

she locked eyes with the reporter's hazel ones. Breaking away from the drummer's sensual gaze, Rebecca tried to speak, but the words wouldn't come out.

Jordanna lifted a brow. "You all right?"

Rebecca nodded and found her voice again, and asked the dark-haired woman if it would be all right if she removed Jordanna's bra for her.

"Mmm, be my guest," the dark-haired woman purred.

Rebecca maneuvered herself in front of Jordanna and traced the outline of Jordanna's silk-covered nipple with her finger. She watched with satisfaction as the drummer sighed and closed her eyes at the touch, and then slowly undid the two hooks in the front of her bra. She held her breath as she watched the dark-haired woman's breasts fall out of the cups and her nipples harden as soon as they hit the cold air. Her eyes were immediately drawn to the silver hoop that adorned the drummer's left nipple, and her fingers soon followed, wanting to feel the hoop and the perfect nipples for herself.

The hoop felt cold against her warm fingertips, and she watched as Jordanna's breathing began to grow heavier with the sensation. She gave the hoop a little tug, and then let go, running the tip of her finger around Jordanna's areola, making the dark-haired woman shiver.

Rebecca pulled her fingers back as the drummer began to respond to her touch.

"Don't be afraid," Jordanna crooned in a low, soothing voice. She placed her hands on top of Rebecca's and loosely linked them together, guiding them to her. She felt Rebecca's body jump slightly as their linked hands came to a stop, cupping the dark-haired woman's breasts.

"So soft," Rebecca whispered as she caressed another woman's bare breasts for the first time in her life, and decided that she liked the feeling very much. "So good." She looked at Jordanna, and her breath caught at the sight. The drummer had her eyes closed and her head tipped back slightly, and her long, dark hair was flowing loosely down her back. At that moment Rebecca realized that she was about to make love with the most beautiful woman in the world.

Jordanna opened her eyes to see Rebecca sitting there just staring at her.

The reporter was mesmerized by the power of the drummer's gaze and realized that Jordanna could make love to her with her eyes alone, not needing to use touch or taste to do so. She shivered as the blue gaze caressed her body like a gentle lover, making her feel things she had never felt before for anyone.

"Are you okay?" the drummer asked the silent woman.

Rebecca leaned forward and placed a kiss on the drummer's lips. "You are breathtaking."

Jordanna looked down and blushed, then gave a light snort of a laugh. She looked up and smiled shyly at the reporter, who began to tug on the drummer's sweatpants.

"I take it you want these off?" the drummer teased, and nibbled gently on an available earlobe.

"Yes," Rebecca mumbled breathlessly.

Jordanna lifted a brow at her and slid off of the bed. She turned around and pulled Rebecca up with her, pulling the blonde in close for a hug. Rebecca wrapped her hands around Jordanna's bare back and ran her hands up and down it, feeling the silky-smooth skin against her fingers.

Jordanna moved back, and Rebecca slowly ran her hands down the dark-haired woman's hips, pulling the sweatpants down as she went along, smiling as she realized that the woman didn't have any panties on.

"Oh, God," Rebecca sighed loudly, seeing the dark-haired woman's whole body in its total naked splendor. "You are beyond beautiful, Jordanna. Words can't describe what I am feeling right now."

The drummer blushed. "Thank you," she said quietly. "I think I know exactly how you're feeling." She leaned in for another hungry kiss. "You know, I'd like to see you, too."

Rebecca moaned slightly. "Oh, yeah," she said as she looked down at the long tee shirt she was wearing.

Jordanna pulled the tee shirt over Rebecca's head and took a deep breath at the sight of the reporter's bare breasts. Rebecca blushed when she saw the dark-haired woman smiling at the sight of her hardened nipples.

"You...are...so...beautiful," the drummer said slowly as she moved toward the reporter and left a trail of kisses down her neck. She stopped and looked directly in Rebecca's eyes for the young woman's blessings before continuing. The reporter nodded and closed her eyes before she felt a moist mouth brushing against the outline of her breast. "Oh. Mmm, yeah. I like that, Jordanna," the reporter whispered, as the mouth made its way to a nipple, licking, nibbling, and teasing it. Jordanna worked her way to the reporter's other breast, feasting on it like a kid in a candy store.

"Does this please Madam Jorcula?" the reporter teased, remembering one of their first civil conversations.

Jordanna raised her head and looked into Rebecca's eyes.

"Yes, Jorcula is more than pleased. She does love to suck, you know," the drummer added before she stood up and kissed Rebecca on the mouth quickly, and then nibbled and licked her way back down Rebecca's neck and breasts.

Rebecca felt waves of desire shooting right to her groin as Jordanna's mouth took in as much of her breast as she could, and she pulled on the drummer's ebony hair slightly to let her know where she wanted Jordanna to go next.

"A woman that knows what she wants." Jordanna looked up at her and saw the desire in the blonde's eyes and smiled. "Are you sure?" she asked, waiting for Rebecca's answer. When the reporter nodded her head, Jordanna slid her hands under Rebecca's body, scooped her up, and eased the smaller woman down the bed. With a smile, she eased herself down between the reporter's legs, caressing them with her hands, following the caresses up with kisses. When she reached her final destination, she tugged Rebecca's panties off and threw them onto the clothes pile on the floor. She looked at Rebecca's body and sighed at the beauty right before her eyes. Rebecca heard the sigh and then parted her legs without instruction, and the drummer began placing butterfly kisses on the area just above her patch. Rebecca's body shook slightly from the new sensations she was feeling. No one had ever made her feel as excited and alive as Jordanna was making her feel. "Jordanna, please. I need you," she pleaded, her voice filled with desire.

The drummer picked Rebecca's legs up and put them over her shoulders. She kissed the inside of her thighs, taking the time to enjoy the scent of the reporter's arousal. She looked up and smiled at the reporter, who looked back at her with a carnal need that the dark-haired woman had never seen before, and then she brought her mouth to Rebecca's center. Rebecca's hips jumped as she felt the dark woman begin to caress her sensually with a gentle tongue, exploring areas that the reporter never knew existed and feeling sensations that she had never felt. "Mmm. God. So good," she moaned, hoping that the drummer would never stop with her ministrations. Jordanna tasted every inch of the reporter, and the sounds of pleasure Rebecca made were like music to the drummer's ears and only fueled her fire tenfold. "I want to feel you...inside me," the reporter said, feeling her impending release was going to come much sooner than she hoped.

"Patience, Rebecca," Jordanna purred.

"No-o-o...now," the young woman pleaded.

Jordanna shrugged her shoulders and laid her body down next to the reporter's. "It would be my pleasure," she said, moments before she slid a finger inside of her new lover.

"More..."

Jordanna lifted a dark brow. "All right," the dark woman responded and slipped a second finger in, letting the reporter set the pace. "How's that?"

"One more."

The drummer slipped a third finger in. "That good?"

Rebecca began riding on Jordanna's hand and a smile came to her face. "You're perfect."

Jordanna smiled at what she figured was a verbal slip and felt Rebecca's walls begin to tense around her, so she began to bite gently on the reporter's neck before moving to a nipple, sending new jolts of desire to the blonde's already sensitive center. "Let it go, Rebecca, I've got you," the drummer purred, remaining inside the smaller woman until the final tremors rocked her body. Jordanna pulled the reporter into her arms and held on tight, whispering words of love and comfort in Rebecca's ear.

The reporter's eyes were still filled with desire as she looked at the woman in bed with her. Rebecca sat up and pulled the drummer with her, wrapping her legs around Jordanna's midsection and her arms around the dark woman's neck. She leaned forward and captured the drummer's mouth with a kiss, and this time she ran her tongue along Jordanna's lips, pleading for entry. Jordanna let her take control and moaned into the reporter's mouth as she started her exploration. They parted when oxygen ran low, and Rebecca pushed the drummer onto her back. She laid her body down on top of her brand-new lover's body, enjoying the feeling when her nipples brushed against Jordanna's and the delightful feel of Jordanna's slick, warm skin rubbing against her own. She began sucking on the drummer's pulse point. Feeling her pulse increase, she kissed her way down the dark-haired woman's upper body and hesitated momentarily when she reached her breasts. Waiting no longer, she traced her tongue around the dark-haired woman's nipple, feeling Jordanna's breath catch and seeing the way she responded to her touch.

Rebecca could feel her own heart pounding uncontrollably, and apparently Jordanna did, too, because the dark woman lifted the reporter's chin up so she could look into her eyes. "You're doing fine, Rebecca." The reporter smiled at her and brought her head back down to the drummer's nipple, this time taking it in her mouth. She sucked and bit on it gently before she turned her attention on Jordanna's other nipple and began tugging on the silver ring with her tongue. "Oh, God." The drummer's body arched off the bed and she moaned softly, opening her eyes and then closing them again.

Rebecca worked her way down, licking and kissing the curve of the drummer's hip. She felt the dark-haired woman's hands caressing her back and buttocks as she made her way further down the drummer's body. A vision came into her head as her kisses led her down to the patch of dark hair, and she stopped what she was doing. The vision was of Jordanna and the woman in the bathroom.

"You don't have to, Rebecca," the drummer whispered, noticing the reporter's hesitation when she reached her groin area. "Do whatever you're comfortable with. No pressure, okay?"

"But I want to taste you, Jordanna. I, I just...what if I can never do it?"

"That'll come with time, Rebecca, and we have plenty of that. And if you can't, that's okay, too." She smiled and ran her hand down Rebecca's cheek.

Rebecca grabbed her hands. "No, I *really* want to taste you, Jordanna."

"Um," Jordanna muttered, and thought of a compromise. She ran her fingers down the length of her sex and locked eyes with Rebecca as she slowly brought her hand to her own mouth, rubbing the moisture on her lips. "C'mere."

Rebecca climbed up the length of the drummer's body, and Jordanna pulled her close. "Taste me," she whispered in a throaty, desire-filled growl, and leaned in for a passionate kiss. She felt Rebecca's tongue run across her lips before it slipped into her mouth, and they both let out a moan. "Mmm. Heaven," the reporter managed to say between kisses. "Not enough, Jordanna...more."

Jordanna took Rebecca's hand in hers and guided the timid woman's hand down to her womanhood. "You can touch me, Rebecca. I want you to feel what you do to me."

Rebecca closed her eyes and stroked Jordanna's center gently, enjoying the warm, silky texture against her fingers. It felt exquisite. She looked up into the drummer's hooded eyes and wanted nothing more than to please the dark-haired beauty.

She quickly slipped her finger past Jordanna's folds, and the drummer jumped forward slightly before she closed her eyes and moaned. "Mmm, yeah. So good, Rebecca. More, please."

Rebecca slipped another finger inside the dark woman and felt her jump again. "All of them," the breathless drummer pleaded.

"All of them?"

"Use...all of your fingers, Rebecca. I need you to fill me completely. I need you..."

Rebecca did as she was asked, sliding all of her fingers into Jordanna's wet center, and began rubbing her thumb against the length of the drummer's clitoris.

"Oh, yes. That's it, Rebecca," Jordanna said between moans. Rebecca began thrusting her fingers in and out, keeping up with the rhythm Jordanna set as she rocked back and forth. "Oh, yes. Rebecca," the dark-haired woman cried out as spasms ripped through her body, sending her over the edge. She fell weakly to the bed and pulled Rebecca down with her, Rebecca's fingers still inside her. She felt a few tremors as Rebecca slowly extracted her fingers from her center, touching the still sensitive area.

"Rebecca, I really need to hold you." Jordanna held her arms open for Rebecca to climb into. The drummer almost started to laugh as she felt tears begin to well up in her eyes, knowing that she had just made love for the first time.

Rebecca looked up at the woman whose arms she was cradled in. "You're crying." The reporter placed a kiss on the dark woman's cheek and wiped the tear off with her finger.

"Yeah." The drummer smiled at her, her emotions running wild. "You don't know what this means to me. You just gave me more than I could ever ask for, Rebecca. I love you," she whispered, the words coming out of her mouth before she could stop them.

"Oh, God," Rebecca cried out, never expecting to hear the declaration from the drummer. "I... I love you, too, Jordanna."

THE SNOW WAS still falling when the drummer woke up. *This feels wonderful,* she thought, looking down at the still-sleeping reporter tucked in the crook of her arm. *She feels wonderful.*

"Jordanna?" the reporter mumbled sleepily.

The drummer moved an errant strand of hair out of Rebecca's eyes. "I'm sorry, I didn't mean to wake you."

Rebecca sighed contently as she realized she was in the drummer's arms in her big, warm bed. Her finger soon found its way into the hoop of Jordanna's nipple ring. "How come only one?" Rebecca asked.

Jordanna shuddered at the jolt from the contact.

"I guess it is true that it enhances..."

"Yes," the drummer said, shuddering again, as Rebecca kept playing with the ring. "Yes, it does. I guess you like it, huh?"

Rebecca smiled. "Yeah, I think it's *very* sexy. Why only one, though?"

"I wanted to make sure I liked it before getting the second one done," the drummer teased.

Rebecca quickly flicked her tongue over the dark woman's pierced nipple, enjoying the shudders that rocked the drummer's body. "Did it hurt?"

"Yes, it was pretty painful. Maybe it wouldn't have been so bad if I would have had it done professionally, but I had Susan do it. She's not very gentle," she said, remembering the wicked smile on Susan's face as she jabbed the needle through her flesh. Even the bottle of Jack Daniels she had consumed before having it done did nothing for the pain.

"Yeah, I know. I saw what she did to your house, remember? She wasn't very gentle there, if I do say so myself." The reporter poked at her other nipple. "Get the other one done." She winked at Jordanna. "By a professional, of course."

The drummer's eyebrows shot up. "I'll do it if you'll get one," she said, and winked back.

Rebecca laughed.

Jordanna raised her brows again. "What's so funny, Rebecca?"

"Me, have a nipple ring? I'm a farm girl, Jordanna."

"You live in New York City now, not on a farm. Even so, farm girls do have nipples, don't they?" Jordanna laughed and pinched the body part being discussed. "Unless I'm dreaming about this," she said, and climbed on top of Rebecca, straddling her legs. She bent down and took one of Rebecca's pink nipples in her teeth and tugged gently. "Get one for me, please?"

Rebecca shuddered and held up the white flag. "Okay, okay. Only one for me, though."

"Oh, yeah," Jordanna said triumphantly. "I know just the place that we can go to. It's not near here, but we could stop there on the way to the Garden. You're gonna look so sexy with one, not that you don't without it. No backing out on me, okay?"

"Deal," Rebecca answered, hoping she wouldn't chicken out at the last minute.

They both stayed quiet for a few minutes, content just to lie there in each other's arms. "Me," Rebecca snorted, "Have a nipple ring. What will my family think?"

Jordanna smiled and kissed her on the forehead. "Does your family have to know? It's not something you usually share with Mom and Dad, you know?"

Rebecca laughed. She thought about going home for the holidays and showing off her future jewelry. *Look what I got,*

*Dad.* Her eyes twinkled at the thought. *Oh, and Dad, meet my lover, too.*

Even better.

"Besides," Jordanna half joked, "I'll be the only one that will see it."

*Did she just say that?*

The two lay there quietly for some time, enjoying the cozy feeling they felt in the warm bed while outside a blizzard roared on.

"Jordanna, can I ask you a question?" Rebecca asked lazily.

"Mmm," the drummer purred. She ran her fingers gently across Rebecca's lips. "What's that?"

Rebecca hesitated. "Is Jordanna your real name?"

The drummer's movement stilled and her eyes took on a dazed look. A few minutes passed.

"Hey," the reporter said, putting her hand on Jordanna's cheek. "You don't have to answer that if you don't want to."

"No," the drummer whispered.

Rebecca ran her fingers through Jordanna's ebony hair, enjoying the silky texture against her skin. "Okay," she said, letting the drummer know that she wouldn't question her about it any further.

Jordanna's eyes welled with tears. "I mean, no, Jordanna is not my real name. Why?"

Rebecca smiled at the drummer and took her hands in hers. "I just wanted to know the real name of the woman that I just made love with, that's all."

One lone tear ran down Jordanna's face, which Rebecca caught with her finger before placing a kiss on the wet streak it left in its wake. Both women stayed quiet for a while, just basking in the warmth and solace that they found in each other.

"Julia," the drummer finally said, pulling the young woman into her arms.

Rebecca looked at the ebony-haired woman questioningly. "Julia?"

Jordanna chuckled lowly. "Julia is the woman you just made love with. Jordanna is my name legally now, but my birth name is Julia Smith."

"Smith, huh?" Rebecca asked, laughing. "Am I really supposed to believe that is your last name?"

Jordanna rolled her eyes. "Just don't ask me if it's my motel name, okay? That's one of the many curses of having the last name Smith."

"Thank you for sharing that with me, Jordanna." She kissed the drummer on the cheek. "Thank you for opening your heart up to me."

Jordanna smiled. "Thank you for making me want to open my heart." She leaned down and kissed the reporter on the forehead.

Rebecca blinked as tears filled her eyes. "Jordanna?"

"Hmm?"

"Can I tell you something very, very personal?"

"Of course you can. You know you can tell me anything, Rebecca."

Rebecca lay there quietly for a few seconds, weighing her decision to tell the drummer her biggest secret. She had always wanted to tell someone, and for some reason she felt safe with the dark-haired woman.

Jordanna pulled her closer. "Honey?"

*Honey? I've never used that word in my life.*

"You are not the first musician I've slept with."

Jordanna sat up abruptly, pulling the reporter up with her. "What? Why are you telling me this?"

"David is not Cindy's father."

"Not her father?" Jordanna looked at her and blinked. "Who is, Rebecca?"

"Evan Carlisle."

"Evan Carlisle?"

"Stop repeating what I say, Jordanna! You know, Evan Carlisle, the singer. Overdosed on heroin last year."

"I know who he is, Rebecca. I just...well, I'm kind of shocked, that's all." She laughed nervously. "Does anyone else know? David?"

"No, he doesn't know."

"Wow," the drummer clucked. "So Evan never knew he had a child?"

Rebecca shook her head. "Not mine, no. I think he had a few with some other women, though."

"Yeah," the drummer snorted. "I'm sure he did. He *was* the male version of me."

"Did you know him?"

The drummer nodded. "I met him once, yeah. At the Grammys, I think. Some awards show." She didn't tell Rebecca he had spent the whole night at the after-show party begging her to sleep with him, something that she could proudly say she turned down.

"Jordanna?"

"Hmm?"

"I trust that you will not tell anyone."

"It stays between us, okay?" The drummer lowered her head

and kissed Rebecca soundly. "Thank you for sharing this with me, Rebecca," the drummer said, taking Rebecca's hand in hers and squeezing it tight. "I feel privileged to know you trust me with it. I'll guard it, and you and Cindy, with my life."

# Chapter
## Ten

THE REST OF the day was peaceful, the two women sharing more than they had shared with anyone before. Rebecca told Jordanna about the circumstances that led to Cindy's conception. She had been on a two-day assignment for the magazine, and the popular singer sweet-talked her into going out to a bar on an off night, where he fed her tequila after tequila. He took a very drunk Rebecca back to his hotel room, and they spent the night together having unprotected sex. She found out a month later that she was pregnant. David never suspected a thing.

After a relieved Rebecca finished spilling her guts to the drummer about Evan, they made love again in the early afternoon; this time the glowing reporter was much less inhibited. Afterward, they lay in each other's arms cuddling and talking more, until they both took a catnap. When they woke, the snow had tapered off, leaving a 29" mess in its wake.

Jordanna went outside to try to shovel a bit of the driveway, enough to allow access to and from the house until the snow-removal service could get there. Rebecca offered to help, but Jordanna promptly refused, suggesting that the reporter use the time to rest and work on her article.

Rebecca placed a call to John and filled him in on the progress she was making, telling him that she was at Jordanna's house and they were indeed bonding, like he had joked when he first told her of the assignment. Of course, she didn't quite tell him how much they had bonded. She made herself a cup of tea while Jordanna was outside and set out to work on her trusty laptop. Except the words didn't come. Out of the corner of her eye, she could see her new lover shoveling snow in her tight jeans, sweater, construction boots, hat, and big, bulky jacket. "Well, this just ain't happening," she said to herself, closed out her file, and put her laptop away. "I think she needs some help." She ran up the stairs as easily as ever, her body fully recovered; it was hard to remember that she'd been under the weather when

she woke that morning. She headed for her room to change into
something warm, realized she was not properly prepared for a
snowstorm, and decided to raid the drummer's closet for a
sweatshirt.

As she grabbed a sweatshirt out of Jordanna's closet, she
accidentally knocked over a metal box that was on a shelf above
the drummer's clothes. The loud thunk caught her by surprise.
"You're such a freaking klutz, Rebecca," she said out loud.
"Look at the mess you made." Looking down, she saw various
photos all over the floor. She bent down and picked everything
up, and got a better look at the photos. One shot was of a very
young Jordanna at Christmas time, all smiles, with a man and
woman, who, the reporter assumed, were her parents. She
turned the photo over to see if there was anything written on it.
There was. It said *Thomas, Patricia & Julia – Christmas 1979.*
Flipping through the rest of them, she noticed that it was the
only one she had with her family. The next few were of a
teenage Jordanna, standing in the arms of an African-American
man. "Who could that be?" She flipped the photo over to see if
there was an inscription, but there was none. She also picked up
a folded old flyer, yellow from age, from a club called the
Dollhouse, featuring a stripper named Blue that danced there on
Friday and Saturday nights. The final thing she picked up off
the floor was a ripped newspaper clipping, also yellow from age,
from the late 1980s. The headline of the story read, *Brentwood
man killed in drug-related gang hit.* "Why would she save all this
stuff?" Shrugging her shoulders, she put all the items back in
the box and put it where she had found it.

She quietly slipped outside without the drummer noticing
her. *Brrr, it's cold,* she thought. *Ooh, heavy, wet snow. Perfect for
snowballs.* Picking up a handful of snow, she formed it into a
nice-sized snowball and nailed the drummer in the back.

"What in the hell?" the drummer screamed, turning around
to see her lover standing there, smiling innocently. "Oh, you'll
pay for that one," Jordanna said, as she dove her hands into the
snow and took off after Rebecca. Catching up to the smaller
woman with no problem at all; she grabbed the back of the
reporter's shirt and dumped the snow down her back.

"Aaaahhhh!" Rebecca screamed, pulling the sweatshirt away
from her body to let the snow fall to the ground. "You are gonna
get it for that one."

"What did I do?" Jordanna laughed. "You started it. So,
come on, Rebecca. Let's get wet," she said with a wink.

"Okay," the reporter said, running and jumping on top of
the drummer, knocking them both into the snow. "I've got you

right where I want you," she purred into the dark-haired woman's ear. Jordanna used her body weight to flip them over so she was now on top. She leaned down and captured the reporter's cold, yet very warm, lips with her own. "Whew, I think we melted quite a bit of snow here," the drummer said after breaking off the kiss.

"Hey, you wanna build a snowman?" the reporter asked jokingly.

The question brought back memories of the drummer's youth. Building a snowman was a ritual at the Smith household whenever it snowed, and Jordanna remembered when she and her father would go outside and build a snowman and have snowball fights.

Rebecca walked over to the drummer and put her cold hand on Jordanna's arm. "Jordanna? Are you okay? You look about a million miles away. Talk to me, Jordanna. Please don't shut me out."

The drummer pushed herself off of the snowy ground and held her hand out for Rebecca to take. "Just thinking back to my childhood. Something I haven't thought about it a long time." Jordanna shook her head and pulled the reporter's ungloved hands into her own, rubbing them with her own for warmth. "You must be freezing, let's go inside."

JORDANNA BUILT A fire in the den after they both changed out of their wet clothing. She realized she had never enjoyed being snowed in as much as she did now, with Rebecca at the house. The endless possibilities made the dark woman smile wickedly. But it was just the reporter's presence that soothed her hard soul. Spending time with Rebecca made her heart sing, made her feel more alive than she had felt in years. She realized that this was exactly how she wanted to live, and to do that meant letting down her guard and telling Rebecca the truth about her past, something she wasn't sure she could do. She didn't know if she could handle the pain of someone else's rejection, especially from the woman that she had grown to love.

*Deal with that later. Just enjoy your time with Rebecca while you can.*

"You want to go a round of pool?" Jordanna asked, remembering what it felt like to *teach* the young woman how to play the night at the bar in Cleveland. This would be a lot more fun with just the two of them.

A smile played across the reporter's lips. "Sure, I don't know if I remember how to play, but I'll try. You can always show me again, can't you?"

Handing a pool stick to the reporter, Jordanna stood behind her and whispered, "I'd be delighted to teach you anything. You are a mighty fine student." She gave the reporter a quick smack on the butt. "Now let's see if we can make this interesting, hmm? How about each ball we sink, the other removes a piece of clothing."

Rebecca playfully slapped her on the arm. "Hey, do you think that is fair? I'll be completely naked, and you'll be fully clothed, in that case!"

Jordanna laughed and raised a mischievous brow. "And that would be a bad thing? Listen, I'll go easy on you."

Rebecca looked the drummer up and down. "Plus, you've got more clothing on than me," she said, grabbing hold of the drummer's black leather vest. Jordanna began to take the vest off, but Rebecca stopped her. "No, don't take that off yet. I like the vest. Just...the shirt goes with it when it's time to take it off, okay? Fair is fair."

The drummer smiled. "Okay, you got it. I lose the vest and shirt at the same time." *She likes me in vests? I'll have to wear them more often.* The raven-haired woman kissed the smaller woman on her neck and then went over to the pool table to rack the balls. "You want to break?" she asked, lifting an eyebrow.

Running her fingers through her strawberry-blonde hair, Rebecca smiled nervously. "Nah, why don't you do it?" she replied.

Noticing that she seemed nervous, Jordanna walked over to her and put her hand on her shoulder. "There's nothing to be nervous about, baby. It's just a game of pool. If you don't want to play we don't have to, or we could forget about the terms of the game if it makes you uncomfortable."

Blushing slightly, Rebecca turned and looked into Jordanna's eyes with desire. "I do want to play with you, so break them balls, blue eyes. Oh, and try not to move the table, okay?"

The drummer loved how cute Rebecca looked when she blushed. "I'll try, but I can't promise anything," she said as she made the break. "You're up first."

As usual, Rebecca scratched the ball. It landed on the floor next to one of the four stereo systems in the house. "Uh, sorry. I guess I'm a little rusty," Rebecca said, smiling sheepishly.

The drummer walked over to her, took her by the hand, and escorted her to the table. "Here, try again." She wrapped herself around the reporter's body and guided her shot, which she sank. "See, you just needed a little coaching." She walked over and grabbed her stick to make her shot.

Rebecca cleared her throat. "Excuse me. Aren't you forgetting something?" the reporter asked, bending down to remove one of Jordanna's boots.

The drummer's eyes twinkled. *This is going to be fun.*

A while later, Jordanna was down to her undergarments and her black jeans. Rebecca was in her denim shirt and undergarments. "This is so much fun, Jordanna. You look so good like that," she said happily, and nibbled on the drummer's neck.

With a pleased sigh, Jordanna brought Rebecca's hand to her mouth and kissed her fingers. "And you look wonderful like that, Rebecca. In fact, I think you should dress like that all the time."

Rebecca ran her hands along the drummer's hips, making the drummer jump. Jordanna couldn't resist the onslaught of passion the reporter was torturing her with. She bent down and slowly brought her lips to the young woman's. In no time, Rebecca had worked her tongue inside the drummer's mouth. Their tongues danced until they couldn't breathe any longer, and Jordanna broke the kiss. "Your turn. Let's finish this game," she said, her voice filled with desire. Her eyes were blazing, and she was breathing heavily.

"I think that you are letting me win this game, my big bad drummer," the reporter said, unbuttoning the drummer's jeans and slowly sliding them down her long legs. She kissed the insides of Jordanna's thighs. "So beautiful," she said in between kisses.

Jordanna closed her eyes as she felt the kisses making her legs weak. "In this game, it's a win-win situation for both of us, don't you think?" Stepping out of her jeans, she walked over to the table. With extreme incentive, she had no problem sinking the shot.

"Come over here," she demanded, and Rebecca was by her side in no time. Slowly, she began to unbutton the reporter's denim shirt. Losing her patience when it took too long, she ripped it open, buttons flying everywhere. "I'll buy you a new one," she said with a shrug, breathless at the sight of the reporter in her forest-green silk bra and panties. Her hands went straight for Rebecca's breasts, and she pinched her nipples through the silk. Rebecca's breath caught. "Mmm. Oh, yeah," Rebecca purred as Jordanna kissed the bare skin between the reporter's breasts. "You taste so damn good, Rebecca."

Rebecca turned suddenly and walked to the table, making each stride more seductive than the last. "My turn," she said, as she stuck her tongue out at the drummer.

Right as she was going to make the shot the drummer jumped up on the table and eased herself down by the pocket that Rebecca needed to sink the ball. "Focus on your target," she purred. Jordanna had black lace panties and a form-fitting, see-through black camisole on, complete with spaghetti straps. It showed off every curve of her body. Her long black hair hung down and clung to her skin in strands, due to the light sheen of sweat that had already formed on her body. Rebecca couldn't take her eyes off of her. All she wanted to do was touch and taste every inch of the drummer.

Rebecca propped the stick on the ground and leaned on it. The delicious sight before her eyes made it hard for her to concentrate on the game. "Why are you making this so damn hard, Jordanna? How the hell am I supposed to make the shot with you distracting me like that?"

Jordanna got up onto her knees and straddled the pocket. "C'mon, all you have to do is get the little ballie through my legs and in the hole, Rebecca," Jordanna teased.

"That's all I have to do, huh?" Rebecca said as she climbed on the table and lay down on her stomach. She inched herself as close to the drummer as she could, strategically placing herself between Jordanna's legs. Intentionally running the stick lightly between the dark-haired woman's legs, she made the shot. Aroused by the sound of the drummer's moans, she pulled Jordanna to her and slid her hands slowly up the drummer's stomach, stopping just short of Jordanna's camisole. "Ballie is in the hole, now where's my prize?" she asked sensually. She smiled and wiggled her eyebrows at the drummer before she let the tall woman's breasts free of their confinement. "Come to mama," Rebecca said before she took one into her mouth.

The drummer burst out laughing. "Come to mama? You're too much, Rebecca."

Rebecca ignored the outburst and kept at her task, only stopping for a moment to look Jordanna in the eye. "You want me to stop?"

The dark-haired woman thrust her breasts back at Rebecca immediately. "No, no, don't want that...go back to mama!"

The two of them were still tangled together on the table when Jordanna announced that it was her turn. "C'mon, mama," she said and held out her hand to help the young woman off the table. Rebecca began tickling the drummer. "I'm winning!"

Jordanna wriggled herself free. "You haven't won just yet," the drummer responded as she made her shot. The ball slowly rolled down the table and went in its intended pocket. She vaulted over to the reporter and pointed to her bra. "Off!" she barked.

Rebecca took the hint and unhooked it slowly, while Jordanna watched. The dark woman's eyes closed when she caught sight of Rebecca's supple breasts, feeling an instant jolt of desire shoot right to her center. "Oh, God, Rebecca, you make me so hot. I want you so bad."

"Patience is a virtue, my drummer," Rebecca said, moving out of the reach of Jordanna's playful hands. Looking out the window, Rebecca noticed a couple half-covered in snow, trying to walk their dog. They were looking directly into the house. "Oh...my...God."

"What's the matter?" Jordanna quickly moved across the room to see what had upset the reporter. A wicked grin eased its way onto her face when she saw what had startled Rebecca. "Let 'em watch. Maybe they'll learn something." She eased herself behind the reporter, rubbing her hardened nipples against Rebecca's back, and began nibbling the blonde's neck and caressing her breasts. "C'mon, let the exhibitionist in you shine."

"But..."

Jordanna laughed. "But what? Let's finish this game and give the nice little family a little thrill in the process." She escorted her very embarrassed lover to the window with her and began placing wet kisses on her breasts. "You know you want to."

"You are an animal, Jordanna Fox!" Rebecca squealed.

The drummer got down on her knees and began pulling Rebecca's panties down with her teeth. "Arrrrooo!" she growled playfully.

Rebecca went silent for a moment. "Hey, wait, I thought we were going to finish the game. You cheated."

Grabbing the reporter by the hand, Jordanna led her back to the pool table. "If you *insist* that we must finish this," she pouted. Jordanna grabbed her stick and sank the last three balls left on the table with one shot. "We won. Now let's give them that show."

A FEW HOURS LATER, the tired couple woke up in each other's arms in Jordanna's bed. "Hey, beautiful, how are you feeling?" the drummer asked, placing a kiss on the reporter's forehead.

Rebecca closed her eyes and moaned. "I feel fantastic. You?"

The dark-haired woman pulled her into her arms and smiled brilliantly, thinking about their all-night adventure that took them from in front of the window, to the pool table, the kitchen for a quick snack, and finally ending the night in Jordanna's bed. "I've never felt better." Jordanna started to untangle herself from Rebecca to get up. "Let me get you some coffee."

The reporter draped her arm across Jordanna's stomach and stopped her. "No, don't move. I'm very comfortable in this position." Lying there in her lover's arms, Rebecca remembered what they had done in front of the window. "I can't believe you made me do that."

"Do what, love?" Jordanna asked, unsure of what Rebecca was talking about.

Rebecca blushed. "You know. The window, us, bare skin, tongues and hands everywhere, those people watching."

"Oh, that." Jordanna chuckled and contemplated whether she should let her lover off the hook so quickly. Running her hands through Rebecca's mussed hair, she decided that she would. "You know, Rebecca..."

"Hmm?" the reporter purred, relaxing into Jordanna's soothing touch.

"First of all, I didn't *make* you do that. And the second thing is that we can see out of the windows of this house, but you can't see into the house," she explained, and tried not to laugh. "I don't know what they were looking at, but it wasn't us."

Rebecca sat up. "What? You're telling me that they didn't see us?"

"Don't sound so disappointed, my little exhibitionist. I think that you got into the idea of someone watching us. Admit it, oh, modest one," the drummer teased and thought for a few moments. "You know, the show at Madison Square Garden might be an option. We could always make love on the stage in front of twenty thousand people. Just think, the spotlight shining down on us, our sweat-soaked bodies sliding against each other. I certainly wouldn't object."

Rebecca playfully slapped her on the arm, harder than she intended. "You are so bad, Jordanna. I think that's why I love you so much." She pulled Jordanna closer to her for a kiss. "Mmm, if you keep kissing me like that, I just might take you up on your idea," the reporter happily admitted.

# Chapter
# Eleven

THE DRUMMER WAS singing to a tune by Tupac Shakur, nervously banging and tapping on the steering wheel of the 3000GT as they headed west on the Long Island Expressway.

Rebecca couldn't help but notice the nervousness. "Jordanna, calm down. She'll love you."

"I'm not nervous," Jordanna said, tapping away.

Rebecca laughed. "Yes, you are," she said, and placed her hand over the Jordanna's. "Stop tapping like that. You're making me nervous."

"*I don't know where we're going but she's makin' me come...*" the drummer sang along with the music again, turning her head to wiggle her eyebrows at the reporter.

"That's disgusting, Jordanna," the reporter said, although she had to admit she enjoyed hearing her lover sing such provocative lyrics.

Jordanna pleaded her innocence. "Hey, I didn't write the song."

Rebecca laughed. "You know, listening to these lyrics, it's no wonder you think rap is good to *dance* to. You're such a pervert."

"You wouldn't have me any other way, though, would you?"

"Nope, I wouldn't." Rebecca chuckled. "You are so full of yourself. You are nervous, though. Don't try to change the subject."

"You think I'm nervous because I'm singing and drumming on the steering wheel? Rebecca, I think that you forget that I'm a drummer. I've written some of my best songs this way." Jordanna turned to glance quickly at the reporter. "Do you really think she'll like me?"

Smiling, Rebecca tried to comfort the drummer. "Her mother does, why shouldn't she?"

Being an only child, Jordanna had never been around many

young children in her life and wasn't sure if she would be comfortable around Rebecca's young daughter. She had never thought about having children of her own. In her mind, it was never really an option. Why was it so important for her to be able to win over the heart of a child she didn't know?

*She's Rebecca's, that's why.*

The drummer took Rebecca's hand in her own and kissed it. "You always know what to say to me to make me feel better, baby."

Both women were silent as they drove through the dimly lit Queens/Midtown Tunnel and headed into New York City, feeling the tightness of the lanes. Once they emerged from the tunnel, Jordanna let out a breath. "You're going to have to navigate from here, Rebecca."

"Okay, it's not that far from here. Just take this straight to Fifth." Watching the streets go by, Rebecca told the drummer to make a right at the next block, the block where her ex-husband's apartment was. "There's a spot over there," Rebecca said, pointing to a parking spot a Mercedes had just vacated seconds before. The drummer backed the 3000GT in with little room to spare. "Now you know why I like Long Island; you don't really have to worry about parallel parking there," Jordanna said, flashing her famous crooked smile at Rebecca.

After emerging from the car, they put some change in the parking meter and started on their brisk walk down the Manhattan street. Jordanna felt her stomach starting to act up. *Why am I so nervous?* "Did you tell David that I was coming?"

Rebecca nodded. "I told him I was bringing a guest. I just didn't tell him it was you. Beware, they are both fans of the band so they may get all star-struck on you. Although, I guess you must be used to that by now."

Jordanna had been thinking about something she thought would be important to discuss *before* they actually went into the apartment. "Rebecca?"

Rebecca stopped, turned around, and caught sight of her tall, dark lover. *God, she is beautiful.* "Hmm?"

"Have you decided what you want to tell them about us?" Not sure she really wanted to hear the answer to her question, the drummer looked away and began to play with a button on her leather jacket.

The reporter cleared her throat. "What do you want to tell them?"

Jordanna looked directly into Rebecca's soul-searching hazel eyes. "I, I want you to tell them the truth." Taking the reporter's hand in hers, she told the blonde exactly what she wanted. "I want you to tell them that we are together, Rebecca. That we...love...each other." She looked at the reporter expectantly.

Rebecca was more than surprised. "You do?"

Jordanna brushed her lips over the top of Rebecca's head. "Yeah, I do."

Rebecca stood silent for quite a while, trying to digest what the drummer had just said.

Jordanna didn't know how to feel about the reporter's silence. "Rebecca. I'd, well, I'd understand if you want to back out of this."

The comment momentarily confused Rebecca. *Is this her way of getting out of the relationship?* She looked away from the drummer to keep Jordanna from seeing the tears forming in her eyes.

Jordanna put her hand on the reporter's face, turning it so Rebecca could look at her. She couldn't help but notice the tears. "What's wrong?"

Rebecca looked up at her. "Do you want out of this relationship, Jordanna? Please, tell me the truth."

"No!" the drummer immediately said.

Rebecca looked down at the ground. "It's just, well...what you said about backing out of the relationship before."

Jordanna broke out into a smile and put her arm around Rebecca's shoulder. "I only said that because I thought maybe that's what you wanted. It's not what I want at all."

The reporter let out the breath that she had been holding in. Forgetting that they were in the hall in front of her ex-husband's apartment, she threw herself around the drummer. Before she knew it, they were engaged in a tongue-clashing, passionate kiss.

An older man leaving the apartment across the hall saw the two women standing there, kissing in the hallway, and he turned around and went back into his apartment. The sound of the door slamming brought them both out of the sensual haze they were in. "Did somebody see us?" the reporter asked, laughing.

A wicked smile grew on the drummer's face. "I think so. I told you that you were into the exhibitionist thing."

Knocking on the door of her ex's apartment, Rebecca decided to dispute the statement. "I am not."

"You are..." The door opened and David stood there, mouth open upon seeing the unknown guest his ex had briefly mentioned.

"Too," Jordanna finished her sentence.

Rebecca and Jordanna walked through the door and into the apartment. "Dave, you can close your mouth now, it's very unattractive," the reporter teased her ex-husband.

"But, that's..."

The drummer interrupted him by holding out her hand for him to shake. "Jordanna Fox," she said, introducing herself. "Nice to meet you, David."

"Mom-my!" Cindy shrieked as she ran through the room and jumped into her mother's open arms. "I missed you, Mommy."

Rebecca spun her daughter around and gave her a bunch of little kisses. "I missed you too, pipsqueak."

Cindy looked at Jordanna for a few seconds. "I just saw you on MTV. You're in a video on a horse."

Rebecca let her daughter down on the floor.

"Mommy, she's on MTV," the little girl said, pointing to the drummer.

Rebecca explained the situation to Cindy. "That's right, honey. She's a drummer in a rock band. Mommy is touring with the band so I can write an article on her. I'm staying at her house right now."

Turning to Jordanna, she introduced her young daughter to her lover. "Cindy, this is Jordanna Fox."

"Hi, J-Jor," Cindy said, unable to pronounce the drummer's name.

Jordanna smiled at the young girl. "You can call me J or Jor."

Cindy walked up to the drummer like she had known her for years. "Okay, Jor. Can you come color with me?"

Rebecca was about to protest when Jordanna picked Cindy up. "I'd love to color with you, Cindy. Lead the way." Rebecca caught her eye and smiled as Cindy was telling the drummer which room to go into.

David joined the reporter in the living room, taking a seat next to her on the couch, anxious to ask Rebecca about her guest. "What are you doing hanging out with her, Beck?" he asked, unable to contain the excitement in his voice. "She's not at all like the press makes her out to be. Did I hear you say you were staying with her right now? I wish Anna were home to meet her. She's working nights this week."

"Slow down, David. You're making my head spin."

"I mean, it's just, how often do you have someone as famous as Jordanna Fox in your house, you know?" David shook his head. "Wow."

Rebecca smiled. "I can understand your excitement, Dave. Don't worry about Anna. She will definitely get the chance to meet Jordanna," she said. "And, believe me, as far as her personality goes, Jordanna wasn't the easiest person to get along with when I first met her. In fact, we didn't get along very well at all at first."

"What do you mean by that?" David turned and looked at her. "What changed things?"

*Uh-oh.* "I don't know. We just realized we had more in common than we originally thought." *Much more in common.* "I'm staying with her so I can finish my article on her for the magazine, so Anna will probably have the chance to meet her."

They could hear giggling coming from Cindy's room. "I see Cindy already put a claim on her," David said, laughing.

"She was pretty nervous about meeting Cindy," Rebecca told her ex-husband.

"Why would *she* be nervous about meeting our daughter?" he inquired, surprised at the comment.

*Should I tell him? Not yet.* "She's not used to being around kids, David."

Cindy and her pet horsie came riding into the living room. The little girl jumped off of Jordanna's back and ran up to her mother. "Can you and Jor stay for dinner tonight? Pleeeeease?"

Rebecca looked at Jordanna to see her reaction. "How about we all go out and get something to eat, my treat," the drummer suggested, and then got up off of the floor.

"Can we, Daddy?" Cindy asked her father.

David wasn't about to disappoint his daughter, or say no to having dinner with Jordanna Fox, for that matter. "Let me get our coats."

They all climbed into the GT, with Jordanna in the driver's seat and David in the front passenger seat. Cindy and Rebecca sat in the back, because they were the smallest of the group and would fit more comfortably in the tight space there. "Sorry, we should've brought the Pathfinder. I wasn't thinking," the drummer apologized. "You two okay back there?"

Rebecca looked into the rear-view mirror into Jordanna's eyes. "We're just fine."

"So," the drummer said before she backed out of the spot. "Where do we want to go?"

Cindy voiced her opinion. "Jekyll and Hyde's!"

Jordanna nodded. "Okay, Jekyll and Hyde's it is. You just have to tell me where it is."

"Have you ever been there, Jordanna?" the reporter asked with a smirk. "It's um, interesting, to say the least."

"Nope. How *interesting* could it be?"

"You'll see. Make a right at the next block," Rebecca said, and laughed.

The four of them had an enjoyable dinner at Jekyll and

Hyde's. Cindy was having a ball with all the special effects at the theme restaurant and found it especially funny when one of the ghoul waiters came up behind the drummer and pretended to pick bugs out of her hair and eat them. Even Rebecca got a good laugh at that, more from the look of embarrassment on the drummer's face than from what was actually going on. Jordanna fought the uncontrollable urge to break the ghoul's arm, not doing so only after seeing the look of sheer delight in the child's eyes.

Having their fill of talking gargoyles, tacky B-movie skits, and screaming masks hanging on the wall behind them, they piled into the 3000GT for the ride back to David's apartment. Sitting in the front with the drummer, David couldn't stop questioning her about music and her life on the road. Answering his questions as politely and as best as she could, Jordanna shot Rebecca a look in the rearview mirror.

Sitting in Rebecca's arms in the back of the car, Cindy talked non-stop about all the crazy things that they'd seen at the restaurant. "Mommy, I like Jor a lot. It was funny when that person was picking bugs out of her hair. Can she come color with me again?" the child asked.

Rebecca looked at the drummer to see if she had heard the comment. When she saw the huge smile break out on the ebony-haired woman's face, she knew Jordanna had. "I'm glad you like her, honey. So do I. You have to ask Jor if she would like to color with you again," the reporter explained, while twirling her daughter's dark curls around her finger.

Cindy climbed forward and maneuvered herself in between the front seats. "Mommy said she likes you, Jor," the young girl innocently admitted. "So do I. I asked her if you would color with me again, and she said to ask you. Will you?"

Blushing slightly at the child's innocent comment, Jordanna turned her head quickly and ruffled Cindy's hair. "I'd love to color again with you anytime, honey."

"Good, I'm glad," Cindy exclaimed.

"How would you guys feel about coming to the show at the Garden Wednesday night, backstage passes, the works? You think it would be okay for Cindy to see the band live?" the drummer asked, glancing in the mirror to look at her lover.

"Yeah! Can I, Mommy?" the child asked, giving her the puppy-dog-eyed look.

Rebecca smiled directly into the blue eyes looking at her in the mirror. "I don't see why not. What do you think, Dave?"

"That would be great. Would it be a problem to bring Anna, too?" he asked the drummer hesitantly.

"Not at all." The drummer glanced quickly at her lover's ex-husband. She realized he was pleasant-looking and seemed like an okay guy, but couldn't picture the reporter married to the man. "Rebecca told me about her. She was included in the invite."

David let out a breath. "Cool, thanks. She'll be upset when I tell her about tonight, but that should make her happy."

"You can pick up the tickets and passes at the 'will call' booth about an hour before the show. They'll be waiting for you," Jordanna said, backing the car into a parking spot not far from the apartment.

Rebecca hugged and kissed her daughter goodnight in the doorway, and smiled when Cindy jumped into Jordanna's arms and kissed her, too. "Night, Jor. Night, Mommy," she said, and then went into the apartment with her father.

THE TWO WOMEN made popcorn and picked out a movie to watch when they got home. "I told you she'd love you, Jordanna," Rebecca said as she fed her lover popcorn. The reporter sat on the floor with her back leaning against the couch, and Jordanna slouched between the reporter's legs, propped up against Rebecca's chest.

Jordanna finished chewing her popcorn before answering. "Yeah, I'm glad, too, Rebecca. I was a little nervous for a while there, but I think you noticed that, huh?"

Rebecca laughed. "Just a bit."

"She really is a sweetheart, Rebecca. You done good with her," she said, accepting more popcorn from the reporter. Jordanna turned around when Rebecca didn't say anything. The reporter had tears streaming down her face. "Sweetheart, what's wrong?"

"You mean David's done good with her, Jordanna, not me."

Jordanna wiped a tear from Rebecca's cheek. "No, I mean you've done good with her, not David."

Rebecca got up quickly, and Jordanna nearly landed on her back on the floor. "How can you say that, Jordanna? Don't you see? I chose my career over my own daughter. I couldn't take care of her on my own because I'm not home often, so I left her with a man who is not even her real father!"

"You did what you thought was right, baby."

"That doesn't mean it was right, Jor. I could have quit my job and found a nine-to-five job, but I chose not to. World's Greatest Mom of the Year award I will never win."

The drummer stood up and pulled Rebecca into her arms. "Stop beating yourself up, baby. What's important is the fact that you love your daughter, and she's living in a loving home with people who care deeply about her. That's much more than a lot of kids have."

"It's all a lie, though," Rebecca managed to get out through the tears.

If anyone knew anything about lies and deception, it was Jordanna. She kissed the reporter on the top of Rebecca's head and put her arm around the smaller woman's shoulder, walking her back over to the couch. "Shh, baby. You can let it out, okay? I'm here for you."

After Rebecca calmed down, they sat comfortably watching the movie, a movie each of the two women had seen more than once. They relaxed as the unquestionably romantic tale played out across the television screen, and Jordanna felt Rebecca hold on to her tight as the young reporter cried — again — after the death of one of the main characters.

"I know that's going to happen, but I still cry anyway every time I watch the movie."

"Mmm, I know what you mean." Unshed tears glistened in Jordanna's eyes, as she thought about the movie, Rebecca, and losing someone you love more than life itself.

She would want to die right along with that person.

REBECCA WALKED UP to the tattoo/piercing building hesitantly, frowning at the sight of the painting of a huge skull on the front. Jordanna put her hand on the reporter's back and gently guided her through the door. "Get your butt in there. You're not backing out on me now."

"Can I help you?" The owner of the store greeted them in all of his colorful splendor.

"Yikes," Rebecca whispered to the drummer, after observing that there wasn't an inch of his real skin color showing, not even on his face. The man was pierced on every visible part of his body, and the reporter didn't even want to think about what could be hidden under his clothing. She turned and looked at her smirking lover, who was enjoying Rebecca's changing facial expressions as she noticed each different thing about the man.

Jordanna waited for her lover to answer and spoke up when Rebecca didn't. "She's here to get her nipple pierced."

Rebecca spoke up. "*We* are both here to get our nipples pierced."

The man looked at the two of them and a pleased look came over his face, thinking that this must be his lucky day. Tattoo Man squinted at the drummer, who hid her eyes behind dark sunglasses, and had her hair in a braid down the back. A faint look of recognition crossed his face. "Do I know you? Didn't you used to work at Utopia?"

Jordanna let out the breath that she was holding. *Whew.* "Uh, nope, never worked there."

Looking at her again, he shook his head. "You just look so familiar to me. So, who wants to go first?"

They both answered him at the same time. "She does."

Jordanna shoved the smaller woman forward. "I already have one, you go first."

Rebecca shot the drummer a pained look. "Come with me, please?"

The drummer chuckled and grinned. "Of course, I'll come with you," she said and followed the tattooed man into a room in the back, where he instructed the reporter to sit in a dentist-like chair.

Rebecca didn't notice the expectant look on the man's face.

Jordanna burst out laughing. "I think you're going to have to bare your breasts for this, baby."

Rebecca blushed profusely. "Oh. Oh, yeah. I don't know where my head is," she said, and lifted her shirt up over her head before undoing the snaps on her bra. She noticed the way Tattoo Man's lip twitched in anticipation, waiting for the moment she was finished with her bra. She also noticed her lover telling the guy to get his thoughts out of the gutter with just a quick icy look, having removed her sunglasses only minutes before. He quickly looked away from the tall woman's intense stare and fumbled with the utensil he was going to use for the piercings. "Are you ready?"

"As I'll ever be." Rebecca's eyes widened and her body tensed up as he walked toward her. Jordanna walked over and held her hand. "You all right?"

"Um, yeah. I think so," Rebecca said quietly, putting up a brave front for her lover. Within moments, the man was done. "Ow. Ow. Ow." A small tear rolled down her face, and the drummer wiped it off with her finger. It was more from her body's reaction to the piercing than the pain. Jordanna tilted the reporter's chin up to her with her finger so she could look in Rebecca's eyes. "It's done. You okay?"

Rebecca looked down at her now-pierced body part and laughed. "Yeah. Wow."

Jordanna did the same but smiled instead of laughing. "It looks really...nice," the dark woman said, leaning down and placing a kiss on the reporter's lips before whispering in her ear. "And *very* sexy. I like it a lot."

Tattoo Man approached Jordanna. "Your turn. Why don't

you sit in the chair now."

The drummer sat down in the still-warm chair, and Rebecca started to leave the room. Jordanna called out to her, stopping her from leaving. "Hey, where are you going, baby?"

Rebecca paused at the door and turned around. "I'm giving you your privacy."

"Who said I wanted privacy? I need a little support for this, too, you know."

Rebecca wasted no time and was by her side instantly, entwining her hand in the drummer's. She watched as Jordanna got hers pierced, only turning her head at the last moment, not wanting to see the excess skin and tissue come out the other side of her nipple. When it was over, Rebecca wiggled her eyebrows at her lover. "Sexy."

"That wasn't too bad, huh? Do you think you'll get your other one done?" the dark woman asked Rebecca.

"Only if you get your cl—"

"Rebecca!" Jordanna cupped her hand over Rebecca's mouth. "No way! I draw the line here. Nothing below the belt. Not for me," the drummer said, shaking her head violently.

"What about a tattoo?"

"Rebecca!"

"Why not?"

"I promised myself a long time ago I would only mark myself for a really special reason, so that's why you won't find a tattoo on my body right now," she explained. "I can always let my piercings close up, but tattoos are so forever, you know?"

"That's true." Rebecca was intrigued by her lover's answer. "I'm just surprised, though. You seem like a tattoo type of girl."

"It must be the bad-girl image that others have painted of me." Jordanna smiled and shook her head. "Hey, am I going to be accused of being a bad influence on you? Since you've met me you've become a pool-hustling exhibitionist, and you are also sporting a sexy new nipple ring. Let's not talk about having a relationship with a woman. I'll be expecting more than one toaster for this one."

Rebecca furrowed her brows. "Toaster? What are you talking about?"

Jordanna chuckled. "It's a lesbian recruiting joke. Long story, forget I said it."

"Maybe you could get a tattoo of a toaster?"

Jordanna shook her head. "You're a nut, Rebecca, you know that?"

"Yep." She smiled. "Certifiable."

# Chapter
# Twelve

JORDANNA MANEUVERED THE GT through the city streets on the way to the band's sound check for their first show at the Garden. As they stopped for red lights, she watched all the people that worked in the city with interest. Women walking in power suits and sneakers, men with loosened ties, all on a break from their normal nine-to-five workday. Each one with lives so different from her own. People with lives more like her lover's. She looked to her right; Rebecca was staring blankly out the window.

"Are you okay? Is the new jewelry bothering you?"

"It throbs a bit. Actually, it throbs a lot, but it's not that bad. You?"

The drummer pulled into a parking garage as close to the Garden as she could find. "Same as you. It takes a few days and then you kinda forget it's there, until something, or *someone*, touches it," she said, her eyes twinkling.

Rebecca wondered why Jordanna had insisted on driving to the Garden herself when the rest of the band were all coming in limos. When she'd asked, the drummer had replied only, "Quick getaway." Getaway from what?

The two threw their passes on and walked past the guards posted at the door, down the long corridor that led to the backstage area. The first person they ran into was Jerry, whose eyes were immediately drawn to the women's entwined hands. He didn't say anything but gave the drummer a look of warning. She tilted her head and narrowed her eyes, daring him to say something to her.

He didn't.

Jordanna veered past the usual ensemble of groupies that somehow managed to sleaze their way backstage, avoiding temptation. That was no longer an option; she had Rebecca.

When the opening act took the stage for their sound check, Jordanna grabbed a bottle of sparkling water from the backstage area. Taking a surprised Rebecca's hand in hers, she led the young reporter to the back of the arena. They spent time together laughing, talking, and kissing, not necessarily in that order. The drummer grinned wickedly when she felt Rebecca's hands straying up and under her shirt. "Mmm, that feels so good, Rebecca. I'm gonna be a pile of mush on stage if you keep that up."

"Shut up and kiss me, drummer."

Jordanna grabbed the reporter by the hand, pulling her into her lap. The two leaned slowly into each other, and even though the position was an uncomfortable one for them both, they didn't seem to notice, or care. The kiss was a slow, passionate one as their tongues danced and hands roamed.

They didn't notice the spotlight shining on them or hear Kelly's voice over the PA system screaming for the drummer to get her ass on stage for the sound check. Taking a moment's break from their passion, Jordanna squinted into the bright light shining directly on them. "What in the hell?"

Rebecca jumped up quickly and rubbed the aches out of her protesting legs. "Damn pins and needles." She looked down toward the stage area and saw the band standing on the edge, waving them down. "I would say that they are looking for you, Jordanna, huh?"

The drummer got up right after her, experiencing the same aches as her lover. "Ya think?"

The two growled as they heard Kelly's voice over the PA again. "I hate to break up the major love fest, but you are needed on the stage, Jordanna."

The dark woman cursed and muttered under her breath. "You don't hate it as much as I do."

The adventure of trying to climb back down the stairs wasn't an easy one. They were both feeling the effects of their kisses and sore limbs as they stumbled down each step. "Whoa," the reporter said, as her slightly stiff body nearly sent her tumbling, taking Jordanna down in the process. "Sorry, are you all right?" She held her hand out to the laughing drummer, helping her up.

"I'm fine, Rebecca."

"I've never seen *you* like this, though."

"Must be the steps and the lack or circulation in my legs...and your kisses. I told you I'd be a pile of mush."

A round of laughter erupted from the stage. "Told you Jordanna's *fallen* head over heels for Rebecca. Literally," the voice over the PA said.

The drummer knew that her band-mates couldn't see her rapidly growing blush, but the reporter could. "It's true, you know," the dark woman shyly admitted.

Time for Rebecca to blush. "Right back at ya, drummer."

REBECCA TOOK HER place at the side of the stage to watch Plenty of Nothing's sound check, which she had done numerous times since taking on her assignment. This time it felt different to her. She wasn't watching Jordanna Fox, the sex-crazed egomaniac. She was watching Jordanna Fox, her lover. She thought about how things had changed between the two of them in such a short time. When they had first met, she found the woman to be the most frustrating, arrogant, and beautiful woman she had ever met. Now she was all that and then some. She felt a sense of being at home when she was around the woman. She couldn't explain it; it was just something she felt, and it felt very right.

She as pretty sure that Jordanna felt the same way. She hadn't quite said as much, but the way the dark woman's face lit up or her eyes sparkled when they looked at each other told Rebecca more than words could ever say.

She learned that another one of Jordanna's strange quirks was to do the drum-tech part of the sound check herself, rather than have Gary do it. Apparently Jordanna was a perfectionist when it came to things like that.

She enjoyed watching the dark woman go through the tedious ritual.

The sound guy's voice boomed over the PA. "Right bass."

Jordanna nodded her head and went about her task. Thunk, thunk, thunk, thunk.

"Left bass."

Thunk, thunk, thunk, thunk.

"Floor tom."

Thunk, thunk, thunk, thunk.

She did the same thing for each drum and cymbal. When she was done, she did a few drum rolls and fills around the set, rocking the house with a quick drum solo before she put her sticks down.

The sound guy called out again. "Sounds good, Jordanna."

Another nod of the dark woman's head and she slid out from behind the wall of drums and was by Rebecca's side instantly. "Hi."

"Hi, yourself."

Not long after, they heard the sound of guitars and her name being called yet again. "That was quick. I guess they need me now," she said with a childlike smile. Jordanna leaned down and kissed the reporter quickly before she went back to her drums.

Kelly shook her head as she watched the affectionate display between the two women. "Knock it off, you two. We have a sound check to do." She walked toward Rebecca on her way to take the stage. The guitarist swung her instrument over her back and pushed a strand of her curly fair hair out of her face before she spoke. "You like her, huh?"

Rebecca nodded. "Yes. Yes, I do."

Kelly leaned against the reporter and whispered in her ear. "I've never seen her like this. Love looks good on her. You two make a cute couple."

Rebecca laughed. *Cute couple? Jordanna would love to hear that. Goes against that reputation thing she's got going.* "Well, thanks. I think so, too."

The band kicked into "Fight or Take Refuge" as soon as Kelly finished talking with the reporter. Since the release of the video, the song had steadily climbed the charts, and they had decided to open their shows with it. The fast tempo and catchy lyrics got the crowd going every show.

Their sound check consisted of stupid chitchat in between the partial songs that they did. The band followed along when Jordanna spontaneously began the opening drum part to Led Zeppelin's "Rock & Roll." The drummer looked over to the side of the stage and saw her lover smiling at her and singing along to the lyrics. Rebecca got a kick out of listening to Jordanna trying to copy Robert Plant's falsetto, not an easy task.

Rebecca thought the best part of the sound check was when Jordanna came out from behind the drums and Gary took over the drumming duties. She yanked her jeans down slightly and pulled her underwear high enough so that the name showed over her jeans. She smiled and spoke into the microphone. "Since I don't own any BVDs, I guess these will have to do." She then launched into an old rap tune, which was on the set list for the night's show.

When they finished with the sound check, Kelly made it a point to tease the drummer. "You're in an extremely good mood tonight. Any particular reason?"

Jordanna played dumb. "I don't know what you are talking about, Kelly."

"I think it's got to do with a certain strawberry-blonde that happens to be standing on the side of the stage right now waiting for you," she said, pointing to Rebecca. "I was telling her before that I thought that you two made a cute couple."

"Oh, please!" Jordanna gagged. "Cute couple, my ass!"

"So are you trying to tell me that you guys are not a couple?"

The dark woman was getting frustrated with her friend's teasing. "No, that's not what I'm saying at all, Kelly, and you know it."

Rebecca walked up to the two of them. She turned to Jordanna and pointed to her visible undergarments. "So, are you going to pull your jeans back up, or do I have to do that for you?"

Jordanna pulled the reporter into her arms. "I prefer when you pull them down, Rebecca."

"Well, I've heard enough of this conversation," Kelly said and put her hands in the air. "I'm outta here, guys."

THE BAND EXITED the stage after their third and last encore, the fans still looking for more. Jordanna and her bodyguard pushed their way through the crowd of fans lucky enough to score backstage passes. The drummer spotted Rebecca standing in the corner of the room, a sleepy Cindy snuggled up in her arms with her head resting against the reporter's shoulder. David stood next to Rebecca and had his arm around a tall, brown-haired woman.

Anna was the first to notice Jordanna walking toward them. She tapped David on the arm to let him know that the drummer was heading their way. "Wow, she's really tall." David laughed at the comment and then watched the eye contact that went on between Jordanna and Rebecca.

"Hi," the drummer said, smiling first at her lover and then her family. Cindy stirred and looked up at Jordanna. "Hi, Jor," she said, leaning forward to give the tall woman a kiss on the cheek.

"Hey, kiddo. How did you enjoy the show?"

The child broke out into a big smile. "It was really, really cool, Jor."

The drummer smiled back and ruffled Cindy's hair. "I'm glad you liked it, sweetie."

Rebecca and Jordanna turned to face David and his girlfriend. Rebecca made the introductions. "Anna, this is Jordanna Fox."

Jordanna stuck her hand out for the woman to shake. "Nice to meet you, Anna." The woman nodded, suddenly struck mute. Jordanna looked at Rebecca with eyes that pleaded for help.

Rebecca took the hint and led her family over to where Kelly was standing. "C'mon guys, let me introduce you to the rest of the band before Cindy falls asleep."

The drummer winked and mouthed the word "thanks" to her. "I'm gonna go take a quick shower, and then I'll be back out, okay?"

"Okay. Don't take too long, though, please," Rebecca whispered.

Half an hour later the drummer reappeared, showered but still in the same leather pants that she had worn for the show. She had on a large Plenty of Nothing tee shirt that she managed to grab from a vending area. She leaned down and whispered in her lover's ear. "Can you believe I forgot to bring a change of clothes?"

Rebecca laughed and teasingly sniffed into the air. "Is that what that smell is?"

"Very funny, Rebecca." Jordanna absentmindedly ran her hand through Rebecca's hair. "Did everyone meet the rest of the band? Cindy looks totally beat." The drummer caught the look on her lover's face, and she realized what she had been doing. *Oh, shit. Busted.* "They saw?"

Rebecca nodded her answer as David came up behind the drummer. He took Rebecca by the arm. "I need to talk to you, Rebecca," he said keeping his gaze on Jordanna. "Privately."

Rebecca shrugged out of his grip and crossed her arms in indignation. "Anything you need to say to me, David, you can say in front of Jordanna." Silence fell upon them. Rebecca could feel her temper beginning to rise. "Well? What did you want to say to me?"

David frowned and sighed. "Shit, Becky. You answered my question without me even having to ask it."

The reporter started tapping her foot on the floor in annoyance, only to feel the comforting hand belonging to her lover begin to rub her back. "Humor me, Dave. What *exactly* was your question?"

David looked down at the ground. "I've noticed how the two of you look at each other, and I know I just saw her run her hands through your hair, Rebecca."

*And your point is?*

Rebecca relaxed into the feel of the drummer's hand rubbing her back. *Well, you gotta tell him sometime. Just do it.* "Yes, David, Jordanna and I *are* lovers, if that is what you were wondering." The reporter thought that David's eyes were going to pop right out of his head after she said that. She could see the veins in his neck begin to bulge.

"Great!" he screamed, when he finally found his voice. "Just fucking great, Rebecca. Were you always into chicks?"

*Men!*

Rebecca turned and looked at the drummer. "No," she sighed. "Not that it is any of your business, but Jordanna is my first."

David rubbed his chin. "And how in the hell do you expect me to explain this to Cindy?"

*You're not the father, you're not the father,* ran through the dark-haired woman's mind, but she controlled herself and kept those thoughts to herself. Jordanna cleared her throat and spoke for the first time. "Don't," she said, her voice deep. "Let Rebecca and me handle that task, David. This way, if she has any questions, she can ask us."

Rebecca looked up in surprise. *Us, as in us...you and I us?*

Jordanna spoke to David again. "Would it be a problem if Cindy spent the weekend at my house with us?"

Rebecca was speechless. *She's serious about wanting me in her life, isn't she?* "Uh, yeah, I think that's a great idea." She turned to her ex-husband. "David?"

He looked away. "Well, I dunno."

The reporter didn't wait a second to react. "What don't you know about it, David? Remember she is my daughter, too. Or do you have a problem with my relationship with Jordanna? You went on and found someone else. Did you expect me not to do the same?"

"No."

Rebecca stepped forward and stood face-to-face with her ex-husband. "Just not with a woman, right? That's the problem isn't it, right?"

The dark woman put her hands on Rebecca's shoulders. "C'mon, baby, calm down. This isn't the easiest news to lay on someone. Give him a chance to get over the shock of it."

"Cindy will be staying with us this weekend, David," the reporter demanded. "Whether you freaking like it or not."

David shook his head. He knew there was no winning with his ex-wife when she had her mind set on something. "Okay, she can stay with you this weekend."

Rebecca let out a deep sigh, turned, and looked at her lover before finally focusing on David. "Good. I'll call and let you know when we will be there to pick her up. I'm gonna go say goodnight to her, and then we are out of here."

After she finished saying goodnight to David, Anna and Cindy, Jordanna excused herself to join the band while they posed for photos and signed autographs. Rebecca watched as the drummer did her best to avoid having to deal with the forward groupies that were vying for her attention. "You know, you are going to have to deal with them some time, Jordanna," the voice from behind her said.

The drummer turned to face the loving hazel eyes of the

woman that spoke to her. Jordanna looked at Rebecca and
smiled. "I know I will," she said, quickly putting her arm
around a fan that wanted his picture taken with her. "You see
that one redhead over there?" she asked, pointing to a group of
women huddled together in the corner of the room. *The one that
just touched me, or should I say tried to touch me, in places that I only
want you to touch now.*

Rebecca nodded.

"She follows us just about everywhere we play."

Rebecca blinked. She wasn't sure if she was going to like
this story. "And? Go on."

"She's spent the night with me quite a few times. She's
pretty wild. I remember waking up dead drunk one time with
her and a friend of hers sprawled across my bed."

"I don't know if I really want to hear about this, Jordanna,"
Rebecca admitted honestly.

Jordanna blushed. "Sorry."

"How does she get backstage all the time?" Rebecca turned
to get a better look at the woman they were speaking about.
*Tramp. She's nothing but a hussy slut groupie.*

*Nothing special to look at either.*

Jordanna's lips twitched. *She's gonna love this.* "I put her on
our perpetual guest list."

"Ah, I see. One of your special friends, huh?" the reporter
chuckled, not really understanding why she was finding it
funny. Maybe because she would rather laugh than cry. "But
still, they are always going to be around, Jordanna. I understand
that it's part of the lifestyle of a musician."

Jordanna pulled Rebecca in for a hug, ignoring all the people
that were standing around watching the scene. "But I don't want
to live that lifestyle anymore, Rebecca. I *can't* live that lifestyle
anymore." She put her arm around the reporter's shoulder and
started walking. "C'mon, let's go home."

# Chapter
# Thirteen


REBECCA NOTICED THAT the dark woman's hands were shaking as she they drove the three-hour-plus drive from the Garden to her Amagansett home. "Are you okay?" She looked at her lover's face; Jordanna looked tense and a million miles away. "Do you want me to drive?"

The dark woman shook her head as if clearing her mind. "Huh?"

Rebecca put her hand on the drummer's knee and squeezed it lightly. "I just asked you if you were okay."

*Uh, no, I'm not okay, Rebecca, but how do I explain that to you?* "Uh, yeah. I'm fine, Rebecca, why?"

Rebecca wondered if the drummer was coming down with something, but somehow she had the feeling there was more to it than that. "It's just, well, you seem a million miles away, your hands are shaking, and you have sweat running down your face. Are you okay to drive?"

Jordanna shook her head again like she had done a few minutes before. "I can drive," she said gruffly, and shifted in her seat to get comfortable. She realized that wasn't going to happen; the aching in the lower half of her body wasn't going to let it happen. She tried hard to get the visual images and the redhead's seductive words out of her mind, focusing on getting home and making it through the night without doing something she'd regret.

Rebecca didn't find Jordanna's assurances comforting but decided not to push the drummer further on the subject. "Okay, but if you need a break, just say it and I'll drive."

JORDANNA'S HANDS WERE still shaking as she tried to unlock the front door. "Shit!" she muttered under her breath, hoping the young woman wouldn't notice.

Rebecca grabbed the keys from her and opened the door.

After they both were in the house, Rebecca handed them to her lover and touched her arm. "What is wrong, Jordanna? Don't try to tell me it's nothing."

The dark woman just glared at Rebecca as she walked past, heading up the stairs to her bedroom. "I'm gonna get changed."

Rebecca headed for the kitchen and called out to Jordanna. "I'll make us some tea. Maybe we can watch a movie or something?"

She got no response from the drummer.

Jordanna locked the door behind her once she was safely in her bedroom. She knew she couldn't let the young reporter see this and cursed herself that she'd let it happen. Too many years of over-indulging herself while on the road. How could it *not* happen? The images, the temptation...it was all too much for her to handle. Did she really think it would just go away now that she had found love?

*Yes.*

But it hadn't; her body was more than telling her that. She went into the bathroom and looked at her reflection in the mirror. Rebecca was right. She *was* shaking and sweating profusely.

*Maybe if I just take care of this by myself.*

She went back into her bedroom, unzipped her leather pants and lay down on her bed, and slowly eased her hand down to feel her own wet curls that protected the area just aching to be touched. She needed release, but just not this way. She needed to feel the power again. Needed to feel the control. Her body craved it, like a junkie yearning for a fix. She needed to let the darkness inside her loose again.

*You want this. You need this. You've got a beautiful piece of ass downstairs waiting for you. She says she loves you. See how far she's willing to go for you, Jordanna,* the darkness taunted once again.

But her heart and her head fought it.

*Don't do this to her, Jordanna. She deserves better than this. She's not one of your sleazy groupies.*

She closed her eyes and sat with her head in her hands for a few minutes, praying to God for control, hoping that the overpowering urge would pass.

But it didn't.

"Rebecca!" She screamed her lover's name at the top of her lungs as she got up and walked to her bedroom door to unlock it. "Come up here, *now*! Please!" Her lips twitched into a twisted grin as she let her dark side take control of her actions once again.

Not knowing what was wrong, Rebecca took the stairs two

at a time. "What? What's wrong?" As soon as she walked in the room, the reporter saw the look in her lover's eyes and noticed the drummer's unzipped pants. *What the hell?* "Jordanna, talk to me, please."

The dark woman didn't say a thing with her mouth, but the blue eyes filled with desire said all that needed to be said. That's all that Rebecca could feel, those intense eyes burning into her like a hot flame. Wanting. Needing.

The next thing the reporter felt was her body being slammed against the wall, and then hands ripping at her clothing. The buttons on her denim shirt flew all over the room, and the drummer pushed Rebecca's bra up violently. She could feel Jordanna's heavy breathing against her neck and felt the cotton of the drummer's shirt against her now-bare breasts.

"Let me fuck you," the drummer growled, not waiting for her answer before taking Rebecca's sore nipple into her mouth and tugging hard on her new jewelry.

The drummer's body was present in the room with Rebecca, but her mind was elsewhere.

Jordanna imagined a small, dark-haired woman she had taken in...what town was that? Was it this tour? She couldn't remember. What she *did* remember was that she had no trouble coaxing the woman back to her hotel room after one of their after-show parties. She also had no trouble coaxing her out of her clothing, and when Jordanna spanked the woman mercilessly, she did enjoy the feel of the sting. What was her name? She couldn't remember that either.

The images of that night remained in Jordanna's mind as her out-of-control body continued its assault on her lover.

Rebecca felt her body shudder, unaware if it was from pleasure or pain. "What? Fuck me? Oh, God, Jor. Yes, please..."

Another tug on the reporter's jeans and Rebecca felt the cool air against her completely exposed body. Jordanna put her leather-covered thigh in between her lover's legs and forcefully spread them apart, cursing when the jeans around Rebecca's feet got in her way. "Get these fucking things off," she commanded, smacking the young woman's foot so she would lift it up, allowing Jordanna to pull Rebecca's shoes off and free her legs to give her access to the young woman's sacred treasure. "That's better."

In the hotel room, the drummer had the woman tied to the bed with a blindfold on. "You certainly are willing to do anything for me, aren't you? You all are," she purred as she caressed a breast with her whip, smiling when the woman's nipple stood at attention for her. The woman merely shook her head.  The whip worked its way further down her body.  The drummer felt herself shiver as she heard the woman moan.

Rebecca moaned when she felt the drummer slide down to her knees, her hands never leaving the reporter's sensitive body. The moan turned into a full-blown groan when she felt Jordanna's tongue make contact with her beyond-wet center. The scene was both scary and exciting to her, and she realized that she wanted nothing more than for the drummer to take her at her terms.

In that hotel room, the drummer had the bound woman spread-eagle on the bed.  Jordanna was on her knees between the woman's legs.  She leaned forward and whispered into the woman's ear before she nibbled on it.  "Tell me what you want me to do to you."  The bound woman cried out as she felt the dark woman's insistent nibbling make its way down her neck.  "I want to you to love me with your whip, Jordanna, and then I want you to fuck me with your body."

The dark woman looked up at her lover, her intense blue eyes screaming with desire.  "You like that, don't you?  You want me to fuck you until you scream, don't you?"

Rebecca felt paralyzed when she heard the drummer's words.  The reporter's legs were getting weaker, as if they were going to give at any time.

"Up, now!" the drummer commanded, grabbing hold of the younger woman's leg and putting it over her shoulder.  "Stay like that until I tell you to move."  Rebecca had one hand on the wall and the other on Jordanna's shoulder to hold her weak body up.

The drummer could feel herself responding to the situation, the need to be the one in power grabbing her once again. Rebecca watched her lover as Jordanna closed her eyes and arched her body backward, letting out an animalistic moan that Rebecca thought all of Long Island could hear, as a powerful orgasm ripped through her body.

*Did she just?* "Jordanna?"

"I guess I didn't explain the rules to you, little girl," the dark-haired woman growled.  "You don't speak without being spoken to first, got that?"

Rebecca nodded.

"Good girl."

Jordanna's mind remained in the hotel room in that unknown town as she invited two of her fingers to join her tongue in her quest to dominate the small woman.

"Oh, God, Jordanna.  Don't stop," Rebecca pleaded as she felt the dark woman start to pull away from her.

The reporter nearly lost her footing as Jordanna began to get up. "What did I say about talking?" she asked as she started to walk away from the reporter. "Stay there," the dark woman hissed. "Do not move an inch."

Rebecca watched Jordanna as she walked to the other side of the room and opened her dresser drawer. The dark woman spoke in her lowest register. "Close your eyes."

The sexy voice spoke straight to Rebecca's already aroused body. "What?"

"Close your eyes!"

Rebecca did as the drummer said. She could hear her lover's breath, heavy and ragged.

"Get down on your knees," the dark woman commanded, rummaging through her dresser drawer. Jordanna ran her hand across the cold metal handcuffs, and a chill went through her body. Her hand finally came to rest on the soft leather strands of her flogger, and she caressed them sensuously. She lifted out the items that she wanted and shut the dresser drawer. "And keep your eyes closed."

"What?"

"Do as I say! I'm running this show!"

Rebecca couldn't believe that she was actually doing what she was doing, but within seconds she was down on her knees, waiting for her next instruction from the dark woman.

"Like a dog," the drummer growled.

*You've got to be kidding me?*

"Jordanna?"

"You heard me, do it!"

The small woman got down on her hands and knees. Her body was responding wildly to the dark woman's commands. She could feel the heat her own body was giving off, and the wetness between her legs reminded her that if Jordanna didn't touch her soon, she was probably going to die from need. "Jordanna, please," she whispered as she felt her lover's presence behind her.

Leaning over Rebecca, Jordanna ran her hand between the small woman's soaking-wet legs and whispered in her ear. "You spoke without being spoken to again, and you must be punished. What do you want me to do to you?"

"Take me," the reporter pleaded quietly.

"Say the word."

*The word?*

"Say the word!"

"Take me, please?"

"Open," the dark woman commanded as she offered the reporter a finger dripping with her own essence. Rebecca willingly accepted the finger, enjoying the feel of the digit in her mouth, and her own taste, until Jordanna pulled it away. The dark woman ran her fingers between the reporter's legs once again. "I *will* teach you how to share," Jordanna said, before she slid her finger into her own mouth.

"Mmm, you certainly are ready," the dark woman purred. "Aren't you?"

"Please..."

Rebecca thought she was going to lose her mind if Jordanna kept up the slow torture. She moaned when she felt the leather of Jordanna's pants against the back of her thigh.

"Since you asked me so nicely, I'll grant your wish," the drummer said as she slapped the smaller woman hard on the ass, listening as the reporter moaned at the contact.

After a few seconds Jordanna slapped her again. "Oh, God. C'mon, Jordanna, ple—oh, yes," she screamed as she felt something whip across her back, leaving a heated, stinging sensation in its wake. She then felt Jordanna spread her legs and penetrate her hard with what she assumed was a toy of some sort.

"You want this, don't you?"

"Oh, God. Ye-yes," Rebecca answered in a whisper.

"Good," the velvet voice said. "I only want to please you. Now tell me, how do you want it?"

The reporter could barely speak. "What?"

Taking it slow, the drummer pulled Rebecca into an upright position and ran her hands over the younger woman's breasts. "How do you want it?" she whispered in Rebecca's ear, keeping her rhythm in sync with the reporter's. "Fast, slow, hard, gentle? Tell me how you want it. Tell me..."

Rebecca had no clue what she was saying, thinking, or doing. She was ready to go over the edge and was glad that the dark woman, crazed or not, was the one to take her there. "Fuck me. Fuck me. Fuck me!" the young woman screamed.

Hearing Rebecca's voice screaming those obscenities brought the dark-haired woman's mind from that hotel room and back to reality.

*What the hell did I just do? This is Rebecca. The woman I claim to love. Not a cheap quickie.*

*Oh, God, what have I done?* Jordanna felt tears streaming down her cheeks, and all she could do was stay with Rebecca until they both collapsed on the floor.

"Oh, God, Rebecca. I'm so sorry. I shouldn't have... I didn't mean..." The seriousness of the situation hit the drummer hard. "I am so sorry."

Rebecca saw how vulnerable the drummer looked at that moment down on the floor in a heap, the strap-on she used still hanging lazily between her legs. "It's okay. C'mon, Jordanna. I'm okay, see? I'm okay, really," the smaller woman crooned, cupping the crying drummer's cheeks in her hands. Something clicked in Rebecca's head. *Now I know why she was acting like that. Now I know why she doesn't behave herself on the road. She can't.*

"God, I-I am so sorry, Rebecca," the drummer said, really feeling fear for the first time. Fear of losing something so special, something she had no idea she needed more than anything in her life. "Did I hurt you?"

The reporter locked eyes with Jordanna. "No, you didn't hurt me." *Except for this painful stinging across my back.* "You just scared me a little, Jordanna."

"Oh, God," the drummer whispered quietly as they remained in each other's arms on the floor. Jordanna felt her heart breaking. "Rebecca, I'm sorry I scared you. Can you forgive me?"

The reporter ran her fingers through the drummer's dark hair. "There's nothing to forgive, Jordanna. Addiction is not an easy thing to admit or control."

"What?" Jordanna could feel her anger building at the sound of the word. "I'm not..."

Rebecca kissed her gently before she could say anything more. "I didn't understand what was the matter with you before, but now I do."

Jordanna got up and walked away from the young woman. "I'm *not* an addict, Rebecca. Don't call me an addict. Susan's a fucking addict!"

The reporter followed Jordanna and pulled the drummer around so she could look into her eyes. "Yes," she said, clearing her dry throat, "yes, you are, Jordanna. You might not see it that way, but you are."

The drummer's eyes became cold and her voice harsh. "And I suppose you will tell me, Rebecca, just what exactly am I addicted to?"

"Sex, Jordanna. You are addicted to sex."

"No, I'm not," Jordanna tried to object. "I can stop."

Rebecca picked the flogger up from the floor and said the first thing that came to her mind. "Why didn't you, then?"

"I..." The drummer noticed the tool in Rebecca's hand. "Rebecca, did I hit you with that?"

The reporter answered her quietly. "No."

Jordanna lunged forward and turned Rebecca's body around, only to be greeted by four fresh stripe marks going down her back. "Damn it, Rebecca, don't lie to me! I did hit you with it!"

"I know you didn't do it to hurt me, Jordanna. You didn't even know you were doing it."

"And that's supposed to make it right?" The drummer closed her eyes and let the tears fall. She backed up against the wall and slid down it. "Don't fucking make excuses for me, Rebecca. There are none." She sat there quietly for a while, with her hands covering her eyes, and then stood up.

Rebecca walked up behind the drummer, who stood in front of the window, looking out. She wrapped her arms around the tall woman's waist and laid her head against her lover's back. "Jordanna, this only proves that you are addicted. If you weren't, then why would you do that? Not once did you say my name. When we make love you always say my name, Jordanna. Always. It was like you were someone else, somewhere else, with someone else."

The drummer couldn't argue any longer. She couldn't hold back a new set of tears. *Oh, God. I am an addict.*

"It wasn't you, Rebecca. The person I was just with wasn't you. Can you understand that? I never wanted you to see me like this, or for you to be involved...especially not as a participant. I really thought I could handle it, Rebecca," the drummer said, her voice weak and shaky. "I really did. I guess I was wrong. I'm sorry for what I just did to you. Did to us."

Rebecca pulled Jordanna closer; unable to hold her own tears in. "Jordanna, you didn't do anything to us. Please believe that. I love you. Trust in that."

"I do," the drummer admitted. "I never wanted to hurt you, Rebecca," she said, still facing the window.

"Jordanna, please look at me."

The drummer remained as she was, looking out the bedroom window.

"Look at me, Jordanna!" Rebecca pleaded.

This time the drummer listened and turned to look at her.

"You did not hurt me," Rebecca insisted, looking her lover in the eyes. "Please believe me."

Jordanna felt her heart pounding hard. "Rebecca, I love you, and I don't want to lose you. I can't stand the thought of losing you."

Rebecca leaned her forehead against the dark woman's and started to laugh. "You are not going to lose me. Got that?"

The two moved away from each other, and Rebecca noticed the look on the drummer's face. It was a look of relief, but there was still a great deal of sadness in Jordanna's usually sparkling eyes. "I'm going to go shower and put some clothes on, but we need to talk about this more, Jordanna."

The drummer cringed at the mention of a shower. "Take a cool shower. Your back is going to sting."

Rebecca nodded and started to walk toward the bathroom, turning around when Jordanna called out to her. "Let me know when you're done. I have to take care of your back. It needs salve."

"I will," the reporter answered, and then closed the door behind her.

Jordanna stood quietly by the bathroom door and listened as Rebecca prepared for a shower. She heard the water turn on and knew the moment the water hit the young woman's back by the gasp she heard. She pulled a pair of jeans and a sweatshirt out of her closet and went into the bathroom downstairs to shower.

Once Rebecca became acclimated to the water and the intense stinging in her back, she began to lather up. As she showered, bits and pieces of conversations she had shared with the dark-haired woman came flooding back. Rebecca now knew that her lover had an addiction and knew that she needed to get help for it before it consumed her, or consumed them both. She thought about what the drummer had said about Susan's addiction to cocaine.

*"An addict will do just about anything for their fix, Rebecca. Anything. They always seem to find a way."*

She realized now that what Jordanna said didn't just come from understanding what it was like to be addicted, but from actually knowing because she herself had an addiction. She also knew that she would fight it along with the dark woman, even if Jordanna didn't want her to.

Shutting the shower off, she dried her wet body as best as she could without making contact with her back. She opened the door slightly and peeked out, but her lover was nowhere to be found. "Jor?" She saw the jar of salve sitting on a table next to the bed and grabbed it. "Jordanna?"

The dark-haired woman walked back into the room fully dressed. "Lie down on the bed."

Rebecca did as she was told, lying on Jordanna's bed on her stomach. She felt the end of the bed dip as her lover settled her weight on it. "This is going to sting."

The reporter grabbed onto the pillow tightly and only jumped a bit as Jordanna began to gently apply the salve. Jordanna took her time, making sure she didn't apply any extra pressure to the wounds and then stopped.

Rebecca felt the drummer's movements still and then felt the strange sensation of something wet splashing across her back. "Jor?" She turned her body slightly and looked into the wet eyes of her lover.

"I'm so sorry," the drummer said once again as she looked back into concerned hazel eyes. "I can't believe I did this to you." She put the cap back on the jar of salve and got up from the bed. "I think that's good for now. Get dressed." She turned around and walked out of the room.

After she threw a robe on, Rebecca went back to the kitchen to finish the tea she had started to make before the drummer called for her. Jordanna was already in the kitchen, sitting with her elbows on the table and her head in her hands. Her car keys were on the table in front of her. Rebecca immediately walked over to the drummer and started to give the dark woman a hug, but Jordanna shrugged her off. "Don't."

Rebecca felt the sting of the word and stepped away from the drummer. "Jordanna, please don't shut me out."

The drummer sat there silent for a few minutes as Rebecca finished making the tea. The smaller woman placed the two cups on the table and sat down next to Jordanna. "At least drink your tea."

Jordanna took a sip and spoke. "I'm driving you home tonight."

"What?"

"I think it would be best if you leave, Rebecca," she said coldly. "Get as far away from me as you can, before I hurt you again."

Rebecca felt tears stinging her eyes and tried to blink them away. "You don't mean that."

"I do mean it, Rebecca," the drummer said, her voice hoarse. "I want you to go."

"No."

"What?"

"I said no. I don't want to go."

"Rebecca, please..."

"Do you really want me to go?"

Jordanna didn't answer, but instead stared into space.

The reporter felt desperation starting to set in. "Do you really want me to go?" she screamed. "Answer me, damn it!"

"Now I know I'm supposed to spend my life alone, just like she said I was supposed to," the drummer said. Her voice was emotionless. "Nobody deserves living with a low-life shit like me. Least of all someone beautiful and wonderful like you."

Rebecca slapped Jordanna across the face, trying to get her to snap out of it. "No! Don't you dare say that about yourself."

"But it's true, Rebecca." Jordanna started to rock back and forth on the chair. She started to cry again. "I didn't realize that it had become that bad. I didn't know."

Rebecca took Jordanna's hand and rubbed it between her own. "Jordanna, you told me who you were before we entered into this relationship. You told me that you were into rough sex. You also gave me the courtesy of thinking about that and deciding for myself whether or not I wanted to get involved with you." She stopped speaking and closed her eyes to gather her thoughts. "Please give me that courtesy now. Let *me* decide whether or not I want to stay here with you. Don't tell me you're taking me home without discussing it with me first. This isn't just about you."

"I know it's not just about me, Rebecca. It's just...I can't control my actions. Do you understand how that feels?"

Rebecca shook her head. "No, I don't understand it, Jor. Tell me how it feels. Explain it to me."

Jordanna stood up and looked out the window, rubbing the kinks out of the back of her neck with her right hand. "I guess the best way to explain it would be to compare it to a seizure patient. One minute you're standing there and everything is fine, and then, boom, two seconds later you're down on the ground unable to control yourself."

She turned around and walked back to the table, sitting down in the chair next to Rebecca. "You don't realize how quickly your life can be turned upside down. All it takes is the blink of an eye and everything changes," she continued. "It's a helpless, frightening feeling to walk around with everything being so uncertain. I feel like a big question mark sometimes."

"God, that sounds awful."

"It is awful. I've got so much temptation in front of me when I'm on the road, Rebecca. It's hard for someone like me to say no to it. I've never really had to say no, until now."

Rebecca put her hand on her lover's arm. "Because of me."

Jordanna nodded. "Because of you."

"So, what you are saying is that you've always given in to the lust because it's easily available to you and has been so much a part of your life for so long. Tell me if I'm off-base here, Jordanna."

"No, you're right, Rebecca. I've never felt the need — or desire — to be faithful before I met you, but now I do." The drummer shook her head solemnly. "I thought I could control those desires now, but I just proved that I couldn't. How do I handle this? I'm pretty much okay when I'm at home, but once we hit the road and all I have is women offering themselves to me, showing me their bodies, the temptation is just way too inviting. Like you said, I can't ignore them forever." A single tear escaped and dripped onto the table.

"Did you..." The reporter started to ask Jordanna a question, then thought twice about it and stopped.

Jordanna looked into her lover's eyes, urging Rebecca to ask her question. "Did I what?"

"Nothing."

"C'mon, you can't start a question and then stop like that. What were you going to ask?"

Rebecca blushed, pretty much knowing the answer to the question without having to ask. "Did you...well, you know...every night when you were on the road?"

Jordanna rubbed her head and looked down, surprised that she was finding it hard to talk eye to eye with the reporter about this. "Yeah, pretty much."

"Why?"

"I dunno. It was there for the taking, I guess. And your body...well, at least mine, goes on a high when you're on stage. Especially if the show is a really good one, that high is even more intense 'cause the crowd is going wild and your adrenaline is really pumping. Once I get off the stage, that adrenaline is still pumping, you know? I need something to help me relax and to release that energy." She paused and thought about her next statement. She had never been willing to admit this to anyone before, including herself. "Another reason would be loneliness. Being on the road for months at a time can be a real drag when you're all alone, Rebecca."

"So tell me the truth now, Jordanna. Do you really want me to leave?" Rebecca asked suddenly, her heart pounding in anticipation of the answer.

Jordanna stood up, picked up the car keys, and walked out of the kitchen. She hung the keys back on the key holder by the front door and went back into the kitchen. She saw Rebecca looking at her expectantly as she walked back in. She pulled the reporter into her arms, hugged her as tight as she could without hurting Rebecca's back, and whispered into her ear. "No, baby, I don't want you to leave."

Rebecca's breath caught. "Good, 'cause I don't want to leave, in case you didn't notice. We will get through this together, Jordanna, whatever it takes. Just know that I love you and I am here for you," she said, placing a tender kiss on her lover's lips. "C'mon, love, I'm tired. Let's go to bed."

She led the dark woman up to her bedroom, watching the drummer climb into the bed before doing the same. She felt

Jordanna's breath catch as she snuggled up behind the drummer, her arm coming to rest on the dark-haired woman's stomach. Jordanna turned and pulled Rebecca close, letting her body relax as she felt the warmth and love radiating from the small woman next to her. Within minutes, the two were sleeping soundly in each other's arms.

# Chapter
# Fourteen

WAKING UP EARLY wasn't a curse for Jordanna when she was on the road. Late night after-show parties and the ever-constant revolving door of visitors tired her enough to keep her in bed past the crack of dawn. Once home for a few days, though, her body got into the routine of waking up just before the rooster was ready to crow.

The room was still dark when she opened her eyes. The bright red numbers on her clock read 4:15. Yawning, she stretched as much as she could without disturbing the sleeping form next to her. Her body was telling her it was time to get back into the swing of things. Easing herself gently out of the bed, she went into the bathroom to take a quick shower and change into her running clothes. Walking out of the bathroom, she pulled her windbreaker over her head before she stopped and gazed at her still-sleeping lover. Rebecca's face was bathed in the moonlight, making the drummer's heart skip a beat when she looked at her. *She is beautiful. Not just on the outside, but on the inside, too. She proved that to me last night.*

Last night.

The drummer sighed when she thought about what had happened, and prayed to God that she hadn't hurt their growing relationship too much. She knew that Rebecca was a forgiving woman, but did she even deserve forgiveness?

Jordanna sighed again as she grabbed a piece of paper and wrote a quick note to the reporter, letting Rebecca know where she was in case she woke before Jordanna came back.

As she slipped out the back door of the house, she felt a chill from the cool breeze coming from the ocean and hoped that the soon-to-be-waking sun would make its presence known quickly. The temperature had risen so much in the past few days that no trace of snow remained from the late-season blizzard they'd experienced just days before.

She took to her run with sure, even steps. Her body, beaten

from being on tour for over a year, was adapting quickly to its old routine. Looking up into the yellows and pinks of the sunrise, her mind quickly went back to the events of the previous night and how she had almost ruined the best thing to ever happen in her life.

Because of the young reporter, she looked at things differently now. Knowing that the road ahead would be difficult for both of them, she was still happy that there was a road ahead. She couldn't remember the last time she *truly* felt happy, but she did now, and that was all that mattered.

*That's if I don't fuck it up.*

Rebecca saw the other side of the moody drummer, the side Jordanna didn't let anyone get close to. What most people saw as conceit and arrogance, Rebecca looked beyond, and saw Jordanna for who she truly was—someone that *had* to be an arrogant rock star to boost her low ego. The drummer smiled when she thought of that. Nobody would ever suspect that someone like her—tall, dark, gorgeous, and a drummer in one of the world's most famous rock bands—could ever have a confidence problem.

But she could, and she did.

Looking back, Jordanna had looked at life for the past fifteen years through clouded and cynical eyes. Now, for the first time in her life, everything was crystal clear to her. Could the love of one person do all of that for her? And, more importantly, would she be able to hold on to that love?

Jordanna's good mood quickly faded. *I can't lose that love. I need her here—with me. Does she want that, though, especially after what I did last night?*

*Ask her to stay with you and find out.*

Her dark thoughts returned. *She will say no, so don't even bother, you loser.*

Jordanna fought against that ever-present dark side, trying to be hopeful, but... *What if she does say no?* A lone seagull landed in her path, blinked at her, and then flew away.

She slowed her pace to a fast walk when she saw the town of Montauk in the distance. As the buildings got closer, she walked up to the dune area and cut in between two small oceanfront hotels to walk along the street where people were just beginning to come to life. Making her way past the tourist shops, she went into the bakery and took a deep breath, inhaling the intoxicating smell assaulting her senses. She walked out of the store with a box full of donuts and pastries, chuckling lowly. *So much for the run. This is like eating a whole bag of potato chips and washing it down with diet soda.*

HAZEL EYES WATCHED from the driver's seat of the black BMW as the drummer walked into the bakery. *She's alone. That means Rebecca's alone at the house.* A gloved hand picked up the cell phone lying on the passenger seat of the car. *Did she tell you she's being threatened yet, Rebecca? No, she's too busy defiling your body to do that, isn't she? Does she make you scream out her name in passion, Rebecca? She's good at that, you know. That's her specialty. Slut.*

The gloved finger began to dial the drummer's number as soon as Jordanna emerged from the bakery. Let's see what she's told you about me, pretty one."

WAKING UP TO an empty bed, Rebecca opened her eyes slowly. She looked at her lover's side of the bed. "She's up early," she mumbled to herself. Noticing the note that Jordanna left on her pillow, she picked it up and read it.

*Rebecca —*

*Went out for a run on the beach. Will stop at the bakery to pick up something, so don't eat too much before I get back. I hope you like pastries.*

*Jor*

Rebecca smiled as she folded the note up and put it on the bedside table. Slipping out of bed, she walked to the window and let the morning sun douse her with warmth. She went into the bathroom and took a long shower, wincing only slightly as the hard water massaged her bruised back.

She then wrapped herself in a towel and went into the guest bedroom to pick out her clothing for the day. As she was slipping into her jeans, the phone rang. She knew the dark-haired woman was out for her run but assumed that her staff would answer the phone. It rang twice. Figuring it might be Jordanna calling, she picked up the phone since no one had bothered to answer it yet.

"Hello?"

A muffled voice came over the receiver.

"Don't think that this is over, Jordanna. You're going to have to pay for what you did. Mark my words, you won't live to see the year 2001, and neither will your little girlfriend, so enjoy her while you can, you fucking tramp."

Rebecca didn't know what to say. "Wait. Who is this?"

The line went dead before she could finish her question.

The phone fell out of the reporter's hand. *What the hell was that all about?* Then the realization hit home. *Someone is threatening to kill Jordanna and me.* She threw a bathrobe on to cover up her naked top half, and quickly ran down the stairs to see if her lover had returned. As she ran into the kitchen, she nearly knocked over Jordanna's housekeeper, Rosa. "Oh, I'm sorry."

Rosa turned and gave the reporter the once-over. Jordanna's housekeeper was much younger than Rebecca had originally expected, and a lot more attractive, with long, curly, dark hair, and big, pouty lips. The way the woman's dark eyes shot daggers at her made her wonder if her lover had ever taken a roll in the sheets with her housekeeper. She certainly wouldn't put it past Jordanna.

After what seemed like an eternity of scrutiny, the woman finally spoke. "Jordanna is out for her morning run."

The reporter took an immediate dislike to the housekeeper and forgot for a brief moment about the phone call as she answered the woman. "Yeah, I know she is, she left a note for me on her pillow." She winked.

Rosa glared at her. "Oh. I see. Well, there's coffee ready if you want it. Jordanna said that she was going to pick up breakfast. That means pastries. The woman has..." Rosa paused and licked her lips, finishing her statement dramatically. "Quite the sweet tooth."

At that moment, Jordanna came in through the kitchen door. "What do I have, Rosa?" She dropped the box of goodies on the kitchen table and grabbed two mugs of coffee for the reporter and herself. She gave Rebecca a quick kiss and teased the housekeeper. "What have you been telling her about me, Rosa?"

"She was just telling me that you have a sweet tooth." Rebecca looked directly at Rosa and continued. "But I already know *exactly* what you like to eat, Jordanna, don't I?"

Seeing the devilish gleam in Rebecca's eyes, the drummer got the very distinct feeling that there was something going on between her lover and her housekeeper. She looked at Rebecca and shrugged questioningly. "What did I miss?"

Rebecca smiled and winked at her. The smile quickly faded as she remembered the phone call. "That can wait until later. We have something much more important to talk about now."

"What's up?" the sweaty drummer asked.

Rebecca's face was all business. "Jordanna, you got a phone call when you were out."

Jordanna's eyes twinkled. "Oh, yeah, from who?" she asked in a teasing voice.

"That's what I need to know, Jordanna. What in the hell is

going on here?"

The drummer didn't understand. She grabbed Rebecca by the arms and looked at her. "What do you mean? Who was on the phone, Rebecca?"

The reporter's legs started to feel weak. "Someone called threatening to kill you, Jordanna. To kill me, too. Who the hell would do something sick like that?"

Jordanna blinked. "What else did this person say, Rebecca?"

The young woman started to cry. "The person said that it wasn't over and you — we — wouldn't live to see the year 2001. Oh, yeah, and that you had to pay for what you did."

"Was it a man or a woman, Rebecca? Could you tell?"

"I don't know. The voice was kinda muffled, and once what the person was saying registered in my mind, well, that was it. What the hell is going on, Jordanna?"

Jordanna pulled the shaken reporter into her arms. "Shh, it's okay, baby. Let's sit down and I'll tell you what I know." Leading her to the couch in the living room, Jordanna let Rebecca sit down first, and then the drummer sat next to her. She pulled the young woman close and stroked her lover's hair.

Jordanna started to explain. "I have been receiving death threats for about a year now."

The reporter gasped and clutched the dark woman. "It's okay, baby, let me finish," the drummer said immediately, feeling Rebecca relax slightly in her arms.

Jordanna continued. "First it was stupid little threats through the mail with letters cut and glued on paper that said *Die, bitch* and things like that. The police wrote it off as a crazy fan and pretty much closed the case, but right before you joined us on tour, I got another threatening letter, this one more personal. This person, whoever it is, knows about my past."

Rebecca thought about the damage Jordanna's ex did to her house. "Do you think it could be Susan?"

Jordanna shook her head. "I thought that at first, but by what the threat said, this person knew me when I was younger. Before I knew Susan."

"What do the police think?"

Jordanna didn't answer right away. "I...didn't tell them about that threat, and I can't tell them about this one."

"I don't understand. Why?"

The dark woman didn't know what to say. "I couldn't tell them about it, Rebecca. It said too many incriminating things." She looked away from her lover.

Rebecca was confused. "It can't be *that* bad, Jordanna. Who did it incriminate?"

"Me," the drummer answered, her voice a breathy whisper.

Rebecca pulled away and looked at her lover. "You? What...why?"

Jordanna closed her eyes. "Years ago I did some things that I'm not too proud of, Rebecca. I was a pretty fucked-up kid. Associated with some nasty people and got myself into a lot of trouble."

"Tell me."

Jordanna shook her head. "I can't tell you, Rebecca. At least not right now."

The reporter didn't want to get angry with her lover but couldn't control it. "I think that since they are threatening me *because of you*, that you *owe me* that fucking answer, Jordanna. Now!"

The dark woman winced at the words. "I'll tell you soon, Rebecca, but right now we have to get ready for the sound check."

"To hell with the sound check, Jordanna! What if this person is at the Garden?"

Jordanna caressed the reporter's face. "Why do you think all the bodyguards have been hovering around me, Rebecca?"

"Don't they always?"

The dark woman shook her head and laughed. "No, not like this. One guard actually wanted to stay in my hotel room with me when I had a...guest...to make sure she wasn't the crazed fan. I told him that he just used that as an excuse 'cause he wanted to watch two women get it on with each other. You should've seen it, his face turned so red."

Rebecca got up and turned away from the dark woman. "This is *not* funny, Jordanna."

Jordanna followed her and pulled the reporter into her arms again, whispering in Rebecca's ear. "I'm sorry. I know it's not. We *will* get through this, baby, trust me." She looked into the young woman's hazel eyes. "Can you do that?"

Rebecca immediately felt calmer and nodded. "Yes, I trust you with my life."

Jordanna couldn't help but feel elated by the words, especially after what she had done to Rebecca the night before. She wanted that trust more than anything she had ever wanted in her life. "Good." She whispered in her lover's ear. "I love you, Rebecca."

"I love you, too."

JORDANNA WALKED OFF the stage dripping with sweat

and scanned the room for Rebecca. When she didn't find the young woman, she headed directly for the showers. Standing in the shower room, she felt someone come up behind her and touch her gently on the small of her back. "I was just looking for you," Jordanna said, her voice purring. She turned around to see Candy, the redheaded groupie that she told Rebecca about, the one that followed the band around from show to show. She stood there with her blouse unbuttoned and desire in her eyes.

Surprised that it was not her lover, Jordanna found herself speechless. "Uh, I thought you were somebody else."

"I'll bet," the woman said, as she began to work the drummer's sweat-soaked tank top off of her body. Jordanna pushed the woman away. "When I said no to you yesterday, Candy, I meant it. Get your fucking hands off of me!"

"You had no problem fucking me senseless all those other times, Jordanna. What's the problem this time?" the woman asked angrily.

Rebecca watched the redheaded woman follow her lover into the shower. "That little hussy bitch," she said to no one in particular, before she started off behind them. When she entered the shower room, she heard their voices but couldn't see them because the showers veered off to the right. She held her breath as she rounded the corner, catching the woman's last comment to Jordanna. The reporter cleared her throat and then spoke. "I'm her problem."

Jordanna turned and smiled as Rebecca approached them.

"Who the fuck are you?" the redhead questioned, anger in her voice.

Jordanna answered for her. "She's my lover, that's who she is. And if you don't mind," she paused and ran her thumb across Rebecca's chin. "I'd like to be alone with her," the dark woman said, dismissing the woman.

"I thought that bleached-blonde bimbo was your lover, Jordanna?" the woman hissed.

Jordanna snorted. "You mean Susan? She's history, and so are you. Now get the fuck outta here." She watched the woman turn and walk away. "Oh, and Candy?"

The redhead turned around, a look of hope glimmering in her eyes. "Yeah?"

"Don't bother to check on the guest list the next show. Your name won't be there."

"Your loss," Candy said before she cursed and turned away, slamming the door behind her.

"My loss," Jordanna said in a childish voice before she burst into laughter. "That was good, baby. She didn't expect that from you."

"Is that what happened yesterday?" the reporter asked hesitantly. She wanted to know if a visit from someone like Candy was what set the dark woman off.

Jordanna looked at Rebecca and then closed her eyes. "Yeah."

"I thought so. She came in here when you were showering, didn't she?"

The dark woman nodded. "Yes."

"What happened?"

Jordanna's lips twisted before she grinned. "Nothing."

"Did she touch you?"

The drummer snorted. "Yes." *At least she tried to.*

"How?"

Jordanna pulled the young woman close to her, leaned down, and gently brushed her lips against the reporter's.

Rebecca sighed. "Like that?" she asked.

"No."

The drummer slowly eased the reporter's shirt over her head and then did the same with her own. "Shower with me?"

"Here?"

The dark woman worked the hooks on her lover's bra with expert ease, ridding Rebecca of the offending garment. She smiled as her eyes caught sight of the silver hoop hanging from the reporter's nipple.

*God, that is so incredibly sexy on her.*

"Yeah, here, unless you got any better ideas. I know I won't be able to make it all the way home to Amagansett without ravishing you on the side of the road. I don't know about you."

Jordanna popped the button on Rebecca's jeans and slowly pulled the zipper down. She slipped her fingers on the inside of the jeans and started to ease her out of them, pleased that the young woman wasn't wearing any panties. "Mmm, you came prepared. I like that," she purred softly in Rebecca's ear.

Rebecca grabbed the drummer's hands. "Wait."

Jordanna's head snapped up, and her mind instantly returned to the previous night. "Rebecca, I understand if...if you don't want to be with me after what I did to you."

"No, that's not it, love." The reporter took the drummer's hand in hers. "You wanted to know if I had any better ideas. Well, I think I do."

"Oh?" The drummer's eyebrow rose. "Do tell."

Rebecca smiled. "My apartment."

"Huh?"

The reporter rolled her eyes. "My apartment, dopey, is

pretty much around the corner from here. A shower I know is clean, a nice comfy bed, some romantic music, candles. What do you think?"

"I definitely think you're onto something, lover; that's what I think."

Rebecca followed Jordanna out of the showers, and they started to leave the building. "Wait," the reporter said, as they walked past the backstage bathrooms. "There's something I need to do first."

Jordanna leaned against the wall. "I'll wait out here for you."

Rebecca grabbed the drummer's hand and pulled her to the door, pushing it open and walking in. "No, come in with me."

Jordanna narrowed her eyes. "What are you up to?"

Rebecca winked at her and dragged her through the bathroom to an empty stall. "You'll see." She let Jordanna's hand go and walked in the stall, letting the door close behind her.

Jordanna sighed. "What did you do, bring me in here so I could listen while you pee?"

The door opened slightly, and Rebecca crooked her finger at the drummer, telling her to come inside.

"Rebecca?"

The reporter shook her head and opened the door wide. She grabbed a surprised Jordanna by the hand, yanked her into the stall with her, and pointed to the drummer's jeans. "Take your jeans and panties off and get up on the toilet."

"What?"

"You heard me, just do it."

The drummer smirked and did as she was told, locking the door behind her before she hopped onto the seat.

"No." Rebecca opened the door. "Door stays open."

Jordanna's brows lifted straight to the sky before a mischievous grin grew on her face.

"Ever since I saw what I saw when we first met, I can't get the picture out of my head. Are you with me so far?" the reporter asked.

"Sure am," Jordanna answered, feeling her center begin to throb in anticipation already.

"I don't ever want to see that woman's...head...in my mind anymore, do you understand?"

The drummer licked her lips and nodded.

"I want to see a different head in my mind when I think of someone going down on you in the bathroom, or anywhere else, namely mine. Now lean your back against the wall and slouch down a bit, Jordanna."

After the drummer did as she was told, Rebecca walked up to the toilet and straddled it. She spread the drummer's legs apart, dipping her fingers into the drummer's treasure. "You're so wet for me, love."

"For you," the drummer mumbled quietly and closed her eyes, grabbing onto the walls.

Rebecca kissed the drummer on the inside of her thighs slowly, grazing Jordanna's center with her tongue for a brief second.

Jordanna let out a loud moan. "Oh, God. Rebecca. Please don't tease me like that."

Rebecca could feel the drummer's leg muscles quivering from the strain of keeping herself up in the uncomfortable position and now had a new respect for her lover.

She made it look so easy.

Jordanna lifted her leg just slightly to allow the reporter easier access. "Rebecca, I can't hold on here that long...this has to be a quickie, baby." Removing one hand from the wall, she pushed her lover's head in close before bracing against the wall once again. Rebecca held onto Jordanna's shaking legs for her as she licked and sucked hard on the drummer's womanhood, making the dark-haired woman come hard and fast. The reporter hung on to Jordanna as the strength drained right out of her body and she started to slide down the wall, helping her lover down onto her rubber-like, unsteady feet.

Once the drummer was able to stand up on her own, Rebecca handed Jordanna her clothes and watched as she got dressed.

The drummer looked at the smirking reporter and laughed. "Are you happy now, baby?"

"Yes, very. And you?"

Jordanna pushed Rebecca against the wall gently, rubbing her body against the reporter's, and bent her head down for a kiss. She ran her tongue along Rebecca's lips, tasting herself on them before the young reporter let her in completely. When they broke away, she looked into Rebecca's hazel eyes. "Does that answer your question?"

A still-smirking Rebecca pulled the door open, and they walked out of the stall, ignoring the looks and comments from the other people in the bathroom. Jordanna stood next to Kelly as they washed their hands at the sink, and locked eyes with the guitarist in the mirror. She laughed and shrugged. "Wasn't my idea, Kel."

"Sure it wasn't," the guitarist drawled as she finished her business and walked away.

# Chapter
# Fifteen

THE TWO WOMEN spent all night at Rebecca's apartment, relaxing and enjoying their time with each other. The next show at the Garden wasn't until Sunday night and they had some free time, so the women decided that they would hit a play before heading back to Jordanna's house.

"You've never seen it, right?"

"No, I haven't seen it, and I really want to, but you've seen it so many times...that's stupid, Jordanna. Why don't we see something neither of us has seen," the reporter argued.

"Rebecca, I loved *Les Mis*. Get it? I L-O-V-E-D that play, so it wouldn't be a hardship for me to spend three and a half hours seeing my favorite play again with my beautiful lover at my side."

Rebecca rolled her eyes. "You're such a mush sometimes, you know that?" She continued looking at the plays listed in the paper and tried again. "What about *Rent*, have you seen that yet?"

The dark woman shook her head. "Yes, I've seen that one, and I've seen almost every play that's on right now."

"*Phantom*?" Rebecca asked pathetically, hoping she could come up with something Jordanna hadn't seen.

"Yes, baby, I think everyone's seen that one, haven't they?"

"Okay, you win. You've seen 'em all. *Les Mis* it is, then," the reporter said with a grin. "What about something to eat?"

"How about we eat somewhere on the Island on the way back to my house, a diner or something?"

Rebecca linked her arm in the dark-haired woman's and led her to the door. "Sounds good to me."

THE TWO WOMEN followed the usher to the second row center in the theater. Rebecca decided that she liked having a famous girlfriend with a little pull. "These are great seats," she said as she sat down. "I've been waiting so long to see this."

"Did you bring tissues?"

Rebecca turned and looked at the drummer. "Tissues? Why would I bring tissues?"

The dark woman shifted in her seat a bit and stretched her long legs out to the side trying to get comfortable in the tight space. "This play is bittersweet, baby. Don't get too attached to any of the characters."

"Are you trying to tell me that you, Jordanna Fox, cried through this play?"

Jordanna rolled her eyes and laughed. "Do you really think that I'm that insensitive? This is an emotional play. I do have a small heart here, you know," she said, pointing to her chest.

The theater lights dimmed, and the actors took the stage. The reporter leaned in and whispered in the drummer's ear. "You've got my heart, too, Jordanna."

The dark woman swallowed the huge lump growing in her throat and cursed herself for not bringing any tissues. She didn't even hear the opening lines of the play.

Something made Rebecca tear her eyes from the stage and look at her lover's face. *Are those tears in her eyes? The play just started. It's not that sad yet.* "You're crying already?"

"I got something in my eye," the drummer said quietly.

Three hours later, Rebecca sat wiping the tears from her own eyes as the play wrapped up.

They stood up, along with the rest of the crowd, to applaud the actors taking their bows on the stage. Jordanna could tell by the huge smile on her lover's face just how much she liked the play. "So, what did you think?" she asked, as they were walking out through the lobby.

Rebecca smacked her on the arm. "You know what I think. It was..."

The drummer finished for her. "Incredible?"

"Yeah. Incredible."

Darkness had fallen over the city by the time the play ended. The two walked the five short blocks back to Rebecca's apartment hand in hand. "I can't believe that you live so close to that theater and have *never* seen that play."

"I guess I was just waiting to see it with the right person—" the reporter was interrupted by a group of young boys barging in between the two of them.

"Fucking queers!" one boy yelled, slamming all of his body weight into Rebecca and nearly knocking her down. No sooner had the words come out of his mouth then the boy found himself face down on the pavement with a very angry drummer on his back.

"Apologize to the lady," she growled.

The boy's friends took off down the street, leaving him alone with the reporter and the enraged drummer. "No way! I ain't apologizing to no fucking lezzie."

She pushed her knee harder into his spine. "Apologize!"

"Jordanna, stop. Don't hurt him," Rebecca pleaded.

The kid tried to get a look at the woman that had him pinned to the ground. "Jordanna? As in Jordanna Fox?"

Jordanna ignored his question and increased the pressure on his back. "Say you're sorry, now, or I'll kill you right here, you little dickless asshole!"

Rebecca tried to get her lover off the boy. "Jor, baby, he's just a stupid kid."

"I know that, Rebecca, but someone's gotta teach him a lesson."

"That's not what I meant, Jor. Please," the reporter begged, leaning down and making eye contact with the drummer. "Don't hurt him, please. For me."

Jordanna sighed heavily and got up off of the kid. "Consider yourself lucky she was here. Now get the fuck outta my face before I change my mind," she snarled, watching the boy start to run off down the street.

Rebecca leaned up against the newsstand that they were standing next to. "What in the hell just happened, Jordanna? Why did you respond like that? You didn't need to threat..."

Jordanna rubbed her forehead and turned to Rebecca, her normally warm blue eyes blazing. "The kid was a rude little jerk, Rebecca, and he needed to be taught a fucking lesson. Apparently his parents never taught him manners."

"But did you need to threaten him violently? The kid knows who you are now."

"What's he gonna do? Turn me in?" The dark woman grabbed her lover by the arms. "That's the only way I—these kids know. So yes, I had to get a little violent with him, Rebecca; otherwise, he'll never learn."

They walked the rest of the way to Rebecca's apartment in silence.

THE DARK-HAIRED WOMAN took a sip from the can of soda Rebecca placed in front of her and rubbed her aching head. "Are you mad at me?" she asked as she sat down on the couch.

Rebecca took a sip of her own soda. "No, I'm not mad at you, Jordanna, I just didn't expect you to do what you did."

"I'm sorry," the drummer said quietly as she took a good look around the room for the first time. "You have a nice apartment, Rebecca, very homey. I only really saw your bedroom, the bathroom, and the shower last night."

"Thanks. It's all right. Nothing like your place, though," Rebecca answered mindlessly. "Jordanna?"

"Hmm?"

"Can we talk about your past?"

The dark woman sighed and looked up at her lover. "C'mere," she said, as she held her hand out and pulled the reporter down next to her. She finished her soda and put the can down on a coaster. "My past is a very long, very fucked-up, very difficult thing for me to discuss, Rebecca."

The reporter ran her hands through the drummer's dark hair. "I have all the time in the world for you. Seriously, though, I *need* to hear it, Jor, please?"

Jordanna closed her eyes and looked down, visions of the past flashing in her mind. "I...I don't know if I can do this."

"Yes, you can, baby. You can tell me anything, don't you understand that? I love you, no matter what you tell me. I love you."

*I hope to God that's true.*

Jordanna cleared her throat, feeling the bile rise in it. "I did some things, things that if anyone ever found out about them would..." She paused and took Rebecca's hand in her own and kissed it. "This is off the record, right?"

Rebecca leapt up off the couch and paced in front of her lover. "Jesus Christ, Jordanna! What kind of a person do you think I am? You think that I would write about your past? I can't believe this! My lover doesn't fucking trust me. That's just great!"

The drummer tried hard to remove her foot from her mouth. "Rebecca, please. I do trust you. Sit down. I don't know what I was thinking when I said that. I'm sorry." She locked eyes with Rebecca, who was standing there in a defensive pose. "Please, sit down. I'll tell you."

Jordanna thought about just how much she was going to tell the reporter, and a real feeling of sadness came over her when she thought of Rebecca's reaction. Would the reporter be so horrified and disgusted that she would leave her? Rebecca had already been a victim of her addiction, and that hadn't sent her running for the hills, but...

Everyone else in her life had run so far.

"Rebecca?" They both spoke at the same time, breaking the silence that fell upon them. "Jordanna?"

They both chuckled. After sitting back down on the couch and taking the drummer's hand in her own, the reporter spoke.

"You first."

Jordanna kissed each knuckle on the reporter's hand slowly. "I don't know where to start."

"Start from the beginning, love."

The drummer smiled and rolled her eyes. "How did I know you were going to say that?" "Okay, the beginning. Yeah, well, um..."

Rebecca put her reporter's hat on. "Tell me about your childhood, Jordanna."

The drummer sat silent for a few seconds and then began. "I grew up on Long Island. You know that, though. That's how I know Kelly and Rache; we went to school together." She smiled sheepishly. "We lived in a very suburban area. My father was a foreman at one of the factories by my house, and my mother worked part-time at the library."

Rebecca moved closer to the drummer and put her head on Jordanna's shoulder. "Go on," she whispered, encouraging her lover.

All the images of her youth flashed before the drummer's eyes again. Playing one-on-one with her father in the driveway. Him not coming home. Her mother's boyfriends. Her best friend's older sister. Her mother beating the crap out of her. Living on the streets. Meeting Karla. Working for Dre.

*Julia Smith's death and Jordanna Fox's birth.*

"I, um, well, you know I'm an only child, right?"

Rebecca nodded. "Yes."

"I grew up in a middle-class family, did all the things a typical teenager did. I was on the honor roll in school, but never had to study," she said with a little grin.

Rebecca chuckled. "I hated the kids that were like that. I always had to study." She patted Jordanna on the knee and urged her on.

"I was very involved in school activities. I was team captain of the girl's basketball team and the only female percussionist in the band. That's when I first met up with Kelly and Rachel. We formed a band together and played at the school and some little eighteen-and-under clubs in the area. My best friend sang lead vocals. My father..." Her voice became emotional and she stopped talking.

The reporter pulled Jordanna close and noticed tears in the dark-haired woman's eyes. "What happened to your father, Jor?"

"I loved him so much, Rebecca," she blurted out as tears let loose and streamed down her face. "He left home one day and never came back. Not a word, no note, nothing. I never saw him again.

"My mother blamed me for it, Rebecca. She said that he hated having me as a daughter and he left because of me," she continued. She wiped the tears with the back of her hands. "We were so close when I was young; we did everything together. Why would he hate me?"

"He didn't hate you, Jor." Rebecca kissed her lover gently on the cheek. "How well did you get along with your mother before he left?"

Jordanna looked at her. "We tolerated each other, I guess. She wasn't a very warm woman. Whenever Dad and I would do something together, she never wanted to come. She always stayed home." She swallowed a few times. "He bought me my drum set when he saw that I was interested in taking drumming further. Paid for my lessons at the Drum Center. He was there when I was in the recitals they had every year. She never really showed an interest in anything I did. She never came to anything I was in."

Jordanna seemed like a small child to Rebecca as they spoke of her youth, not the hard-edged, adult woman that everyone thought she was. "Sweetheart, it sounds like she would be the reason he left, not you. She just blamed you instead of taking the responsibility for it."

Jordanna cracked a small smile. "I hope so." She sighed. "Still doesn't change the fact that he's never been in touch with me since, though. I found out a few years ago that he remarried right away and had a couple of children afterwards. My guess now would be that he was probably having an affair back then. I think they both were, actually."

"Sounds like a good guess. What happened after he left, love?"

The drummer got up and walked to the other side of the room. "She met this slob named Bruce at a bar, and he moved in the house not long after. The pig didn't have a job. He would sit at home in the afternoon when she was at work, and he'd drink beer, eat, and watch porn."

"Sounds like a real winner to me," the reporter commented.

Jordanna frowned. "That's an understatement. After a while, he sorta forced me..."

Rebecca's breath caught and she burrowed herself further into her lover's embrace. "No, don't tell me..."

Jordanna shook her head and interrupted Rebecca. "No, he didn't force himself on me, if that's what you're thinking. But he did," she sat back down, "force me to sit and watch the movies with him. After a while he would jack off right in front of me.

Never once touched me, though." She closed her eyes. "I'll never forget, he had the biggest penis I'd ever seen, and his back was so hairy...ugh. He's probably a good part of the reason I prefer women."

"You think?"

"No." She laughed a bit. "I started to question my sexuality before my father left home. But he certainly didn't make me find men more desirable, that's for sure."

"I guess not."

"After a while," the drummer continued, "he started to watch the all-girl porn. I think watching that turned me on more than it did him. When the video would end, I would say I had to study and go upstairs just so I could, um, release myself, if you know what I mean."

Rebecca blinked at her. "Did you like watching those movies?"

"Not at first. After a while, though, it got so that I actually looked forward to it, I hate to say."

The reporter had never understood what the draw was to those movies. She had seen quite a few of them when she was married to David because he liked watching them, but she never got the attraction. They seemed so unreal to her, and definitely did nothing to turn her on. "So that's when you started to realize you were gay? Because you liked watching women have sex with each other on screen?"

Jordanna shook her head. "No, I started to realize it when all the girls in my school started dating the guys and lusted over all the hair-band dudes. I, on the other hand, had a huge crush on my best friend's older sister and found myself attracted to female rockers."

"Oh," Rebecca said, and sat quietly for a while, letting her mind digest all the information. "Did your best friend's sister..." Rebecca started to say.

"Her name was Laura."

Rebecca continued. "Did Laura know you had a crush on her?"

The drummer pursed her lips. "Yeah, I think she must have known. Whenever I would go over to Tracey's—Tracey was my best friend, by the way. When I would go over there, Laura would always join us, and she'd pay a lot of attention to me, always trying to make some physical contact of some sort. She was three years older than me, and had just graduated. Most girls that age wouldn't be seen with a younger sister and her friend, you know?"

"Tell me about it," Rebecca chuckled. "I always hated it

when Lisa and Ryan would follow me around when I was with my friends."

"My point exactly. The only thing was, I didn't see it that way back then. It only occurred to me after..."

Rebecca cocked her head to the side. "After what?" she questioned.

The dark-haired woman looked down at the ground and cleared her throat. "One afternoon my mother and Bruce went out somewhere, so I sneaked into the closet where I knew he kept those videos hidden. I was watching one and practically jumped through the roof when the doorbell rang." She stretched her legs out to get more comfortable. "Laura was at the door."

"And? Tell me what happened."

"She seduced me, Rebecca."

"Seduced you?" Rebecca chuckled a bit. "How?"

Jordanna closed her eyes and let the memory overtake her, bringing her back to that day.

*Julia opened the door wide and let Laura in the house. "What's up, Laura?"*

*"I just want to talk to you, Julia. Your mother's not home, right?"*

*Julia shook her head. "No, she just went out with Bruce. What did you want to talk to me about?" she asked nervously. Laura had never come to her house alone before.*

*Laura sat down on the couch next to Julia, put her hand on the young girl's thigh, and started to rub it. "I think you know."*

*"Uh..." Julia mumbled and looked away, not sure how to react to Laura's boldness.*

*"Do you like it when I do that to you?" Laura asked, running her other hand through her long strawberry-blonde hair. "Julia, I like you a lot, and I think you like me."*

*Julia looked down at Laura's hand, which had made its way to the inside of the dark-haired girl's thigh. She looked directly into Laura's brown eyes. "I do," she whispered and closed her eyes. She could feel the heat rising up her neck as she began to blush.*

*"Touch me," Laura whispered as she guided Julia's shaking hands to her breasts. "Don't be afraid. I won't bite...hard."*

*"I've never done this before," the teenager admitted as she began to caress Laura's breasts through her shirt. She could feel the blonde's nipples reacting to her touch.*

*"You're doing just fine," Laura said in a low voice before she leaned in for a kiss. She kissed the teenager softly, taking her time before she worked her tongue into a stunned Julia's mouth.*

*"Oh, God," the teenager muttered, responding to all the new*

*sensations.*

"This is just the beginning, Julia," Laura said, as she pulled her shirt up over her head and exposed more bare flesh than the teenager had ever dreamed of seeing. Julia moaned at the sight of Laura's small, creamy breasts. Her nipples were red and pouting, just waiting to be devoured by the inexperienced teenager.

"I need you to do something for me, Julia," the blonde said.

"I, uh, okay."

Laura pushed Julia down to the floor and onto her knees. "I need you to suck my tits, Julia. Will you do that for me?"

"Oh, God." The teenager felt a jolt of desire shoot through her body at the words. "I-I... Shit. I, yes," she stuttered, and waited for the older girl to instruct her further. When she didn't, the shaking Julia hesitantly placed light kisses on the older girl's stomach, and worked her way up to her breasts.

"Suck them, please, Julia! Now!"

She shyly took a nipple into her mouth and sighed, sucking on it gently on it while Laura guided her hand to the other one. "Yes, Julia, like that...that feels so good."

The teenager could feel the slow ache begin to burn between her legs. "I want you," Laura moaned, and began pulling Julia's tucked Union Jack tee shirt out of her jeans and up over her head. "Gotta get this off," she said, as she unhooked the teenager's bra and let it fall to the floor. She pulled Julia closer to her so that their nipples touched, sending a quick jolt to both of their throbbing centers.

"Oh, yeah, that's much better," Laura crooned, before she went for the button on Julia's jeans. Unzipping them and easing them off of the tall teenager, she flipped Julia over so that she was now on top of her. "Lean back," she commanded, pushing the young girl down on the couch. Laura slipped her fingers under the top of Julia's panties and pulled them down slowly, revealing the young girl's dark curls.

Laura took the sight in and then sighed. "You are so beautiful, Julia. Did you know that? I remember when you were that skinny, gawky best friend of my kid sister. Look at you now. So grown up and so ready for me."

"Thank you," Julia responded as she began to blush. Embarrassed at being so exposed, she looked into Laura's eyes and started to tug on her jeans. Laura quickly disposed of her jeans and panties. "Do you see how much I want you, Julia?" She ran her fingers through the moist area between her legs. "Taste me, Julia. This is all for you," she said before offering the young girl her finger.

Julia tasted the offered finger and moaned.

Laura laid her body on top of the teenager's. "Now, I want

*nothing more than to taste you. Will you let me?"*

Julia nodded her consent as the girl shimmied her way down the teenager's body. She realized that Laura obviously had quite a bit of experience at this. "Open your legs for me, let me inside," she said and the teenager obeyed. "Mmm, Julia. You're so wet for me." Laura kissed her way up the insides of Julia's legs before she finally kissed the young girl's center. Julia's hips left the couch at the contact. "Oh, my God. Laura!"

They were much too involved to have heard the front door open and slam shut. When they looked up, they saw a gawking Bruce and Julia's furious mother standing in the doorway.

"What in the fucking hell is going on here, Julia?" her mother screamed, after she caught sight of the two naked girls on the couch. Laura leapt up and ran for her clothes.

Julia's mother was shocked. "Laura? Get dressed and go home now. I'll deal with you later. I'm sure your father is going to love this!" She grabbed her daughter by the hair and pulled her up off of the couch.

"Damn it, Julia! I trusted you, and this is what you do?" the furious woman said before she slapped the teenager across the face. "My daughter's a fucking queer!" Slap! "I hope you're proud of yourself." Slap! "How many girls have you fucked before, Julia?" Slap! "Huh, you little dyke slut?" Slap! "Did you enjoy yourself?" Slap! "I hope you did, you lezzie!" Slap! "I can't believe this fucking shit!" Slap! "You're going straight to fucking hell now, Julia. Do you realize that?"

"Mom!" Julia put her hand in front of her face to deflect the last blow. She knew her lip was bleeding because she could taste the blood in her mouth. Her blue eyes turned to ice. "Don't you ever," she said, grabbing her mother's hands, "lay your fucking hands on me again, Mom! Ever!"

Bruce stood there and watched the interaction between his girlfriend and her daughter; her beautiful, naked daughter. His eyes took in every inch of her body. He shifted his stance, worked his jaw. Swallowed hard. Then turned away. Fast.

Her mother watched him run up the stairs, looked at her daughter, and let her hands drop to her sides before she collapsed onto the couch. Julia took that moment to go to her room, taking the few things she owned and putting them into her black duffel bag.

"Where in the hell do you think you're going?" her mother asked as she watched Julia emerge from her room with the packed bag slung over her shoulder.

"I don't know. Maybe Tracey's."

Her mother snorted. "What, so you can go fuck your little

*girlfriend again, Julia? What does Tracey think about the two of you?"*

*"Tracey doesn't know,"* Julia answered, fighting to keep the tears from falling down her face.

*"You really think their parents are gonna let you stay there after I tell them what happened?"*

*"I really don't care. I can't stay here. Not with you. Or Bruce."*

*"You walk through that door, Julia, and you will never, ever, walk back in here again!"* her mother threatened. Julia smirked, only feeding her mother's fire more. *"I'm not joking, Julia!"*

*"Fine,"* Julia responded on her way to the door. *"Have a nice life, Mom."*

Her mother jumped up and blocked her, pulling her by the hair. *"You're just like him. He couldn't stand being around you, did you know that? That's why he left me."* She pointed her finger in Julia's face. *"Because of you. It's your fucking fault he left!"*

Julia looked at her mother with pity. Her mother caught the look and snapped. *"Don't you dare pity me, you fag! You are sick and perverted. All of your kind are! Now get the hell out of my house! I am not your mother. This is not your family."*

*"I don't want to be a part of this family,"* Julia said, as her hand started to turn the doorknob. She turned around and faced her mother. *"Oh, and Mom, tell that fat slob Bruce that one of his porn videos is still in the VCR, will ya?"* Julia laughed. *"He's probably upstairs jacking off right now after seeing Laura and me on the couch."* She winked at her mother. *"He's got a really big penis. Is that what you like about him, Mom?"*

*"Get the fuck out of here, Julia!"*

The dark-haired teenager opened the door and walked out of the only life she knew.

Rebecca sat there, stunned at what Jordanna had told her. She remembered the fight she had with her own parents when she told them that she was going to school in New York after she graduated. Jordanna's mother had just let her fifteen-year-old daughter walk right out the door. "God, that's awful, Jordanna. She just let you go like that? Just because she caught you having sex?"

"I haven't seen her since that day," Jordanna said with only the slightest bit of regret in her voice. "And I don't think it was because she caught me. I think she just wanted me out of her life, too, after my father left." She looked down. "I gave her the perfect reason to fight with me by doing what I did. That was her way out."

"That is terrible."

"I know," Jordanna agreed, thinking back all those years. "She was so self-righteous and had no reason to be. I mean, she asked that disgusting slob Bruce to move in with us. I think she knew what he was doing during the day, in front of me. She wasn't shocked when I called her on it right before I left. My mother was sick, and a pretty selfish and vain person. I think all she cared about was what people would think about her, and forget what they'd think if they found out her daughter was gay, or a fag, as she called me. I shamed her, Rebecca. It was the perfect excuse." She laughed a bit. "She never worried about what they thought about that pig moving in with us right away, though. Isn't that convenient?"

"Is that..." The reporter bit her lip. "Is that also why you don't like to be called names?"

The dark woman turned her head to the side, not following the question. "What do you mean?"

"Remember when we went to that Italian restaurant on the pier in Montauk?"

The drummer smirked. "Yeah, how could I forget? You certainly made it quite memorable."

"Before we went, you warned me that people might think we were a couple. You also said you don't react well to being called a fag or something like that. Do you remember that?"

"Yeah, I remember. What does that have to do with anything?"

Rebecca pushed Jordanna's dark bangs out of her eyes. "Tonight you nearly killed a young boy because he called us queer."

"So? I don't like being called names. Most people don't. I'm not following your point, Rebecca."

"I think it's because of your mother. You said that when she was hitting you she called you every name in the book, so when someone else says it to you now, you go a little wild."

Jordanna laughed. "I thought you were a journalist, not a psychologist. You're too much, Rebecca."

"Don't you see, Jordanna? As a journalist, it helps to be able to understand what makes a person tick to really write a good article on them."

The drummer let a wicked grin cross her face. "So," she said, pulling Rebecca on top of her, giving her a quick kiss. "What makes me tick, Dr. Freud?" She kissed her again, this time with a little more passion. "Huh, Rebecca? Tell me what makes me tick."

Rebecca took a deep breath after that last kiss. "Don't try to change the subject, Jordanna. I think this is important."

"Yeah, I guess." The drummer pulled away from Rebecca, disappointed. Rubbing her temple, she thought about what the reporter was trying to say to her. "So you think, what? That I overreact when someone calls me a name because subconsciously I'm remembering all the nasty things my mother said to me the last time I saw her?"

Rebecca nodded. "Did it hurt?"

The dark woman sighed. "Did *what* hurt?"

"Did it hurt you when your mother said those things to you?"

Jordanna jumped up, rubbed her head, and grabbed another soda out of the refrigerator. "Of course it hurt, Rebecca! As cold as she was to me, she's my mother, and to hear those things coming out of her mouth was far worse than any beating she could have given me."

Rebecca got up and stood next to the drummer, taking her hand in her own.

Jordanna looked in the hazel of the reporter's eyes and agreed with her. "I guess you're right, Rebecca. I just never really thought about it."

The young woman rubbed the drummer's stomach. "Are you feeling all right? Do you want to head home now, Jor?"

Jordanna picked up her car keys off of the kitchen table and handed them to Rebecca. "I don't think I can drive, Rebecca. My head is killing me. I think I might be getting a migraine."

Rebecca grabbed the keys from the dark woman. "No problem. I can drive. You might just need to eat," she said, exactly the moment her own stomach rumbled. "And think I need to eat, too."

# Chapter
# Sixteen

REBECCA LET THE drummer doze during most of the drive on the Long Island Expressway. She was happy to have some quiet time to think about what her lover had told her. Was it only two days ago that the drummer had lost control of herself sexually after the show at the Garden? Since then, they had both received death threats, she'd witnessed for herself the dark woman's temper with the young boy, and she'd found out that Jordanna's parents both had abandoned her at a young age. *No wonder she's fucked up. I would be, too.*

She remembered Jordanna talking about stopping to get something to eat at a diner that she really liked in Hauppauge. When she saw the exit the drummer had mentioned, she got off. "Jordanna, wake up," she said, nudging the drummer gently on the shoulder. "Baby, we are at the exit you said to take."

Jordanna's blue eyes fluttered open. "I fell asleep?" She felt her stomach want to rebel. "I feel a little sick."

Rebecca rubbed Jordanna's knee, offering comfort. "You need to get something to eat. We are at Route 111, like you told me. How do I get to the diner from here?"

The drummer looked around. "Make a left here, and we'll have to make another left about a mile and a half down the road on Veterans Highway. It's a main intersection. The diner is called Nirvana. It's on the right-hand side of the road." She put her head against the window and let her eyes close again.

Rebecca shook her head. "Yeah, great, you sleep. I just hope we don't end up in Connecticut."

"I'm not sleeping, just resting my eyes," the drummer mumbled minutes later.

"Oh, okay. Right."

"And unless you got on the ferry or drove straight into the water, we'd never be able to get to Connecticut that easily from here," Jordanna said in a sleepy voice.

"Smart-ass."

"You know it."

Rebecca drove down the dark, winding road, passing a few small intersections until she saw a main one. "Hmm. Is this it?" she spoke out loud.

"Does the sign say 454?" the sleepy voice asked.

Rebecca looked at the sign at the light, and 454 happened to be one of the many numbers on it. "Yep, I think so."

"This is it, then."

The reporter made a left and spotted the pink-and-blue neon sign with palm trees on it that read Nirvana. She pulled into the parking lot and found a spot as close to the front as possible, shaking her lover again when she put the car in park. "C'mon, Jor, we're here."

Rebecca got out of the car and walked to the other side, opening the door for her lover. "Are you all right?" She held her hand out to help the drummer out of the car. "Do you want to just go home?"

"No, I'm okay," the dark-haired woman responded. "I *really* could use some coffee. Caffeine usually helps when I have a headache."

"Yeah, I could go for a cup myself."

The two walked through the parking lot and up the steps. Rebecca held the door open for her lover and waited for her to walk in. Jordanna stopped abruptly and turned around to face the reporter. "Did I tell you that this is my hometown?"

Rebecca shook her head. "No, you neglected to mention that."

"Yep, this is where I grew up." Jordanna snorted. "Whaddya think? Maybe I'll run into some old friends tonight."

"Are you sure you want to eat here, then?"

The drummer answered as the host was seating them. "Yeah, it's a good diner. The food is excellent."

Hearing her answer, the host turned and smiled at her. His gaze lasted longer than it should have. "Thank you. It's always nice to hear such nice compliments like that," the man said, pulling a chair out for Rebecca and turning back to look at the drummer again. Jordanna stared back. "Your waitress will be right over," he said as he walked away, frowning pensively.

Rebecca noticed the way the host looked at her lover. "What was up with him, Jordanna?"

Jordanna shook her head and furrowed her brows. "I don't know." She pulled her seat closer to the table. "He looks a bit familiar to me but I can't place him."

The diner was packed with people, unusual for the late hour. After they decided what they were going to eat, they waited for their waitress to finally come to take their order.

"Can I get you something to drink first?" the woman asked. Jordanna looked up at the waitress, who had turned and looked away. A flash of recognition appeared in the drummer's eyes, and she looked at the woman's name tag. "Tracey?"

The waitress looked at her, her brown eyes opening wide. "Oh, my God. Julia?"

"I don't use Julia anymore; it's Jordanna now," the drummer said to her childhood friend.

"Yeah, I know all about you. Jordanna Fox, the *big* freaking rock star. The one who screwed my sister and then took off, never to be seen again. You and your whole trashy family broke my family apart. Do you know what happened to her?" Tracey asked in a sarcastic tone. "Do you know what happened to Laura?"

*Trashy family? I screwed her? She came to me.* The drummer didn't want to fight, so she just went along with what the waitress said. "No, what happened to her?"

"After *your* mother told my parents about the two of you, Laura ran off to find you. We never saw her again. At least not alive."

Jordanna shifted uncomfortably in her seat. "What?"

Tracey wiped the unexpected tears out of her eyes. "AIDS, Julia. She died of AIDS."

The reporter's head shot up, and she looked at her lover. Jordanna locked eyes with her and shook her head. "You don't think?"

"I don't know what the hell to think, Julia!" Tracey spat, not realizing that Jordanna was speaking to Rebecca. "All I know is that my sister is dead, and you're not only alive, but a millionaire jet-setting around the world! Where's the fairness in that?"

The drummer looked down. "I'm sorry."

"Your being sorry won't bring her back!" the woman screamed. Other patrons of the diner were now listening to their conversation. The host came over to see what was causing all the commotion. "Tracey, what's going on here?"

Rebecca spoke up for the first time. "I think it would be better if we leave, Jordanna."

"I knew I recognized you, you sleazy bitch," the host said to the drummer after the mention of her name, and handed them their coats. "Yes, I suggest you do just that."

Jordanna looked at the host and finally realized who he was—Tracey and Laura's father, Kevin. She surmised that their family must have bought the diner from the previous owners.

"Good to see you, too, Mr. Erickson," she said, flashing a phony smile.

Tracey turned and spoke to the reporter as they got up to leave. "Are you her girlfriend?"

Rebecca nodded. "Yes, I am."

"I suggest you run as fast as you can. She's really bad news," the waitress warned her. "And get yourself tested."

Jordanna put her arm around Rebecca's shoulder and started walking toward the door. "C'mon, let's get the hell out of here." She stopped and turned to look at the waitress. "Good seeing you again, Tracey," she said sarcastically, but her voice softened before she finished. "I really am truly sorry to hear about Laura."

Neither of the two women said anything until they got to the car. "Give me the keys," the drummer said, walking to the driver's side.

"No."

"What?"

The reporter was adamant. "No! You've got a migraine and you're angry. You still haven't eaten anything, and you are not driving!"

"So then drive, Rebecca! Get me the fuck out of this town," Jordanna snarled at the reporter as she stomped to the other side of the car.

Rebecca started the car and pulled out of the parking lot recklessly. "Where are we going?"

"What?" the distracted drummer questioned.

"Damn it, Jordanna, I have no idea where the hell I am! Which way do I go?"

"Oh, make a right at the light and follow the road down a few miles." The drummer knew she had to calm down. She had no right to take her anger out on her lover. "I'm sorry, Rebecca."

"For what?" the reporter asked coldly.

"For you having to hear that, and for me losing my temper with you."

Rebecca felt her heart rate slow down. "It's okay." She paused. "About what she said about Laura..."

The drummer knew where the conversation was going. Her lover had every reason to be concerned. "Rebecca, I've been tested. I get tested every few months."

"I thought that two women couldn't..."

"That's what most people think," the dark woman answered quietly. Jordanna turned her body to look at her lover. "Rebecca, two women can contract and pass along the virus, too, if they aren't careful. No one is exempt from this disease."

Rebecca scratched her chin. "When we make love, are we careful?"

Jordanna sighed heavily and looked down in shame. "No, baby, we're not."

"God, I never really even thought about it until now, you know?"

The drummer pursed her lips and shook her head. *She's so innocent.* "I know, and that's my fault. I know better. We should have been more careful right from the start." She turned and looked out the window, watching the buildings pass by as they drove. "Like I said before, I get tested quite often, so hopefully there's nothing to worry about. There's one thing I can tell you, though; Laura didn't give it to or get it from me. She was my first."

Rebecca's eyes widened at the revelation. "When your mother caught you...that was your first time?"

"Yeah, it was, although we never really got the chance to finish what we started."

Rebecca started to laugh. "I don't know why, but for some reason I can't picture you ever being a virgin."

The drummer's eyes twinkled in the light. "Well, believe it or not, I was," the dark woman said with a chuckle. "I could tell that Laura wasn't, though. She seemed to be a bit more experienced. I was a nervous wreck and didn't know what to do. It's true I wanted her and had a crush on her for a long time, but I never expected her to just show up at my house and seduce me like that."

"That's what I was going to ask you."

"What?"

"Why you were so careless. Why couldn't you have found somewhere more private to do your business, like your bedroom?"

"Stupidity?" Jordanna thought back to the year or so after the incident. "You know, I asked myself that same question so many times after it happened." Her eyes took on a far-away look. "Especially when I was out on the streets looking for my next meal."

Rebecca stopped at a red light and looked at her lover. "What did you do after you left home?"

The drummer could feel her stomach doing flips. "Do we have to talk about this now, Rebecca?"

"If we don't talk about it now, when will we?"

Jordanna sighed and closed her eyes. She took a deep breath and began. "All I had to my name when I left home was around $400, some clothes, and a junky old car I had saved up my allowance for. I had just got my permit and didn't have my real license, but at that point I didn't give a shit. I remember driving around until I couldn't keep my eyes open anymore."

*She drove around with no specific destination until day turned into night. Her eyes burned from the driving and the crying that she had done.*

*She thought about what she was going to do. Things like where she was going to sleep, how she was going to feed herself once her money ran out. Things that she had never had to worry about before.*

*She decided that the park-&-rides designed for commuters at some of the exits along the Long Island Expressway would probably be the best place to park without being noticed by the law. Exhausted from driving all day, she pulled into the closest one in Brentwood, which happened to be one town over from her hometown. In her mind she knew that it wasn't such a good idea because of the town's crime-ridden reputation, but she was too tired to care, and too hungry. She hadn't eaten since morning, before Laura made her pleasurable but fateful visit.*

Was that only this morning? *she wondered as she ripped open the bag of Cool Ranch Doritos that she had bought when she stopped at a 7-11. After she finished the Doritos and washed them down with a large soda, she climbed into the back seat of the car and settled her tall frame down as comfortably as she possibly could.*

*Tired as she was, she couldn't seem to fall asleep. The repercussions of the day's events had hit her hard. Blue eyes stared out the window of the back seat looking up at the stars, hoping she would find some answers in them. All she found was a cold, dark, heartless sky and an intense pain in her heart. She couldn't believe that she had gone from the emotional experience of exploring her sexuality for the first time to being disowned by her family and forced to sleep in a parking lot all within one day. It was all too much for a fifteen-year-old to comprehend.*

*She thought about what her mother said to her as she was walking out the door.* I knew she blamed my father's leaving on me. Fuck her! I am not sick and perverted. I'm not.

Am I?

*The sounds of the commuters woke Julia up in the morning.* People that have homes and families to go to, *she thought, feeling sorry for herself.* "Ouch," *she said out loud as she was trying to work the kinks out of her abused neck.* "Sleeping in the car is the pits."

*She spent the next few months of her life living from day to day, not sure where her next meal would come from. She found herself spending most of her time wandering the streets of Brentwood, liking the diverse mix of backgrounds of the people that resided there. It was a town where someone like her could easily get lost, because she was one of many people living off of the streets.*

*It was on the street that she met a woman named Karla. Possibly three or four years older than Julia, she made her money any way she could. Whether it was by selling her body or running drugs for her dealer, she always found a way. The two instantly took a liking to each other, Karla because she saw a little of herself in the young girl, and Julia because she needed a friend. The older woman lived in a small studio apartment in the basement of a house, and quickly invited the homeless girl to stay with her. Julia spent many nights alone with Karla, who took it upon herself to teach the inexperienced girl how to satisfy a woman. Other nights she would accompany the older woman on some of her drug runs.*

*After seeing that her friend had a knack for the scare tactics needed to pull off the drug buys and runs that they did, Karla introduced Julia to her dealer, Dre. She knew that the young girl was uncomfortable living off of her, so she thought that maybe she could get a job of her own through Dre.*

*Standing in front of a convenience store in a small shopping center in Brentwood, the two women waited for Dre. "That's him," Karla said when she saw the black BMW pull into the parking lot. Dre got out of the vehicle, stood to his full height, and looked the two women over. Towering over the women in height, his 6'6" frame made even the tall girl seem small in comparison.*

*The man's dark brown eyes looked Julia over like a fresh piece of meat. "Tall," he said, looking her up and down. "Nice," he commented as his eyes hit her chest area. He looked at Karla. "I approve. You always had good taste." He turned to speak to his subject. "Karla tells me that you're looking for work?"*

*"Yes," she whispered, nervously shifting from foot to foot. She cleared her throat. "Yes, I'm looking for work."*

*"What are you willing to do?" the deep voice asked. His brown eyes never left her blue ones.*

*She walked up to him and spoke in her lowest register. "What would you like me to do?"*

*Karla stepped in between the two of them and spoke up. "Dre, Julia comes with me on some of the runs that I do. She's got the attitude for it. If you need another runner, she'd be perfect."*

*Dre walked past Karla and ran his hand down Julia's ass. "Good. You got the job. Fuck up once and it's your head, Karla." He led the young girl to his BMW. "Now, Julia, why don't you show me what else you're willing to do?"*

*She lifted her eyes and looked at his again. He smiled.*

"That's the man in the photos?" Rebecca thoughtlessly blurted out after Jordanna had finished speaking. She remembered the box that she'd accidentally dropped in the drummer's closet, and the photos that had fallen out of it, especially the one of Jordanna and the unidentified African-American man.

Jordanna raised a questioning brow at Rebecca. "What photos?"

The reporter didn't know if her unpredictable lover would be angry with her for going into her closet, but she didn't want to lie to the drummer. "The ones in the box in your bedroom closet."

Jordanna turned and glared at Rebecca, feeling her anger rising at the intrusion. "What? Why in the hell were you going through my closet?"

"Calm down, Jor! I knocked the box off of the shelf when I borrowed your sweatshirt the day of the snowstorm. Some photos and other things fell out of it. I just cleaned it up and put it back. I couldn't help but notice what was in it."

"Oh," the drummer said, closing her eyes and leaning her head back against the seat. Her head was pounding worse than ever. "Yeah, that's him in those photos, if they're the ones I'm thinking about."

"Why hide them away, though?"

"It's a part of my life I'd like to forget."

"Then why do you keep them?"

*God, why all the questions now? I really have a headache.* "Because." She paused. "This way I won't ever forget what I did."

"What you did?"

Frustrated with all the questions, the drummer slammed her hand down on the dashboard. "Damn it, Rebecca! Can't you stop the questions, stop being a reporter, and just be my lover and my best friend tonight?"

The reporter could feel tears coming to her eyes and was starting to question whether being with the secretive drummer was worth all the frustration she was feeling. "I thought that is what I was being, Jordanna."

Immediately regretting her actions, Jordanna looked around to see where they were. "Get off at the next exit, Rebecca," the drummer requested, but the reporter didn't listen and drove right past the exit. "Please get off at the next exit, Rebecca," Jordanna pleaded.

The young woman sighed, put on her directional, and pulled into the right lane. She put her directional on again when she saw an exit coming up and got off of the expressway. When she got to the end of the ramp, Jordanna motioned for her to pull into an abandoned gas-station parking lot.

"Look at me," the dark woman asked quietly. "Please."

The reporter sighed and unbuckled her seatbelt before turning in her seat to face the drummer. "*What* do you want, Jordanna?"

"I need to say something to you, and I want you to listen." The dark woman could see the tears and hurt in her lover's eyes. She lifted the armrest that was the barrier between them and held out her arms. "C'mere."

Rebecca looked around. "What if someone sees us?"

"It's dark out. We aren't doing anything illegal, and, besides, we're in an abandoned parking lot. Who's gonna see us? I just want to feel you in my arms right now, Rebecca."

"Oh." The young reporter sat in the same position for a minute and then climbed into her lover's arms.

"You feel good," the drummer said as she kissed the reporter's forehead lightly and held on tight. "I'm sorry I've been acting like such a child, Rebecca. I'm hungry and tired and my head feels like it wants to explode, but that's no excuse for me to take my anger at life out on you like I've been doing tonight. Forgive me, please?"

Rebecca wanted to remain angry with her lover but couldn't. "God, Jordanna, you make it extremely difficult to stay angry with you."

Jordanna gave Rebecca her best puppy-dog-eyes look. "Then please don't."

Rebecca sighed. "I really hate it when you make that face." She turned and kissed Jordanna on the lips gently. "Let's go find us something to eat now, okay?"

# Chapter
# Seventeen

REBECCA SENT HER tired lover upstairs to bed and headed for the sunroom. To work. Not on her article; she opened her laptop and began to research sexual addiction. She'd need to know much more than she did if she was to help Jordanna. Or to handle her own feelings. "Coping mechanism for stress. Didn't you tell me that already, Jor? Just in different words." Rebecca continued reading. "Keeps feelings inside," the reporter snorted. "Oh, yeah, that's her all right."

Rebecca scrolled down and read further. "Addiction usually starts with self-satisfaction. You did say you did that after watching those girl-girl videos with Bruce." Rebecca scratched her head and thought about that. "I think with all the women you've had falling at your feet, you don't have to worry about that now, do you, Jor?"

The reporter didn't hear her lover come down the stairs and walk up next to her; she jumped when the drummer spoke.

"That's not necessarily true," the dark woman whispered hoarsely. She peeked around Rebecca's head and looked at the screen. "What are you doing?"

Rebecca looked up and saw Jordanna standing there wearing only a short, black, unbuttoned silk robe revealing a lot of bare skin. "Uh," Rebecca mumbled, distracted by the vision in front of her.

*I like this robe.*

She breathed in heavily as the drummer's slightest movement made the robe part more, making her view even more distracting as a rosy nipple peeked out, calling her name.

*In fact, I like this robe a lot.*

"I'm doing research. I thought you were tired?"

Jordanna seemed oblivious to the havoc she was wreaking on Rebecca's hormones. "Couldn't sleep."

Jordanna wanted to see what the reporter was researching and sat down next to her. "Can I see what it says?" she asked, feeling curious and sad at the same time. Her eyes were beginning to moisten as she tried to read what the website had to say. Recognizing herself in most of the words, she knew that she had to accept the fact that, yes, there was a problem. It was something that she'd known for years, but always denied.

She read the information on the screen along with Rebecca and wondered why the reporter stopped scrolling where she did. Jordanna reread the last line and looked at Rebecca.

"Addict is usually never satisfied with sex." *Oh, God, she must think that she doesn't satisfy me.*

The drummer put her hand on Rebecca's cheek and turned her head so she could look directly into her eyes. "Rebecca, you are a wonderful lover; don't ever doubt that. You make me very happy, in and out of bed."

Rebecca smiled and cleared her throat, which had become unusually dry, and then continued to scroll down. Jordanna put her hand over Rebecca's right hand, the one controlling the mouse. "Stop, go back up a little." Rebecca brought the arrow to the arrow-up key and clicked on it until Jordanna told her to stop. Rebecca read what Jordanna was looking at.

"Believe it or not, the driving force behind most sex addicts' compulsion is a desperate need for love."

"Oh, God, is this true?" Rebecca closed her eyes, saddened by the thought. "You don't feel loved?"

Jordanna turned away from her lover, unable to look into her caring hazel eyes. "I didn't," she whispered and turned back around. "For a long time."

Rebecca's eyes started to tear; she blinked, which only made everything become a blur. She wanted to cry; she wanted to take on some of her lover's pain for her, but she knew she couldn't. "Jordanna, please tell me you feel loved now."

"I do now, yes."

Jordanna got up and went into the bathroom and grabbed a few tissues, handing them to her lover when she came back out.

"Thanks," Rebecca said and accepted the tissues, wiping her eyes with them. "Jordanna?"

The dark-haired woman put her hands up, stopping the reporter from saying what she was going to say. "Rebecca, I...since you came into my life I've felt more than loved. You don't even have to say it. You've shown me in so many different ways. It shows in your eyes when you look at me, your actions when you do things for me, and in your caresses when you make love with me. Without you even saying the words, I just know."

Rebecca ran her hands through her lover's bangs and smiled. "Just making sure. Um, getting back to that website and everything I've read. They talk about pornography a lot, Jordanna. Are you into porn?"

"Well, you already know I was introduced to porn early in life, thanks to my mother." The dark woman blinked once, and an errant tear ran down her face. *Damn these emotions.* She stood up and took Rebecca's hand. "Come with me."

Jordanna led her into the living room and grabbed a set of keys. She opened the locked door of a large wooden cabinet that stood off to the side of the room, pulled out one of at least a hundred tapes that were in the cabinet, and handed it to her lover.

Rebecca gasped. "Oh, God!"

"Yeah. So I guess that answers your question."

Rebecca was speechless. She flipped the tape over to confirm what she thought she saw. There, in living color, was a familiar dark-haired, blue-eyed woman looking back at her. "This is you."

"Yeah, it's me. That's not the only one I was in," the drummer admitted. "I did four or five of them."

Rebecca walked over to the cabinet and glanced at the rows of tapes, running her fingers over them. "I would think that this cabinet was owned by a man, Jordanna."

"Nope, they're all mine."

Rebecca cringed at the thought. *There's just so much I don't know about this woman.* "Why?"

"Why, what?"

The reporter took her pick and pulled one out. There again, staring back at her, was her lover. A tall, very naked, dark-haired man with a perfectly sculpted body stood behind her in a strategic position. "Why would you do one of these films?"

"Money," the dark-haired woman answered frankly. "At least that's what it was at first." She paused, and her eyes took on a far-away look. "Then it became a need. And here I am today, ten or eleven years later, finally realizing—no, admitting—that I am addicted."

Rebecca didn't say anything; she just put the video back, closed the doors of the cabinet, and locked it. Quietly, the reporter walked over to her partner, put her arms around the dark-haired woman's waist, and pulled her into a hug. They stood there in each other's arms for quite a while feeding off of their love of one another before Jordanna spoke. "Thanks," she whispered in the reporter's ear.

"For what?" the reporter asked, lifting her head off the drummer's shoulder to look up into her eyes.

"For knowing that I needed a hug just now. For loving me

like you do—faults and all. For loving me after what I've said and done to you. For caring enough to research and try to help me through what just might be the biggest fight of my life. I don't deserve someone like you, Rebecca, but I thank God that you stumbled into my life."

"I thank God for that, too, Jordanna," the reporter said before she broke their contact. "And you are deserving of it, but that's something that you'll learn with time." She smiled and started to walk toward the stairs with the drummer right behind her. "Are you ready for bed now?"

"Yeah, I think I'll be able to sleep now. I love you, Rebecca," the dark-haired woman said, and she stopped and took the reporter's face in her hands, brushing her lips gently across Rebecca's.

THE STALKER SAT looking at a recent publicity photo of Jordanna and smiled. "Enjoy life, Jordanna, 'cause there's not much of it left for you. Just like there wasn't for them. I will never let you forget that, even when you are rotting in hell."

The stalker went into a closet and pulled out a Glock 9 mm and loaded it. Things were falling into place.

"You are mine."

Looking at another photo, one taken backstage at the Garden that included the drummer and her new lover, the stalker frowned. "It's really a shame you had to get involved with the tramp, Rebecca, because now you have to die, too."

# Chapter
# Eighteen

JORDANNA WALKED INTO the living room. "I'll bring my cell phone with me in case you need to reach me," the drummer said. "I left the number of the radio station in the kitchen."

"Yes, Mommy!" Rebecca put her hand on her hip and laughed. "What time is my curfew tonight?"

The drummer cracked a smile at Rebecca's implications. "I'm being overprotective, aren't I?"

The reporter crossed the room and put her arms around her lover's waist. "Yes, you are. But I have to admit it's nice feeling protected."

"Mmm." Jordanna bent down and kissed Rebecca. "I'm glad," she said, feeling the reporter's response to her kiss. "I'd much rather stay right here with you, though."

"You'll be late," Rebecca said as she smacked her lover on the backside and gently pushed her out of the room. "I'll be fine, Jordanna, really. Don't worry about me."

"Okay, see you later, baby," the dark-haired woman called out as she walked out the front door. "Lock the door behind me, please."

"Yes, Mom," Rebecca teased playfully, but locked the door to appease Jordanna. She watched the champagne-colored Pathfinder back out of the driveway, and waited for Jordanna to turn onto the main road before picking up her cell phone. Her heart pounded as she made the call she had wanted to make since she had heard her lover's answers to the questions regarding addiction.

She let the phone ring and waited. "Jackson, Hill and Associates," the tinny voice on the other end of the phone answered.

"Jim Hill, please."

"May I ask who is calling?"

"Rebecca Hurley."

"Hold on, please."

Rebecca rolled her eyes when she heard the painful sounds of Air Supply coming through the receiver. "God, Jim. Can't you switch the station?" she muttered to herself. "What a cruel thing to do to your clients."

"Always a critic, huh, Becky?" Jim answered with a hearty laugh. "How are you doing, stranger?"

Rebecca leaned back on the couch, making herself more comfortable. "That's my job, Jim, and I'm doing great. How have you been?"

"Fine, fine. So, to what do I owe this pleasure?"

"I need a favor from you. Can you look someone up for me?"

"Uh, yeah. Whaddya need?"

Rebecca frowned, feeling the guilt of her actions already. "Everything you can get, Jim. Police record, medical history, the works."

"Hold on a sec, Becky." Rebecca could hear her friend searching for something to write with. The one thing she always remembered about Jim was that he could never keep his desk clean. Moments later she heard him say, "Gimme the name."

"Jordanna Fox."

"Jordanna Fox, as in the musician? Tall, dark, blue eyes, gorgeous but major trouble?" he asked and laughed.

"Yeah, that's her."

"Can I ask you why, Becky? Getting into a new kind of reporting?"

She leaned forward and fiddled with a snag in her shirt. "She's my latest assignment, Jim. That's all I can say."

"You meet her yet?" he asked. "I hear she's a complete bitch. Beyond gorgeous, but a bitch nonetheless."

Rebecca smiled. *That's what I thought at first, too.* "Yeah, I've met her. She's really not that bad once you get to know her. I'm staying at her house right now."

"She know you're doing this?"

"No, she doesn't, and she won't find out. Right, Jim?"

"Not from me."

"Great." Rebecca paused. "I appreciate that."

"Just be careful with her, Rebecca. She's got a real bad reputation," he warned his friend, as he quickly skimmed over Jordanna's police record.

Rebecca sighed, tired of being warned about her lover. "She's fine, Jim. Let me know what you come up with, okay? Call my cell. You still have the number, right?"

"Somewhere," he said, and she heard pages turning. "Yep, got it. I'll call you when I have something. Hey, when are we going to get together? I never get to see you anymore. I miss you."

"Soon, Jim, soon. I miss you, too. Thanks for the help. Bye."

Rebecca put the phone down on the table. She felt restless and uneasy, and thought about Jim for a while. She had met Jim when she was still going to NYU and had dated him briefly after her marriage with David ended. She'd thought before of using his private-investigation agency for information to write a few articles on a couple of deadbeat musicians that John had assigned her to, but her conscience wouldn't let her do it. She wondered why it would allow her to do it this time, with her own lover.

She decided that she would sit in the sunroom to work on her article and to wait for Jim to get back to her. She picked up her laptop, Jordanna's cordless phone, and her cell phone, and headed into the sunroom. As she walked through the living room, she noticed the keys to the video cabinet were still on the table.

*I shouldn't.*

She continued to the sunroom, setting her laptop down on a small desk. She went over to the stereo and flipped the dial to 102.3, the radio station that Jordanna and Rachel were heading to. "Cool station," she said when she heard a Led Zeppelin tune playing. "They have good taste." Once the song ended, the disc jockey announced that Rachel and Jordanna would be there momentarily to do an interview, and mentioned the growing group of people waiting outside the station to meet them. Rebecca's heart did flips when she heard it, knowing that her lover was weak to any temptation that might come her way.

Trying to get her mind off of things, she sat down at the desk and started to work on her article. She sang along with the song on the radio, the popular female singer singing about a woman's eyes and her lack of control once she looks into those sad eyes.

The reporter was wondering whether the vocalist knew her lover or not. All she saw was Jordanna's blue eyes as she listened to the lyrics.

She continued to sing the song, the vocalist crooning about the visions of her lover's body in her head, and how they were driving her insane. "Oh, God, that's it! It's entirely your fault, Melissa," she said to herself, blaming the artist and her lyrics for her actions. She closed out her file and headed into the living room. "I have some nerve calling Jordanna weak, don't I?" she said to herself.

She walked up, looked at the keys to the cabinet, and shook her head.

*This is wrong.*

She turned to walk away, and stopped.

*Oh hell, she left them here. Maybe she* wanted *me to watch them.*

Taking the keys and opening the closet, she picked out the video that Jordanna had handed to her the night before and put it into the VCR.

The television came to life, and Rebecca settled down on the couch. "Where in the hell do they get this God-awful music?" she muttered as the opening credits rolled. She fast-forwarded through the first few bump-and-grind sessions on the tape, and then caught sight of a familiar dark-haired woman on the screen and rolled it back a little. She sucked in her breath at the first sight of her lover on the screen. Jordanna didn't look any older than eighteen, her body slimmer, less filled-out than she was now.

It was a "women in prison" film, and Jordanna was one of the sexy young inmates. She watched as the warden of the prison, who looked about twenty-five years her senior, disciplined the young Jordanna by taking a paddle to her bare backside.

Rebecca could feel her body reacting as she watched her naked lover bump and grind with just about every actor and actress in the film, and then she thought about the drummer.

*This is this how you feel most of the day, isn't it, Jordanna?*

She watched it all the way to the closing credits, and decided a cold shower was definitely in order. She rewound the tape and had just put it back in the cabinet when she noticed that there were more tapes hidden behind the ones in the front. They each had different city names and dates marked on them, all in Jordanna's handwriting. She pulled out one labeled *Houston 8/27/96* and eased it out of its case, slipping it into the VCR. The first thing she heard was her lover's voice, telling whoever was in the room with her to get on the bed. She watched two women, one fair and one brunette, walk across the room and climb on the bed. She heard Jordanna's voice again, but didn't see her.

"Take her shirt off...slowly," Jordanna commanded. The blonde hesitated, but then did what the drummer asked her to do.

"Very good, ladies," the drummer purred. "Now, you do the same, and remember what I said; don't rush."

The brunette's hands were shaking as she unbuttoned her friend's blouse. Rebecca heard Jordanna's voice again. She spoke slowly and precisely, and a picture of her lover sitting in a

chair across from the bed formed in her mind. She pictured
Jordanna dressed in a shiny black rubber corset wearing spike
high heels and watching the two women pleasure each other,
whip in her hand, coiled and ready to strike.

*All they need to do is call her "Mistress."*

"You two have never fucked each other before, have you?"
the drummer asked.

Both women shook their heads "no."

"Mmm," the dark woman moaned. "Watching you fuck each
other for the first time will be a real treat for me, then. Now,
remove her bra, hook by hook. I want to see those luscious tits."

"You've got such a way with words, Jordanna," Rebecca said
out loud, as she sat staring at the television, trying to decide
whether she wanted to continue watching something that her
lover had taped for private viewing or not. She decided to
continue, curious to see if Jordanna ever showed herself on the
tape.

The brunette took her friend's bra off, and the camera
panned in for a close-up of the blonde's breasts. "Mmm, her tits
are beautiful, too. Now suck them," the drummer commanded
once again, and the brunette did as she said.

"Are you going to join us, Jordanna?" she asked, after doing
as Jordanna asked.

"If you're good girls and do as I say, I *might* join you. If you
want that, then don't disappoint me."

Rebecca was hoping that her lover hadn't joined them, for
obvious reasons, but a small part of her was hoping to see her in
the video. To see how she was with someone other than herself.
*God, that commanding voice is just* way *too sexy.* It was the voice
Jordanna had used the night she lost control. The confident,
soothing bedroom voice that had turned the reporter on to no
end, like it was doing to her now.

It was then that she heard another voice, a man's voice, on
the tape. Her eyes opened wide as a naked Gary got on the bed
with the two women, and smiled into the camera. Jordanna
instructed the brunette to pleasure the blonde at that point, and
the camera turned off. Rebecca was just about ready to turn the
video off after a minute or two of static, but then the camera
turned on again.

"You know the rules, Gary," the dark-haired woman purred.
*What rules?*

Gary grabbed his wallet, pulled out a condom, and handed it
to Jordanna, who proceeded to put it on him.

*Ah, okay, those rules.*

"Oh, Christ! She slept with Gary, too?" she said out loud as she sat looking at the scene on the screen. Her lover stood up to her full height and began to kiss him. His mouth started to stray down her neck, and then he took an attentive nipple in his mouth, as she sighed contently. She wrapped her body around the slightly shorter man and lifted her leg up high, taking all of him in easily. He grunted, and she let out a loud moan as he began to pump his manhood in her.

Rebecca felt like she wanted to throw up. She wondered why Jordanna never mentioned her relationship with Gary before. Was there a relationship? Would she jump back in bed with him as soon as she hit the road again? She heard Jordanna's low voice in her head.

*No, I wouldn't.*

She hoped that was true.

Rebecca practically jumped out of her skin when her cell phone rang. She turned the video off and ran into the sunroom to grab the phone. "Hello?"

"Got a pen?" Jim asked immediately, not bothering with the greetings. "Take this down. The bitch has quite a nice record. Did you know that her real name..."

"Is Julia Smith? Yes, I know that, Jim." *And don't call her a bitch.*

Jim sighed and murmured something about hoping that the reporter was not getting into something she couldn't handle. He wondered aloud just how close they had actually become. When she declined to respond, he turned to the records and began to read them for her.

She sat quietly at the desk and wrote what Jim was telling her, not really hearing what he was saying. He gave her brief details about each incident, mentioning that she was arrested for the first time at age twenty for possession of narcotics, and made some kind of comment about Jordanna's fetish for having sexual encounters with women in public places.

After she hung up the phone, she looked down at the words on the paper.

*Brentwood, NY: Arrested June 1989, possession of narcotics.*

*New Orleans, LA: Arrested February 1993, lewd behavior, assault on a police officer, resisting arrest.*

*San Diego, CA: Arrested May 1995, lewd behavior, indecent exposure, resisting arrest.*

*Miami, FL: Arrested August 1996, possession of narcotics, lewd behavior, disturbing the peace, resisting arrest.*

*Kansas City, KS: Arrested December 1997, disturbing the peace, destruction of private property, resisting arrest...*

# Chapter
# Nineteen

JORDANNA ADJUSTED THE headphones she was wearing and looked at her watch for the tenth time in five minutes. The disc jockey asked them questions about the tour and when they thought they would cut their next CD.

"I have half a dozen songs that I've been working on that I wrote while we were on the road," the dark-haired woman answered. "I know Linda has a few, too."

"But we're going to take a couple months off before we even think about going into the studio," Rachel interjected.

"Do you guys like touring?" the disc jockey asked.

"I like performing live," Rachel started to explain. "But I don't particularly care for long tours anymore, though."

Jordanna smiled at the disc jockey, because he knew her well and already knew her answer to the question. "I love touring," she said to the listening audience. "Although, I must admit I've been enjoying the break a lot."

The disc jockey cut to a commercial and walked out of the room. Rachel tried her best to control the smirk that was forming across her lips.

Jordanna raised her eyebrow at her. "What?" the drummer asked. "Why are you smirking like that?"

"'Cause someone's in love," Rachel said, chuckling.

Jordanna blushed. "Knock it off, Rachel."

The disc jockey walked back into the room. Ron Sutcliff was an old friend of the band, and one of the few men Jordanna had dated. "What did I miss?" he asked, noticing the mischievous look in Rachel's eyes and the blush on the drummer's face.

"Nothing," the drummer said.

"You chicken-shit," Rachel countered, shaking her head. "Tell him."

"What?" Ron's curiosity was definitely piqued.

"I met someone," Jordanna said shyly.

Ron looked at her like her hair was on fire. "Yeah, you meet a zillion women every day, so?"

"I think she's the one, Ron," she admitted.

Ron lifted up his hand, signaling that they were about to come out of commercials. "Hey, we're back at WNYX, and we'd like to thank our two very special guests for stopping by. Thanks Rachel, Jordanna. It's always a pleasure to have you guys with us, and we look forward to the three upcoming sold-out shows at the Coliseum."

"Thanks for having us," Jordanna responded as Ron queued a song from their first CD. After it began, he jumped out of his seat and crossed the room to talk to the drummer. "Did I hear you right, Jordanna Fox? You think you met the one?"

"Yeah, I do."

"Wow," the shocked man said. "Does she feel the same?"

"I think so. At least, I hope so."

Rachel flung a CD case at the drummer and shook her head. "H-e-l-l-o! Let's talk about clueless!" the bassist teased. "She feels the same about you, Jordanna; believe me. It's written all over her face every time she looks at you."

"That's wonderful, Jordanna. Although I have to say, I was kinda hoping for a reunion," Ron admitted. "But I'm so happy for you."

The drummer reached out and messed up the top of Ron's long, curly brown hair. "You know if I ever decided to marry a man it would be you, Ron."

"I know," he said, holding back a pleased smile. "But a guy can hope, can't he?"

Jordanna laughed and gave him a hug. "You'll like her, Ron. She's really great."

"There'll be a lot of women with broken hearts outside, you know. Most of them are waiting for you to come out."

The drummer kissed Ron on the cheek. "I better go let them down easy then. It was good seeing you again, Ron."

"Yeah, good luck, girlfriend. So, will I be invited to the wedding?"

Jordanna narrowed her eyes. "Wedding?" she asked, slightly confused. "Oh, of course. You can be my best man. See ya, Ron."

The drummer joined Rachel, who was already outside in the parking lot signing autographs and talking with their fans. Jordanna could feel the people immediately closing in around her, and for a brief moment she felt like she was being watched.

*I think I should take these threats more seriously.*

She shook her head and walked forward, heading toward

her Pathfinder. Rachel caught the look in her eyes. "Jordanna? You okay?"

"Yeah, I'm fine," she said as a young fan handed her a photo to sign. She looked down at the boy and asked him his name. *He has to be around the same age as Cindy,* she thought.

"Brian," he answered, giving her a big smile.

She smiled back, and the boy's mother asked her if she would pose for a photo with him.

"Sure," she answered. "Why don't you get someone else to take it and get in the photo too," Jordanna suggested. The woman handed another fan her camera and stood next to the drummer and her son.

"Thanks so much, Jordanna," the woman said after the picture had been taken.

They stood outside in front of the radio station for over an hour, making sure not to disappoint any of the fans that made the special trip out there to meet them. Jordanna turned down quite a few invitations from both male and female fans looking to get to know her better.

After they signed the last autograph, Rachel and Jordanna got into the Pathfinder. "He's a nice guy," the bassist said, watching Jordanna put her seatbelt on and adjust her seat.

"Huh? You mean Ron?"

Rachel nodded. "Yeah, he's a really great guy."

"Yeah, he is," the drummer agreed.

"Why did you date him, Jordanna?" Rachel asked. "I mean...you knew you were gay, but you dated him anyway."

"He's a lot of fun to be around, Rache. I told him right from the start that I'm a lesbian, but he said he was okay with it. We had a really good time together, but it was more like two friends going out and not romantically, you know?" the drummer explained.

"Sorta like the way you and Gary are?"

"No," the drummer answered immediately. "My relationship with Ron is, was, absolutely nothing like that."

"Did you sleep with him?"

Jordanna raised a brow. "Which him?"

"Ron, you idiot! Everyone knows about the arrangements you and Gary have."

*Arrangements? That's a polite way of saying it.* "What arrangements?" the drummer asked, interested in what was being said about her relationship with her drum tech.

"Well, it's no secret that you guys go out cruisin' together, if you know what I mean."

"I know what you mean, Rachel. And? What about it?"

"Rumor has it that you and Gary will share the same woman sometimes."

Jordanna smirked. "Yeah, so?"

"So you and Gary have slept together, in a way..."

The drummer rolled her eyes. "Christ, Rachel, let's talk about beating around the bush. Yes, Gary and I have done the dirty, if that's what you want to know." She shook her head. "Ron and I came close, a lot of foreplay, but we never went all the way. I knew he deserved better than what I could give him, so I couldn't go through with it."

"You? You couldn't go through with it?" Rachel laughed. "Speaking of that subject, I'm very proud of you."

"Huh? Why?"

"'Cause I thought I might have had to take a taxi home with all the invitations you got today."

"Yeah, well," Jordanna stammered, feeling the blush begin to build.

"You've got it bad, Jordanna," the bassist teased.

Jordanna revved up the engine and pulled out of the parking lot. "Think I should take Sunrise Highway all the way home? There're so many lights on the highway out here."

"Okay, I get your hint. Subject is closed," the bassist said.

Jordanna reached over and pulled her cell phone out of the glove compartment. "Do you mind if I make a phone call?"

Rachel grabbed the phone from her. "You drive, I'll dial. What's the number?"

"My house."

Rachel dialed Jordanna's home number, listened to see if it went through, and then handed the phone to the tall woman.

Rebecca answered the phone on the third ring. "Hello?"

"Hi."

Jordanna could hear the smile on Rebecca's face. "Checking up on me, Jor?"

"You know it, baby."

"Everything is just fine, Mom, so stop worrying. Are you on your way home?"

"Yeah, we just left. I should be home in a little over an hour. Any progress on your article?"

Rebecca frowned and hesitated a bit. She hated lying to her lover. "Yeah, I'm making headway."

*She's watching the videos, I can tell.*

"Good, I'm glad. I wouldn't want my being such a distraction to interfere with your work," the drummer teased as the red light they were sitting at turned green. "I better go, baby. I'll see you soon."

"I'll be waiting here for you. I love you."

Jordanna turned her head, leaning as close as she could to the driver's-side window. "I love you, too," she whispered softly, then pressed the end button on the phone and turned off the power. She handed it back to Rachel. "Can you put that back for me?"

Rachel laughed and put the phone away. "You know I should, by all rights, tease the hell out of you right now, Jordanna."

"But you won't," the drummer said dryly. "Unless you *really* feel like walking the rest of the way home."

"No, can't say I feel like doing that. It's kind of far."

As they drove along the highway, Jordanna noticed a bunch of kids running on the track of a high school that was visible from the road. It made her think about the accusations that Tracey had made about her when they went to the diner. "Rache?"

"Yeah?"

"Do you remember Laura Erickson from Hauppauge High?" the dark-haired woman asked.

Rachel scratched her head and turned to look at Jordanna. "Tracey's oldest sister?"

"Did you know that she died?"

"Mmm, yeah. She died of AIDS, right? Not long after you took off, if I remember correctly. Why?"

"Because I just found out about it last night. How come you didn't tell me about it?"

"I figured you knew already, since you and Tracey were so close. How did you find out?"

Jordanna snorted. "We visited the old neighborhood last night on the way back from Rebecca's apartment. We went to the diner."

"Nirvana?" Rachel asked, excitement in her voice. "Wow, I haven't been there in years. Is the food still as good as it used to be?"

"I wouldn't know; we never got the chance to eat anything there."

"Why? What happened?"

"The Ericksons just happen to own the place now," the dark woman answered. "Tracey's a waitress."

"You've got to be kidding me! What happened when she saw you?"

Jordanna sighed at the thought. "Let's just say that she wasn't very happy to see me," the drummer said, and quickly ran her free hand through her inky black hair. "She pretty much blamed me for what happened to Laura."

"Why would she think that?" Rachel asked, and then thought further. "Oh, shit, Jordanna! You didn't?"

"C'mon, Rachel! I had *nothing* to do with her death, but apparently when she ran off it was to find me."

Rachel had never known the whole story behind Jordanna's mysterious disappearance when she left home at fifteen. She was curious, as all of Jordanna's friends had been, but not one of them had the guts to question the moody drummer about it. When someone actually did find the nerve to question her, she gave vague answers as to why she left and where she went during that time period. Her mother simply told anyone who asked that her daughter ran away.

"I guess something happened between you and Laura," Rachel said, wondering if Jordanna would actually supply her with the answer to that.

"Yeah, you could say that."

Rachel had to laugh to herself. "Mmm, so Rebecca heard the conversation that you had with Tracey?"

Jordanna nodded. "Yep." She opened the window for some fresh air. "I feel bad because I took my anger out on her, and she had absolutely nothing to do with it."

"You didn't hit her or anything?"

"Oh, God, no! I was just acting like a complete bitch," the dark-haired woman responded.

A smile formed on Rachel's face. "You mean you were acting like your usual self?"

"Yeah, I guess. She kept asking me all kinds of questions, and I'm just not used to that so I kinda lost my temper. I know that she does it because she cares, but I'm just not used to people caring for me like that. You all know how hard it is for me to let someone in. I want nothing more than to be able to let down my guard with her, Rache; I really do. I just don't know how to explain that to her."

"Explain it exactly the way you just did, Jordanna."

"Yeah?"

"Yeah."

The drummer wasn't lying about her hatred of driving on Sunrise Highway. "Shit, we were catching all the green lights there for a while." She slowed the Pathfinder down to stop at a red light. "Hey, do you mind if we stop at this shopping center for a few minutes?" Jordanna asked, noticing a florist there.

Rachel opened her window for some air. "Nope, I don't mind."

The drummer pulled into a parking spot right in front of the florist, put the Pathfinder in park, and climbed out of the vehicle. "I'll be right back."

Rachel watched as Jordanna walked into the florist, amazed at the change in the dark-haired woman. She would never in a million years have imagined that anything could make the drummer want to settle down, but it seemed like her relationship with Rebecca had done just that.

Jordanna walked out of the florist with a stuffed teddy bear in one hand and a dozen red roses in the other. As far as Rachel knew, the drummer had never given any of her female friends anything, except her body, a couple of hours of her time, and then an escort to the door. But something romantic?

Forget about it.

The drummer opened the door, put her purchases in the back, and then slid into the driver's seat. "Not a word from you," she said right away, having noticed the huge grin on her friend's face.

"You love her," Rachel said.

Jordanna smiled at the thought, and it lit up her whole face. "I now know what love feels like, Rachel, and it feels so right. I love her more than anything."

Rachel put her hand on top of Jordanna's, patting it in a friendly manner. "I'm really happy for you, Jordanna. You deserve it."

Jordanna rolled her eyes and laughed.

"No, I'm serious, Jordanna. Everyone needs love in her life. Lust is fine, but it doesn't make you feel complete like love does."

"Yeah, I'm learning that," the drummer admitted. "I never understood that before, but now I do."

"You know, Jordanna, it's really nice to be able to talk to you like this. I feel like the woman that I once knew is working hard to find her way back. I guess I'll have to thank Rebecca for that when I see her."

"I guess you will," the dark-haired woman said quietly.

They both sat silent for a while, thinking about what had just been said.

"Jordanna?"

"Yeah?"

"That teddy bear is so-o-o-o cute." Rachel laughed out loud.

"Shut up, Rachel."

# Chapter
# Twenty


REBECCA CHECKED THE time and shut off the video she was watching.

*God Jordanna, what are you doing to me? I've never seen so many naked people in my life as I have since I met you.*

Figuring that Jordanna would be home soon, she rewound the tape and put it back in the cabinet where she had found it. "She's home," she murmured when she heard the garage door opening.

Rebecca quickly ran into the sunroom, picked up a book, and crawled up on the couch. She heard the front door opening and footsteps in the foyer.

Walking through the door, Jordanna looked down at the teddy bear in her hand and began to feel like a schoolgirl with her first crush. *Am I really giving this to her?*

*Yeah, I am.* "Rebecca?"

"In the sunroom," the reporter called out.

Jordanna walked to the sunroom, standing half in and half out of the room, holding the bear and flowers behind her back. "Hi."

Rebecca looked up from the book that she was pretending to read. "Hey, how'd the interview go?"

"Good," the drummer answered. "Did ya hear it?"

"Why are you standing there like that?"

Jordanna felt her face flush as she walked into the room. "I, um, picked you up a little something." She handed Rebecca the flowers and the teddy bear.

"Oh, Jordanna! He's so adorable!" The reporter took the bear in her hands and hugged him close. "And the flowers are beautiful. Thank you."

Jordanna kneeled down on the floor next to her lover. "Not half as beautiful as you are, Rebecca," she said, taking the reporter's hand and kissing it. "I love you with all my heart, and

I just wanted to make sure that you knew that."

Rebecca's eyes saddened as she thought about how she had just looked into the drummer's past life, her private life, behind her back.

Jordanna didn't miss the look. "What's wrong, Rebecca? Did I say, do, something wrong?"

The reporter put her hand on the drummer's cheek. "No, honey, *you* did everything right." Tears streamed down her face. "*I* did everything wrong."

Jordanna pulled Rebecca into her arms, questioning her with her eyes. "I don't understand, Rebecca. What could you possibly have done wrong?"

"I...when you were gone I watched some of the videos in that cabinet. I found the ones you had hidden, the home movies, Jordanna," Rebecca said, feeling completely embarrassed. She looked up, waiting for her lover to react, and saw that Jordanna was smiling.

*Smiling?*

"Jordanna? Did you hear what I said?"

"Yeah." The dark-haired woman wiped the tears off of Rebecca's face with her thumb. "I heard what you said. Rebecca, why do you think I left the keys there?"

"You *wanted* me to watch them?"

"Yes."

"Why? Now I don't understand. I mean, I'm glad you're not mad that I watched them, but I don't get it."

Jordanna kissed her on the forehead. "You know it's hard for me to say how I feel, Rebecca, and it's very hard for me to talk about myself. You had so many questions, and I figured if you saw those films some of them might be answered." She shook her head and closed her eyes. "I honestly didn't know how you would feel after you saw them, though. Some of the earlier ones... I didn't always join in on the action and, um, you mentioned self-satisfaction the other night and, well, I..."

The reporter found Jordanna's rambling adorable. "I understand, Jordanna. You don't have to say any more." Rebecca smiled and leaned forward once again, this time to place a light kiss on the dark-haired woman's lips.

"Mmm," the drummer moaned into her lover's mouth.

"Jordanna?" the reporter said, breaking the kiss.

"Hmm?"

"That wasn't the only thing I did while you were gone." Rebecca could feel her heart begin to pound. Even she was angry with herself for contacting Jim about Jordanna's past. She couldn't even imagine how her lover was going to feel about it.

"Yeah? What else did you do?" the drummer asked, with a look of mischief in her eyes.

Rebecca got up and looked out the window at the crashing waves, wanting nothing more than to throw herself into them. "I have a friend."

Jordanna laughed. "Okay?"

"He's a private investigator," the reporter continued, her back still turned to her lover.

Jordanna's smile quickly faded. "And?"

"I called him and had him do a background check on you," the reporter admitted.

The drummer was up and by Rebecca's side in a flash, turning her around so she could look at her. "What? Why? What kind of check, Rebecca?"

Rebecca felt tears falling again and wanted to control them but couldn't. "Medical history, police record, the works."

Jordanna closed her eyes. She could feel her body starting to shake in anger and fear. "Why did you do that?"

"Because I wanted to know."

"You could've just asked me," the drummer said, visibly upset.

"I tried to ask you the other night, and you got mad at me, Jordanna. I'm sorry, I was wrong. I shouldn't have done it."

Jordanna couldn't argue with that; she did get angry at all the questioning. "So, what did you find out?"

"A lot, actually."

"You know I've been arrested, I take it," the drummer said, a little bit of sarcasm in her voice.

"Yes."

"Do you know *exactly* what happened?"

"No."

"Do you want to know?"

"Yes."

The drummer grabbed Rebecca by the arm a little more forcefully than she should have and sat her down on the couch. "Stay there," she said, and walked over to the same spot Rebecca had been standing in and looked out the window.

Jordanna stood quietly for a while and then spoke. "I got arrested for possession when I worked for Dre." She cleared her throat. "I had to spend four months in prison for that, Rebecca." She paused. "I actually was sent to jail for six months, but I got out after four for good behavior."

"You spent time in prison?"

"Yes, I did." Jordanna turned around and looked at her quiet lover, who was looking at the carpeted floor. "Then I was arrested again in New Orleans."

"Tell me about that arrest, please."

Jordanna sat down on the couch next to her. "Have you ever been to New Orleans during Mardi Gras?"

"No," the reporter answered.

"Well, it's one big fucking party. Drinking, drugs, sex. You name it, it's happening there."

"That I know. Go on," Rebecca said.

"Right before we got our recording contract, we did a little tour that took us down south. It happened to be when Mardi Gras was going on." Jordanna stopped and sighed. "One night after an early show, Gary and I went to this bar to have a few drinks. Gary's originally from New Orleans so he knows all of the hot spots there. Anyway, we met these two women, and they were really into the spirit of the festivities." She paused again, her mind going back to the events. "Do you really want me to continue, Rebecca?"

"Yes, I do, but speaking of Gary, can I ask you something?"

Jordanna narrowed her eyes at the sound of the younger woman's voice. "Sure, what?"

"Why didn't you tell me you two were together?"

Jordanna burst out laughing. "Gary and I were *never* together!"

"But I saw you with him on a video, Jordanna!"

The drummer put her hand on Rebecca's knee and gave it a quick squeeze. "We're only friends, Rebecca. Every once in a while we'd have sex, but that's it. Nothing more."

"Ah, okay." *A day in the life of Jordanna Fox.* "Continue what you were telling me before, please."

The drummer sighed. "Okay. So anyway, to keep up with the Mardi Gras tradition, Gary decided to ask these two women to show us their, um..."

"Tits," Rebecca offered.

"Yeah, he asked them to do that. Some women will oblige and others won't. These two were more than happy to oblige." She looked into Rebecca's eyes and saw uneasiness there. "Are you okay?"

"Yeah, I'm fine," Rebecca answered, and then rubbed her head. "Why do you do that?"

"Do what?"

"You get embarrassed saying words like *tits* in front of me when you had no problem saying that, or even worse words, to those women in the video I watched."

"You're *not* one of those women, Rebecca. You're my lover and my best friend. I respect you more than that."

"Oh," Rebecca said quietly and looked down. *Well, that's good to know.* "Please, do continue, lover."

Jordanna sat silently for a second, wondering if Rebecca was being sarcastic or not. "We bought them a few drinks and, by that time, I was shit-faced and feeling no pain, so I asked the one woman to show me her tits," she said, getting the word out with little hesitation. She let out a little laugh and blushed slightly.

"Okay." She started again after she regained her composure. "I asked her to show me them again, and she did. This time, I couldn't control myself and I..."

"You what, Jordanna?"

"I suc—kissed them right there at the bar. She responded to what I was doing and that only got me going more. I picked her up and walked over to the pool table and laid her down on it. I lifted her miniskirt up, knowing full well she didn't have any panties on, and I went down on her right there in front of everybody in the bar."

"Holy shit, Jordanna!" Rebecca knew she shouldn't have been shocked by this revelation, but she was. "Right in front of everybody?"

"Everybody," Jordanna confirmed. The drummer felt her heart pounding, almost as if it were going to take off and fly right out of her chest. "The people in the bar were cheering and going wild. They were *really* into it, and, to be honest, so was I." She closed her eyes.

"What about the woman?"

"She didn't protest, Rebecca. She begged me to keep doing it."

"So then how did you get arrested?"

"A couple of off-duty cops happened to walk in as it was happening. The next thing I knew, they had me on the ground and I was fighting with them. I punched one of the cops in the face. Gary was fighting with the other cop."

"Resisting arrest."

"Yeah, and assault, amongst a whole slew of other offenses."

"That's stupid."

"You're not kidding."

"Were you the only one that got arrested?"

"No, Gary and the woman I was with got arrested, too. I called home and had my lawyer post bail for all of us."

"Oh." The reporter wondered where, exactly, Jordanna could possibly have obtained the money to post all of their bail before the band had their recording contract. She kept her thoughts to herself.

"Do you want to know about the other times I got arrested?"

"Yes. No. Yes, I think."

Jordanna smirked a bit at Rebecca's answer. "You know Aerosmith's song 'Love in an Elevator'?"

Rebecca couldn't help but laugh. "You didn't?"

Jordanna nodded. "I did. That's why we had to stay at a different hotel in San Diego on this tour, not that you would've known that, though. We've, or should I say I've, been banned from that hotel for life."

"What if a little kid tried to get on the elevator?"

"At that point of my life I didn't give a shit who was getting on as long as I was getting off," Jordanna admitted dryly.

Rebecca put her hand on her lover's arm. "What about now?"

The drummer's eyes narrowed questioningly. "What do you mean?"

"I mean, would you give a shit now that you've met me and my daughter? If you had Cindy with you and went to get on an elevator and there were two women — or anyone — doing what you did, would you care at all?"

*I guess I deserve this question, don't I?* "I would want to beat the living shit out of them, Rebecca." Jordanna looked her lover directly in the eyes. "I wouldn't do most of the things I used to do now that I've met you."

"That's good to hear," Rebecca responded. "Miami?"

Jordanna took a deep breath. "Got caught by the ocean one night. I thought sex on the beach and marijuana were legal in Miami," the drummer teased. "Apparently they're not."

Rebecca smiled at that. "What about the last arrest in Kansas around a year ago? Why on earth did you trash a hotel room?"

The dark-haired woman got up and walked quietly back to the window. "I didn't," she whispered.

"You didn't trash the hotel? Then what? I don't understand."

Jordanna didn't speak for a minute. "It was a cover-up, Rebecca."

The reporter stood up, walked over to her lover, and placed a warm hand on the drummer's shoulder.

"I was in the hotel lounge one afternoon when I met these two women that were vacationing there," the drummer began. She turned around, looked at her lover and let the tears she was holding in begin to fall. "At least, that's who I thought they were."

"What do you mean?"

"It turned out that they weren't vacationing there. They

were locals, just waiting for Jordanna Fox to show up in town."

Rebecca narrowed her eyes at the dark-haired woman. "You lost me here, love. Can you fill in the blanks a little?"

"Okay, I met these women in the lounge. We had a few drinks, did a lot of flirting, and I ended up inviting them to my room." She closed her eyes. "I had sex with both of them."

Rebecca swallowed the lump in her throat, moved off to the side, and leaned up against the wall where Jordanna was standing to listen to what the tall woman had to say.

The drummer sighed heavily and began the rest of the tale. "The next afternoon, as we're leaving the hotel for our sound check a policeman steps in front of me and slams me against the wall. Then he proceeds to handcuff my arms behind my back and starts to read me my rights.

"I had no idea why I was being arrested," she continued. "I was totally embarrassed; everyone was standing around watching. Apparently there was a photographer lurking around somewhere because there were photos of me being led to the police car in handcuffs all over the papers the next day.

"When we arrived at the police station, I saw the two women that I told you about there with their families. This small woman, who I assumed was the mother of one of the girls that I had sex with, came flying towards me, knocked me into the wall, and slapped me hard across the face." Fresh tears started to fall down the dark-haired woman's cheeks. "That's when it hit me what I was being arrested for."

Rebecca knew by the tears that the drummer was shedding that this was not an easy story for her to tell. She put her hand on her lover's arm. "Jor, honey?"

"One of them was a minor."

*Oh, God.*

"I was arrested for statutory rape."

Rebecca felt her world come crashing down on her. She knew her lover was by no means an angel, but for Jordanna to be arrested for rape, well, that was something she never wanted, or expected, to hear from the woman that she shared a bed with, the woman that she gave her heart to.

The woman that owned the other half of her soul.

The admission plunged Rebecca into a darkness she had never experienced before, a darkness that she knew she had to walk through with Jordanna in order for the both of them to survive.

The reporter felt her legs start to give out and she grabbed onto a small table, the closest piece of furniture she could find. Jordanna took her by the arm and walked Rebecca to the couch, helping the unsteady young woman into a sitting position before returning to the spot where she was originally standing in front of the window.

"Rebecca, I *didn't know* she was under age."

"How old was she?"

The drummer didn't answer her.

"How old, Jordanna?" the reporter repeated forcefully.

"Fifteen."

"*Fifteen*? Jesus Christ, Jordanna, you slept with a child!"

The drummer crossed the room with the speed of a cheetah, bent down, and grabbed Rebecca by the arms. "Goddammit! Don't you think I know that, Rebecca? Do you think a day has gone by since then that I've forgotten that I fucked a fifteen-year-old?" she hissed, her voice cracking with emotion. She looked into the terrified eyes of her lover, let go of the reporter's arms, and stood up straight, making her way back to the spot in front of the window once again. "I'm sorry."

Rebecca looked up at her with an angry, yet frightened, look in her eyes. "So, what happened? Shouldn't you be rotting in jail right now?"

The comment felt like a blazing arrow ripping straight through the drummer's heart. "Yes, I should be rotting in jail right now." *For more things than just this, Rebecca.*

Rebecca got up and walked over to the drummer. "I'm sorry. I didn't mean that the way it sounded."

"Yes, you did mean it," the drummer said sadly. "And I should, by all rights, be in jail right now. Luckily for me, I'm a rich woman that can afford the fast-talking, expensive lawyers. After they arrested me, the girl admitted to the police that she lied to me about her age. She told me she was twenty-three."

"That still doesn't make it right," Rebecca said angrily. "Besides, you really believed that a fifteen-year-old was twenty-three?"

"Yes, I did believe it, Rebecca," Jordanna said, defending herself. "I figured if she was in the bar she had to be over at least eighteen, right?" the drummer admitted, and walked back to the couch to sit down. "Rebecca, have you seen the young girls these days? She might have been fifteen, but she had a body of a thirty-year-old." She closed her eyes, envisioning the beautiful young girl writhing under her body in ecstasy. "And when she offered me that body, I took it. I didn't force myself on her, though."

The reporter stood looking straight ahead, her hazel eyes void of any emotion. A tear slid down her face.

"My lawyers," the drummer continued, "convinced the

girl's family to settle out of court. The deal was that they'd drop the charges and forget it ever happened if I paid them an obscene amount of money."

"I take it they are a rich family right now."

The drummer nodded solemnly. "Yes, they are."

"What about the district attorney? Wouldn't they want to bring you up on the charges even if the family dropped them?"

"The former DA is now a rich man also, Rebecca. And it's funny how, if a little money is involved, the records of the actual charge can change to a different one, just like that," Jordanna said, snapping her fingers as if making something disappear. "Our judicial system really is a joke, if you think about it." She looked up at her lover, who looked as if she didn't know if she should stay in the house with her, or if she should run as far and as fast as she could. "I'm not proud of what I did, you know."

Rebecca sighed heavily. "I never thought that you were. It's just..." she stopped and sighed again.

"It's just what?"

Rebecca sat back down on the couch next to the tall woman. "I really don't understand how you could continue to sleep around after that as if nothing ever happened."

The dark-haired woman turned her body on the couch so she was facing her lover. "I continued sleeping around because I couldn't stop," she said quietly, in a voice filled with emotion. "Can you understand that?"

Rebecca got up and walked to the window again, looking out at the sea to escape the intense blue gaze of her lover. "I do understand, Jordanna."

"You're free to go, you know. I can certainly understand it if you don't want to continue to share a bed with a rapist." Jordanna watched as Rebecca's body stiffened, and small shudders ran down her own spine. "Just because I told you I loved you doesn't mean you have to stay with me," she continued. The drummer cleared her throat, removing all traces of emotion from her voice. "I know sometimes love just isn't enough."

The moment of truth had come, and Rebecca realized that she was going to have to learn, and learn really fast, what the term *tough love* actually meant.

They had discussed, albeit very briefly, the drummer seeking help for her addiction. Jordanna agreed, after the night she'd lost control with Rebecca, that therapy would be the best direction for her to go, but they hadn't discussed it since.

Today was the day that Jordanna would have to decide whether to shit or get off the pot.

The reporter tore her gaze away from the ocean and turned to look into the tear-stained face of her lover, who was rocking back and forth on the couch with her head in her hands. Rebecca walked over and kneeled on the floor in front of the drummer, taking the tall woman's hands in her own. "You know I love you more than anything, right?"

Jordanna lifted her sad blue eyes to meet sad, yet compassionate, hazel ones. "Yes."

"Do you love me?"

"More than life itself."

"You have a decision to make then, love."

"I know I do, baby."

Jordanna sat back down on the couch, and Rebecca climbed onto her lap and leaned her head on the dark-haired woman's shoulder. "You know I'll be here for you, supporting you all the way, right?" the reporter whispered into the tall woman's ear.

"I know you will."

"You also know the only way we will be able to have a future together is if you get help, Jordanna."

"Rebecca..."

"No, Jor, please don't start this again. I just told you how I felt about you. I don't think I'm asking for much. Are you willing to get help or not?"

"Yes," the drummer said quietly as she watched two seagulls picking at something in the sand. "I'll do whatever it takes, Rebecca."

The reporter smiled and kissed the drummer on her tear-streaked cheek. "Jordanna?"

"Hmm?"

"I think you were set up."

"Set up?"

"By that girl and her family. A quick and easy way to become rich, you know?"

Jordanna chuckled slightly, and Rebecca looked up at her. "I'm sorry, it's not funny. It's just that I said the same thing as I was going back and forth to the lawyer's office all those days. I told my lawyer what I thought, and he told me I should just leave well enough alone since they had agreed to drop the charges."

"Jerry told me to keep my mouth shut about it too, in a threatening sort of way," she added. "He told me to consider it a learning experience and that I had better start thinking with my head and not with my pussy; otherwise something like that would be bound to happen again."

Rebecca found herself snuggling tighter in the dark

woman's embrace, not understanding the serious need to be in Jordanna's comforting arms, especially after what she just learned about the drummer.

*Am I going to be able to make love with her now without thinking of that young girl?*

"Jor?"

"Mmm?"

"I think you were enticed and made a very bad decision that day, and paid for it. I believe you when you say that you thought she was twenty-three. You have never given me a reason not to believe you."

The dark-haired woman blinked, and her top lip twitched. "Rebecca?"

"Mmm?"

"Thank you for being who you are." The dark-haired woman placed a kiss on the top of her lover's golden hair. "And for believing in me. Lord knows I don't deserve it, but thank you, anyway."

# Chapter
# Twenty-one

THE SOUNDS OF music caressed the reporter's ears like a lover. Rebecca dressed quickly and made her way down to Jordanna's studio. She could hear a soft acoustic tune that was familiar to her coming from behind the closed studio doors.

She waited for the song to finish and then pushed the door open gently. She heard Linda's voice first. "That's about Rebecca, isn't it?"

Rebecca looked at the drummer, who was sitting on a stool with her guitar in her lap, and smiled as their eyes met. She waited for Jordanna's answer.

"Yeah, it's about Rebecca."

"You know it's a chart-topper, Jordanna," Linda commented. "You should have fallen in love a long time ago."

Jordanna shifted her gaze from her lover to Linda. "I know it has potential. As far as me falling in love...well, a lot of things would have been different if I'd met Rebecca years ago." She whispered softly, "A lot of things."

"I know what Rache and Kelly will think, but what do you think of the song, Rebecca?" the guitarist asked, knowing Rebecca was standing behind her by watching the drummer's eyes.

"Yeah, what do you think, baby?" Jordanna asked, hoping that Rebecca truly liked it. It hadn't been a hard song for her to write. The words had come quickly for her, and it practically wrote itself. Yet, on the other hand, it was a difficult song to write because it couldn't come close to conveying how she truly felt about the reporter.

Rebecca walked over to the drummer and wrapped her arms around her, almost knocking her off of the stool. "Do you really feel that way about me?"

Jordanna smiled. "With all of my heart, baby."

Rebecca could feel tears coming to her eyes. "I don't know what to say, Jordanna. I love it. It's the most beautiful song I've ever heard."

"I was hoping you'd like it."

Rebecca laughed. "Like there was any doubt?" She kissed her lover gently on the forehead. "What's it called?"

"I'm not 100% sure yet, but I think 'The Other Half' is a pretty appropriate title for it." The drummer shrugged her shoulders. "Or maybe something with your name in it."

Linda offered her idea for a title. "How about '*Rebecca's Song*'?"

Jordanna nodded her head and pursed her lips, seriously considering that title. "I like that one a lot," she said, and walked over to Rebecca and ruffled the top of her hair. "I think that one's a keeper."

Rebecca looked up. "You wouldn't dare?"

"Sure I would," the drummer answered with a chuckle.

Jordanna and Linda spent another hour or so trading songs back and forth. They were both pleased with what they had heard so far, and Rebecca enjoyed seeing the creative process in action.

Linda packed her guitar up, and Rebecca saw her to her car before returning to the house with plans to finish the article that had brought the two lovers together in the first place. Jordanna, revved up and ready from the good practice session, decided to get behind the drums and practice a bit more to keep her stick work in shape.

The reporter found it difficult to concentrate on her article when her lover was in her studio behind her drums. She got up, followed the sound through the house until she found her destination, and stood in the door to watch her lover play. Rebecca watched in amazement as the drummer's hands crossed over each other in different patterns without missing a beat and without ever opening her eyes.

"Hey, where'd you just go, baby? You were out of it for a minute there," the drummer said with a chuckle.

"I-I, you..." Rebecca stammered as her eyes digested the body standing in front of her. "God, Jordanna, you look so sexy all sweaty like that," she said, running her hands along the drummer's moist biceps, feeling the heat radiating off of her lover's skin.

"What are you doing?" the drummer asked, as Rebecca's fingers made their way under her tank top.

"What do you think I'm doing?" the reporter whispered in her ear.

"And here I was afraid that you wouldn't want me to touch you after I told you about Kansas," she smirked.

The reporter kissed her on the cheek and then moved down to Jordanna's neck, sucking gently. "You worry too much sometimes."

Jordanna backed away slowly. "C'mon, Rebecca! You know I have that appointment that *you* made for me with the therapist in a little over an hour to discuss my sexual habits. Do you think I'll make a good impression going in there with a hickey and smelling of sex?"

"It would prove a point," Rebecca said, her eyes full of laughter. "And speaking of points," she teased, tugging on her lover's nipples through the cotton tank top she was wearing.

"Stop that!" Jordanna smacked her hands away. "As much as I want to throw you over my shoulder, lay you down on my bed, and make mad, passionate love with you, Rebecca, I can't right now."

"Oh, all right," Rebecca pouted. "You are already on the road to recovery. You just aren't supposed to have willpower against *my* advances."

Jordanna laughed and ran her hand along the reporter's backside. "Don't worry, I'll make it up to you later. Actually, um, do you want to go out tonight? Like on a date?"

"A date?"

"Yeah, we could get something to eat and then go out to a movie or dancing or something. Whatever you want."

"Dinner and dancing sounds like fun to me, but I still don't have anything to wear," the reporter said, pointing to the drummer's old sweatshirt she was wearing.

"We could go shopping in town after my appointment," Jordanna suggested. "There's a couple of trendy stores right on Main Street in Bridgehampton, not far from the doctor's office."

"Okay," Rebecca agreed. "Sounds like a plan to me."

"MS. FOX? COME with me, please."

Both women stood to follow the white-coated woman. The doctor's assistant put her hand on Rebecca's shoulder. "You can't go in there."

Jordanna turned and looked at the woman, controlling her temper. "I *want* her in there with me."

Just then, the doctor, a woman in her early forties, walked out of her office. "Ms. Fox? I'm Dr. Rosen. I would like to talk to you alone for a few minutes first, and then your friend can come in."

Rebecca shrugged and sat back down in the waiting room, retrieving the magazine she had been reading. She watched her lover follow the doctor into her office.

Jordanna looked around the doctor's office, noticing a bookshelf in the far corner of the room. She laughed to herself as she realized more than ten copies of the book *I'm Okay, You're Okay* adorned the shelf. She sat down in the seat across from the doctor and linked her fingers together, waiting for the woman to speak.

The doctor sat reading a file that Jordanna assumed was her own. She watched as the woman pushed the glasses perched at the tip of her nose back up. "So, Ms. Fox," she began.

"Jordanna, please."

"Okay, Jordanna. Can I ask you why you are here today?"

*Oh, shit, here we go. Get me the hell out of here.* The drummer shifted uncomfortably in her seat. "I have a problem and I need help."

"What kind of a problem?"

"An addiction."

"To what?"

Jordanna rubbed her temple and sighed. "To sex."

"I see. What do you hope to obtain by coming to these sessions, Jordanna?"

"Recovery, salvation, I don't know," the drummer said, feeling close to surpassing her tolerance level already.

The doctor wrote a few notes down on the form in the drummer's folder and then looked up again. "Why do you think you are addicted to sex, Jordanna?"

*Argh!* "Because," she said, speaking slowly, "it dominates my life. Because I can't get enough of it. Because nothing ever satisfies me. Because I can't stand myself anymore."

"Jordanna, tell me about yourself, please. What exactly is your occupation?"

The drummer rolled her eyes. "I'm a musician."

The doctor looked up again. "I thought you looked familiar. I think my son has a poster of you hanging up on his wall."

Jordanna shrugged. "It's possible."

Dr. Rosen sat forward in her seat. "Ms. Fox. — Jordanna — do you ever engage in sex with your fans?"

"Yes, mostly."

The doctor scribbled more notes. "I see. I always thought it was the female groupies that were more forward than the males, but I guess that's just another myth."

"No, it's not a myth. They are much, much more forward," Jordanna confirmed, noticing the questioning look in the doctor's eyes. "The answer to the question you are thinking right now is *yes*."

The woman got up from her seat and sat down in the chair

next to the drummer.    "And what was I thinking about, Jordanna?"

The drummer had to bite the inside of her mouth to control the little smirk that wanted to work its way across her lips.  She could see that she made the doctor a bit uncomfortable, and for some reason that was exactly the way she liked it.  Jordanna leaned forward and whispered.  "Whether I sleep with women or not."

The doctor rose quickly and returned to her seat.  "Well. I see."  She focused her attention on the paper in the drummer's file again and cleared her throat.  "What made you come to the conclusion you had a problem?"   She looked up, her face a careful mask.  "And that you needed to get help for it?"

"It's not a what, but a who, that helped me come to the conclusion," the drummer replied, thinking of her lover.  "The woman that is sitting out in the waiting room is the person who, shall we say, opened my eyes.  Which, by the way, can she come in here with me now?"

The doctor tapped her pencil on her desk.  "Who is she in relation to you, Jordanna?"

"She's my lover."

"Oh, I see.  You might not want your lover in here for the next part of this.  I'll be asking you questions regarding your behavior — things you've done in the past.  Some of it might not be pleasant for her to hear."

Jordanna shook her head.  "I understand that. The thing is, I want to be able to make a commitment to her, and I know the only way to do that is to be truthful with her.  I did a lot of things in my past, and I'd rather her find out now here, while she's with me, than find out from someone or somewhere else. We need to go through this together."

The doctor picked up her phone.  She pressed a button, and her assistant's perky voice came over the phone.

"Yes, Doctor?"

"Brenda, have Ms. Fox's friend come in here now, please," the doctor requested.

The two women heard a quick knock on the door, and then the reporter stepped into the office.  The doctor motioned for her to sit on the empty seat next to her lover.  "Have a seat, Ms...."

"Rebecca," the reporter said.  "Thank you."

"Well," the doctor said as she pulled a file out of one of her desk drawers.  She pulled out a form that reminded the drummer of pop quizzes in high school.  "Rebecca, it is not normal policy to have anyone but the patient in with me so early in our sessions, but Jordanna really wants your support in this.  As I just told Jordanna, I need her to answer some very personal questions so I can determine how I can help her in her recovery."

Rebecca nodded. "I understand that."

"If you have any comments or questions, you need to wait until the questioning is over, okay?" the doctor asked.

Rebecca nodded once again. "I'll keep any comments I have to myself for now."

The doctor spoke. "Jordanna, please try to answer these as honestly as possible. You will only be lying to yourself if you don't. Most of these are yes or no answers. I won't hit you with the deep talks just yet," the doctor said, and cracked a quick smile.

The reporter held out her hand for the drummer to take, showing her that she was there to support her. Jordanna took her hand and smiled.

"Okay, let's begin," the doctor said, picking up her pencil. "Do you own any pornographic movies?"

"Yes."

"Pornographic magazines or books?"

"Yes."

"Do you, or have you, ever masturbated while watching or reading porn?"

"Yes."

"Have you ever engaged in group sex?"

"Yes."

"Voyeurism?"

"Yes."

"Exhibitionism?"

"Yes."

"Sadomasochism?"

"Yes."

"Bondage and domination?"

"Yes."

"Top or bottom?"

"Top."

The questions and answers were flying by so fast, Rebecca's head spun. *What the hell kind of a question is that?* "Um," she cleared her throat, "what does that mean?"

"Basically she was asking me which role I play in the BDSM scene, dominant or submissive," the drummer explained. "The top is the dominant one, the master or mistress if you want to call them that. The bottom is the submissive one, or the slave."

"Oh." *God, am I that naïve?* "Okay, so you're the dominant one then. I think I knew that."

The doctor resumed her questioning now that Jordanna had

explained what she meant to Rebecca. "Have you ever paid for sex?"

"Yes."

"You have?" Rebecca asked abruptly.

The doctor gave her a warning look.

"Oh, sorry."

"Now where was I?" the doctor murmured, looking for her last check mark. "Oh, yes, here we are. Have you engaged in public sex?"

"Yes."

"Have you ever been arrested for a sexual offense?"

"Yes."

"Um, engaged with or fantasized about sex with children, animals, or corpses?"

Jordanna felt her lover's hand tense up at the question. She looked at Rebecca, who could tell the drummer was unsure of how to answer the question.

Rebecca shook her head no.

*I didn't know that she was underage. I didn't know.* "No."

"Jordanna, have you ever forced yourself on someone?"

The drummer's head turned, and she looked at her lover. "Uh..."

Rebecca answered the question for her. "You did not force yourself on me that night after the Garden. I was a very willing participant," the reporter said, flashing a mischievous smile. "Besides, if I would have said *no* to you, would you have continued?"

"I don't know, Rebecca," the drummer answered honestly, sadness in her voice. "I'd like to think that I wouldn't have, but I was so out of control that I'm honestly not sure."

"Oh."

The doctor watched the exchange with interest. "Can I ask what happened?"

Jordanna sighed. "My band did a show the other night, and a woman came on to me when I was in the shower after the show. Before I met Rebecca I would've just given in to it, but this time I graciously declined. I couldn't get the thoughts out of my mind, though, and my body was craving the action. When we got home, I tried to take care of it without hurting Rebecca, but I lost control and..."

"We had a lust-filled night of wonderful sex, Jordanna; that's what happened," the reporter finished. "And don't think I didn't enjoy it 'cause I sure as hell did. I was beyond turned on by it so don't go blaming yourself thinking you hurt me."

"Rebecca, that wasn't sex. That was fucking," the drummer

said, looking directly at her lover. "I don't ever want to do that to you again. If we feel aggressive and feel like having lusty sex every once in a while, then that's fine, but I don't *ever* want to be so void of feeling with you again and just fuck, because that's what happened that night. I didn't even realize it was you I was with."

"Oh," Rebecca said, sighing quietly. "I guess I kinda like being fucked, then, though," she added with a little smirk, trying to make the obviously upset drummer feel better.

"Rebecca!" Jordanna squeezed the hand that she was still holding. She saw Rebecca wink at her and then turned her attention back to the doctor. "Please pardon my...our language, by the way."

"That's okay, it's nothing I haven't heard before." The doctor leaned back in her chair, took her glasses off, and continued with her questioning. "Jordanna, did you have a different partner every night while you were on the road?"

"Pretty much, yeah."

"Did you ever consider seeing any of these people again?"

Jordanna ran her hand through her long mane of hair. "I did with one or two, but in total, no, I was usually finished with someone after one time."

"Have you ever had a long-lasting relationship?"

The drummer laughed. "I was with my last lover for over two years, but we never saw each other 'cause I was either on the road or living here on the Island in my off time. She lives in California."

The doctor gave Jordanna one of her best fake doctor smiles. "How long have you two been together?" the doctor asked, meaning her and Rebecca.

Jordanna looked at the reporter. "What has it been, three whole weeks now?"

"Three weeks?" the doctor repeated, her voice showing her surprise. "You two seem like you've known each other forever."

"It feels that way to me, too," the drummer said. "I've never felt this comfortable with someone so quickly."

"Just a few more questions, Jordanna. Then I'll have Brenda set up another appointment the same time next week so we can continue. Is that good for you?"

"I'll have to check my schedule," the dark-haired woman said. "I'll call if I can't make it."

The doctor nodded. "Okay, just a few more and then you can go." She picked up her pencil and looked at the paper she was writing on. "Have you ever engaged in homosex—oh, I guess this question doesn't really apply with you, does it?"

The drummer smirked. "I guess you should ask if I've engaged in heterosexual activities then," she teased. "Which, yes, I have, in case that's a question."

The doctor smiled. "Are you satisfied?"

"Satisfied with sex?" Jordanna felt Rebecca flinch at the question, and she squeezed her hand. "I, uh, when I'm with Rebecca, yes, but before I met her, definitely not. I was always in search of something more, something new and different."

Dr. Rosen rubbed her chin slowly as she looked at the next question on her list. "Do you drink, Jordanna? Or partake in illegal narcotics?"

"I have an occasional drink or two when I'm out," the drummer responded solemnly.

The doctor checked a box on her list and shook her head slightly. "If you are serious about helping yourself, that is one of the luxuries you will have to give up. Alcohol impairs your judgment and is also a source of addiction. You will always want to be in control of your actions, and you cannot do that if your judgment is impaired."

Jordanna nodded. *Crap.* "I understand."

"This is the last one," the doctor promised when she finished scribbling on the paper. "Have you ever tried to or entertained the thought of committing suicide?"

"Yes," Jordanna answered solemnly, and then she closed her eyes.

Rebecca grabbed her by the arm. "You thought about it or tried to?"

"Tried it, Rebecca, but obviously I failed. I guess your private-investigator friend must have missed that little piece of info in his investigation of me, huh?" Jordanna said, sounding a bit more sarcastic than she had meant to be.

The doctor cleared her throat, and the two women turned their attention to her. "Jordanna, I'm not going to lie to you. You have a very long road ahead of you, but I think you know that already; otherwise you wouldn't be here. Recovery isn't easy, nor does it happen overnight. You have to be *willing* to make it happen, and from what I've seen and heard from you today, I think you are. Plus," the doctor said, turning her gaze to Rebecca, "You have so much to gain if you do."

The dark-haired woman looked at her lover and smiled. "That I do."

"You know what you have to do this week to get your recovery started, right?"

The drummer's eyes lost some of their shine. *My videos.* "I have to do a little house-cleaning, don't I?"

"Yes, you do," the doctor answered. "You have to get rid of anything that might tempt you, and those videos and magazines will do just that. I know it will be hard, but let Rebecca help you."

Jordanna stood up and headed for the door with Rebecca right behind her. "All right," she said. "Thanks, Dr. Rosen."

The doctor followed them and had started to close her office door when Rebecca turned around to speak to her. Jordanna was already heading to the waiting room to make another appointment. "Doctor? What about sex? Should Jordanna and I, um..."

The doctor narrowed her eyes at the reporter. "Continue your normal routine, Rebecca."

Rebecca nodded.

"Denying her a healthy sexual relationship would be damaging to her. As long as you are with her, she should be fine. When you are separated for periods of time is the most common time for an addict to lose control." The doctor pulled out a pamphlet and handed it to the reporter. "I want you to read this, Rebecca. It's for the spouses of sex addicts—what to expect, how to handle certain situations that may arise with her."

Rebecca took the pamphlet from her. "Thank you, doctor."

REBECCA WAITED FOR the drummer to pull the car out of the parking lot before she started to ask questions. "Jor?"

"Hmm?"

"When did you try to kill yourself?"

Jordanna shifted in her seat at the mention of the subject. "Last January."

"Right after the rape charges were dropped?"

"Yes."

"How?"

"I swallowed a bottle of pills and washed them down with quite a bit of Jack Daniels. Kelly found me, and they rushed me to the hospital." She sighed. "They had to pump my stomach. Although I'm sure if you had my medical history checked out it said that I was brought in to the hospital due to malnutrition. Just another lie to cover up something foolish and selfish that I've done."

"Why did you try to kill yourself?"

"You have to ask that? Rebecca, because of my addiction, I let a fifteen-year-old fool me into believing that she was an adult, and I slept with her! I hated myself so much that I wanted to die, and that was the only way I could think of to make the addiction go away."

"So you knew you had an addiction?"

"I knew it. I just wasn't ready to admit it."

Rebecca couldn't hold her tears in. "I'm so sorry."

"For what?"

"I'm sorry that I had Jim investigate your background. I'm sorry for what you went through," Rebecca admitted and paused. "And I'm most sorry that I didn't know you then, that I wasn't there for you."

Jordanna felt slightly overwhelmed. "I'm just glad you're here for me now, baby." She pulled the car into a spot on the street, thankful for the opportunity to end the depressing conversation about the lowest time of her life. "Ready to shop?"

HAZEL EYES WATCHED the drummer and her lover walk out of the doctor's office, get into the red GT, and pull onto the narrow residential street. The stalker waited for the drummer to make a right onto the main road before putting the car into drive and doing the same. The stalker was thankful that Jordanna had purchased a bright-colored car because it was easy to spot. Following a couple of cars behind, the driver pulled the black BMW into a vacant parking space next to the sidewalk after the drummer did the same a little further up the road.

The couple exited the car and strolled along the sidewalk on Main Street, unaware that they were being watched. The drummer walked slightly behind her partner and put her hand on the small of her back as they entered a trendy clothing store. Through the window it was possible to see the dark-haired woman standing near her lover while she looked at clothes. Moments and a few words later, the drummer threw her hands in the air in defeat and then turned and walked away from the smaller woman. She walked up to the shop's clerk, handed her a credit card, said a few words, and then walked out of the shop.

Jordanna stopped to put her sunglasses on in the shop's doorway, and her gaze went in the direction of the BMW, lingering there for a minute before she turned and went in a deli a couple stores down. Hazel eyes watched as the tall woman stopped to talk to a couple of people that flagged her down in the store's doorway before she walked out of view. Fifteen minutes later she emerged from the deli with a bag in her hand, which she put in the car before going back into the store in search of her lover.

The stalker lowered the passenger-side window. The two women walked out of the store, hands full with bags.

"What did you get?" the tall woman asked.

"I'm not telling.  You can't see what I'm wearing until tonight."

*I wonder where they're going tonight? I guess I'll just have to follow them and find out, now, won't I?*

A dazzling smile flashed across the drummer's face. "I thought I'd only have to go through that on our wedding day."

The stalker watched as the reporter's face took on a stunned look.  Just as stunned as the face that was watching them.

*Wedding day? The bitch is happy. Well, I can't have that. I was happy once, and you took all of that away. Now it's going to get taken away from you, Blue.*

# Chapter
# Twenty-two

JORDANNA SAT ON a chair in the hallway, looking toward the stairs. It seemed as if it took Rebecca at least an hour to come into view, and the drummer could feel her heart pounding hard in anticipation.

The dark-haired woman's breath caught when she saw her lover, who was wearing a form-fitting black dress. "You look absolutely beautiful, Rebecca," the drummer said, and started to rise to help Rebecca into her coat.

"Thank you." Rebecca held out a gold chain. "Could you help me with this?"

Jordanna set Rebecca's coat down and smiled as she took the chain in her hand, realizing it was the pearl from that kiosk at Sea World. "Sure, baby, I forgot about this."

She pushed Rebecca's long hair to the side and placed the chain around Rebecca's neck. "You take my breath away," she whispered into her lover's ear as she fastened the clasp on the necklace. She placed a few small kisses on Rebecca's neck and then moved away from her lover, circling her so she could look at her with the necklace on. "So beautiful," she whispered, and helped Rebecca into her coat.

Jordanna put her leather jacket on and then held out her hand for the young woman to take.

Rebecca graciously accepted Jordanna's hand, and the two walked out of the house into the night. The reporter couldn't get over how different her lover looked in the designer suit she was wearing and couldn't help staring.

"What?" the dark-haired woman said, noticing the reporter's gaze.

"I hope you don't get insulted by this, but you look so, um, handsome tonight, Jordanna," Rebecca answered. "And beautiful, of course," she continued, her face beginning to blush.

"Handsome?"

"Yeah. I mean that in a good way."

Jordanna chuckled.  "I'm not insulted, Rebecca.  I don't mind being your main man," she said, cracking a smile.  "I had every intention of wearing my leather mini for you tonight, but this outfit called to me when I saw it hanging there.  I don't know why."

"Well, I'm glad," Rebecca said.  Jordanna opened the car door for her lover and waited for her to climb in.  "I *really* like it."

"THIS PLACE MUST be nice in the summer," the reporter commented, as Jordanna backed the GT into a parking spot near the side of the bar.  The bar, aptly named Crooked Hill, was a small, refurbished home located on oceanfront property that was nestled comfortably between two hotels.

They could hear the muffled sounds of the loud music as they got out of the car, and Rebecca could feel her stomach starting to knot at the thought about going to her first women's bar.

Jordanna noticed that the reporter was nervously playing with the strap on her purse.  "There are other clubs around here, Rebecca.  Do you want to go somewhere else—a regular bar?  I just figured that this would be the best place for us to come if we wanted to dance together."

The reporter closed her eyes at the thought.  "Nope, I've been wanting to dance in your arms all day.  I just, well, I just really don't know what to expect to see in there," the reporter admitted.

"Well, this to me is the worst part," the drummer said, as she pulled the front door open and let Rebecca walk in before her.  She put her arm around the reporter as they walked in, and all eyes turned their way to check out who was coming through the door.

"Oh, God, I see what you mean," Rebecca said, trying to avoid all the eyes that were fixed on her and her lover.  "I feel like I'm on display big time."

Jordanna chuckled and took the reporter's hand, quickly leading her down the back stairs to the second dance floor.  "You ready to be on display again?"

Rebecca took a deep breath.  "Yeah.  As ready as I'll ever be."

They walked through the door that led to the lower level and, for the second time, all eyes turned to them.  Rebecca watched as some of the women recognized Jordanna and pointed her out to friends.

*You can look all you want, ladies, but she's mine.  All mine.*

The drummer leaned down and asked Rebecca what she
wanted to drink, suggesting that the reporter snag a table for
them, preferably in the corner for privacy.   The dark-haired
woman let go of her lover's hand as they went their separate
ways.

Jordanna could see that Kristin, the club's long-time
bartender, saw her and was waiting for her to approach the bar.
"Oh, my God, look what the cat dragged in!  It's been a while
since we've seen you here, Jordanna," the bartender said as
Jordanna walked up and leaned against the bar.  She looked the
dark-haired woman up and down.  "You're looking good."

"Just finished a fourteen-month tour," the drummer replied.
"Haven't been home much."

Kristin leaned forward to whisper in the drummer's ear.
"No strippers here tonight, only on Saturdays now."

"I'm not here to see them, Kristin," the drummer said dryly.

Kristin raised a brow so high she might as well have spoken
her words aloud.  "What have you done to the real Jordanna?"
After a long moment, she shook her head and cleared her throat.
"So, who's the babe in the black dress that you came in with?"

Jordanna raised an eyebrow, looked over to where Rebecca
was sitting, and noticed another woman sitting much too close to
Rebecca for her comfort.

*She's mine, bitch, so you just better back the fuck away from her,
if you know what's good for you.*  "That's my lover," she answered,
her lip curling slightly as she spoke.  "And that woman better
remove herself from her presence before I get back."

"What happened to Susan?"

"Kicked her out of my house."

"And this is your new little, um, flavor of the day?"

"No.  Rebecca's the real deal, Kristin.  I love her."

The eyebrow climbed skyward again.  "Looks like that
woman's got her eyes on her, too, Jordanna."

The dark-haired woman looked back at the table again, and
the woman was sitting even closer to Rebecca than before.  She
grazed her hand across the reporter's thigh.  "That's it, call the
coroner.  She's a dead woman."

Kristin laughed at seeing the jealous side of the dark-haired
woman.  "This is a switch."

"What's a switch?" the drummer inquired.

"Usually you're the one flirting with someone else's partner.
How does it feel to be on the other end this time?" the bartender
teased.

The drummer narrowed her eyes at Kristin.  "Ask her," she
said, pointing to the woman sitting next to Rebecca, "how it feels

when I knock her from one end of the bar to the other."

Kristin laughed and pulled out a bottle of beer for the drummer, placing it on a napkin in front of her. "What can I get for your lover?"

Jordanna threw money down on the bar and pushed the beer bottle back toward Kristin. "O'Douls for me, and a Coke for Rebecca."

"Coming up!"

Jordanna sat down in the seat that the woman had vacated and took a long pull on her bottle. "She hit on you?"

"Yep," Rebecca said, fighting to hold back a smile at seeing Jordanna in such a jealous state. "That she did."

Jordanna straightened up in her chair and turned around to look for the woman who had just left the table. Rebecca put her hand on Jordanna's. "It's okay, Jor. Please don't do anything. She didn't know I was here with you."

"Sure she did." Jordanna sat back down in the chair and relaxed. "Bitch."

The reporter laughed and took in her surroundings, thinking about how, if someone had told her two months ago that she would be at a women's bar with her rock-star lover, *female* rock-star lover, she would have laughed in their face.

Rebecca's eyes took in the all the women on the dance floor, some moving seductively with their partners and others just dancing to have a good time. Behind the dance floor was a small stage that was bare. "No band tonight?" she asked the dark-haired woman, who was busy running her hand along Rebecca's thigh under the table.

"What?"

Rebecca looked at the stage. "No band playing tonight?"

"Oh, uh, they only have bands here during the summer, and they play outside on the deck. That stage is for the strippers that they have," the drummer explained, her face starting to blush.

"Strippers? Do I even have to ask whether you watched them or not?"

Jordanna shook her head and laughed softly. "I think the only question would be is whether I took them to the pay-by-the-hour down the road or not."

"I don't want to know," the reporter said, feeling a hand move to caress the inside of her thighs. She shuddered and took a sip of her water, returning her gaze to the dance floor. "Dance with me?"

The drummer set her beverage down on the table, stood up, and took off her jacket to reveal a sleeveless red tank top. She held out her hand for the reporter to take. "I'd be honored."

Rebecca held on to Jordanna's hand tight as they made their way through the crowd to the dance floor. The song that had been playing when they first started to walk to the floor ended, and a more upbeat rap tune that Jordanna immediately recognized came blasting out of the speakers.

"How do you dance to this?" the reporter asked, very unsure of herself. Jordanna moved behind her lover, put her hands on Rebecca's hips, and began to grind her groin area into the reporter's backside to the beat of the song.

"Ooh, I like that," Rebecca said out loud, hoping her lover could hear her.

She did. Jordanna ground herself against her lover even harder, feeling a slow fire begin to burn within her.

Wanting to get in on the action, the rest of the crowd followed suit, and soon they were all doing the same moves. Rebecca laughed as she thought about what the drummer had said when she was looking through her CD collection. "So, rap *really is* good to dance to," she yelled to her lover.

The dark-haired woman smirked. "You think so?"

"Oh, yeah," the reporter answered. *Just ask my throbbing center.*

"Told you so."

The song wound down and a slower tune came on. Jordanna remained behind the reporter, wrapped her arms around her waist, and began to sway slowly with the music, singing the song that was playing into Rebecca's ear.

Rebecca lost herself in the sound of her lover's voice and melted into the feel of the dark-haired woman's body pressing against her...Jordanna's hands caressing her thighs...the drummer's breath on her neck...the smell of her perfume.

*Oh, God, this is bliss.*

So absorbed in each other, neither woman noticed that the vocalist's voice was no longer heard, Jordanna was singing the song *a capella*, and that they were the only ones on the dance floor. The patrons of the club recognized a special moment when they saw one and quietly left the dance floor to listen to the high-profile drummer sing the words that she wished she'd written to her lover, because she felt them with all of her heart.

Jordanna lost sight of everything around her, and she dove headfirst into everything that was Rebecca. She knew now, beyond the shadow of a doubt, that her life would be lost without the reporter in it.

She took the reporter's hand, spun her around so that they were facing each other, and then blue eyes met hazel. Rebecca wrapped her arms around her lover's neck and slowly freed

Jordanna's hair from the confines of the ponytail, watching it fall around the woman's shoulders. The drummer pulled her lover close, and she caressed Rebecca's cheek with her fingers before she leaned down for a gentle kiss.

"Move in with me?" the drummer asked when the kiss ended, surprised when she heard her own voice say the words, knowing she was setting herself up for a very big fall.

*Did I just say that?*

Rebecca looked up at the drummer with a shocked look on her face, unsure of what her lover had just said to her. *Did I hear her right?*

"What did you just say?" she asked, wanting to confirm whether she really did need to have her hearing checked.

"I-I asked you to move in with me," the drummer repeated, blushing profusely.

*That's what I thought she said.*

"Yes," the reporter answered, not hesitating for a moment. A smile lit up the drummer's face and Rebecca's heart swelled, knowing that she was the cause of the beautiful smile.

"Oh, God," the drummer whispered, burying her head in Rebecca's hair. She picked the reporter up and kissed her. She kissed her with a passion and a love so strong that she thought she would pass out from it. When they broke apart, Rebecca whispered in her ear. "Take me home, Jordanna."

DOZING IN THE driver's seat of the black BMW, the stalker was jolted alive by the sound of laughter from patrons leaving the bar. Eyes caught sight of the two women, one dressed in a black suit and the other in a form-fitting black dress.

*You have excellent taste in women, Jordanna, I must admit.*

They were both laughing and walking hand in hand to the red sports car.

*They look* really *happy. I wonder what that's all about?*

The stalker snorted when the couple got in the car and kissed each other like two teenagers in heat. *Get a room, damn.*

Eyes watched the GT pull out of its parking spot and make its way onto Montauk Highway. The BMW pulled into place two cars behind the GT and followed it until it made the quick left onto the private drive that Jordanna's house was located on. The BMW slowed briefly, its driver watching the red car until its taillights were out of sight before speeding up and heading west.

# Chapter
## Twenty-three

"LET IT RING," the dark-haired woman said gruffly. "The machine will pick it up." She returned to the task she had been performing before the rude interruption. "Now, baby, what were we doing?"

"You were right here." Rebecca tangled her hands in inky black hair and pulled her lover's mouth back down to her nipple.

*"Pick up the phone, Jordanna. I know you're there. I heard you making your little girlfriend squeal like a pig. You both look so beautiful when you're in the throes of passion."*

"Who in the hell is that?" the reporter asked, shocked at the muffled, yet distinguishable words she just heard on the drummer's answering machine.

"Fuck!" The dark-haired woman jumped out of the bed and picked up the phone. "Who the fuck are you?"

Rebecca watched her lover's eyes as they scanned the room, looking for any sign of an intruder. She opened her closet, grabbed the first pair of jeans she could find, and somehow managed to get them on without dropping the phone.

*"Oh, don't cover up that sexy body on my account, Jordanna."*

"What the fuck do you want from me?" the drummer snarled. She reached into the back of her closet, grabbed a box similar to the one that Rebecca had dropped, and pulled out its contents. Rebecca gasped when she saw the drummer pull out a gun and load the clip into it before she did the same to a second gun that had seemed to have appeared out of nowhere. She slipped them both down the back of her jeans.

*"I see you're bringing out a piece of your past, Blue,"* the muffled voice said. *"You thought you buried that past, didn't ya?"*

"What, exactly," Jordanna paused, "do you want from me?" She pulled a thin white tee shirt over her head, not caring that it was winter and that she didn't have a bra on.

*"I want you to experience what I experienced all those years ago. Prepare to watch your girlfriend die right in front of your eyes, and*

*then, maybe, if you're a good girl, maybe I'll put you out of your misery."*

Click.

"I'm going to kill you, you fucking son of a bitch," the drummer screamed as she slammed the phone down. "Stay here, Rebecca. I have to check the house."

"But, wait." Rebecca watched her lover leave the room. "Please be careful." *I just found you, I can't lose you.*

Jordanna slowly walked the halls of her home, keeping close to the walls. *I can't believe I'm playing fucking cops and robbers,* she thought as she made her way through all the rooms on the second floor. Using a gun as a scare tactic during a drug buy was a lot different than sneaking around trying to apprehend a stalker, one that she wasn't even sure was in the house. For some reason, one that she couldn't explain, she felt at ease with the situation, though. The only thing she didn't feel at ease with was the fact that she didn't have Rebecca in her line of sight, and she considered going back for her. Deciding to move ahead, she checked each room and closet but found nothing.

Feeling pretty safe that no one was in the house, she went back to her bedroom to check on her lover. Rebecca, who had dressed quickly when the drummer was on the phone with the stalker, ran into her arms. "Are you okay? What's going on, Jordanna?"

Jordanna held onto the reporter tightly and looked around the room, figuring that there had to be a video camera hidden somewhere. "It was another threatening phone call."

"I figured that out. But why the gun?"

"Because," the drummer explained, "whoever it was knew what we were doing."

"Don't you think that could have been an easy guess, though? We haven't exactly been keeping our relationship a secret."

"Rebecca, the person could see us. They knew we were making love, and they saw when I put my jeans on and pulled out my gun. You can't see into the house from outside, which you know already, so I figured the person was either in the house or there's a camera in the room."

Rebecca moved away from her lover and sat down on the bed. "What are we going to do, Jordanna?"

The dark woman took her lover's hand and grabbed their jackets. "C'mon," she said, leading the reporter down the stairs quickly and out of the house. She stopped Rebecca from going any farther than the door and took a quick look around to determine whether it was safe. Not seeing anything suspicious,

she went back for Rebecca, and they continued out the door.
"Do you know how to use a gun, Rebecca?"

Rebecca didn't answer her right away as they walked
toward the GT. "No, I've never used one, Jordanna," she finally
answered. "I could never shoot someone."

Jordanna sighed. "Then I'm taking you to Rachel's or
Kelly's so you'll be safe."

"No way! It's the middle of the night, and I'm not leaving
your side, Jor."

"Rebecca, please don't argue with me on this!"

"What are you planning to do?"

"I honestly don't know," the dark-haired woman admitted.
"Fuck! I can't believe this. This is all my fault," the dark woman
said.

Rebecca put her hand on the drummer's arm. "Don't say
that, Jordanna."

"But it's the truth. This all has to do with my past, and I've
put you at serious risk. I should have been up-front with you
about this from the beginning, but, no, I was my usual selfish
self and had to have something that I've never had before and
put you in danger by doing that."

"It wouldn't have changed anything. I'd still be here with
you, by your side. You know that by now, don't you?"

Jordanna looked into Rebecca's eyes. "I think I do," she
said, her own eyes welling with tears. "You know, tonight was
such a special night for me. I can't tell you how happy you made
me when you said *yes*."

"Probably about as happy as you made me when you asked
me," Rebecca answered, tears forming in her own eyes. "Um, I
think we better figure out what to do about this jackass soon
because I plan on spending the rest of my life with you, Jordanna
Fox. No one, and I mean no one," she said quietly, "is taking
this away from me."

The drummer shook her head in agreement, too choked up
to speak.

Jordanna started the car and made her way down the
driveway. Rebecca spoke first, breaking the silence. "Are you
sure this definitely has to do with your past?"

"Yes," the drummer said solemnly. "The person called me
Blue. That was what I was known as out on the streets when I
was working for Dre. Karla gave me the nickname."

*Blue?*

Rebecca closed her eyes and saw the folded ad from that
strip club that had fallen out of the box that she knocked down
in Jordanna's closet. "Did you say they called you Blue?"

Jordanna looked at her. "Yeah, why?"

"In that box I knocked down there was an ad for a club called the Dollhouse and..."

The drummer didn't let her finish. "There was a dancer named Blue on the ad. Yep, that would be me. I guess I neglected to tell you that I also used to strip for a living, huh?"

"Holy shit, Jordanna!" Rebecca turned her head and laughed hysterically. "Jesus! Is there anything else I don't know about you?"

The dark-haired woman sighed but didn't speak.

*You will tell me your little secret, Jordanna, be sure of that.* "Okay." Rebecca paused for effect, knowing that Jordanna wasn't ready to tell her the secret she'd been hiding over the years. "Are you sure we just can't call the police?"

"No! No police, Rebecca," the dark-haired woman snapped. She cleared her throat and took the reporter's hand in her own. "I'm sorry, this just has me a bit on edge."

"It's got me a bit on edge, Jor, that's why I thought it would be easier if we just let the police handle it."

"It definitely would be a hell of a lot easier, Rebecca, but I told you that it'd probably get me into trouble if the police got involved."

The reporter just shook her head, wondering to herself what her lover could have possibly have done that would get her into trouble with the police. After hearing about her statutory-rape arrest, she wasn't sure if she really wanted to know. "Um, Jor, does anyone else know what you did?"

"I would assume the person calling has a bit of a clue. For the life of me, I just can't think of who it could be. Everyone I knew from that time is dead now. Dre, Karla, they're both gone. Why?" Jordanna asked.

Rebecca's head shot up. "They're *both* dead?"

"Yeah, I, uh, Dre was, um..." The drummer rubbed her chin nervously. "Well, he was killed in a shootout."

"Dre was the one I read about in that old newspaper article you had in that box?"

"Yeah, he was. I know you want to ask me about my past, so go ahead. I won't get mad or yell this time."

"Well, I am just a bit curious," the reporter admitted, taking advantage of the drummer's openness. "What happened once you started working for Dre?"

Jordanna glanced quickly at the reporter. "He had me running drugs at first. Pick-ups and deliveries. Same thing I did with Karla, only this time I got paid for it."

"Except now you did it by yourself? No backup?" Rebecca

inquired.

"No. I usually went with Dre," the drummer said hesitantly. "He sorta took a liking to me and wanted to train me himself."

Rebecca felt a touch of jealousy. "What do you mean he 'sorta' took a liking to you?"

"I was his type," the drummer said, pausing to scratch her chin. "Sexually speaking, of course."

"Oh, of course."

"That was over ten years ago, baby."

"I know. I don't want to be jealous about your past, but, for some reason, I am." The reporter leaned her head on the taller woman's shoulder.

The drummer chuckled. "You have no reason to be, but it tells me how you feel about me, and that makes everything that I did and went through worth it. It took meeting you to make me realize it," Jordanna said with a smile. "I would be jealous if it was you."

Rebecca lifted her head up and looked into the drummer's eyes. "You would?"

Jordanna kissed her on the forehead. "Yeah, I would." That answer made the reporter smile a smile that would melt the coldest of hearts. Jordanna hesitated. She took a deep breath and continued. "Well, like I said, Dre took a personal interest in me. First thing he wanted was to make sure that I knew how to handle myself should I get into a sticky situation. Of course, that meant carrying a gun, which obviously was something that I never had the need to do before then. He gave me one of his .38's and took me to a makeshift range in this abandoned warehouse that he'd set up. It didn't take long for him to think that I was ready to hit the streets with him. I guess I proved myself to him as time went by and I got more involved in his business."

"When, exactly..." Rebecca started to ask before Jordanna finished the question for her.

"Did I get more involved with him personally? Is that what you were going to ask?"

The reporter blushed. She knew it was really none of her business. "Yeah, that's what I was going to ask."

Jordanna smiled, and her eyes looked colorless in the moonlight. "Once I started working with Dre I practically lived at his house. I would get calls from him in the middle of the night to go out on runs. So he asked me to move in with him. It only made sense. He knew that I lived with Karla and that we were lovers. Luckily, Karla understood why I had to go."

"I don't know if I would understand," Rebecca admitted. "I

wouldn't want you to go."

"No?"

"No."

"Well, she worked for Dre, so she knew how demanding he could be. She could see that he wanted to make me his right-hand man, so to speak." She paused. "And she knew that whatever Dre wanted, Dre got, so there was no use in fighting it." The sun was coming up over the horizon; the drummer realized that they had been talking for hours. "You hungry?"

"Yeah, how'd you know?"

"Lucky guess," the drummer said teasingly. "You like pancakes?"

"Who doesn't?"

JORDANNA PULLED THE GT into the parking lot at the diner and groaned. "It's crowded already, damn." She spotted one available parking space at the end of the lot. "You wanna go somewhere else or see how long of a wait it'll be?"

"Let's see how long of a wait it is. I'm definitely in the mood for pancakes. You said they have all different kinds, right?"

The drummer pulled the car into the spot and then shut the engine. "Yep."

They walked into the restaurant, and a tall, dark-haired woman greeted them. "Hey, good-looking."

Jordanna rolled her eyes. "Hey, Nancy, how are you doing?"

"Can't complain. Finished with the tour?"

"A few more shows and then a break." She pulled Rebecca close to her. "Nancy, I want you to meet Rebecca, my partner."

The woman held out her hand, and Rebecca took it. "Nice to meet you, Rebecca. Just the two of you today?"

"Yeah, the usual, in the back, if you have any booths there, please."

The hostess sat them in the last booth in the place and gave them both menus. She started to walk away but then turned around. "Hey, are you guys playing at the ranch concert again this year?"

"From what I heard, yes, I think we were asked to play again this year."

"That's cool. Looking forward to it," Nancy said, and then walked away.

Rebecca reached her hand across the table and put it on her lover's. "Jor?"

"No, I never dated her," the dark-haired woman said and

smiled. "Believe it or not."

"How did you know I was going to ask that?"

Jordanna looked her directly in the eyes. "Because I know you, Rebecca, and you know me."

"Yeah, you do, don't you? I like that." Rebecca smiled. "What's the ranch concert?"

Jordanna passed her a menu. "It's an annual concert they hold here in Montauk every August."

"Oh."

"They clear out this field right here on Montauk Highway for it. They usually have four or five performers. It's fun, like one big barbecue with good music."

"I wonder if they'll want me to cover it for the magazine?" Rebecca shook her head. "That's if we don't get ourselves killed first."

"We're not going to get killed." Jordanna spoke quietly, in a reassuring voice. "We'll both be at the concert in August, and every other day after that."

They both sat silently for a while as the waitress took their order and brought them coffee. Rebecca's mind went back to the conversation that they were having about her lover's past. "What happened to Karla?"

The drummer looked away. "She..." She swallowed the lump that quickly formed in her throat. "She was beaten to death by a john," she finally got out, and paused. "I saw some of it happen."

Rebecca put her hand on Jordanna's face and turned the drummer's head toward her. She could clearly see the pain in her lover's eyes. She couldn't imagine what it must have been like for Jordanna, watching the only person that truly cared for her, at that time, die. "I'm sorry. That must have been a hard thing to see."

"If only I would have gotten there five minutes earlier," she mumbled, not explaining what she meant.

Rebecca wondered if her lover was blaming herself for Karla's death. "Jordanna, it's not your fault. You were just a kid, what could you have done?"

"I could have stopped it from happening." A lone tear made its way down her cheek. Rebecca lifted the dark-haired woman's hand and brought it up to her lips.

"Krhm." The waitress cleared her throat before putting their food down on the table. "Banana-nut pancakes for you," she said, placing Rebecca's plate in front of her. "And chocolate-chip pancakes for you. Would you like some more coffee?"

"Yes, please," the dark woman replied. "Thanks."

They ate for a few minutes in silence. Rebecca, as usual, had a million questions running through her mind that she wanted to ask her lover. "Jordanna?"

The dark woman looked up from her plate. "Hmm?"

Rebecca noticed that Jordanna had a little bit of whipped cream from her pancakes on her chin and started to chuckle.

"What?"

The reporter leaned over the table and tried to nonchalantly remove the whipped cream with a kiss. "Mmm mmm, good."

The drummer blushed. "What was that for?"

"You had whipped cream on your face, and it looked too delicious to ignore, so..."

"And I'm the one going to a sex therapist?" the drummer asked incredulously.

The reporter laughed. "Well, I didn't do things like this until I met you."

"Yeah, yeah, blame the big bad drummer," Jordanna teased and then laughed lowly.

"You know, I was going to ask you something before I got distracted," the reporter said and then paused. "Oh, yeah. What happened to the man that killed Karla? Did he go to jail?"

Silence.

Jordanna closed her eyes and looked down. "No. They found his severely battered body near Karla's," she said so quietly Rebecca barely knew that she spoke.

The reporter couldn't believe what she thought she had just heard her lover say. Words failed her as she tried to swallow the information. *Did she mean what I think she meant?*

"You?"

Jordanna could feel the butterflies in her stomach going wild. *Say goodbye to the best thing that has ever come into your life, Jordanna.* She looked up at the reporter. "Yes."

Rebecca's face took on a horrified look and tears started to well in her eyes. "Oh, my God, are you trying to say you've killed somebody?" The reporter's voice got louder with each word.

Jordanna placed her hand on the reporter's and leaned over the table to whisper to her lover. "Rebecca, please! Nobody knows about it, and I'd like to keep it that way."

The reporter realized that as much as she thought she knew the woman sitting across from her, she really didn't know Jordanna at all. There were so many differences between them. *So, now I'm sleeping with a murderer. What's the big deal? Doesn't everybody?*

The dark woman could see all of the different emotions

written across Rebecca's face. "Rebecca, please say something."

Rebecca looked at her blankly. "What?"

"Say something. Anything."

"What in the hell do you expect me to say? What does it feel like to beat someone to death?" She snorted. "Give me a damn break, Jordanna! I don't fucking know what to say!"

Seeing the reporter all huffy made Jordanna laugh. "Well, that's a start."

"It's not funny." She gave the drummer a dirty look. "A man is dead."

The drummer glared back at her. "So is my ex-girlfriend," she said gruffly. "Don't forget that." Her voice softened. "When I pulled the scum off of Karla and saw her bruised and bloody face, Rebecca, I just lost it. I couldn't control my rage." She sighed. "Karla pleaded with me not to kill him, and I didn't at first. I just knocked him to the ground."

The reporter urged her on without saying anything, just by the look in her eyes.

"I went over to Karla to help her. I pulled her into my arms and just tried to comfort her, Rebecca. She made me promise not to kill him, and she told me to get out from under Dre's influence before it was too late for me." She took a sip of her coffee, the liquid soothing her dry mouth. "Here she was, lying there in so much pain near death, worrying about me."

"She told me to take care of myself, and then her eyes closed for the final time, Rebecca," she continued. "She died right there in my arms. I eased her onto the ground and looked at the man that killed her, remembering the promise I made to her that I wouldn't kill him." The drummer took a deep breath of air, finding the need to supply her pounding heart with extra oxygen. "I couldn't keep that promise."

Rebecca fought the serious urge to hurl everything that she had consumed that morning. For the first time, she didn't want to hear what the drummer was saying. "Let's just go home, Jordanna."

"Oh, no, we're not going back to my house, or at least you aren't. Did you forget about the phone call?"

Rebecca stabbed at her pancakes with her fork and pushed them around on her plate. "No, I didn't forget it."

Jordanna felt her hammering heart begin to slow to a normal pace. "I was thinking of renting a room at a hotel, maybe away from the East End, somewhere on Central Long Island until I talk to Rachel or Kelly about you staying with them." She finished her coffee and set the cup down. "Although I would like to go check to see if I can find the camera first."

"Jordanna, I am not leaving you, so forget it. Besides, do you want to put Rachel, Kelly, and their families at risk?"

The drummer threw her napkin down on the table. "No, I don't want that." She grabbed the check, left a tip for the waitress on the table, and got up. "C'mon, let's go."

THE DRIVE BACK was an extremely quiet one, with Jordanna concentrating on the road and Rebecca staring out the window, lost in her own thoughts.

The silent treatment was just about all the drummer could take. She could imagine how Rebecca felt about her at the moment. Hell, she knew how she felt about herself, and it wasn't good. *Rebecca hasn't even heard the worst of it yet.* Sadness really began to take over. She herself had learned how to deal with the guilt of her past by covering it up with a different name, a different life, and, as she had just learned so recently, by taking it out on the innocent women she lured into her bed. She realized that this life that she was thinking about was shallow and lacking without love. Without Rebecca.

*I can't lose her. I just can't.*

Rebecca couldn't help but wonder what she had gotten into by getting involved with Jordanna. To think that she originally had thought the woman was your typical arrogant rock star. Well, that made her laugh now. Never had she expected to find out the woman had a sordid past filled with gangs, sex, rape, drugs, and violence.

*Okay, so the sex I knew about.*

But still, she knew in her heart that her feelings for Jordanna would not lessen no matter what Jordanna told her about her past. They were real. They were her anchor in this storm. They had to be. She reached over, took Jordanna's hand in her own, and watched the smile grow on the drummer's face. Seeing her smile at such a small gesture made Rebecca realize that Jordanna needed the reporter in her life as much as she needed the drummer. It was as simple as that.

Wasn't it?

Jordanna pulled GT over to the side of the main road near her home. "Stay here," she said, opening the car door. "I'm going to check to make sure the house is safe, and then I'll come back for you, okay?"

"Please be careful, Jor."

The dark woman shook her head and winked at Rebecca before she slammed the door shut. "I will."

Rebecca watched as Jordanna pulled her gun out of the back of her jeans and made her way up the private drive. After the drummer was out of sight, her thoughts went to the person that was after them.

Was this person really any more dangerous than her lover was?

She nearly jumped through the roof when Jordanna got back in the car, threw something on the back seat, and started to drive down the road. "What happened? Where are we going?"

"I found the camera. It was in a vent in the bedroom. It's now in pieces on the back seat," the dark woman explained. "The house was clear otherwise."

"That doesn't explain where we are going, Jordanna."

"I'm going to the police and turning myself in. I thought about it as I was checking the house, Rebecca. I couldn't stand it if anything happened to you. You shouldn't have to pay for something I did years ago."

"No."

"What?"

"No. Damn it, Jordanna, turn the car around! You are not going to turn yourself in." Rebecca cleared her throat. "Losing you would be the worst price that I'd ever have to pay for anything in my life. Do you understand that?"

"I have *no right* to put your life on the line, Rebecca."

"Let me decide that, Jordanna."

"Damn it! Please be reasonable."

"Turn...the...car...around," the reporter growled. "Now!"

Jordanna almost slammed the car into a pole. "Okay, okay, I'm turning it around." The dark woman drove a few blocks and pulled up at a scenic overlook to turn around.

"It's pretty here," the reporter said to change the subject, noticing the view of the bay.

Jordanna looked out at the scenery that she had seen hundreds of times before in her life. It was, because of Rebecca, she realized, the first time she could really appreciate the its beauty. "Yeah, it is."

Why did this have to happen now that she had found love? She questioned why her past hadn't bitten her in the ass years ago, when she didn't give a shit about herself or anyone else. *No sense in asking why now, a lot of good it will do.*

"Jordanna?"

"Hmm?"

"What are we going to do?"

The drummer let out a deep breath. "Well, we're going to go back to the house and wait. Let the bastard come to us. I really wish you would reconsider staying somewhere else, though, baby."

"Nope, forget it.   I'm not leaving you.   I told you that already."

# Chapter
# Twenty-four

THE DRUMMER STRETCHED her long legs out across the carpeted floor in the living room. She sat with her lover curled up next to her, looking at the contents of the box that Rebecca had accidentally dropped on the floor, hoping that something in it would jolt her memory.

Nothing did.

"He was a nice-looking man," the reporter commented, as Jordanna looked at one of the old photos of Dre and herself. "Kinda looked like a bigger version of Tupac Shakur, huh?"

"Huh?"

Rebecca pulled the photo out of her lover's hand. "Are you all right, sweetheart?"

Jordanna sighed and rubbed her forehead. "Just a little frustrated, I guess. Why can't I remember anything?"

"Don't give up, keep looking."

Jordanna pulled out the flyer for the club she used to dance at and unfolded it, laying it down on the floor. Rebecca traced the letters on the fancy design of the club's name. "How'd you get this job?"

"Dre. He owned the place." Jordanna turned her body slightly as she started to feel the beginning of pins and needles setting in. "Actually, he was a silent partner. He figured I'd be a big draw for the place."

Rebecca pushed Jordanna's hair back, then nibbled and sucked gently on the dark-haired woman's neck. "I bet he was correct."

The drummer leaned her head to the side, letting out a little moan. "Mmm, yeah, he was." She put her hands on the reporter's cheeks, pulling her face closer to her own until their lips met. Jordanna felt the reporter's tongue running gently along her lip seeking entrance, which she willingly gave in to. Coming up for air, the drummer chuckled. "I thought you were angry with me?"

"I am."

Jordanna smirked. "Remind me to make you angry more often then."

Rebecca wiggled her eyebrows at the drummer. "Hey, did you lap dance when you worked at that club?"

"Nope, lap dancing wasn't really popular then." She leaned forward, kissed her lover again, and whispered into her ear. "I'll lap dance for you, though."

"You will?"

The drummer cracked a smile. "Sure. It'll cost, though."

"You want me to pay you for it?"

"Services rendered, baby. I don't come cheap."

Rebecca ran and got her wallet. "How much?"

"Hmm, the going rate is like forty bucks. Add on the celebrity status and, lemme see. How about ravishing me all night as payment?"

"It's a deal!"

They both jumped at the sound of the doorbell. "Who in the hell could that be?" the drummer muttered. She pushed herself off of the floor, stretching a bit to get the blood circulating again, pulled out her gun, and headed to the door.

Rebecca stood up and followed her lover. "Jordanna, please be careful. It could be the person who is doing this."

The tall woman switched direction and quietly made her way to the window. She used the barrel of her gun to move the curtain, hoping to get an undetected glimpse of who was at the door. "We weren't supposed to practice today," the dark woman whispered when she saw who was standing there.

Rebecca could see her lover's tense body relax immediately. "Who is it, Jor?"

The drummer moved away from the window, slipped the gun down the back of her jeans, and walked to the door to let the guitarist in. "Linda?" Jordanna greeted her band mate hesitantly. "Did I screw up my dates or something? I thought we were supposed to get together again next week. The whole band."

"Nope, you didn't screw up any dates. Mind if I come in?" The drummer nodded and Linda walked past her. "I'm here to keep my promise, Jordanna."

"Your promise?" The drummer's eyes narrowed. "And, um, what promise was that?"

Linda backhanded Jordanna across the face and then grabbed Rebecca, putting a gun to her head. "This promise, Blue."

*What the fuck? Linda? Linda? No, it can't be. I would*

*remember.*

"What's the matter, Blue? Cat got your tongue or something? You don't remember me from back then, do you?"

Jordanna wiped her bloody mouth and then started to lunge toward the two of them, wanting nothing more than to get the gun away from her lover's head.

"Back the fuck away, Jordanna," Linda warned the fast-approaching woman. "Or she bites it now."

The drummer stopped where she was. She looked into the frightened eyes of her lover and then settled her gaze on Linda. "Let her go, Linda. It's me you want," she said, speaking directly to the angry woman holding Rebecca hostage.

"I *will not* let her go, Jordanna." Linda shifted her feet. "I won't let her go because..." She paused as the painful memories flashed through her brain. "I watched you kill the love of my life, and now you're going to watch me kill yours."

The reporter was stunned and confused. "The love of your life was a dirt bag that beat up on prostitutes?" the reporter asked incredulously, finding this hard to believe.

"No, Rebecca." Linda laughed. "I see your lover hasn't told you everything about herself. She didn't tell you how she put a gun to Dre's head and pulled the trigger, did she?" She laughed again and looked the drummer straight in the eyes. "She didn't tell you how warm his blood felt against her skin, exactly like yours is going to feel on mine." She ran the gun down Rebecca's cheek. "Now, do you remember me, Blue?"

Jordanna closed her eyes tight as a quick picture flashed in her mind.

*The dark-haired woman cursed when she heard the phone ring. "Whoever you are, you have great fucking timing." She looked up into the dark brown eyes of the woman straddling her stomach, running her hands along the curve of the dark-haired woman's hips. "I gotta pick it up, Karla, it's probably him." She waited for her lover to climb off of her body and rolled over onto her side to pick up the phone. "This better be an emergency."*

*The deep voice on the other end of the line laughed. "Did I catch you at a bad time, Blue?"*

*"Your timing could be better, Dre. What's up?"*

*"You got a drop to do tonight. Bring Karla with you."*

*The dark-haired woman heard music in the background on the phone. "Where the hell are you? At the club?"*

*"No," he laughed. "I'm at my bitch's place."*

*"Where's that music coming from?"*

*"Lynn plays the guitar, Blue. She's practicing."*

*"Yeah?" the dark-haired woman snorted. "Well, tell Lynn she plays like shit."*

The drummer opened her eyes. "Holy shit, I remember."

"Jordanna?" Rebecca swallowed a couple of times. "That...that can't be true." She turned and looked at her lover. "Please tell me this isn't true."

Jordanna closed her eyes, unable to look Rebecca in the face. "It is true, Rebecca," the drummer confirmed. "I killed him."

"But it was in self defense, right?"

Jordanna stood perfectly still, hoping the guitarist would give her the chance to reach for her gun. "No, I knew exactly what I was doing when I did it," she said solemnly. She could see the look of complete disappointment in Rebecca's eyes. "It was the only way, Rebecca."

Linda lost it. She walked over to the drummer, dragging Rebecca along with her, and put the gun to Jordanna's head. "What the fuck do you mean, the only way?"

The drummer spoke calmly, wanting to explain this more for Rebecca's sake than for the guitarist's or her own. "It was the only way I could get out from under him, Linda."

The guitarist slapped the drummer across the face once more, making her bleed again. Blood trickled down from Jordanna's lip. "That's not true. He would have let you go. He told me that you wanted out."

The drummer laughed, tasting the blood in her mouth. "You really think he'd have just let me go?"

"He told me that you were free to leave whenever you wanted."

""Jordanna shook her head. "There's a lot you didn't know about Dre, Linda. There's no way he'd ever let me leave."

"You're lying," the guitarist hissed. "He wouldn't lie to me."

"It's the truth, Linda."

Linda put the gun to the drummer's head again. "Shut the fuck up, Jordanna. I've had enough of your shit over the years. You think you're so fucking hot."

Rebecca closed her eyes, hoping that it would stop the insistent pounding in her head. *Why is this happening to us?* She thought about trying to escape, but knew that a bullet traveled faster than both she and Jordanna could run. "Oh, Jordanna? You know that Oriental whore of a girlfriend that you were fucking with?" Linda shifted the gun back to Rebecca's head.

"Karla?" the drummer responded sadly.

"Was that her name?" Linda snorted. "Well, what does it

matter? Dre had her taken care of for your entertainment."

Rebecca watched Jordanna's face as anger wrote itself across it, and her eyes went from a darker blue to a cool shade of ice.

"Are you telling me that Dre had Karla killed?" Jordanna was ready to lunge at the guitarist and take her out with her bare hands. "And set it up so that I would see some of it?"

"Ooh, Jordanna, you're so smart! Give the girl a prize."

"Fuck you, Linda."

The guitarist laughed wickedly. "You see what you got yourself into by getting involved with this slut, Rebecca?" Linda ran her hand down the reporter's cheek and then waved the gun around carelessly. "It's a shame 'cause I like you, I really do. I think we could've been good friends, maybe even something more." She felt the reporter's body shudder. "Just know it's nothing personal with *you*. Jordanna is completely responsible for your impending death. I told you that she'd end up hurting you in the end."

"Damn it, Linda, if you like her, then why would you want to hurt her? Just let her go," the drummer pleaded. "Take me in her place."

"Now, now, Jordanna, you know that I can't do that. I'll kill you, but not until you've watched your little lover here die. I want to enjoy watching every second of your precious pain."

The guitarist waved the gun around while she continued talking. "You know, Jordanna, I think I owe you an explanation as to why I slept with you. I have to admit, I was curious 'cause Dre did mention that you were *all that* in the sack, and, yeah, I gotta admit, he was right: you are one hell of a fuck." She stopped and paused. "Don't you agree, Rebecca?"

Rebecca remained silent.

The guitarist yanked on the young woman's hair, pulling her head back. "Answer me, Rebecca! Jordanna is wonderful in bed, isn't she?" she snarled.

The reporter looked at her lover and nodded. "Yes, she is."

"But you see, Rebecca, that's all she is. She uses people to get her way. She degrades all of the women she sleeps with to make her feel better about herself. She's a controlling, selfish bitch that isn't capable of loving you, or even making love to you."

"That is absolutely not true, Linda. Jordanna and I make love all the time."

Rebecca felt Linda's arms tense, and got a good look at the guitarist's well-muscled body. "She," the guitarist pointed at Jordanna with her gun. "She wouldn't know the meaning of love if it bit her on the ass."

"But *I* would," the reporter said quietly.

"Shut up!" the guitarist screamed. "This isn't about you! I thought I told you that."

Linda saw Jordanna's hand slowly start to reach behind her back for her gun. She pulled Rebecca directly in front of her and put the gun to her head. "Pull that gun out and you'll be cleaning her brains from your carpeting."

"Just fucking do it then!" Jordanna sneered. *Please forgive me, Rebecca, I know this sounds insane, but I think this is the only way to keep you safe.* "I really don't give a shit if you kill her, Linda, she means nothing to me! She's just one out of the hundreds of notches on my belt."

Linda narrowed her eyes in confusion. "But you brought her here."

Jordanna shrugged. "Yeah, so? What in the hell does that mean?"

"You've never brought any of your whores home with you."

"There's always a first time for everything, Linda. Jerry said I needed good press. What better way to get that than to make the journalist writing the article scream out your name in passion every night, huh? The nice little article Rebecca wrote on me has been submitted already. She can't change it now, even if she wanted to." She laughed and looked at her lover. "You were so damn easy."

*Damn it, Linda, let her go! Come after me.*

Rebecca's eyes opened wide, and Linda stared at her blankly. "I really thought meeting her had changed you, Jordanna. Apparently not."

"Get real, Linda! I can't believe that you, of all people, would actually think I could have feelings for the little bitch, other than sexual ones, of course. Remember who you're dealing with here! I don't have feelings at all."

The reporter was stunned. "This was all a fucking game to you?" Rebecca managed to get out as tears began to stream down her cheeks.

"Oh, please, Rebecca, don't start the crying bullshit or act all shocked with me!" The drummer put her hands on her hips, trying to think of something that would make her lover realize that she didn't mean what she was saying. "I mean, you really didn't expect me to ask you to move in with me or anything like that, did you?"

Rebecca was confused. *Huh? I don't understand. You did ask me to move in with you. And the nice little article on you hasn't been submitted yet.*

*But Linda doesn't know that, now does she?*

Rebecca cocked her head to the side. *Is this in your plan, Jordanna?* Her somber eyes brightened when she realized that it was. "You really think I would want to move in with someone as sleazy and as low-class as you, Jordanna?"

Jordanna grinned wickedly, realizing that her lover had caught on. *Good, Rebecca, now go back at me. Let's make her think she has no leverage.* "As low-class as me?" Jordanna let out a wild laugh. "She's all yours now, Linda." She paused and winked at the guitarist. "Take my advice, don't pass this one up. Her pussy is sweet, real sweet." She shrugged. "She's just not my type."

"You fucking, ungrateful slut!" Linda elbowed Rebecca in the jaw and nailed her in the back of the head with the butt of the gun, letting her drop to the floor. She pointed her gun at the drummer, who managed to pull hers out when Linda hit Rebecca.

Jordanna started to squeeze the trigger on the gun. "Don't make me kill you, Linda."

"Kill me?" The insane woman laughed at Jordanna. "You killed me the day you killed my fiancé and my child! You can't kill me no more, Jordanna!"

*Her fiancé? Her child?*      The drummer's eyes narrowed. "What in the hell are you talking about?"

"Dre and I were engaged, Jordanna. We were expecting a child. Right after you killed him I lost my baby! It's your fucking fault, you murdering bitch!"

The drummer stood there in shock, staring straight ahead, unable to move. Unshed tears clouded her vision. *Oh, God, this nightmare just gets worse by the minute. I'm just a complete fuck-up all around.*

"I deserve to die." Jordanna didn't realize she had said the words out loud.

"And you will," the guitarist promised, pulling the trigger. "Right now."

Linda's words and three gunshots were the last things Jordanna heard before her world went black.

# Chapter
# Twenty-five

REBECCA WONDERED WHY traumatic experiences in life always seemed to play out in slow motion. She knew she was being led through crowds of media and into the police station. Her hands were behind her back, in handcuffs. She closed her eyes as cameras flashed in her face.

"Is it true that you and Jordanna Fox were lovers, Ms. Hurley?"

"Were you living with Jordanna?"

*Go away. Just go the fuck away.*

"Did you do it?"

"Did you kill her, Rebecca?"

*No more questions. Leave me alone.*

Next thing she knew she was sitting in an uncomfortable yellow chair in a mostly empty interrogation room, except for a small desk and two more chairs—not remembering how she got there in the first place.

She looked at the officer sitting directly across from her. "Am I under arrest?"

"You're innocent until proven guilty, ma'am. Tell us what happened at the house."

She closed her eyes. All she saw was Jordanna's body lying on the floor, in a pool of blood. "Which one?"

The officer narrowed his eyes. "Which one what?"

"Who died, damn it?"

"We can't say until her family is notified."

Rebecca slammed her hand down on the desk. "I am her family, you stupid fuck!"

"Ma'am, I suggest you calm yourself down and tell us what happened."

"I want to call my lawyer."

A phone was pushed in front of her. Two hours later, with her lawyer by her side, she recalled the events of the shooting and its aftermath, leaving out any mention of Jordanna's involvement with Dre.

Rebecca remembered that she had been standing over the two still bodies, the gun still in her hand, when the police and the paramedics arrived on the scene. She'd nearly had a heart attack when they burst through the front door, weapons drawn. She was handcuffed and thrown in the back of a police patrol car.

From there, she watched one body quickly being wheeled out on a gurney and loaded into a waiting ambulance. The second body came out of the house in a black bag.

Two officers got in the front of the car and pulled away from the house. Rebecca turned, staring at the oceanfront home with tears in her eyes, until it was out of sight.

She hadn't expected it to end like this.

BLUE EYES FLUTTERED open. They looked around at the bright, unfamiliar room in confusion, finally focusing on the woman sitting in the chair next to her bed.

"Hey there, gorgeous," the exhausted reporter whispered, squeezing the hand that she had been holding most of the night, once she was released from police custody.

Jordanna saw the large purple bruise on Rebecca's jaw and reached up to touch her lover's face. "You're hurt," she said in a whisper, her voice groggy from the anesthesia still coursing through her veins. Rebecca ran her hand through the drummer's disheveled hair. "Shh, love, save your strength. I'm fine. Let me go tell the doctor that you're awake."

The small woman tried to get up from her chair and was held back by the surprisingly strong hand in hers. She turned and looked at Jordanna. "It's okay. I'll be right back."

"Wait." Jordanna looked into her eyes. "Linda?"

Rebecca turned and faced the hospital-room door, then took a few minutes to gather her composure to speak. "She's dead," she answered, trying very hard to hold back the tears that threatened to fall.

"What happened?" The drummer started to say something else but was interrupted by a nurse that had just entered the room.

"Oh, Ms. Fox, you're awake," the nurse said. "Let me go get the doctor."

Jordanna watched the nurse leave the room and pulled the reporter closer to her. "Please look at me, Rebecca." The blonde turned and faced her lover. "What happened?"

Rebecca swallowed a few times, as she thought of the incident that she knew would be etched forever in her brain. "I saw her going after you when I regained consciousness, and I remembered where you put your other gun."

Jordanna's eyes widened. "You shot her?"

"Yes, I killed her," the shaking reporter admitted right as the doctor rushed into the room. She watched him examine her lover's eyes with a penlight and then listen to her heart with a stethoscope.

"How are you feeling, Ms. Fox?" he asked.

"I've had better days, that's for sure."

"One of the bullets hit a main artery. You lost a lot of blood so we had to do a transfusion. We also had to remove your spleen and patch up your shoulder. Other than that," he smiled and continued, "you're fine. You'll be our guest here for a few days."

The dark woman rolled her eyes. "Great. My dream vacation."

The doctor wrote a few things on her chart and spoke without looking up. "The cuisine here gets rave reviews, Ms. Fox."

"Jordanna, please."

"Okay, Jordanna." He turned and looked at Rebecca, standing patiently in the corner of the room. "You should tell your friend here to go home and get some sleep. She's been here with you the whole time."

Jordanna's eyes opened wide. "The whole time? How long have I been out?"

Rebecca walked over and sat back down in the chair next to the bed. She took her lover's hand in her own and rubbed it, not caring what the doctor would think. "Since yesterday, love."

Blue eyes blinked. "Damn."

The doctor turned to leave the room. "I'll leave you ladies alone now." He coughed and cleared his throat. "Oh, the hospital board has set up a press conference and would like for me to discuss your condition, Jordanna. There's been a circus of reporters outside our front door since you arrived here yesterday."

"I can imagine," she said with a snort. "Do what you have to do, Doctor. You can tell them what's wrong with me. You can tell them that I'm a spleenless woman." She smirked a bit. "I've certainly been called worse."

He smiled at her, deciding that he liked the dark-haired drummer despite the things he had read in the paper and what his co-workers told him about her. "I'll do just that, and I'll be back to check on you later. Get some rest, both of you."

"Thanks, Doctor," both women said in unison.

Jordanna took Rebecca's hand. "Baby, were you questioned by the police yet?"

Rebecca sighed.  "Yes, I spent half the afternoon there yesterday, sick with worry because I didn't know if you were dead or alive."

"They aren't pressing charges or anything, are they?"

Rebecca started to shake her crossed leg nervously. "I don't think I would be sitting here if they were, Jordanna. They said it was pretty much a self-defense kind of scenario. That I acted out in defense of my lover against an irrational former lover."

"Irrational? Oh, that's a good one."

Rebecca held up a copy of that day's edition of the *New York Daily News*. The front-page headline read "Lover's Quarrel Gone Bad" and had a recent shot of Jordanna and Linda under the caption, with a tiny picture of the band on the side. Jordanna scanned it over. "I hate that picture. Why'd they have to use that one?" She frowned. "*Newsday*?"

Rebecca held up the local Long Island newspaper.  "Gore and Bush are top news," she said with a little smirk.  "You're on page thirteen."

Jordanna shook her head.  "Fine.  They always brag about the band being Long Island's own, and I get page thirteen!  Let's see if I do another interview the next time they call!  What did that other rag say?"

"Which rag?"

"*The Post*, Rebecca."

"Oh, that rag."  The reporter pulled out the other newspaper and held it up for her lover to see. Jordanna started to laugh immediately, grabbing her stomach. "Shit, that hurts. Leave it to *The Post* to have a headline reading 'Lethal Lesbian Lust.'" She looked the cover over.  "And to think I was worried about the band's reputation if people found out I did a few porn flicks when I was younger."

"You know, Jordanna, there is another photo in here," Rebecca commented dryly, her face sad.

Jordanna cocked a brow as concern washed through her after seeing Rebecca's sad face. "Of what? Can I see?"  Rebecca turned the page and there was her 1989 graduation photo, courtesy of Lancaster High School, apparently the only one that the press could get their hands on of the young reporter. The dark-haired woman read the caption under the photo, naming Rebecca as her current lover.

Jordanna lifted Rebecca's chin with her finger and looked in her eyes. "Are you okay with that? I know David knows about us, but what if it's in the local Lancaster paper and your family sees it?"

"I already called them and told them." She swallowed a few times. "I wanted them to hear it from me, not read it in a paper somewhere."

"And?"

"Let's just say that they aren't very happy." She looked away from her lover and spoke. "My father got very quiet. I know when he does that it either means he's pissed, upset, or disappointed."

"Probably a combination of all three on this one. I honestly can't blame him."

"Mom couldn't even speak to me, she was so upset." She turned and faced Jordanna again. "And my brother, Ryan, read me the riot act, telling me I don't know what I'm doing, that you must have seduced me and now I'm brainwashed."

"What, did they like pass the phone around to each other?"

Rebecca laughed a bit. "Yes. I had to talk to each one of them."

"Shit, that must have been hard. What did your sister say?"

"Lisa? I think she was in shock. She just said that she didn't know that I preferred women."

Jordanna laughed. "So what did you say? That you didn't know either?"

"Pretty much."

The drummer ran her hand through Rebecca's hair. "I didn't think they would be very happy hearing about our relationship. Not only for the fact that I'm the same sex as you, but also my reputation, Rebecca. You look up any magazine article or website on me or the band, and it's almost a given my promiscuity is mentioned." She closed her eyes. "Let's face it, I'm a whore."

"No, you're a woman who has an addiction. There's a difference." Rebecca looked into Jordanna's blue eyes and cracked a small smile for her. "And you're getting help for it."

"You always see the good in everything, Rebecca."

The reporter blinked twice, leaned forward, and kissed her lover on the cheek. "You're a good person, Jordanna. It was easy for me to see."

Jordanna tried to sit up, but she felt pain and lay back down. Rebecca moved closer to the drummer, noticing her face was really pale. "I hope you knew I didn't mean what I said to Linda about you."

"I didn't at first." Rebecca remembered the sting of the words that came out of Jordanna's mouth. "When I thought you were serious, I was wishing that Linda would just shoot me right there so the pain would go away." She reached out and caressed her lover's cheek. "But then when you mentioned moving in with you...well, then I knew it was part of the plan."

"It really hurt me to say those things, Rebecca," the dark-haired woman admitted, pain evident on her face. "I knew I had to get her focus off of you and on to me. I could see she was really losing it, so that's when I decided to belt her with my arrogant side." She paused. "I think that's what she always hated most about me, my obvious lack of caring for other people's feelings and the cocky self-assured way I speak sometimes...and my dirty mouth."

The reporter laughed. "Well, you are a colorful speaker. Some of the things you come out with sometimes. I don't know, Jordanna. I'd think you were a truck driver or something."

"Colorful, huh?"

"Yeah. Colorful." Rebecca leaned in close and whispered in her lover's ear. "I've never been told I have a sweet pussy before."

Jordanna snorted softly. "Did I *really* say that?"

The reporter blushed. "Yes."

*God, I love my sweets.* "Well, it's true, so I meant that when I said it. Rebecca?"

"Mmm?"

"Thank you."

"For what?"

"For saving my life. I'm sorry you had to do something that you thought you could never do because of me."

Rebecca leaned down and kissed the drummer on her forehead. "I couldn't just stand by and do nothing while she shot you. Besides, I'm getting kinda used to having you around, Jor. And if that moving-in offer still stands..."

"What about your parents?"

"If they don't like it, tough. It's my life, Jor, and I if want to live it with you, then that's my business."

"I just don't want to cause you problems, baby." Jordanna realized what she had just said and laughed. "Like I haven't caused you enough already, you know?"

Rebecca put her fingers over the drummer's lips. "Shh, not another word about it. It's what I want. Although I do have one problem with this, Jordanna." Rebecca thought about her lover's housekeeper. "Rosa."

Jordanna narrowed her eyes and pursed her lips. "Yeah, what's the deal between you and her? I noticed some tension that day I came back from my run, but I forgot to ask you about it 'cause we sorta got a little distracted by this whole Linda thing."

"The deal is...well, I don't think she likes me very much." Rebecca cleared her throat.

"Why?"

"You."

"Huh?" Jordanna pointed to herself. "Me?"

"I really think that she is jealous of our relationship, love."

The drummer questioned the reporter with her eyes, and Rebecca knew exactly what she was asking without a word being said. "Tch," Rebecca snorted and shook her head. "Oh, please, Jordanna! She's pretty much made it obvious to me that you've sampled more than her cooking."

The reporter watched Jordanna's lip twitch slightly as she fought to suppress a grin. Jordanna didn't say a word, but her twinkling blue eyes said all that the reporter needed to know. "I can't say I like her, love, but she is an attractive woman. I mean I'm sure you must have at least once..."

"Rebecca!"

"What? I'm just curious, that's all. I really want to know why she doesn't like me. I'm a pretty likeable person, I think," the reporter said with a laugh. "C'mon, Jordanna, surely a little afternoon delight with the maid is not an uncommon occurrence these days."

*Afternoon delight?* Jordanna couldn't help but laugh. "You just don't give up, do you?"

"No, so start talking, lover."

"I think you know my answer."

Rebecca played innocent. "I didn't know that I asked a question."

"Jesus, Rebecca! You can drive someone nuts."

The reporter batted her hazel eyes at her. "I want to *hear* you say it."

"Yes, baby," she said with a groan. "If you must insist on knowing, I have sampled more than Rosa's cooking, as you put it." She sighed. "But why would she be jealous, though? We certainly weren't ever going steady, that's for sure."

"Jor," Rebecca whispered and caressed the dark-haired woman's cheek. *Jordanna really has no clue, does she?* "Usually when a person goes to bed with someone, there are some sort of feelings involved. She has feelings for you."

"She knows what I'm about, Rebecca, and that I don't get attached to anyone, as a rule. I mean we even discussed it after the first time it happened."

Rebecca felt her stomach start to knot. "The first time? So this has been going on for a while, huh?"

"It's been going on for a few years now." Jordanna ran her

hands though her hair nervously. "We stopped for a while when her husband found out. He wanted to kill me." She shrugged her shoulders. "Then, last year, at her insistence, we started sleeping together again."

"Holy shit!" Rebecca's bruised jaw dropped. "She's married?"

"Yeah, she is. I would say around 80% of the women I've been with are straight, married women looking for something new to spice up their lives."

"And you just happen to be that spice?"

"I guess I am," she said with a grin.

The reporter laughed. "Are you always so brutally honest, Jor?"

The drummer laughed. "I try to be." She closed her eyes. "I'll fire her when I get out of here, okay?"

"No, you don't have to do that. Maybe we can sit down and talk to her first, love." She ran her hand down Jordanna's cheek. "I'm hoping that if you talk to her, she'll back off of me."

"So you still want to move in with me?"

"More than anything."

Jordanna's face lit up like a Christmas tree. "Then of course the offer still stands. As soon as you bust me out of this joint, we'll take care of it."

"You will do no such thing. I will take care of it. You get to take it easy for a while."

"But, Mom!" Jordanna teased.

"No *buts*, pretty lady," Rebecca argued, watching her lover fight to keep her eyes open. "You get some rest, love. I'll be back later, okay?"

"'Kay. I love you, Rebecca."

"I love you, too, Jor. I love you, too."

Rebecca started to walk out of the room heard the dark-haired woman call her from behind. "Um, Rebecca?"

"Yeah, love?"

"What exactly does the spleen do?" The drummer blinked twice and stifled a laugh. "It just occurred to me that I don't have one anymore." She shrugged and looked down at her stomach. "I don't feel like I'm missing anything."

The reporter shook her head. "I really don't know what it does, to be honest. I failed all those science classes in school," Rebecca admitted. "I was going to look it up on the 'net when I got home."

"I'm hoping it's one of those useless body parts that you really don't need but have anyway, you know, like your wisdom teeth?" She smiled and wiggled her eyebrows. "And I hope it has nothing to do with anything that would alter my sexual performance in any way."

"Argh! It's always got to be about sex with you, doesn't it?" Rebecca walked back across the room and stood next to her lover. "I'm glad you're feeling better, love," she said, and kissed the dark-haired woman on the lips. "I'll see you later."

# Chapter
# Twenty-six

JORDANNA SAT QUIETLY in the passenger seat with her eyes closed and her head back as Rebecca drove home. "How are you feeling, love?"

"I'm fine. Just glad to be out of that place." The drummer shifted slightly in her seat to make herself more comfortable. "I don't feel like going home right away. How about we stop at the park for a while first?"

"I don't think that's a good idea, Jordanna. You just got out of the hospital."

"We have a lot to talk about, Rebecca. Dre, Linda, our future..."

They pulled up to a light, and Rebecca turned to look at her lover. She was still pale, and her hair was slightly stringy from the lack of a shower when she was in the hospital. She ran her hand across Jordanna's cheek. "We can do that at home, sweetheart."

"Please, baby, I need to get some fresh air after being cooped up in that place all those days. We can just sit on the bench by the water. I promise I'll tell you if I start to feel lousy and then we'll go, okay?"

"You know I can't say no to you, don't you?" Rebecca shook her head and cursed herself for being such a wuss. "Pass your house and stay to the right of the fork, right?"

Jordanna smiled. "Yeah."

The reporter parked the car as close to the park bench as she possibly could and grabbed the dark-haired woman's arm as she started to get out of the car. "Wait, Jor. Let me help you get out."

Jordanna glared at her.

"Humor me, please."

Jordanna sighed loudly, but gave in and waited for Rebecca to come around to her side of the car to help her. Once she was out, the reporter linked her arm through Jordanna's as they began the slow stroll down to the bench by the water. They sat and watched as an older couple approached them and sat down on the bench with them to feed the birds.

Rebecca took Jordanna's hand in hers, and they smiled at each other, knowing that they both were probably thinking the same thing, about growing old together. "I almost lost you," the reporter said, and squeezed her lover's hand tighter, never wanting to let go.

Jordanna turned to look into hazel eyes and saw tears. "No, you didn't, baby." She cupped Rebecca's cheek and wiped the tears away with her thumb. "It's gonna take more than a psycho bitch and a couple of gunshot wounds to separate us," she promised. Rebecca laughed a little and cracked a small smile. "That's my girl! There's the smile that brightens my life," the drummer whispered to her.

"I'm sorry. I just lost it there for a minute," the reporter admitted. "I really don't know what's come over me."

Jordanna pulled Rebecca as close to her as she could without feeling much pain in her stomach, kissing the reporter lightly on the forehead, running her hands through the young woman's hair. "A traumatic experience can do that, Rebecca, but it's over now. The threat is gone. We're both alive, and now we can plan our future."

Rebecca sighed contently. "Our future. God, that sounds wonderful." She played with the dark-haired woman's messy bangs.

"It does, doesn't it?" Jordanna melted into her lover's touch.

Rebecca's eyes followed a kite flying high above the sand in the distance. "Jor, can I ask you a question?"

"Of course you can, baby. No more secrets between us anymore, okay?"

"Do you still do drugs?"

Jordanna rubbed her forehead and sighed. "Occasionally."

"Oh." Rebecca frowned as her heart sank. She had to admit she was disappointed by the drummer's honest admission.

"I don't do it often, Rebecca. I'll snort a line or two of coke at some of the industry parties I'm forced to go to, mostly so I can make it through the night. I don't go out and buy it for myself."

"I saw Linda and Rachel doing some on the plane. I was happy when I didn't see you doing it."

Jordanna looked down at the ground, and ran her hands through her semi-greasy hair. "I used to do a lot of it when I worked for Dre. I did that and uppers to keep myself going since I didn't get to sleep that often back then, with all of the shit

I was involved in."

"You're a musician. I should have expected it."

"I haven't done it in over a year, if it makes you feel better," Jordanna admitted, and then ran her hand along the reporter's cheek. "And I won't ever do it again."

"You promise?"

"I promise."

Rebecca held out her pinky. "Pinky swear?"

Jordanna laughed at the gesture, one she hadn't seen since her school years. She smiled and then wrapped her pinky finger around her lover's extended one. "Pinky swear." She sealed the promise with a quick kiss, which got two looks of disapproval from the couple sitting next to them on the bench.

"Okay, now that I got that off of my mind, maybe you better tell me what you wanted to tell me about Dre."

"I wanted to explain what..."

The reporter cut Jordanna off before she could say another word. "You don't have to explain anything to me. You did what you had to do to survive."

Jordanna ran her hand through Rebecca's hair. "But I do have to explain for my own sake, okay?" she asked and gave the reporter a half smile. "I don't want you thinking I'm some cold-blooded murderer or something."

"I would *never* think that, you know that."

"Please, just hear me out." Jordanna waited as the disgusted older couple sitting on the bench with them got up and started on their slow trek back to the parking lot. She waited for them to be well out of earshot before she started to tell Rebecca the details behind Dre's death.

What had started out to be a simple exchange turned into the perfect opportunity for Jordanna to cut her ties with Dre, who, despite what he might have told Linda, had absolutely no plans of letting the dark-haired woman leave his small operation, or at least leave it alive.

"Dre set up an exchange with this small-time dealer from the Bronx named Cruz. I think the deal was around $500,000 for some blow. Dre usually went into these exchanges with two of his goons at his side, and I would follow behind, unnoticed of course, to make sure nothing unexpected would happen."

Rebecca furrowed her brows. "Blow?"

"Cocaine."

"Sorry, I'm not up on street terms of drugs, love."

The drummer placed a quick kiss on her lover's cheek. The young woman's innocence was one of things Jordanna was most attracted to. "Keep it that way, baby."

"So, what went wrong on this exchange?"

Jordanna shook her head. "I don't really know. When I got to the scene Dre's two goons were dead, as were Cruz's goons. Cruz had Dre pinned down on the ground and was just about ready to take him out when I stopped him."

"How did you stop him?"

"I took him out," she said hesitantly and then continued with the story. "Dre was still on the ground, unarmed. He looked at me with such a look of relief after I killed Cruz." She stopped talking and remained quiet for a few minutes. "That was when I realized I had the *perfect* opportunity to cut my ties with him."

Rebecca took Jordanna's slightly trembling hand into her own. "That's when you..."

"Killed him, yes." Jordanna looked at her lover with self-loathing in her eyes. "I put the gun to his head, told him I was sorry that he gave me no choice, and I pulled the trigger."

Rebecca had figured that was what her lover had done, but for some reason it still shocked her to hear her say it. "What about the coke and the money?"

Jordanna shook her head. "For a fleeting moment I thought about taking it, but I really didn't need it. At that point I realized if I left it there, then it would look like they all killed each other, you know?"

"But, the bullets would have been different, Jordanna, from your gun."

"No." She squeezed her lover's hand tight. "I picked up one of the guns on the ground by Dre's goons and shot Cruz with it from where they were laying, and then I used his gun on Dre."

"What about fingerprints?"

"I always wore gloves."

Rebecca coughed. "So you were never questioned by the police?"

"Nope, never. My *real* name never got out on the street." She laughed nervously. "The only person that knew at that point, I guess, was Linda. She must have been at the warehouse, hiding behind something. When I left the place I assumed I was the only one there." Jordanna blinked tears out of her eyes. "I guess I was wrong."

"I heard what she said to you, Jor."

"About the baby?"

Rebecca wiped the tears away with the back of her fingers. "Yeah."

"No wonder she hated me."

"It wasn't your fault."

"I never knew he was engaged, or about to become a father."
She shook her head. "I knew he had a couple kids with some
other women.  At one point I actually thought I was pregnant
with his child.  I went to the doctor, and that's when I found out
that I can't have children."

"You can't have..." Rebecca started to ask but Jordanna put
her finger over her lips.

"No, I can't," the dark-haired woman said quietly, her eyes
sad.  She put her hands on her lover's arms.  "Rebecca, you now
know *everything* there is to know about me, okay?  You know it
all."

"Wow."  A figure standing behind a tree caught Rebecca's
eye.  "Someone's watching us."

"I know, I saw him before," the drummer answered.  "He
has a camera, so pose pretty."

"Jesus Christ!  It's getting so that I hate the people in my
own profession."  Rebecca shook her head in disgust.  "I guess
that's why I never got into news reporting or tabloid-type
writing."

"You're more of a journalist than a reporter, Rebecca."
Jordanna laughed and bumped heads with her lover.  "Wanna
give him a good shot?" she asked, wiggling her eyebrows at
Rebecca.

Rebecca adjusted her position, pulled the drummer into her
arms, and kissed Jordanna with passion.  "Is that what you had
in mind, love?" Rebecca asked when they broke off the kiss.

"Um, yeah," the drummer said, taking the time to catch her
breath again.  "That was pretty much it."  She sighed.  "Why
don't we, um, do it again, just in case he missed his first photo
opportunity?"

"Wonderful idea," the reporter agreed and leaned forward
once again until she felt the soft lips of her lover's against her
own.  They kissed until they heard footsteps coming closer to
them on the boardwalk, and then broke apart.  Rebecca smiled at
her lover and laughed.  "Don't want to scandalize the whole
neighborhood."

"Nope, we wouldn't want to do that, now would we?"  The
drummer flashed a lopsided grin.  "Actually, they really could
use a good shake-up around here.  Something to get their snooty
little asses in an uproar."

Rebecca looked out at the ocean, admiring a large blue ship
chugging along in the distance.  "Jordanna?"

"Yeah, baby?"

"Karla was Oriental?"

"Yeah, she was," the drummer answered and thought back

to one of the first conversations that she had ever had with the woman who took her in as a teen. "She was born in China. Karla was her American name."

"I don't know why, when you told me about her I was picturing her with stringy blond hair and body odor."

Jordanna burst out laughing. "Geez, Rebecca, do you really think that I would sleep with someone like that?"

Rebecca shook her head. "No, I guess not. I try...well, I try to forget that you have ever slept with anyone but me. Kinda stupid, huh?"

"No, it's not stupid."

"Yes it is." Rebecca pushed a few stray stands of windblown hair behind her ears. "So, um, what did Karla actually look like?"

"She had long, dark hair that was as soft as silk and big brown eyes." The drummer ran her hand down Rebecca's cheek. "But I have *always* preferred blondes." She smiled at her lover. "Blondes with expressive hazel eyes," she said, and kissed each of Rebecca's eyelids. "And the name Rebecca. I've always loved the name Rebecca."

"You're so full of shit, Jordanna." Rebecca laughed, put her hands around her lover's neck, and pulled her in for a kiss. "But I love you anyway."

"So, which rag do you think these photos are going to show up in?"

The reporter shrugged her shoulders. "I'm sure we'll find out. When we're in line at a store, no doubt. What do you think the headline will read?"

"Jordanna Fox has female lover," the drummer teased. "Big news flash, like I keep it a secret or something, you know?" She eased herself off of the bench and stood up. "I have to laugh when I read some of these articles. I've have never hidden my sexuality, to the public or otherwise. I just don't understand it."

"You know," Rebecca stood up and linked her arm through her lover's again for the walk back to the car, "I didn't know you were gay when John assigned me to this article. I tried to push it off on one of my co-workers, this guy that has the hots for you big time. John informed me then that you wouldn't particularly be interested in Jake in that way, though."

"You're kidding, right?"

"Nope," Rebecca admitted as they walked down the sidewalk to the car. "I knew who you were, but basically all I knew about you was that you were an excellent drummer." She paused and chuckled. "I also heard you were, um, trouble and basically a reporter's worst nightmare, but I didn't know you preferred women."

Jordanna smirked at the comment. "And to think that you want to move in with trouble."

Rebecca opened the passenger-side door and waited for her lover to climb in and get settled. "I like trouble," she said with a wink. "More than I ever really knew."

Printed in the United States
40420LVS00006B/88